TILL THE STARS FALL

by

Kathleen Gilles Seidel

AN ONYX BOOK

ONYX
Published by the Penguin Group
Penguin Books USA Inc., 375 Hudson Street,
New York, New York 10014, U.S.A.
Penguin Books Ltd, 27 Wrights Lane,
London W8 5TZ, England
Penguin Books Australia Ltd, Ringwood,
Victoria, Australia
Penguin Books Canada Ltd, 10 Alcorn Avenue,
Toronto, Ontario, Canada M4V 3B2
Penguin Books (N.Z.) Ltd, 182–190 Wairau Road,
Auckland 10, New Zealand

Penguin Books Ltd, Registered Offices:
Harmondsworth, Middlesex, England

First published by Onyx, an imprint of Dutton Signet,
a division of Penguin Books USA Inc.

First Printing, March, 1994
10 9 8 7 6 5 4 3 2 1

Well, Pam, it's been ten years
since I did this last. But surely
once a decade is not too often
to pay tribute to our friendship . . .
and our wardrobes.

ACKNOWLEDGMENTS

I have been vacationing on the Mesabi Iron Range in Minnesota since before I was two, but I still didn't know enough to write about it. Julie Zindar gave me so much interesting information about the history of the region that I regret my inability to write an historical novel. David and Gene Rae Carls and the guys at the bar of the Full Circle Restaurant answered many questions. I wanted to write about the Range because it is beautiful. Marlys Carls-Steiskal shared her warm memories and rich insights, and I learned how interesting it is.

I meet Muriel Roberts as another mom at preschool. She turned out to be also Muriel Von Villas, director of the Opera Theater at George Washington University. She made me understand what it must be like to have a voice, and she traded kids with me once a week. I can't imagine how this book would have been written without her.

I always rely on my family to know about things I don't. Now the next generation is being called upon. My nephew Colin Richardson answered my questions about ice hockey. Kathryn Murray and Buzz Schmidt willingly shared college memories with a person they had never met.

Susan Elizabeth Phillips was writing about little girls when I was writing about teenage boys so we traded information; I hoped I helped her as much as she helped me. Diane Chamberlain, I am sure, will be far too generous to tell anyone how literally I transcribed the insights she offered. Ann Salitsky and my agent,

Adele Leone, believed in the book even in its roughest, scraggliest incarnations. Kathleen Ligare struggled through such a draft. It took me a year to understand what she had seen in twenty minutes. Jennifer Enderlin came in to pinch hit at the bottom of the ninth; my score card shows that she hit it out of the park.

Of course I thank my baby-sitters. Elizabeth Mitchell and Valerie Hart keep turning up in my life, the most glorious bad pennies you can imagine. Meagan Vilsack, Kathy Byrd, and Davis Roberts were as wonderful as always. Cassie Vilsack baby-sat less during this book, but she typed the corrections, so she is forgiven.

During the long journey that this book has been, a fellow traveler and I discovered that we were too much alike to be useful to each other. I wish her well and include with this volume much affection and great regret.

Prologue

Krissa could feel her breath against her palms. She had her hands over her face, her fingertips pressed to her eyelids. It was night and here, alone in the kitchen, there was nothing to distract her from the sound of her breath. She let her hands fall. She curved them around the base of her blue-glazed coffee mug. The cup was cold.

In a minute the phone would ring and she would pick it up and someone she did not know would tell her that Danny French was dead.

The evening news had left no hope. On the fifty-third day of a hunger strike designed to raise money for a shelter for homeless women with children, Danny French was in a coma, hours from death. Back in New York reporters were gathered on the sidewalk outside the shelter where he lay, waiting for the death of this literate, sensitive, impatient man. He was a public figure. His death would be news, publicity to be exploited. He was also Krissa's brother.

Surely he had never believed that it would come to this, to actual death. Every time she had spoken to him, he had been confident, even exhilarated. He had been so sure of success. Then suddenly it was too late. He was in a coma, and he was going to die without her having gone to say good-bye.

Going to die. No, he might already be dead. At this moment, a stranger, a reporter, might be dialing her number to tell her that her brother was dead.

She didn't see him that often, just once or twice a year. They spoke on the phone every month, but that was all her doing. Danny cared deeply about the disturbed, unfortunate people who haunted the streets of New York City. But a sister and her four boys . . . that was hard for him. Ordinary things were not easy for Danny.

But why did he have to do this?

She felt the sound before she heard it, a stirring current of air. The phone was ringing. She stood up. It was on the wall a few feet away. It rang again. She had to answer. Not answering wouldn't change anything; it wouldn't keep him alive. The molded plastic receiver slipped against her moist palm.

"Krissa, it's Quinn."

Quinn?

She never thought of the call coming from him. But wasn't it right, here at the end, that it should be Quinn? He and Danny had sung together, he and Danny had shared the best that life had given either one. Yes, this was fitting, this was right, that although they had not spoken to one another in fifteen years, the silk of Quinn's voice should be the lining of Danny's casket.

". . . have started IV's . . ."

Krissa too had not spoken to Quinn in all this time, and yet his voice was still familiar, deep, velvety rich. And for a moment, for a heartbeat, she was nineteen, twenty again, and none of this had happened. She was twenty-one, twenty-two, and she was devotedly, passionately in love with him, Quinn, her brother's partner.

". . . and they'll be on their way to the hospital . . ."

IV's? Hospital? For the first time she heard his individual words. "What are you saying? Did he give up?"

"No, no. The city did. They are releasing the funds. Danny's getting everything he wanted. He won."

"He's not going to die?"

"No."

A slender shape appeared at the foot of the kitchen stairs. It was Adam, Krissa's middle son—her child of light, the one most like herself. The left knee of his gray sweatpants flapped down from a triangular-shaped tear. He must have heard the phone ring and gotten out of bed.

"It's Uncle Danny, isn't it?" His voice was tight. "Is it over? Is he dead?"

Krissa murmured something into the phone, some words of gratitude and farewell, she wasn't sure what, and she crossed the kitchen, opening her arms to her child, now as tall as she. He was thin and strong, his young muscles tensed.

Children shouldn't have to suffer like this. The anxiety, the dread, the dark, bewildering murk that had been following her day after day had spread to them. They too had been bewildered and confused. They didn't understand any more than she had why Danny had chosen to do this to himself, why he had decided to let himself die. They were children; they shouldn't have had to endure this

Her grief and confusion burst into anger. *You son of a bitch,* her heart shrieked at her brother, *do what you want to yourself. But how dare you, how dare you, do this to my kids?*

WASHINGTON, D.C., DECEMBER 1992

Quinn slid in the antenna on the narrow phone and laid it back down on the piano bench. He had been here all night, playing requiems—Brahms, Verdi, Faure—searching for solace in the dignity of the music. Only through music could he make sense of his grief, grief for a man he had not spoken to in fifteen years, a man he had thought he hated.

How Danny would have jeered at the piano. It was a nine-foot concert grand; it had cost more than many people's houses, and Quinn had it right here in his living room. *How can you?* He could hear Danny's voice in his head. *When people don't have places to sleep at night?*

It hadn't always been like this. They had been the
two lead singers of Dodd Hall, one of the premier
rock bands of the early seventies. Together they had
written more than a hundred songs and sung many of
them over and over, night after night, first in the little
clubs and coffee house of New England, then in the
massive stadiums in the largest cities in Europe and
North America.

Then it had ended. In Madison Square Garden one
night, Quinn had strapped on his guitar, put his hand
over the mike, and in a white-hot flame of anger
hissed at Danny, "Enjoy this one because it's the last.
I will never sing with you again. I will never be on
stage with you again. I will never speak to you again."

And he hadn't. He hadn't spoken to Danny since
that night. He hadn't sung a Dodd Hall song in public
since that night.

So what do you do when your partner—the man
who shared the most glorious moments of your life—
what do you do when he takes fifty days to starve
himself to death? Do you go to New York and sing
at his funeral?

No need to answer that one now. The wily trickster
had pulled it out of the bag again.

Chapter One

The left front of the red Ford station wagon was crushed, the fender twisted, and the shattered headlight hung free of its housing. Krissa French was standing at the side of the road, both hands gripping the back of her neck, her elbows pulled in close to her body. She felt sick. She was fifteen, driving on her learner's permit, trying so hard, being so careful ... and suddenly this other car had ... she couldn't remember if she had seen it or not. How could this have happened?

Her mother was talking to the other driver, exchanging insurance information. Her older brother was standing at the opposite side of the narrow, forest-lined crossroad, rocking back on his heels, his hands in the back pockets of his jeans. Of course he could be calm, he could stand there like he was bored, like none of it mattered. He hadn't done this.

Now he was crossing the road, coming toward her. She didn't care. He could joer, he could taunt. Nothing he said could make her feel any worse.

He spoke. "It wasn't your fault, you know. The other guy had the stop sign. He plowed into you."

"But I should have stopped anyway. Defensive driving—isn't that what I should have done?" Her driver's ed instructor had gone on and on about defensive driving.

"I don't see why you would have," her brother answered. "Especially with Mother telling you to stop slowing down at every crossroad."

Krissa swallowed. "That's right. She did say that, didn't she?"

"You can count on her forgetting, but she did."

If Danny was telling her that it wasn't her fault, then it probably wasn't. He certainly wouldn't be going out of his way to be nice to her.

He was sixteen, less than a year older than she was, but they weren't close. In fact, she didn't think he liked her very much. Most of the time he ignored her. The rest of the time he treated her as if she were slightly subnormal.

She did not dislike him, but he embarrassed her. Leanly built with fair skin, narrow features, and dark eyes, he was their school's loner, one of its few rebels, moving through the halls aloof and sneering, with his overly long hair a defiant tangle of untamed black curls. It seemed a waste to her, his refusing to go along with things. He was very smart and very talented. He had never had a music lesson in his life, but he could play on his guitar every song Bob Dylan had ever written, and even if she didn't like his taste in music, she did love to hear him sing. He had a wonderful voice, but he was not in the choir at school or church.

He never did things the way everyone else did. He would write long, long term papers, working late into the night, getting research from congressmen and trade associations. He would get *A's* on those papers, but having never turned in the routine homework assignments, he would get terrible grades for the semester. Krissa did not understand this. She did all her work on time; she kept her locker neat, her papers in order. No one was ever unhappy with her; no one ever had any complaints about her. Certainly of the two of them, it seemed far, far more likely that Danny would be the one to wreck the family car.

"If you're okay, then I'd better see if I can get this thing driveable," he said. Checking quickly for traffic, he crossed the road to the station wagon, dropped the tailgate, and took out the tire iron. A moment later, he was crowbarring the front quarter panel away from the ruined tire. For all that he claimed to hate cars, he worked quickly and expertly, spinning the tire iron to loosen the lug nuts.

When he was done, he bounced the ruined tire around to the back of the car and slammed the tailgate shut. He was brushing off his hands when their mother hurried over. "Are we going to be able to drive it?" she asked. As always, her voice was tight and urgent.

"It's probably way out of alignment, but we should be able to get home."

"Then let's get going. We need to hurry," Peg French said. "We were late as it was."

It had been Mrs. French's imagined sense of late-ness that had caused her to snap at Krissa for slowing at every empty intersection. Mrs. French was maniacal about time; she couldn't stand the thought of being an instant late anywhere.

She told Danny to drive. Carefully he put the car in gear, testing the steering as soon as they were on the road.

The family lived on the Mesabi Iron Range, an iso-lated and desolately beautiful triangle in northern Minnesota. A forest of Norway and jack pines, popple and birches, grew to the edge of clear, copper-colored lakes. The soil was light and sandy, and beneath it was nature's gift, a deep, rich bed of iron ore. The ore was mined in huge open pits, manmade Grand Canyons.

Ed French, Danny and Krissa's father, was a miner. But two years ago he had been in an accident. He had been driving a truck on one of the narrow roads that wound down the walls of the pit. It had been a Euclid truck, a huge thing with tires the size of a grown man. The brakes had failed.

He had been off work for a year. Last spring he had gone back, but chronic back pain kept him on light duty. He spent the day, all day every day, watch-ing a conveyor belt, making sure it stayed on track,

poking at any of the iron-rich rocks that threatened
to fall off. It was desperately tedious work, the kind
usually given to a high school kid as a part-time summer job. But it was Ed French's future; he would
never be able to do anything else. Each night he came
home, his face set, his eyes bitter and angry.

He had not been an easy man to begin with. Even
before the accident, he had been prickly and moody,
quick to assume that nothing was going to work out
because other people were going to ruin it. He had
no capacity to accept things, to be grateful for what
good fortune he had. Now he sat at the family supper
table, silently brooding, speaking only to blame the
mines for having ruined his back. He blamed everyone: the management, the mechanics, the foremen.
Everything was all, always, someone else's fault.

Because of his temperament and his disinterest in
the warm, active community life of the Range's mining
towns, the French family lived outside town, well past
Levering Lake, in the last house on the power line.
They had a small house set on an open level spot,
surrounded by outbuildings—the big garage, the tool-
shed, and the woodshed. As soon as the red station
wagon came within sight of the property, Krissa heard
her mother draw a sharp breath. At the top of the
drive sat her husband's blue pickup. He had beaten
them home.

Danny turned up the drive. He had hardly switched
off the ignition when the kitchen door popped open
and out came Ed French.

He was a larger man than his lean, sinewy son. Pain had
given his face gaunt lines and, when he saw Danny get
out of the driver's seat, he stopped dead, his face hard,
his eyes glaring. Krissa scrambled out of the backseat.

"So is this your latest stunt?" His voice was hard
and angry. "Is this your new way of making your mark
on the world?"

He was talking to Danny. He thought Danny had
wrecked the car. Krissa spoke quickly. "No, Dad, it
wasn't—"

He charged on. "Isn't wearing your hair like that enough? Or do you have to wreck your mother's car too?"

"Dad, Dad—" She couldn't get him to listen.

He was moving toward Danny now, his step faintly lurching and, open-handed, he shoved Danny's shoulder. Danny fell back a step. Ed shoved him again.

"Dad, please, listen." Krissa hated it when her father got like this. "Dad, it wasn't Danny, it was—"

A hand closed on her arm. It was her mother. "Mom, let go." Krissa shook her arm, trying to break free. "Dad thinks that it—"

"You keep out of it," her mother hissed, her voice a sharp, snapping whisper. "You stay quiet."

Stay quiet? Why? When Dad was blaming Danny? Krissa stared at her mother and suddenly behind her there was a crash. She whirled. Danny was sprawled on the ground and her father was stomping back into the house.

The door slammed. Danny scrambled to his feet. He spun around and stormed across the browning grass toward the woodshed. His books lay scattered on the ground. One was cracked on its spine. Another was full of folded papers. Danny always did that—stuck his papers any place and then he could never find anything.

What had happened? Krissa forced herself to be clear about this. Her father had hit her brother. He had struck him, had knocked him down. And Danny hadn't hit back. Danny—smart-mouthed, impudent, rebellious Danny—had taken it. That made no sense. He could have hit back. But he hadn't.

And her mother. That was the strangest of all. What on earth had possessed her? Why hadn't she let Krissa explain?

"Mother, I—"

Mrs. French held up her hand. "I know what you're thinking. But don't get any notions about going in there to explain." That was exactly what Krissa had been planning on doing. "You know how much your father hates being wrong."

"But—"

"Leave it, Krissa. I'll do the paperwork for the insurance. He'll never have to know that it was you."

"But that isn't fair," Krissa protested. "Danny shouldn't take the blame. I did it. I don't mind admitting that."

"Well, I mind having you admit it, and it's my decision. One word and you'll make everything worse. So come help me with these groceries. You can get your books later."

A hot dish was already in the oven. Krissa and her mother worked quickly and silently. Twenty minutes later supper was on the metal-rimmed Formica table. Her father came in from the living room, Danny came in from outside.

Krissa sat down. This was her family. Father, mother, brother, sister. Her mother passed her the vegetable dish.

She had always known. She realized that now. She had always known, but she hadn't been willing to admit it to herself—they were not like other families.

In other families the dad and brothers did things together, went hunting and fishing, worked on the car. At dinner the dad and brothers talked about chain saws, power augers, and rototillers. Danny and her father never spoke.

Other families went to church suppers and the county fair. The grown-ups had friends like the kids did. The adults would sit up late playing cards in warm kitchens, laughing and talking. In this family only Krissa had friends.

She had always pretended. Pretended that they were like other families. At meals she would talk brightly about cheerleading and student council elections as if her talking could keep them all normal, make them like other families.

They had let her pretend, the three of them, Mom, Dad, and Danny. Night after night they'd let her chatter on like a little kid, even through they knew that it was all a lie.

Tonight she too was silent, listening to the scrape of the serving spoon against the vegetable bowl, the plop of a hot dish dropping onto a dinner plate, the click of the butter dish against the tabletop.

Danny ate quickly, saying nothing. He left the table as soon as he was finished, going back outside. He was not allowed to play his guitar—his *goddam* guitar—in the house and so, until the worst cold set in, he spent hours every evening in the unheated garage.

She did the dishes after dinner as she did every night, cleaning the kitchen carefully and thoroughly even though she knew that her mother would come back in later and resweep the floor, rewipe the counter, and carefully dry the sink. Mrs. French was a perfectionist. Every box of cereal in her cabinet was lined up square with the other boxes, the waxy inner bags carefully rolled and clipped shut. The outside of every jelly jar and every dressing bottle had to be wiped before it was put back in the refrigerator. Nothing, not even the coffeepot or the flour and sugar cannisters, could sit out on the counter all night.

Then Krissa went into her room to do her homework. After an hour or so she heard Danny come in. In another hour she heard the clicking of the television being turned off, the rush of water in the bathroom, and the muted thud of her parents' bedroom door closing on the other side of the house.

Her parents wouldn't tell her anything. If she asked, her father wouldn't look up from the newspaper, and her mother would tense her lips—"We aren't going to talk about that."

And Danny probably wouldn't talk to her either. But she was going to try. She wasn't going to be the only person in the family who didn't know what was going on.

She got up and crossed the hall. She almost never went in Danny's room. It was always a mess. He never made his bed or picked up his dirty clothes. He had books and papers everywhere. It made her mother furious. This was her house, she would rage at him. He had to keep it as she wanted it. But he didn't.

The door was shut. Krissa knocked and when Danny said "Yeah?" she opened it, even though she knew he hadn't meant "come in."

He was standing in front of his desk, wearing the bottom half of a gray sweatsuit. The pants rode low on his lean hips. His chest was sinewy and the muscles in his arms were clean and hard. He was no athlete— he hated organized sports—but ever since the accident, the family had heated with wood to save money. Splitting it was his chore, and he had grown strong from the work.

He was reaching for a book. On the back of his bicep were four bruises, fingermarks where he had been grabbed with a pressure strong enough to rupture the blood vessels. The bruises were yellowing; they were days' old.

He looked across his shoulder, curious as to why she had come to his room. His eyes narrowed as he realized that she had seen his arm.

He set down the book and picked up the sweatshirt that had been draped over the back of his desk chair. He pulled it over his head, the ribbed neck catching on his wild black hair, rumpling it even more.

She spoke. "Dad hits you, doesn't he?"

He shrugged. "Sometimes."

"I didn't know."

"Why should you? What's it got to do with Little Miss Perfect?"

She hated it when he called her that. She might deserve it, but she didn't like it. "This afternoon . . . why didn't you tell him what happened?"

Danny picked up his book again. It was an almanac. "I might ask you the same thing."

"I tried. Mother wouldn't let me."

"She wouldn't?" Danny's voice rose. This interested him. "So she knows?" Then his voice went flat again. "I've wondered."

He was pretending he didn't care, pretending that none of this mattered. Suddenly she was furious. All afternoon everyone had been treating her like a child, not even allowing her to finish a sentence. Why were they acting as if she was so fragile? "What on earth is going on around here?" she demanded. "How often does this happen? When did it start?" Then she knew. "After the accident?"

"Yes, but it's nothing for you to get all steamed up over. It's just a quick fist now and then. It's not like he's going to take the chain saw to me or anything. Mother's right. Let's not rock the boat. I can take it."

"Don't you want to hit him back?" This was what she didn't understand. At school Danny challenged everyone all the time. A teacher couldn't make the simplest mistake without Danny sneering.

"Sure, but think about it. What would happen if I hit back? Either he beats me to a pulp or he has to back down. What's he going to do if I'm stronger? Who's he going to hit next? Mother? You?"

"You aren't trying to protect *me,* are you?"

He laughed a short, harsh laugh. "Now what have I ever done that would make you think a thing like that?"

"Nothing," she admitted. He had always been the least helpful of brothers. "But it's true, isn't it?"

"Don't make me out to be some kind of saint. I probably get a charge out of knowing that I can control my temper when he can't."

"But still ... isn't there something I can do? This isn't right."

"What's right got to do with it?" He shrugged. "But it's only for two more years, and then I'm out of here."

"Out of here? What do you mean? Oh, I suppose you'll want to go to college."

Going to college wasn't an automatic thing for kids around there. Lots got married right after high school and then went to work in the mines. But Danny wouldn't want that.

"You bet I want to go to college. In fact—" He broke off and dropped the almanac onto his desk. "Come in and shut the door. I want to talk to you."

That was strange. Danny had spent the last five years doing all that he could to avoid talking to her. But she shut the door and picked her way around the rubble on the floor to sit on his bed. She started to pull up the sheet, then stopped. That was the sort of thing her mother would do. She sat down on the tangle of blankets.

Danny used an old kitchen chair at his desk. He pulled it closer to the bed and straddled it, crossing his arms across the torn vinyl back. He was looking straight at her, his dark eyes intent. It made her a little uncomfortable. She wasn't used to him looking at her like that.

"Tell me something," he said. "How much do you like it here? Not just home, but school, the Range, all of it? Do you like it?"

"Of course, I do. I—" She stopped. "I never think about things like that," she said honestly. This was her world, and she was determined to succeed in it as well as she possibly could. "But I can tell that it is different for you."

"It is. I want out of here and not just because of what you saw this afternoon. I've felt that way for years. I don't want to work in the mines. I don't want a job with the county government. I don't want to be nice to rich people with their summer cabins. I want out ... and I don't plan on going to St. Cloud or Bemidji."

There were small state colleges in those two towns. "You want to go to the Cities?" That's where the University of Minnesota was. Not many Rangers went there. Minneapolis was too far, and the university was too big.

"Not even that," Danny answered. "I want to go east, to the Ivy League—Harvard, Yale, places like that."

"Danny!" The east coast? The Ivy League? "Where on earth did you get an idea like that?"

The Range was its own little world. People were maybe a bit smug about it because everybody thought—everybody but Danny—that it was such a great place to live, to bring up kids—so clean and safe, with the lakes and the hunting and fishing. And maybe with the smugness was fear, fear about big places where people were ambitious, where life wasn't a matter of working for the mines or not working for the mines . . . Krissa didn't really know, but the east coast? No, people from the Range didn't go places like that.

Danny leaned back and pulled open his bottom desk drawer. He took out two issues of the *Congressional Record* and dropped them on the floor. Hiding beneath them were six or eight paperbound college catalogues. He handed her one. The spine was cracked; pages had been turned down at the corners. He had been reading and rereading it. *Princeton University,* the cover said. The picture on the cover was of a group of students talking beneath a Gothic arch. It looked better than anything she had seen on TV.

But Danny was a kid from the mines. What was he thinking of? She shook her head. "This isn't for people like us."

"Tell me why not." His voice was challenging.

"Well, just because." This was so obvious she hardly knew where to start. "The money, for one. Do you have a clue what places like that cost?"

"Oh, I know. To the nearest dime I know what they cost. But you can get them to pay for it."

"What do you mean 'them?' Not Mom and Dad?" Their father would be on light duty with no overtime for the rest of his life.

"No, of course not. I mean the schools, the universities. They'll pay."

He explained. The best universities could fill their freshman classes year after year with students who were all exactly alike, rich kids, smart kids, kids who went to museums and stuff, whose dads didn't belong to unions.

"But they don't want to do that anymore. They want to appear all liberal and well-rounded. They want to say that they are educating 'The People.' Every freshman class needs a couple of blacks and a couple of hicks. Look at me, I'm perfect. I'm smart. I'm from the middle of nowhere. No one in the family's ever gone to college so I'll look like a major pulling-myself-up-by-the-bootstraps type. They need me . . . or at least they think they do, which amounts to the same thing."

"But places like this . . ." Krissa looked again at the catalogue on her lap. "Wouldn't you be afraid? Leaving home, going to a city . . ." She couldn't imagine it.

"No. Staying here is what scares me."

He sat straight now, no trace of his usual slouch. Krissa knew that she was pretty, with her cheekbones and masses of auburn-tinged hair, but her brother was an extraordinarily striking young man with a wild, gypsy's beauty.

She never thought about the future. She supposed that was strange. The other girls at school did, talking about how they'd have four children, two boys and two girls, and what they would name them. And the guys talked about what kind of cars they would drive.

But none of them ever talked about a future like this. It suddenly made Krissa proud, that her brother was thinking about something this different, that he had the nerve to try it.

She took a breath. "Then I think it's great. I really do."

"Well, it might not happen. I've got to look perfect on paper, and at the moment I don't. The irony of this hit me when school started. Here you'll end up with this great record, and you'll go to St. Cloud like everyone else. I'll be dying to get out, but I'll be stuck in the mines because I'm too much of a smartass to turn my homework in."

"Then start turning your homework in." That seemed easy enough to Krissa.

"It's more than that. It's this whole game you have to play, sucking up to the system for perfect grades and great recommendations."

"But that's simple." Krissa had always gotten straight *A*'s. Surely only a normal family could produce a straight-*A* student. So if she got straight *A*'s, kept her locker neat, joined all the clubs and was nice absolutely all the time, then her family must be normal.

"It's simple for you," Danny returned. "So I've got to ask you . . ." He swung off his chair and paced over to the window, his back toward her. "I mean, I know there's nothing in this for you and here I am, a shit to you most of the time, but I have to ask you." He turned away from the window, but he didn't quite look at her. He was expecting her to refuse. "I really need you to help me with this. It's important, and it will be tough doing it without you."

Danny needed her. Krissa couldn't believe it. Brilliant, talented, independent Danny needed her. It didn't seem possible.

"I know I don't deserve it," he said. "But please . . ."

Of course he deserved it. She owed him. He was protecting her from their father. But even if he weren't, she would have agreed in a heartbeat. No one had ever needed her before, not like this.

"I will, Danny. Yes, yes, I will. Whatever you want . . . anytime."

It started the next night. She took her books into his room, and, amazingly, Danny did exactly what she told him to.

She had a keen sense of what would be on a test and what wouldn't be. "It's not going to be covered, Danny. Why are you studying it?"

"Because it's interesting. This is cool stuff here."

"Then make sure Mrs. Erickson knows that you're learning it."

Throughout the rest of his junior year, she had him

submit outlines and rough drafts of every single paper.
She wore down his impulse to keep his interests to
himself, and soon the high school faculty became
aware of the range and depth of his intelligence.

She made him join every single extracurricular activity he could stomach. He even joined the school
choir, despite his loudly stated belief that the school
music director was not on the same food chain as the
rest of the human species. He complained endlessly,
but he persevered, revealing that he too possessed determination and discipline.

The two of them were a team, sharing their thoughts,
making plans. Krissa loved it. Never before had anyone in this house listened to her. Danny did. He became everything to her. Their father Krissa ignored as
much as possible; their mother she only thought of as
a set of standards to be met.

There was one thing Danny would not talk to her
about—what their father was doing to him. As concil-
iatory as he was being toward his teachers, he conceded nothing to his father. He made no efforts to
placate Ed French, to alleviate his rage. Here was
where he drew the line.

And there were times when Danny would always
keep on a T-shirt whenever he was around her. Krissa
knew that he was hiding bruises. But he never complained. He never seemed afraid. Krissa admired him
for that.

One afternoon in early September of Danny's senior and Krissa's junior year, they were in choir practice. The director, their one truly awful teacher, was
going on and on about the fall concert. It was a warm
afternoon, the windows were open, and they could
hear the blasting in the mines. It was hard to pay
attention. People were whispering, talking, passing
notes. The director droned on. The highlight of the
concert would be the "My Boy Bill" soliloquy from
the musical *Carousel* and it would be sung by—

Krissa didn't even wait to hear the name. Her eyes

shot to Danny. Who else would it be? And this was exactly the sort of thing he would loathe doing.

"By Daniel French."

Danny hadn't been paying attention. He sat up, puzzled. He had no idea why his name had been called. The kid next to him leaned over and whispered. Danny sagged back in his chair. His eyes went vacant and glassy. Krissa had to drop her head to keep from laughing. His face was full of the stupid horror on the head of a stuffed deer.

After practice she found him out in the parking lot, beating his head against the roof of the used Mustang they now shared. "I can't do it," he moaned. " 'My Boy Bill.' I can't. I simply can't."

"Sure you can," she answered calmly. He was going to sing it. These extravagant protests were simply a necessary stage.

"It will be so fake," he groaned. "I can't."

"Come on, Danny, you fake everything."

He lifted his forehead off the car, then suddenly straightened. "Not about music, I don't." The usual mocking exaggeration was gone. He was sincere. "Say whatever you want about me, and it will probably be something I've done. Except with music. I haven't faked that."

"What about 'You'll Never Walk Alone'?" she asked. He had sung that at graduation last year. His performance had been deeply moving, but beforehand he had complained bitterly about having to do it "You said you'd have to fake that."

His eyes shifted away from hers. "Not in the end, no, I wasn't," he admitted. "I'll kill you if you ever tell a soul, but I did manage to connect with it. I sang it to my guitar."

"Your guitar?"

He stuck his hands in his pockets. Across the parking lot some kids were calling out to one another. Car doors slammed. Engines raced.

"I was fourteen the first time Dad hit me. It was a surprise. That's all I felt, surprise. It wasn't until the

third or fourth time that I figured out that it wasn't
going to stop. I didn't have a clue what to do. I
couldn't go to Mother; she didn't want to know. I was
in it by myself. It was just me and my guitar, but after
a while, I decided that was enough. As long as I had
music, I could make it. I could keep my chin held high
and everything else in that song. So I sang it to my
guitar."

The warm September sunshine suddenly felt thin.
Danny was staring up at the school's ornate bell tower.
He seemed so alone. "Can't you do something like
that with 'My Boy Bill?' " Krissa asked. "Find something to latch on to?"

"Have you listened to it? All that pride in being a
father? No, I don't see myself getting there any time
soon."

Krissa could see his point. "Then maybe you
shouldn't try. Tell Mr. Kravitch you can't do it, that
he'll need to find something else. Not singing this one
song isn't going to keep you from getting into
college."

"But a lousy recommendation from him wouldn't
help, and I don't think he wants me questioning his
taste. I don't see that it's such a tough choice. I mean,
it is only one song one night."

But clearly it was a difficult choice for him. All else
that he was doing to get into college, all the careful
crafting of perfect term papers, the community service,
none of that bothered him, even when done without
an ounce of sincerity. It was all part of the game. But
he wasn't prepared to make music one more move in
the game.

The fall concert came, and Danny sang the song
magnificently. Their mother had come, and even she
had had some grudging words of praise for him in the
car afterward. As soon as they got home, he grabbed
a bottle of Coke and went straight to his room. Krissa
followed him.

He had worn a white shirt under his choir robe.
When she got to his room, he was taking it off. He

had it unbuttoned and was pulling it off his shoulders, down his arms. There were yellowing fingerprints on his arm, a purple flowering on his shoulder, and a long red streak across his ribs where he had been shoved against something.

This was brutality. Krissa had never used that word before, but it fit. This wasn't right, that he should be so marked like this. He didn't deserve it. Some of these bruises belonged to her, belonged on her body, not his. He was taking them for her.

As soon as he saw her, he pulled the shirt back on, but he left it unbuttoned, open, the shirttails hanging free. He picked up the bottle of Coke, and the overhead light gleaming against the pale skin of his neck and chest, he chugged part of the Coke, then took a pint of rum out of his desk drawer and filled the bottle back up.

Krissa was amazed. Danny didn't drink. It was part of his plan, his program. He didn't drink, he didn't date. Both were traps, he said. You drink, you go out with a girl, and something could happen and you'd be stuck here forever. But tonight he was drinking.

He dropped to the floor, leaning back against the wall. He acknowledged her by lifting the bottle in a silent toast. He took a drink and then, his shirt still open, tilted his head back against the wall to stare at his poster of Bob Dylan.

"So you did fake it."

"Actually, the bitch of it is that I didn't."

"What did you find to connect with?" The song was about a man who has just discovered that his wife is pregnant. Proud and delighted, he spins grand fantasies of what his son will be like. It was opposite of everything she and Danny knew about fathers.

"It was easy in the end," Danny answered, still staring blankly ahead. "Under all that boasting, the guy knows he's worthless."

"So?" Krissa didn't see the connection. "You're not saying you think you're worthless, are you?"

"Who, me?" He sounded bitter. "I have great value. I'm my father's punching bag."

"Don't say that. That's why he hits you . . . because you are smart, you are talented, you do have a future."

Danny dropped his hands to the bottle and slowly rotated it between his palms. "If I'm such a great guy, then how come I'm abandoning my sister?"

Abandoning his sister? "How are you abandoning me?"

"By leaving you to face Dad on your own. Haven't you thought about that? What's he going to do when he doesn't have Danny boy to knock around anymore? He may hit you. We've got to be prepared for that."

Her father hitting her? She couldn't imagine it. She wasn't going to think about it. She could feel herself drawing in, wanting to shut out Danny's voice. "That's not going to happen. I'm going to be all right."

"Will you promise me one thing?" He looked up at her. "Will you promise me that if Dad ever tries to hit you, you will try and hit him back? Even if you can't hurt him, make the gesture. Show him that you intend to stand up for yourself. He knows I'm not going to, and I think it makes him push harder. You don't have anyone to protect but yourself. So promise me."

She shook her head. She wasn't going to listen to this. "Dad's not going to hurt me. He's not."

"You don't know that. You just don't know that."

But the day Danny mailed his college applications, an odd thing happened. Krissa's father wanted to talk to her. He came back into the kitchen while she was doing the dishes, sat down at the table, and started to speculate about how much prior knowledge Franklin Roosevelt had had about the attack on Pearl Harbor. He went on and on. He was still talking when she was done with the dishes. She dried her hands and leaned back against the damp counter, wondering how she could get away from him, wondering why it felt so strange.

It happened again two days later. This time he was talking about the Kennedy assassination, about the grassy knoll and the trajectories of the bullets. It was like he was trying to pick a fight with her, his tone was so hostile and overbearing. But she couldn't disagree with him; she didn't know anything about it. He was standing in the kitchen door, filling it. She couldn't get past him. The CIA, the mob ... what was he talking about? And why was he saying it to her?

"If you really read the Warren Report ..." Her father's voice was too pitched with anger to be a drone, but it was disconnected, a loudspeaker blasting onto an empty street.

"It's all such crap, such garbage ..."

"That's real interesting, Dad," she murmured, inching her way along the kitchen counter toward the door. "But really ... I need to go do my homework."

"Your homework?" His voice was sarcastic. "You're going to go do your homework? So now are we blessed with two high-and-mighty-go-to-college types?"

"No, no." Her father had never spoken to her this way, so drawling and bitter. Danny, yes, but not her. "I always do my homework, Dad. It doesn't mean anything."

"Well, all those fancy applications your brother sent out, they don't mean anything either. You tell him that."

"Okay." She was at the door now. "Sure. Whatever you say."

Safe in her own room she sat at her desk, then got up and sat on the bed. She should have stood up for Danny. She should have said that his applications meant everything, that the family should be proud of him, but she hadn't. She had just wanted to get away from her father. She would have said anything.

Later that evening she told Danny what had happened.

He was enraged. "He can't do that. Don't listen to him. Walk out. Why didn't you come get me? You can't let him do it."

"Do what?" Danny was so angry that Krissa felt as if she couldn't be upset herself, that she had to calm him down. "All he really did was talk to me."

"He's just starting. Who knows what he'll do next?" Danny stormed. "I'm not going to stand for it."

Krissa had wanted him to comfort her, not for him to get so upset himself. "What on earth are you going to do?" She was a little exasperated. "You'd only end up getting hit."

"I don't care. I have to stop him."

"And if you try, I'll never tell you when it happens again. I'll start lying to you."

"You can't do that," he snapped. He hated being lied to.

"Yes, I can," she said flatly. "If you go pick a fight with him, I'll never tell you anything."

He glared at her, and she went on. "You can't ask me to stand up to Dad and then be mad when I stand up to you."

"But—" He broke off, and suddenly his face relaxed. "Sure I can. I don't have to be consistent." He reached into his bottom desk drawer and started flipping the college catalogues at her. "Get reading, kid. You're going too."

One of the catalogues hit her on the arm. She let it drop to the floor. "What are you talking about?"

"I don't know why it didn't occur to us before. Why should I be the only one going? Your record's as good as mine. Why shouldn't you go too? You'll have to stick it out here for another year, but then you'll be out of here too."

"Me? Go east? But ... but I'm a girl."

Krissa knew how lame that sounded, but it was true. It was one thing for Danny to want to leave the Range, but it was different for girls. In blue-collar families, girls didn't leave home, not until they got married. Oh, yes, she would probably go to college at least for a year or two, but it would be somewhere close and small so it would be like being home, and then she'd come back and—well ... she didn't know, but surely ... something.

"You know why you never think about the future, don't you?" It was as if Danny were reading her mind. "Because yours stinks, that's why. Do you really want a life like Mother's?"

"No, of course not. But my going away to college, that was one of the things Dad was complaining about. He doesn't think I ought to go."

Danny dropped the rest of the catalogues on the bed. "Doesn't that, in and of itself, suggest that going's the right thing to do?"

So their nightly sessions became about both of them. "Come on," he would rail at her, "that topic is too easy. It's not enough to get the grades. You have to show them that you can think."

She didn't know if she was really committed to going back east, but she certainly was committed to the two of them working together. Danny was paying attention to her, he cared about her, he was concerned about her; she would have done anything for him.

She had a wonderful year. It wasn't the sort of fun her old friends were having: going out drinking at the sand pit after the football games or driving along the empty highways at night, turning off the headlights just to make things interesting. Those evening sessions in Danny's room were interesting. Krissa was lit by a glittery, rushing feeling fueled by her brother's wit, his ambition, his energy. They too were racing along the forest roads, but they had headlights. Danny knew where they were going.

Then suddenly he was gone. In April he was admitted to five different schools and selected Princeton. In June he graduated. He spent the summer working in the mines, and in September they were at the little bus depot and he was giving her a quick, hard hug.

"Hold on for a year. It's just a year." His voice was low and fierce. "You can do it."

"I know. I know." She watched the bus pull away from the curb. It went slowly at first, then picked up speed as it passed the Lutheran church. It grew smaller, and then the road bent at the gate to the mine. The bus took the curve, and a second later the road was empty—just the yellow line, the church, and the mine.

"Well, now," her mother spoke briskly, "as soon as we get home, I want you to get started on his room. Really get it clean."

"Yes, Mother."

"I hate to think what the baseboards are like in there. And behind that desk of his ... who knows what you'll find. But I don't want you cutting any corners."

"No, Mother."

"And you get rid of some of those papers of his. All that stuff, I don't know what he's ever wanted it for."

"Yes, Mother."

But she wouldn't. She would clean everything, make it neat, but she wouldn't throw anything out.

She got the vacuum sweeper and the green bucket full of cleaning supplies and carried them to the closed door of his room. *I won't throw anything out.* This was her pledge to her brother. *I will guard your things.* She opened the door.

The room was deserted. The bed was striped. There was nothing on top of the desk, nothing on the walls. Most of the books were gone. The piles of magazines, the spiral notebooks were gone. Krissa dropped the dust cloths and pulled open a desk drawer. It was empty. Even the Dylan poster was off the wall. Everything Danny hadn't taken with him, he had burned.

He wasn't coming back. Not for Thanksgiving, not for Christmas or summers. Never. He had left the Range for good.

She fumbled for the back of the chair. The torn

vinyl bit into her palm. She felt numb, abandoned. What was she going to do here without him?

It proved to be as awful as she had imagined. She had to drive to and from school alone. She had to remember to set only three places at the table. From the time supper was over until school the next morning, she spoke to no one.

There were moments when she almost hated him. She should have been happy. This was her senior year, the best year of her life. But the other kids were all saying that she had gotten stuck-up, that she thought she was too good for the Range.

She was unhappy, lonely. There were things about the Range that she loved: the sunlight falling through the pale green leaves of the birches, the gentle arch of the ferns drifting over the powdery shape of a fallen log, the glowing depths of the abandoned mines. Here was peace and order.

But she couldn't connect that to anything in her life. Her mother's clean countertops were simply sterile. There was no grace or beauty in her parents' home.

Yet she couldn't find answers in the college catalogues. The stirring intellectual life didn't call to her as it had to Danny. There was something missing, a *doing* kind of thing—working with your hands, a flashing needle spinning out a perfect line of stitches, the dusty warmth of a ripening tomato—an earthy, practical beauty.

If only she could have been like Danny with his clear goals. But she wasn't. Her longings were vague. She couldn't articulate what she wanted. *Beauty, warmth, comfort* . . . the words sounded superficial, but there was something she was aching for. She wasn't going to find it by going east, she knew that. But she wasn't going to get it by staying home.

He had no idea what she was feeling. He kept writing her about her applications. *Tell them you've never been to professional theater. That's blowing everyone's mind.* Then she got a note from him, scrawled across a sheet of paper, raggedly yanked out of a spiral note-book. *Ten o'clock, Friday night. The pay phone at the filling station. Be there. I've got to talk to you without them overhearing.*

She knew she should tell him what she was thinking. This would be her chance. But she couldn't. He was the one person who had needed her, who had maybe even loved her. She couldn't disappoint him.

On Friday she went to the filling station. It was strange to be there in the dark. The pumps were closed, and Krissa waited uneasily, embarrassed even though no one was around. When the phone rang, she snatched the receiver. "Danny?"

"It's me. We've got to be quick or I'll run out of dimes. So listen. You're not going to like what I have to say—"

Krissa knew that she too could say things he wouldn't like. *It's awful here and I'm lonely and I don't know if going to college is right. But Dad's as bad as ever. It's like he's out to catch me at something, and I never know when he's going to start, and it makes me feel so unclean.*

Danny went on. "But I want you to do it. You have to do it."

"What is it?"

"When you fill out your applications, in the personal essay, you've got to say what Dad is doing to you."

"But he isn't doing anything to me," she protested instinctively. "At least not much."

"He is too. Look, you're not going to believe how good the people are around here, the kind of schools they went to. You've got to exploit everything you've got. If you say you're from an abusive home, they'll sit up and take notice."

"But I'm not from an abusive home."

"Oh, come on," he scoffed. "What else would you call it?"

"I don't know ... but not that."

Her father was now following her to her room some nights after dinner. He never did anything. He didn't even come all the way in. But having him stand there in the doorway, talking to her . . . she hated it.

"And it doesn't matter what you call it," she went on, "because I'm not going to tell anyone about it." This had always been their secret, one thing that the two of them had never told anyone. "It's nobody else's business."

"Who cares, if it will get you out of there?"

"You're crazy," she told him. "You're absolutely crazy."

"But I'm off the Range, aren't I?"

"You didn't fake 'My Boy Bill' to do it."

"It's hardly the same, and anyway—"

He went on and on, trying to get her to do it his way. He kept having to put in more change, and finally he ran out.

"Get it through your head," she said at last. "I won't do it. If I don't get in, I don't get in. I'm not going to use this as some gimmick to make a bunch of Easterners pay attention to me."

She hung up, exasperated. It was cold and the burglar lights turned the night a thin gray. She hated disagreeing with Danny. She wished they could always be a team, always agree. But she wasn't going to give in on this one. She was right; he was wrong. You didn't tell your family secrets just to get ahead.

That's what she should put on her application, not that her father was abusive, but that she could stand up to her brother. That's what took guts.

She stepped out of the phone booth. There was a pickup idling next to the air hose. A man got out.

She knew him only vaguely. His name was Jerry Aarnesson. He was their family's closest neighbor. About ten years older than her, he had returned to the Range this summer after some time in the military and had bought a piece of land on Levering Lake where he was building himself a place.

"I saw you on the phone," he said. "Do you need some help? A lift?"

That was nice of him. But people on the Range

were nice. "Thanks, but no. I'm okay. I was talking to someone, that's all."

But if I did what my idiot brother wants, then all kinds of people would think I needed help, and I think I'm doing pretty well on my own.

"And you didn't want your folks to hear your call?" Jerry asked.

"That's true," she admitted. "But it was only my brother."

"He went back east, didn't he? How's he doing?"

"Great, I think. He really likes it."

"It's good to get off the Range for a while. You appreciate it more when you come back."

Krissa pulled her sweater tighter around her. "I don't think Danny plans on coming back."

"I didn't either."

He was leaning back against the light pole, his arms folded, looking down at her. He was a big man, tall and blond, with broad shoulders. The Aarnessons were a Swedish family, and you could tell it in the flat, open planes of his face. The harsh light showed a grain to his skin that the boys at school didn't have yet.

It seemed impossible that he and Danny would have anything in common, but they had both wanted to get off the Range.

"Do you want to go get something to eat?" he asked. "Or would it get you in trouble with your folks?"

He was older. He had been in the Navy. Oh, yes, she would get in trouble with her folks.

"They don't need to hear about it," she answered.

She was surprised at what a good time she had, the best time since Danny had left. Jerry told her about his house and that in the Navy he had been on a helicopter-repair crew. Yes, he'd been in Vietnam, but it had been okay. He hadn't minded it. He didn't talk with any of Danny's insight or wit, but he had been places she hadn't and that was more interesting than anything the other kids at school talked about.

Then he took her to show her the work he was doing on his place. He had a little trailer parked on his property, but he was building his garage first. There were places around here where the garage was bigger than the house. On the Range the men built everything. They wanted garages in which to store their tools and boats, and they didn't much care what their wives' kitchens were like.

But Jerry's garage was nothing like the others Krissa had seen. The wood he was using was warm and full of life. Everything was beautifully built. The shelves had been sanded until they were satiny smooth. The craftsmanship in every mitered joint . . . there was something here that spoke to Krissa. Perhaps there was a place for her on the Range.

In a garage? She could hear her brother's voice. *A half-built garage, a place to store chain saws?*

Jerry took her back to the gas station to pick up her car. He got out and opened the door of the Mustang for her. Then he leaned forward and kissed her. It was nice, and she let him put his arms around her and pull her up close to him. But then she heard her brother again. *Is this what you want?* he would storm. *To get knocked up and have to stay here?*

No, no, that wasn't what she wanted. Not until she had seen what else there was.

Chapter Two

BALTIMORE, MARYLAND, MAY 1966

Quinn dropped his tennis racquet in the rear hall. The narrow entry was filled with his equipment: his basketball, his lacrosse stick, his bat and glove. He was an athletic boy, age thirteen, lean and golden-haired. He spent his afternoons playing flag football with his friends across the green lawns that sprawled out from their large houses. A couple of guys had their own tennis courts, and Quinn himself had a basketball hoop attached to the old carriage house in back of his parents' place.

He lived in Baltimore, but not the Baltimore of docks and longshoremen, of row houses with scrubbed stoops and little family-owned restaurants. Quinn's Baltimore was a WASPy world, green and gracious, Roland Park, the Gilman School, cotillions on Friday night and junior tennis tournaments at the club on Saturdays. These people would have never called themselves "rich." "Comfortable," they would admit to, or even "independent." "Rich" was flashy—yachts and couturier fashions. Theirs was a quiet life, understated, civic minded . . . and expensive.

"Come wash up," Quinn heard Jewel call from the kitchen. "Your dinner's hot."

In the half-bath that served the back of the house, Quinn splashed water on his face and hands—as much washing as any hungry thirteen-year-old could endure—and came into the kitchen. A single place setting was laid on the table beneath the large back

window. Jewel, his family's dark, slender maid, put a
steaming plate in front of him. Quinn clasped his
hands and closed his eyes for an instant, giving a lightning impression of someone saying grace, then at-
tacked the food.

Jewel leaned back against the counter. "So the Wil-
son boy, did he get that cast off today?"

His mouth full, Quinn nodded. Although she never
sat at the table with him, Jewel kept careful track of
his friends and activities. "He's supposed to take it
easy. Did you get that album?"

"It's in your room. But it's borrowed. Scratch it,
and we're both dead."

"I'll be careful," he promised.

She leaned forward and rumpled his glowing hair.
"I know that."

They both loved music, any and all music; from Mo-
zart to Elvis, they loved it. Jewel had introduced
Quinn to the wealth of black music. Ragtime and jazz
she knew from their Afro-American roots; she
brought him recordings of blues, gospel, and soul.
These were the voices of the underpriviledged and
the disenfranchised, but Quinn, although a child of
privilege, was drawn to their vibrancy. He loved Jewel
almost as if she were his mother, and he loved her
music with the same passion that any natural-born son
of hers would have.

She was handing him a second helping when the
door to the front of the house swung open, and
through it came Quinn's actual mother, Barbara
Hunter, elegant and ash-blond.

"Quinn, dear, did you have a nice day?"

Quinn pushed back from the table, standing as his
father said he must always do when a lady, even his
mother—*especially* his mother—entered the room. He
leaned forward for her kiss. She smelled faintly of
lavender soap and cornsilk powder.

That's why she was rarely in the kitchen when he
started his meal. She always changed for dinner, putting on a fresh dress before Quinn's father came

home. She took the chair opposite Quinn and waved
him to sit back down and finish eating. Jewel went
back to work at the sink.

Quinn loved his mother too. It was just that ...
well, she didn't quite ... oh, he didn't know.

She folded her hands lightly on the empty table before her. "You're thirteen now, Quinn."

He chewed and swallowed. He knew that.

"So your father and I think that you should join us
in the dining room."

The dining room? "You mean eat with you? The
two of you?"

She laughed softly. "Of course. I wasn't suggesting
that we trade places. I don't think your father has
developed a sudden fondness for the kitchen."

On a normal evening Quinn and his mother stood
up from the table when they heard his father come
home. They would go to the front of the house, meeting Reed Hunter in the wide, light-filled center hall.
He would greet his son warmly and make his pleasant
inquiries about the boy's day. Then Quinn would go
upstairs and face the homework which the Gilman
School, his private preparatory academy, bestowed
aplenty. His parents would have dinner together, and
he would often hear them still sitting at the table late
in the evening, the faint sound of adult talk, adult
laughter floating up the curving stairs to his room.

Eat dinner with them? Be included in that low conversation? He liked the idea, he liked it a lot.

So the next evening when he made his usual clattering entrance through the back door, instead of Jewel
telling him that his dinner was hot, she said that she
had ironed a shirt for him. "It's hanging on your closet
door."

Quinn looked down at his grass-stained rugby shirt.
"I guess I should change, huh?"

"And you have time for a shower."

A shower? That seemed weird in the middle of the
day, but he knew an order when he heard one. So

twenty minutes later, he was back downstairs, clean and hungry.

He was pleased to see the front door opening and his trim father, tanned and silver-haired, stepping into the hall.

"So you're going to join us this evening, son." Reed Hunter's voice was deep and cordial. "That is splendid."

Jewel had come into the hall to take Mr. Hunter's attaché case. Quinn rocked on the balls on his feet, waiting for his mother to lead the way into the dining room. He had spent all afternoon outdoors with his friends, and they hadn't had a thing to eat. He was ready for dinner.

But his mother turned left into the living room, a room Quinn entered only to practice the piano. He stared at her, puzzled. Then he remembered.

Cocktails. His parents never sat down to eat right away. They always had a drink first. He had forgotten . . . a major mistake.

The bottles and glasses were set up on a butler's tray between the two wing chairs. There were bottles and glasses and ice, but no food, no cheese and crackers, no nuts. Concerned, Quinn watched his parents sit in the chairs. He dropped to the sofa, hoping that they wouldn't hear his stomach growl.

His father turned the bottles around on the tray. "I see that Jewel has brought some ginger ale for you, Quinn. How does that sound?"

Inadequate, he thought. "Great," he said.

He crossed the room to take the glass from his father, peering among the bottles, hoping to see a hidden dish of cheese straws.

"So what will it be this evening, Barbara? Sherry or a martini?"

"A martini sounds nice."

Quinn groaned silently. His father was very particular about making martinis, using a bell not a cocktail shaker. He had his own little routine, his own little, time-consuming routine. Unhappily Quinn watched his father, covetously eyeing the olives dropped into the drinks.

"Isn't this delightful," his mother said as she took her glass, "to have Quinn here?" She settled into her chair, twisting slightly so that she was facing her husband. Reed leaned back in his chair, his head turned toward her.

And the two of them began to chat, sharing every detail of each other's day, discussing whom they had seen or spoken to, what they had heard or read. They were endlessly interested in each other. They finished one drink, then poured another, and a third. It was a lovely, golden time for them, the best moment of the day.

It went on for ninety minutes. *Ninety.* Quinn kept looking at the slow-moving mantel clock in disbelief, torn between thoughts of his stomach and his homework. He eyed the piano longingly. His parents went on talking.

It never occurred to him to speak up, to badger his mother into getting him something to eat as most boys would have done. There were standards in this house, standards of appropriate behavior. They were the foundations upon which Britain had built an empire— cold water baths on freezing Scottish mornings and crisp white trousers in the matted jungle. What you did and how you felt had nothing to do with one another. You might be miserable, but you still behaved.

At seven-thirty, his mother at last stood up. The battered Dodge that took Jewel off to unknown parts of Baltimore had come at six-thirty. She had left dinner on the sideboard on warming trays and in silver chafing dishes. The food was dried-up and bland. After their three nightly drinks Reed and Barbara never cared what they ate. Quinn, however, missed the steaming, spicy food served in the kitchen.

The next evening he fortified himself with two apples and a handful of crackers beforehand. So he wasn't hungry, he was just bored. His presence in the living room did not change his parents' conversation at all. They asked him nothing, made no effort to include him in their talk.

The night after that he brought his homework into the living room with him.

His mother shook her head. "Oh, darling . . . this is such a special time of day. Don't spoil it with homework."

Quinn set his books aside. He counted the colors in the needlework pillows and the Oriental rugs. Ten minutes later, a desperate man, he had an idea. "How about if I played something for you?"

His parents often regretted that they didn't hear him play more. But as the thought usually occurred to them when he was going to bed or when someone was playing the piano at the club, their desire rarely got fulfilled.

"That would be lovely, dear." His mother sounded pleased.

Quinn chose a piece that he knew well. He wasn't going to inflict a practice session on his parents. They listened attentively and clapped at the end, smiling warmly at him. Encouraged, he began something else, but after a moment or two, his parents turned back to each other and, as if he were a pianist in a cocktail lounge, began talking softly to each other.

After that, he practiced. His parents weren't listening carefully enough to distinguish between practice and a performance anyway.

Some evenings his mother would have a mild headache and would ask him not to play. Like a man in solitary confinement, Quinn had to amuse himself. There were only so many times he could count the colors in the pillows and the rugs or stare at the rigging of the three-masted schooner encased in the narrow-necked glass bottle on the mantel.

It was then, he thought years later, that he had taken his first steps to becoming a lyricist. When he couldn't play the piano, he played with words. He would create a mental picture of something, then try to find words that would describe it as precisely as possible. He would switch the words, then readjust the picture to fit the new connotations. He listened to the rhythms of the words in his head, combining them into verse.

He was more interested in the sound of his parents' voices than in anything that they said. Looking back on those evenings, he marveled at two people having so very much to say to each other. Night after night they were engrossed in only themselves. After nearly fifteen years of marriage, they were still enchanted by each other.

Reed Hunter imported chocolate. It was a family business started generations ago. Originally there had been an elegant, little factory whose dense, dark chocolate wafers had been distributed in select shops around the Middle Atlantic states. For many prosperous bankers and silver-haired attorneys, Tulip Chocolate was a fragrant memory of the sun-warmed, wrought-iron-fenced afternoons of their privileged childhoods. But the chocolate was only a memory. Reed Hunter had sold the factory, the recipe, and the trademark shortly after his marriage. The company that bought the factory was a large conglomerate with production facilities of its own. They had closed the original factory and had altered the recipe, making the candy more economical to produce. Demand had dropped instantly, and within a year, manufacture was discontinued. Reed had made no attempt to recover the rights to the product. He was content working as a middleman, providing bulk chocolate to small candymakers.

Reed and Barbara were well-liked in their little world. They were charming and generous. Barbara worked tirelessly on charity committees, happily making endless phone calls. Reed was a good golfer and an excellent dancer. He could always be counted on to serve as auctioneer at any fund-raising event. He was graceful and witty.

Only their son knew—and it was years before he could put his knowledge into words—that as a pair they were gargantuanly selfish. They weren't greedy, petty, or unreliable. They had none of the faults that usually accompany selfishness, but that did not change the fact. The two of them were devoted to each other, but only to each other. No one else truly mattered to them, not even their own son.

Quinn continued his round of school, sports, and music, growing better looking each year, acquiring the poise, the effortless charm, that makes the world of the WASP seem so appealing to outsiders. He traveled in a pack of boys who went to the same schools and churches, whose mothers played bridge together, whose fathers golfed together. He did well in school, and in April of his senior year he was accepted at Princeton.

One Sunday shortly after his high school graduation he was at the club playing mixed doubles with his friend Steve Oberlin and a pair of girls. After the match, he and Steve deposited the girls at a table on the terrace and went to fetch drinks. Steve's older brother Chris was at the bar.

Quinn liked the idea of brothers. He didn't have one, of course, and it intrigued him, the notion of life giving you a built-in teammate—a comrade, a fellow soldier who had lined up on your side since birth. So he was pleased when Chris picked up his drink and crossed the terrace with them.

Chris had graduated from Dartmouth that spring and had started work in the trust department of a bank. He was—as he told Quinn years later—intolerably full of himself, feeling quite the up-and-coming young banker.

The bank had hired him in part for his connections and the circles he moved in. He was to build loyalty to the bank among the next generation, among young men like Quinn.

"We have your trust, don't we?" he said to Quinn as they neared the table where the girls were waiting. "If you ever want to go over it, give me a call."

Quinn's trust had been set up by his long-dead paternal grandfather, the last Hunter to have died owning Tulip Chocolate. With the approval of the trustees, one of whom was his father, the other an officer of the bank, the trust could be drawn upon for Quinn's maintenance and education. But the intention clearly was that he would come into a quarter of it at age twenty-one, a quarter at age twenty-five, and the rest at thirty. It would not support him for his life, but if he wanted to spend a couple of years after college as a rare-book dealer or something else not immediately renumerative, his grandfather wanted him to be able to do so.

Quinn never thought about the trust. Money was rarely discussed in his parents' house; it was simply there, taken for granted. Occasionally he overheard his parents being gleeful that the bank was going to let them do something, as if the bank were a stern Victorian Papa who must be cajoled into indulgence. But as far as Quinn knew, Reed and Barbara had no real financial worries.

So he was not in the least interested in going over his trust. Had he not liked the idea that Chris was his friend Steve's brother, had he not wanted to warm his hands at their fraternal fire, he probably wouldn't have gone downtown to have lunch with Chris.

And Chris would have loved it if he had not.

When Chris had suggested the meeting, he had known nothing about the state of Quinn's trust. He had assumed that the interest had been comfortably accruing with, perhaps, an occasional deduction for the tuition at Quinn's prep school. This was what happened in nice families, and surely the Hunters were among the nicest.

But it took Chris ninety seconds to see that he had opened the door to a nightmare. It was his first grim lesson about banking, that bankers are always learning things that they would truly rather not know.

Reed and Barbara Hunter had been draining Quinn's trust fund for years.

The trust had paid for all his school fees, his clothes, his tennis, sailing, and music lessons. One-third of the mortgage, one-third of the groceries, and one-third of the utilities had been charged to Quinn's trust. All of the expenses of the place in Maine, all of Jewel's salary, the dues and fees at the country club, even Barbara's car had been paid from the trust.

Chris was in a hellish position. He thought a wrong had been done, a code had been violated, but he was too junior to criticize the bank or the officer who had approved these expenses. "I suppose that they thought," he said stiffly, "that these were things that they wouldn't have done if they hadn't had a child."

Quinn knew that could not be true. The country club was the center of his parents' social life. The camp in Maine had been in the family for four generations. Neither one of them had ever lived in a house without a staff. They would have expected to belong to the club, keep the camp, have a maid and two cars, whether or not they had had children.

"Did they have to do this?" he asked Chris.

"To maintain their standard of living, yes."

"What about the business?" Quinn had never paid much attention to his father's chocolate-importing concern. "What about all the Tulip Chocolate money?"

"I don't have the right to look at their personal records, but my guess is that it's never brought in very much. They probably lived on their principal until it was gone."

Gone . . . that wasn't a word Quinn associated with money, that it went somewhere and didn't come back. Money *returned*. That's what he had always heard—talk of investments and returns.

How naive could a person be? What kind of dope would have thought that Reed Hunter could run a business? Quinn's stomach knotted with a sick dizziness. He had the sensation that his foot was touching air and that he might fall. Why hadn't he ever thought about this?

He was going to have to start now. He was going to have to think for all three of them. It wasn't right, it wasn't fair. They were his parents, they should have watched out for him. But they hadn't.

He hardly knew where to start. "How much longer can we go on like this?"

"Adding your expenses at Princeton—three years."

Three years! Princeton would, of course, last for four.

"I'm willing to do whatever you want me to," Chris said. "A few words to the right people, a little pressure ... and surely the domestic expenses could be modified, especially as you will no longer be living at home."

But if Quinn didn't pay for running the house, who would?

He spoke to his parents that evening, keeping his voice mild. "The bank says there isn't much money left in the trust Grandfather set up."

"Oh no, darling," his mother said easily, without guilt. "That can't be right. Whoever you talked to must be mistaken."

"No. There's only money for three years of college."

"There's nothing to worry about," his father said. "Your mother and I will take up any slack."

And how would they do that?

This was what was so irritating about them, that they believed themselves. How childlike they were. Years ago they had decided that this was a perfectly acceptable course. Quinn's trust fund had been like the Ideal Parent, a bottomless source that would never stop providing.

Suddenly Quinn wanted to attack. *Do you think that is what other people do? How can you believe that this comfortable, comfortable life is something we are entitled to, something we don't have to pay for?*

This was what drove him crazy—their self-deception, their image of themselves as good, hardworking people who did their share. They considered themselves good sports; they accepted responsibility on the playing field and abdicated it everywhere else. They had left the management of their home and the rearing of their child to an uneducated maid.

How can you think so well of yourselves?

But it was pointless. Such deeply selfish people could never be called to account. Their defenses were total. However thin their explanations might sound to outsiders, the accounts rang true in their own ears.

Three more years wasn't very long. What would happen then? Quinn supposed that if the family was really and truly broke, he could finish college on a scholarship or a work-study program or one of those things he had never paid any attention to. But what about his parents? What would they do? Would they have to move to a smaller house, sell their pictures, drop out of the club? This easy life they had always known, what was going to happen to it?

He went off to Princeton not knowing the answers to any of these questions. But at Princeton, this son of the ruling-class encountered the unlikeliest of saviors: a restless, dark-eyed miner's child, a kid off the Mesabi Iron Range, Danny French.

Chapter Three

Krissa felt her son's thin young muscles ease with the good news. His Uncle Danny was going to live. The hunger strike was over. Everything about Adam's body seemed to lighten; it was as if he were growing younger in her arms.

She stepped back to look at him. He was twelve now. He had Jerry's Swedish-blond hair and his shoulders were broadening with Jerry's strength; but in his mother's eyes, he was still soft, glowing with light, a miracle.

Being this close to a death made her think: What mattered? For Krissa, standing here in this half-lit kitchen in the quiet before dawn, the answer was swift and simple. Her kids . . . nothing mattered as much as they did. That's why she was here on earth, to raise these four boys, to steward their path into adulthood.

"I don't have to go back to bed, do I?" Adam said. "I couldn't sleep."

"I know that." Krissa brushed his thick hair off his forehead and smoothed her hand down to his warm cheek.

She would never have sent him back upstairs to lie awake, thinking about death. Her own mother would have. If she or Danny had come into the kitchen at 4 A.M., no matter how grave the tragedy, her mother's first words would have been "What are you doing out of bed?" Children needed ten hours of sleep a night; they had to clean their plates, and learn to keep tidy, and be quiet. That's what Peg French had thought.

But that was too easy. Raising children was much more complicated than that.

"Shall we play Scrabble?" Krissa suggested. "You get the game, and I'll fix you something to eat."

Food had been a complicated issue in this household ever since Danny's condition had been reported in the papers every day. At seven, Patrick had been too young to have his appetite affected, but the other boys couldn't forget that off in New York their uncle was starving himself to death. Brian, the older of the sixteen-year-old identical twins, had been defiant. He had said nothing, but he had eaten far more than he normally did. What Danny was doing didn't matter, he asserted by asking for second and third helpings. Curt, the shrewder of the twins, ate just as much. Brian's defiance, Curt sensed, would be less remarkable, less objectionable if the two of them behaved alike. Adam had had the opposite reaction. Like Krissa, he had hardly been able to eat at all. She had not interferred; each child had to address this in his own way.

The pale wooden Scrabble tiles made little clicks on the pine table as Adam turned them over. She put the plate at his elbow and sat down across from him. She drew her letters and watched him as he concentrated on his.

She had turned on the rest of the lights, and now the kitchen was full of soft amber light. It was a big room, running the entire width of the house. Jerry, an excellent craftsman, had built the cabinets himself. They were cherry wood, and Krissa had left them unstained, a rich golden red.

Many of the cabinets' upper shelves were narrow and open, lined with tin-topped Mason jars full of dried lentils, macaroni twists, coffee beans, and split peas. Ball jars glowed with Krissa's raspberry jam and her blueberry syrup. Bunches of dried herbs swung from a rack overhead. A swag of red peppers was over the door; a wreath of bay leaves and a rope of garlic hung on either side of the deep window. The oatmeal was in a stone pickle crock; old glass jars in rich tones of cranberry, cobalt, and pine would catch the light from the morning sun.

And Krissa grieved for Danny—not for his death, but for the life he had chosen. He would never know a moment like this, sitting in a warm kitchen playing a game with his son. Yes, she knew that there was suffering in the streets, terrible suffering, that not all children were warm and safe, but even remembering that, she could treasure the beauty in her own life. Danny couldn't.

Adam ate a piece of bread. It was a Swedish rye which Krissa sweetened with honey and flavored with orange and fennel. "Would we have gone to the funeral?"

"I don't know," Krissa answered honestly. "I imagine his supporters would have wanted to do something very public."

Danny was the leader of an organization called the Colony, a group of homeless activists. The surviving members surely would have wanted Danny's death to continue his life's work. They would have carried a pine box through the streets of New York and buried him in a pauper's grave. There would have been no place for private family grief.

If Krissa could have taken him back to the Range and buried him under a stand of slender-trunked birches or if she could have sprinkled his ashes into a silent, snow-crusted mine, if for a moment she could have gone back to childhood with him and loved him in the way that children should be loved and somehow in his death made right what had been wrong with his life, if she could have done that . . . but of course she couldn't.

And he was going to live. There would be no funeral. The endless twisted slagheap of grief and pain that had blocked every thought of Krissa's could melt, and the familiar green landscape of her life return.

She made the simplest words out of her Scrabble letters. The peace of this moment was too luxurious for effort or thought. She wanted to bathe in the serenity. Life was going to be normal again.

At six she sent Adam upstairs to get ready for school. She wanted to cook for the boys, making them pale, fluffy clouds of scrambled eggs or an oven-baked, peach-jam-filled pancake. The sap of the peach juice would crust at the edge of the cast-iron skillet and the pancake would be puffy and brown.

But first she had to call her mother. Reluctantly she went to the phone.

Peg French had taught herself not to care what Danny did. Her son, a temporary source of pride during his successful rock-star days, was again an embarrassment, something she had to disown so that people wouldn't think the worse of her, someone she had to be sure she criticized before anyone else did.

So Krissa spoke simply. "Mom, Danny's going to be okay. The city gave into his demands."

Mrs. French harumphed. "I suppose we're to think that's good news."

Krissa felt herself stiffen. *Danny's going to live, Mother. Can you be happy?*

No, she couldn't. And it was pointless to long for her to be otherwise.

"So how did you find out?" Mrs. French continued. "Some reporter, right? God forbid Danny should have told us himself."

Danny had been in a coma. He could hardly phone home.

"No, it was—"

Quinn.

Krissa felt, for an instant, as if her heart would stop beating. How could she have forgotten this? Quinn had called. Quinn.

She could not tell her mother. "No, a friend of his called."

A friend.

That lilting moment swept over her again, the sud-

den flash she had had when she had heard him speak
his name, a moment that went beyond peace and broke
into joy, the memory of being in love, of running,
laughing, hand-in-hand, starry-eyed.

Quinn.

She hadn't spoken to him in more than fifteen years.
She knew the facts of his life—that he wasn't married,
that he lived in Washington, D.C., that he was a doctor, a surgeon. That seemed so strange. She had
known him as a singer and a lyricist. What had made
him become a doctor?

And why did he call me?

How they had loved each other, she and Quinn. He
had written "Cinnamon Starlight" for her, and
"Clarissa," "Garland," "Scent and Spice," song after
song, the Cinnamon songs they were called. She had
been the Cinnamon-Haired Girl. That was the scent
their generation had for love—cinnamon, and it had
been Quinn's word for her.

After fifteen years they had spoken again at last,
the lyricist of Dodd Hall and his Girl with Cinnamon
Hair.

*Maybe he was being polite. He didn't want me to
hear the news from strangers.*

No, it was not politeness. Politeness was Christmas
cards with mimeographed letters tucked inside. Politeness was an awkward phone call when you were changing planes in the other person's town. She and Quinn
had never done that.

He called because he cared.

No. For sixteen years, she had had to persuade herself that he didn't care, that she didn't either. Otherwise it was too painful, so overwhelmingly wrong that
she should have been in Minnesota raising four boys,
folding construction paper, sewing patches on Scout
uniforms, taking orange quarters to soccer games,
while he had been in Washington, practicing medicine.
They had to not care about each other. That had to
be true.

A thin feeling crept over her, a restless floating dissatisfaction washing away the serenity that had come from playing a game with her son in their warm, light-filled kitchen.

She felt this way once or twice a year. She never had the feeling when the boys were babies. There was something so complete in the caring for their rosy little bodies. It came only when they outgrew their cuddly toddler days. Then she would look up and, every six months or so, notice a small emptiness, a trace of something absent.

It might come at the swimming pool. She'd see other women sitting at the edge of the baby pool, their feet dangling in the water, half watching their children, but mostly talking to their husbands.

Krissa and Jerry had not had a stressful marriage. They hadn't fought, they hadn't disagreed, they hadn't gotten on each other's nerves. But they had never sat at the side of the baby pool talking; they didn't have that much to say to each other.

Jerry had respected her, and she had respected him. But before she had married him, she had been the Girl with Cinnamon Hair. She had moved in a cloud of starry devotion. Respect was not the same.

But this thin, restless feeling didn't last long. She would focus on the boys and soon enough she'd patch herself back into shape and she would feel fine about things again.

She and the boys really did have a good life. When she and Jerry had first moved down to the Cities, they hadn't been able to afford anything but a house that was on the point of being condemned. A once magnificent place, a late Victorian sprawl of high-ceiling parlors and little attic rooms, the house had been cut up into seven efficiency apartments. They had done all the restoration work themselves, moving beams and bathrooms, stripping woodwork, rewiring, retiling, resurfacing. They had been "urban pioneers"—among the first of many families to restore the old houses.

Jerry had been on the sales force of a lawn mower manufacturer. He traveled a lot, often four nights a week. Two years ago the house was done, and he had decided to move back to the Range. Krissa did not go with him. But because he had traveled so much, having him living up there instead of here in St. Paul with her and the boys didn't seem all that different.

She left a message for Danny at the hospital. It would, she knew, pile up with all the other messages and Danny, being Danny, would return the reporters' calls first.

Three days later her phone rang very early in the morning. She was in the basement, working. She had an upholstery workshop down there. When the boys were at school and after they were asleep at night and before they were up in the morning, she went to work stretching, stapling, and sewing. She was fast and flawless. Working only for designers, she charged as high a price as anyone in the Cities. She could have made decent money if she hadn't spent so much time doing mother stuff: helping a teacher set up a complicated art project, having the end-of-season soccer party at her house, generally being around for her kids.

She stopped sewing in mid-seam and picked up the phone.

"Hey, you're awake."

There was no other greeting. "Hello, Danny." How close she had come to never hearing that voice again. "I'm glad to be hearing from you."

"Oh, you know what it takes to kill a Finn," he said breezily. "You have to cut off his head *and* hide it."

She had to laugh. This was an old Iron Range saying about the hardy Finnish miners. "Danny, we aren't Finnish."

"True. But you didn't worry, did you?"

"Yes," she answered. "Yes, as a matter of fact, I did." And she would have liked to tell him what it had been like. She wouldn't be trying to make him feel guilty; she just wanted him to know how much she cared, how much she would have grieved.

But he didn't want to hear it. "Now that was silly.

I'm not going to fail. I wouldn't miscalculate that badly. Of course, it went down to the wire, but we knew it would."

"You expected to end up in a coma?"

"Oh, sure." He was determined to be casual about having been a few hours from death. "They weren't going to let go of that kind of money just because I lost a few pounds. There was no reason for you to worry about me."

This was one of the million things that were so frustrating about Danny—he believed himself. Krissa supposed that he had to, that he needed to believe that his publicity stunts couldn't hurt anyone but himself. And, indeed, their mother had long since walled herself off from him. But the cost of that was too high for Krissa. She would go on caring. Maybe he was a madman, maybe he was a saint. But he was her brother.

She imagined him sitting in his hospital bed. His hair was still as black and wild as ever, his eyes still crackled with mirth and passion, but his hard life on the streets of New York showed in his face. His was now a bitter beauty with the lined and craggy grandeur of a ruined angel.

"So how are you?" she asked.

"Fine. Extremely svelte, but fine. I've got a tube up my nose, and it's starting to bug me. But they say I'll be eating today or tomorrow. Probably baby food or some scientific gruel. It will taste awful, but what can you do?"

Danny had, as an occasional publicity stunt, eaten out of garbage cans. He had no business being fussy.

"You could come here," Krissa said suddenly. He never came to St. Paul unless a lecture or fund-raiser was bringing him to the area, but she liked the idea. It sounded nice. That stretched feeling hadn't left her yet. It had never stayed around this long before. "I can take care of you for a while. I made my own baby food for years."

"God, no. I mean, thank you for the offer." His

rejection had been so crisp that even he felt obliged
to apologize. "I don't intend any reflection on your
baby food, which is undoubtedly a marvel of its kind.
But now's not the time to disappear. This is enough
money to buy and fix up the building, but not enough
to keep it running. I've still got some major fund-
raising to do, and the iron is hot now."

He wasn't even eating solid food yet and he was
planning fund-raising drives. "You're unbelievable,
you know that?"

"Of course," he said simply, proudly.

"But I'm still glad that you're alive," she said. She
was sorry to hear the lightness in her voice. Why did
Danny make it so hard to be sincere?

"You don't hear me complaining."

PLAYBOY: Tell us what your life is like at the shelter.

FRENCH: I have a room in the basement. Most of the
staff—they're all volunteers—live in the shelter. I
don't have any more space than anyone else. I often
think we should have only dormitory beds like the
residents, but I'm overruled.

You have to see this in the context of a full-scale
rock-and-roll tour because that's the background I was
coming from. There's this incredible hierarchy on a
rock tour. My former partner, the road manager, and
I had suites, the guys in the band had single rooms,
the crew doubled up. Those of us who performed onstage and the senior personnel flew first class, some of
the roadies would be on the plane but in coach, while
others would travel on the buses with the equipment
trucks. Some people had to pack their luggage the
night before; others of us didn't.

It was all justified by the money. Each person's importance was defined economically. My former partner
and I were making all kinds of money so we were
important, we were in suites and limos. Why was my
comfort more important than the comfort of the person in charge of packing the drums? That's what capitalism does to you, makes you think that way, and it's
wrong.

PLAYBOY: You keep referring to "your former partner." He has a name, doesn't he?
FRENCH: Who does?

Tom Maddox, "Playboy Interview: Danny
French," *Playboy Magazine,* August 1990,
p. 91.

Chapter Four

Dr. Hunter took the stack of pink message slips out from under the marble paperweight. His afternoon messages had their usual range: the woman he was currently dating, three patients, a few fellow doctors, a salesman from a medical supply company, and Chris Oberlin calling from Baltimore.

Dr. Hunter returned his patients' calls first. He always did. He remembered—unlike some physicians— that there were examining rooms all over the city; no patient had to be in his. And for some, remaining in his required a great leap of faith.

He was an orthopedic surgeon specializing in knees, and often new patients would have been referred to him by their general practitioner. "Why don't you see Dr. Hunter?" And they wouldn't think a thing about it beyond worrying about whether or not their insurance was going to cover the visit. They'd make an appointment and arrive at his office, still innocent.

Some remained so the whole time they were under his care. Others figured it out. Sometimes they recognized his face; other times, recognition didn't come until they saw his full name on the diploma on his office wall or at the top of a prescription. He could always tell exactly when someone recognized him. There would be a quick intake of breath, and he would look up from the knee, ready to deal with whatever followed.

"My God . . . you're *Quinn Hunter*."

He would smile—and it would be a genuine smile; Dodd Hall fans had often grown up to be intelligent, thoughtful people, the kind you enjoyed knowing. "I was, but now I'm a guy who can stop your knee from hurting so much."

He wasn't like Danny. Danny needed to be famous. Danny hadn't left the spotlight for a moment, going straight from music into his political work.

"But I adored you," the patient would exclaim. "I have every album you ever made."

When Americans meet the famous or even the formerly famous, they often become inarticulate, unable to focus on themselves. This was one of the good things about Quinn's speciality. If he had been a G.P., his patients might not have been able to talk about wavering aches or vague symptoms. Knee pain was hard-edged. Its sufferers knew where it was, when it happened. Quinn rarely had trouble getting a consultation back on track.

When he couldn't, when a patient couldn't stop thinking of him as a twenty-two-year-old rock musician, he understood. He passed such patients along to his partners without hesitation.

He returned his patients' calls, left a message with the secretary of the woman he was currently seeing, spoke to the other doctors, and threw out the message from the salesman. Then with ten minutes before his afternoon schedule was to begin, he called Chris Oberlin.

Chris had been managing Quinn's assets since the day he had told him about the depleted trust fund. The gush of Dodd Hall money had enabled Chris to leave the bank and set up shop for himself as a financial adviser. He managed money for many clients now. Chris was very good, and Quinn was very, very rich.

Quinn's call was put right through. "Don't tell me what the stock market has done," Quinn said immediately. "I don't care."

That wasn't true. Quinn lived entirely on the income from his practice. He didn't even need all of it. But he had a sense of stewardship about that fat lump of Dodd Hall money. It compensated for the Tulip Chocolate money that his parents had let slip away. Exactly whom he was stewarding it for was not clear—Quinn had never married—but he was stewarding it nonetheless.

"I wouldn't waste my breath," Chris answered. "I'm calling because I heard from Danny this morning."

Danny.

The marble paperweight gleamed in the light from the thin florescent desk lamp. The white marble had delicate veins of gray spreading outward like branching capillaries.

"Quinn . . . are you there?"

Danny.

Quinn reached forward and switched off the lamp. The marble dulled.

As much money as Quinn had placed in Chris's hands, he couldn't say that he had done Chris a good turn. The other half of the Dodd Hall money belonged to Danny. Although Danny and Quinn had not spoken in fifteen years, they both still trusted Chris, and during all those years, poor Chris had had to go on dealing with Danny. Not many financial managers have clients who don't believe in private property.

"So what does he want?" Quinn could hear his voice. It was off-pitch.

"You heard about his hunger strike?"

"I did." *I played requiems for him two nights running.*

"His Colony is getting enough money to buy the building and get started, but not enough to run it. Danny wants to feed the budget himself."

Danny had long ago cashed in the stocks and sold out of the limited partnerships that Chris had bought for them when they were singing. He had used the money to run the shelters. Now he had no more capital. His only asset was his share in the Dodd Hall songs and the Dodd Hall recordings; his only income was whatever they still generated. How much that was varied each year. If some other artist covered one of their songs and had a hit with it or if a Dodd Hall recording was used on a soundtrack of a movie, there could be a fair amount. Other years there was less.

"So what does this have to do with me?" Quinn asked.

"Danny wants to license some of the songs for commercial use. It would mean a lot of money."

"Commercial use?" Quinn picked up his pen. He used a Waterman. His hands were narrow; he didn't like a Mount Blanc. "What do you mean? Television commercials?"

"And radio. He's already talked to some people—a soft drink company, the manufacturers of athletic shoes—and they're interested."

"You mean he wants to use the songs to sell shoes and soda? Shoes and soda?"

The idea revolted Quinn. So many great songs had already gone that route, having been rewritten and rerecorded to hawk some product—"Stand By Me," "Unchained Melody," "Good Vibrations," and all those great Motown tunes.

Sure, it was only popular music, but people tied their memories to these songs. You partied to them, fell in love to them, broke up to them, cried to them. They were about your life, your dreams ... until an ad agency got hold of them and told you that no, you were wrong, they weren't about your life, your dreams. They were about diet cherry soda.

Chris was speaking. "There could be a great deal of money in it. Money which Danny would put to very good use."

"Affordable housing would be a very good use," Quinn snapped. Sure, shelters were needed, but Quinn believed that Danny and the other shelter-movement people were draining attention and resources away from the genuine solution to the problems of these women and children: building apartments they could afford to live in.

He took a breath. He was not the sort of person

who snapped at his banker. Danny had once brought out the best in him, but no longer. "Off the top of my head," he said in his usual mild way, fighting down the revulsion he felt at the idea of selling the songs, "I'd say no, but I'll think about it."

"He knew that was the best he could hope for."

"I probably shouldn't even do that." But Dodd Hall was over. Those days were gone. Maybe he should let go of the songs. Maybe he should stop caring so much. Danny didn't care anymore. Why should he?

"So"—Quinn heard himself continue—"how did Danny sound?"

As soon as those words were said, Quinn could have ripped his tongue out. Why had he asked? He might care about the songs, but he didn't care about Danny. He truly didn't care. He didn't have time to sit here and talk. He had patients to see.

PRINCETON, NEW JERSEY, SEPTEMBER 1971

It was Friday night, the end of the first week of classes. Quinn left the freshman dorm, feeling excited and confident, looking forward to the evening. Tonight was the final round of freshman auditions for the Nassoons, the oldest a cappella singing group at Princeton.

The Princeton student body had two general types—the guys like Quinn and the "High School Harrys," the kids who had gone to public high schools instead of private prep schools. Quinn didn't know what it was like for the High School Harrys, but for him these opening days at Princeton had been exhilarating, yet comfortable. It had been like swinging on board a new train, one traveling to some place you'd never been. You'd never been on before, but you knew in an instant where your seat was. And it was a good seat, one by the window with plenty of leg room. It was where you belonged.

Earlier in the week two upperclassman had sought Quinn out. They had graduated from Gilman—Quinn's prep school—a few years before Quinn. They remembered his voice and they wanted to be sure that he understood that the Nassoons was *the* singing group on campus. They were directing Quinn to his seat on the train; they had been holding a place for him. Next year other Gilman grads would stand up and wave him into Cottage or Cap and Gown, the eating clubs Gilman grads joined. This was how Princeton worked. It wasn't democratic; it wasn't fair; it was Princeton.

The Nassoons gathered in a room in the basement of Aughty One, a dorm donated to Princeton by the class of 1901. The class had reserved this room with its oak bar and comfortable fireplace for its own reunions, but as its members aged, the Nassoons had taken over the space.

The room was full of people milling about. The upperclassmen were dressed casually; their T-shirts attested their loyalty to Princeton, to assorted bars, ski slopes, or brands of beer. The freshmen were attired more neatly, in alligator shirts and khakis. People were drinking beer and schmoozing it up—personality was a part of the selection process; you had to fit in, and this was your chance to show that you did. The Nassoons weren't a bunch of effete snobs. These were regular guys, athletic and good-tempered. That's why everyone wanted to join.

One freshman was making no effort to show that he too was a regular guy. Standing alone by the fireplace, leaning back against the wall, his arms folded, the only one without a beer in his hand, he was thin and dark-haired, really good-looking except for being dressed like a slob. A plain gray T-shirt hung loosely over jeans which were faded in an odd, rough patch on his right thigh. The other freshmen had all clearly labeled him poison, someone they didn't want to be seen with.

That was a mistake, Quinn thought. Surely part of being a Nassoon was having enough self-confidence and a decent enough set of manners to approach outsiders. Quinn crossed the room and put out his hand. "Quinn Hunter."

"Danny French."

Quinn was capitivated. This guy might be a social misfit, but what an accent he had, a curiously lilting up-and-down cadence, the vowels soaring and swooping in long rounded tones. Quinn had never heard anything like it. "Where are you from?"

"Northern Minnesota. The Mesabi Iron Range."

That sounded vaguely familiar. "Why have I heard of it?"

"How would I know the answer to that?"

Quinn blinked. That was one rude answer. Sure, Danny French couldn't be expected to know how much Upper Midwest geography Quinn had been exposed to, but come on, most people knew what their hometown's claim to fame was.

He tried again. His father had always maintained that it was the duty of every civilized man to follow sports. That way if you found yourself talking to one of the men who unloaded your ships, you'd have something to say. "So what are your closest teams, the Vikings and the Twins?"

"For those who care about such things, yes."

Okay, that was it. Whoever this guy was, he had a chip on his shoulder the size of Memorial Stadium. Quinn excused himself.

The president of the club was standing by the "Womb," a large overstuffed red chair, calling for people's attention. When the room grew quiet, he explained how the audition would work. You weren't going to have to sight-read. Quinn was disappointed. He was good at sight-reading.

A song would be distributed, people would separate into parts to learn it. Then everyone would reassemble for the auditions. "Tenors, you go with Mountmurray. Baritones, follow Matthews. Basses, you're with Hill."

As he spoke, each named senior stepped forward, nodding his head or raising a laconic hand to identify himself. Quinn crossed the room to join the baritones. From the corner of his eye he saw Danny French lever himself away from the fireplace and come in the same direction. So the prickly logger was a baritone. How delightful.

There were five baritones. They introduced themselves to one another and then followed North Matthews up the staircase to his three-bedroom dormitory suite. North passed out the music. It was an obscure Miles Brothers tune, but Quinn knew it. The others clearly didn't. They split up, each crouching or kneeling in a corner, his face to the wall, trying to concentrate on learning the song. Some cupped their hands behind their ears. Quinn heard some humming, a few low lyrics half sung, half mumbled, and an occasional "shit" or "damn."

He went over to introduce himself to North Matthews. "You have a sister starting Sweetbriar, don't you?"

North nodded. "She was in Baltimore this summer. You must have met her then." Obviously North knew who Quinn was and where he was from. "I take it that you know the song?"

Quinn nodded. "It's a fluke. My mother has a black maid. I know that music."

"Then be a sport and see if anyone needs help."

Quinn went over to Tom Goodean. Tom was having trouble with an interval. "It's just a fourth," Quinn explained and sang the line.

He didn't suppose Danny French knew North Matthews' sister. What an asshole that guy was being, waving off North's offer of help, not wanting to have anything to do with the rest of them. Why audition for something like the Nassoons if you were so determined to stand apart?

Of course he probably thinks we're all assholes.

So what? Who cared what Danny French thought?

The freshmen pretty much had the song down when two more upperclassmen arrived. They were tenors, here to let everyone practice singing harmony. Everyone clustered together across from the sofa. North counted a beat and raised his hand. And within a moment Quinn, who had been so smug about having known this song since he was ten, who did not get things like this wrong, hit a wrong note.

He couldn't help it. There was a voice in this room, another voice, full and rich, mellow, magnificent. It was as good as his own. Still singing, he turned to his right, to the sound of that voice.

It was Danny French.

Their eyes met for a moment. *I hear you.* Then like a shot each pair of eyes jerked away.

Quinn tried to concentrate, to focus on himself, his body, his voice, but he wanted to stop and listen to that other voice. It was magnificient, it was distracting ... the style, the phrasing, the tone. And more astonishing than the voice was the singer's musicality, his feel for the music, his understanding of the song.

Determined, Quinn blocked out the sound. His own voice lifted, coming deep from his solar plexus. This was not a competition, the audition hadn't started, but he was singing as he never had before. He was Orpheus, piping his love's way out of the underworld. He was a Siren singing to Odysseus who had lashed himself to the mast of his ship in order to hear this song.

North cut them off. "Take it down a little, will you, Quinn? Let the others hear the tenors. You too, French."

Quinn nodded, and he supposed that Danny did too because North thanked them and lifted his hand again.

Quinn did not restrain his voice one bit. Neither did Danny. Each was determined not to be outsung.

They did sound good together. Their vibratos matched, their phrasing was the same, their style, their feeling—

North stopped it again. He frowned at Quinn. He didn't know Danny, but he had expected more sporting behavior of Quinn. He rearranged the freshmen so that the three others were closer to the tenors. It didn't matter. North got a third tenor in, and that helped, but not very much. Danny and Quinn sang on,

Indians in full warpaint, blockade runners shamelessly flying their Confederate flags.

Finally North gave up. "We might as well go back downstairs."

Quinn left the room quickly. Why did that voice, a voice that went so perfectly with his, have to belong to a jerk like Danny French?

The baritones were the last to arrive in the basement room. The president had already started calling off names, assembling people into quartets. Quinn heard his name and obediently went over to join two guys he knew and one whom he didn't. The president was ready to start. He pointed to one group to come forward, inviting the others to find places on the beat-up sofas that ringed the basement room. A voice interrupted him. "Hey, we need a baritone, don't we?"

Indeed, one of the quartets was a trio. The president frowned, looking down at his clipboard. Quinn was the first to realize what had happened.

Danny French was no longer among the auditioners.

Freshman at Princeton lived in a four-story dormitory called Dodd Hall. The students had suites, two double bedrooms leading off from a good sized living room. Although dark, the rooms were rich with personality. The casement windows were made of leaded glass, the floors were stained oak. Ornate wood trim ran around the baseboards, the windows, and the fireplaces. A dark crown molding encircled the rooms.

The furnishings were not as grand as the rooms. The university provided institutional bunkbeds and desks in the bedrooms; the students furnished the living rooms themselves, buying used sofas and battered chairs at a massive sale held in the gym during Freshman Week.

On the Sunday after the audition, Quinn, alone in his suite, was playing his guitar, strumming it lightly enough so he had no trouble hearing the knock on the door. He leaned the guitar against the wall and opened the door.

It was Danny French, dressed just as he had been Friday night.

"You've heard of the Iron Range," he said in that swooping, rounded accent of his, "because Bob Dylan grew up in Hibbing, our biggest town."

This was an apology. Quinn guessed that Danny French didn't apologize much.

"That's right," Quinn remembered. " 'North Country Blues,' 'Girl of the North Country.' " Dylan's Minnesota songs were full of powerful, bleak images of locked mine gates and empty lunch buckets, people living on half a day's wages. Quinn loved the songs, but they were about something so remote from his experience that they had always seemed like little fictions.

But Danny French had grown up there. The songs weren't fiction to him. Quinn looked at him with interest. "Your father . . . does he work in the mines?"

"Nothing else up there." Danny didn't elaborate. "Is that your guitar?" He squatted down to take a look at it. It was a good guitar, a Martin. He shook his head. "If that were mine, I wouldn't let anyone else touch it."

"Then how fortunate," Quinn answered, picking it up, "that it's not yours." He handed it to Danny.

Danny took the guitar and went to sit cross-legged on the floor under the window. Quinn wasn't much for noticing how other males looked, but Danny French did have something. He had a lean masculine beauty that wasn't at all faggy or queer.

Danny began to strum the guitar, then started to sing; it was an old Everly Brothers song, "Crying In The Rain." Quinn liked its rhymes, especially "fool/-you'll." Danny was singing the melody; Quinn dropped to the floor across from him and picked up the harmony.

Halfway through the first verse, Danny suddenly switched to harmony. Within two notes, Quinn was on the melody. Then Danny changed keys from G to B flat. Quinn followed effortlessly. It was a short song. It seemed to be over in an instant.

Danny spoke. "You got sung in, didn't you?"

That's how you found out you'd been admitted to the Nassoons. The upperclassmen came to your room late that night and caroled you out of bed.

Quinn nodded.

"You must be happy about that, right?"

Quinn started to nod again. "Sure, but—" He stopped.

No, he could say it. Danny had come here and sort of apologized. He had made the first step. Quinn could take the next one. "But I wanted to sing with you."

"Well, yeah ..." Danny was drumming his fingers nervously on the body of the guitar. "But not in there, not like that."

"Why not?"

"It was so Joe College."

"Yes, it was, but why come to Princeton if you don't want that?"

"Good point." Danny's mouth tightened in acknowledgment. "Good point. But you guys ought to hear yourselves. 'My mother' "—Danny's lilting accent flattened into Quinn's mid-Atlantic tones—" 'has a black maid.' "

He had a good ear. "What's wrong with that?"

"It's not that she's black—although I'm sure one could say something about exploitation and racial equality—it's the idea of a maid at all. I expected Southwest Matthews, or whatever the hell his silly name was, to drop into a dead faint, but I suppose his mother has a black maid too."

"I don't know the family, but it wouldn't surprise me."

Danny cursed. "I can't deal with this."

"You don't have to deal with it," Quinn pointed out. "All you have to do is sing with it. You can do that, can't you?"

"Yes," Danny answered, starting to play again. "I can do that."

* * *

From then on, it was all they wanted to do, sing together. They skipped class; they hardly ate or slept. They sang the complex choral works that Quinn knew and all the Scandanavian and Eastern European folk songs Danny had learned back on that Iron Range place of his. It seemed to have been inhabited by every ethnic group to have ever come to America, except for blacks. Danny knew little about black music. So Quinn introduced him to Ivory Joe Hunter, the Orioles, the Clovers, and the Spaniels, the gutbucket-raw sounds of John Lee Hooker and Lightnin' Hopkins. And of course, Danny loved them, charging through Quinn's record collection.

Their different backgrounds, their different personalities, helped bind them together. Each wanted to be the other. Danny secretly envied Quinn his ruling-class ease, his poise and self-assurance. Quinn longed for Danny's deeply rooted sense of the earth. His life on the Iron Range seemed more authentic, closer to nature and passion than anything on the wide, shaded streets of Roland Park. Danny admired Quinn's effortless polish; Quinn craved Danny's energetic sincerity.

One afternoon they were sitting in Quinn's room. Danny stretched out his hand for the guitar and when Quinn gave it to him, Danny began playing a melody that Quinn didn't know. It was solidly rooted in the blues that they had been listening to, but it had a hint of intellectual intricacy that was unfamiliar. Quinn looked at him inquiringly. Danny went on playing.

Then Quinn understood. "It's yours, isn't it?"

Danny nodded, still playing.

"Are there lyrics?"

"None fit for public consumption." Danny stopped playing. "At my best I write tedious imitations of early Dylan."

"That's interesting," Quinn returned. "My melodies are conventional and unmemorable."

"And your lyrics?"

"I like them." Quinn reached into his bottom desk drawer and pulled out a small blue notebook. He flipped it over to Danny. He didn't say—he didn't need to say—that Danny would be the first person to read what was inside.

"Look at that one on the fourth or fifth page," he suggested. "The one with the a-a-b-a rhyme. Sing it with what you were just playing. It should have the right number of syllables."

Danny read through the lyric and stared up at the ceiling for about twenty seconds trying to match the lyric and melody in his head. Then he began to sing.

Twenty sleepless hours later they were staring at each other. Danny spoke: "Shit, man, we're *good*."

Quinn's songs were monologues, carried by a strong first-person voice. There was a definite character in each song, speaking about a specific situation, caught in a concrete moment. When these young men spoke about their lives, the women were not empty place-holders, characterless "Peggy Sue's," interesting only for the emotion they inspired; they too had clearly defined personalities.

Danny's melodies were equally strong and individual. Some were folk based, some were solid white blues—all were sensuous and inventive.

As good as each was on his own, they were better together. Quinn could ruin a lyric by overrefining it. Danny would grab it from him—"It's done, man, it's done"—keeping him from tinkering away the blast of raw energy that every idea began with. Danny tended to put too much in a song: he would have enough musical ideas in each for three or four songs. Quinn could pick it apart. "This is the riff, this is the chorus, this is the verse, this is the bridge, get rid of all that other crap." Danny would and the result would be cleaner and surer.

Within a month, they knew that this was no hobby. This was their destiny, their life work, their profession. They set a goal for themselves, to have a record contract in a year. Then they sat down and worked back-

ward from there, writing out step-by-step what they
would have to do to achieve that. *Make a tape, research the club scene . . .*

"Wait a minute, stop," Danny said suddenly. Quinn
had been the one writing out the list. "Your hand, let
me see your hand, hold up your hand."

"My hand?" Quinn was puzzled, but he put down
his pen, held up his right hand, palm out, fingers
spread.

Danny put his left hand against it, matching them
palm to palm, fingertip to fingertip.

Quinn's hand was honey-brown while Danny's was
blue-veined and pale, but in shape they were the same,
exactly the same. Their palms had the same breadth,
their slender fingers tapered to the same length. The
hands mirrored each other's perfectly; they could have
been the right and left hands of a single person.

It was as if some tiny bit of genetic material, some
little scrap of the first Eve, had remained intact as it
traveled through the millenniums of human history.
As it branched out, forming the races and tribes, it
had preserved itself in duplicate, using the bodies of
Russian and Irish peasants, of Anglo-Saxon scholars
and Norman lords. At last it reappeared in these two
young men to mark them as brothers.

It's Danny French that you notice first. He is talk-
ative and energetic, with long-fingered hands that
swoop birdlike, raking through his dark hair. After a
while you find your attention wandering to Quinn
Hunter, the guy across the room. He too is watching
the Danny French show, smiling drily, still amused
even though he has to have seen it a hundred times
before.

Suddenly you remember that he's the lyricist. All
the words, those hip, intellectual, cool thoughts, those
are his.

You ask him the same question that elicited such a
pyrotechnical answer from his partner. He responds,
" 'My views are pretty much the same as Casey's.' "

He's a baseball fan! He quotes Micky Mantle! Is

this what we need now, more people who quote Mickey Mantle? Is it cool to like baseball?

He laughs. "I'm from Baltimore. Don't you dare make me out to be a Yankees fan."

And suddenly you start to think, "Hey, I like this guy."

You expect to hear from Danny French. Life-of-the-party Joes don't give up easily. But he's quiet, and in response to your inquiring glance, his dark eyes laugh. He's the kid whose big brother has just shown up, and, oh, is he proud of him.

"Do you compete with each other?" you ask.

Quinn, the lyricist, answers. "We're both competitive. We feel a lot of pressure about what other people are doing, and we do compete with ourselves, trying to better our times and all that. But with each other? No, I don't think so. We're playing on the same team."

"But what if you started competing with each other?"

They exchange glances. "Bad news," says Danny.

"Pulverization, extinguishment, nullification, obliteration, mass demolition," Quinn adds.

"The boy does have a vocabulary on him, don't he?" Danny says admiringly.

—Molly Duttonberg, "Close Harmony and Nuclear Pulverization: A Conversation with the Ultra-Cool, Ultra-Hip Dodd Hall," *New York Magazine*, August 1975, p 53.

WASHINGTON, D.C., DECEMBER 1992

Quinn said good-bye to Chris and hung up the phone. He leaned back in his chair, lacing his fingers across the top of his head. What was he going to do? Let Danny sell the rights to the songs?

Hundreds of thousands of now early-middle-aged listeners still loved Dodd Hall songs. They smiled and turned up the car radio when one came on. They heard those songs, and for a moment they were in college again, walking through the shadows of Gothic spires or up the shallow steps of a white-columned brick building.

Did those people want to hear those songs rewritten to peddle consumer goods?

Or for that matter, did Quinn? Every single word had come from his heart. He had poured into those lyrics his feelings about life and independence, his deep disillusionment with authority, and, above all, his passion for Danny's sister.

Who would want "Cinnamon Starlight," the first song he'd ever written for Krissa? That was easy—the McCormick seasonings people. Danny probably already had them lined up. Or maybe Interstate car batteries would pay more. They could just change "Cinnamon Starlight" to "Overly Dim Carlight."

Krissa . . .

I remember when I first sang the song to you. We were in that unheated loft in New York City, and I could see your breath, little white clouds in the air.

Or a furnace company. Why not a furnace company? Instead of starlight, the song could be about a pilot light. It would be so romantic, so stirring and meaningful.

You were wearing one of my sweaters. It hung to your knees . . . And your hair was flowing, curling around your face and over your shoulders. You had stars in your eyes . . .

His afternoon patients were already in the examining room, waiting for him. He had to stop thinking like this. Chris had called him with a business deal. He had decided against it. There was nothing more to it. He stood up.

. . . Stars that lit a galaxy . . .

He slipped the cufflinks out of his shirt. In a minute these thoughts would be gone. He would stop remembering; he wouldn't be able to smell her hair. He laid the cufflinks on the desk by the marble paperweight. One more minute and the memories would be gone, he would be free. He turned back one cuff, then the other. Okay, he was all right now.

This was getting to be a problem. Usually these thoughts, overpowering memories of his Dodd Hall days, of Danny and Krissa, sudden surges of longing and regret, came only once or twice a year. That pace he could handle. But since about the fortieth day of Danny's hunger strike, when it became clear that Danny wasn't fooling around, that he might actually die, Quinn was getting them once or twice a *day*. That wasn't so good.

Just because Quinn didn't sleep on a heating grate to demonstrate solidarity with the unfortunate didn't mean he had no charitable impulses. A few years after Dodd Hall broke up, he set up the James Laurence and Frank Churchill Foundation—named after the elderly gentleman in *Little Women* who had given Beth her piano and the young gallant in Jane Austen's *Emma* who had sent Jane Fairfax hers. Through his foundation, Quinn gave away pianos, bestowing them on schools, churches, community centers, symphonies, and theaters across the country. Any music major with ideals about public service and a gift for teaching could get a job in an inner-city youth center or a crowded day-care facility; the funding was provided by the Laurence and Churchill Foundation. If a child blossomed under this teaching, if he or she stuck with it and really loved it, the foundation provided money for tuition to a college or a conservatory.

Unlike his former partner, who was willing to sleep on a heating grate provided the entire world knew about it, Quinn remained anonymous. His boyhood piano teacher ran the foundation for him. She was exceedingly discreet. So far no one had traced any of the foundation's activities back to Quinn. Her husband had a cousin in Maine and she had used him to arrange for the purchase of the three uprights that stood in the common rooms of Danny's shelter in New York.

And if this new shelter opened, it would get pianos

and guitars, bells and tambourines for the children to play, and a full-time music teacher. Surely that would be enough. Quinn would be doing his share.

Danny wouldn't think so.

You're a rich white guy. Why are your feelings about these songs more important than women having a safe place for their kids to sleep?

Quinn drew a hand across his eyes. Fifteen years and he was still hearing Danny's voice in his head.

A day later he found among his office mail an ivory envelope addressed to him at Georgetown University Hospital, where he did some clinical instruction. The mailroom there had forwarded it to his office.

It appeared to be a personal letter. There was no "Dr." before or "M.D." after his name. The penmanship was in a feminine, flowing hand. Of course that was a tactic of some junk mailers—make the letter look personal so that the recipient would open in.

He turned the envelope over to check for a return address. An instant later he was ripping it open. A letter opener lay at his elbow. But he wasn't using it. It was too far away.

> Dear Quinn,
>   I wanted to thank you for calling me when Danny was taken to the hospital. I was sitting right by the phone, and if I wasn't very gracious, it was because I was so certain that the news would be the opposite of what it was.
>   I waited to write until I heard from him. He called yesterday. He sounds fine and is unable to understand why anyone was worried about him.
>   Again thank you.
>
> As ever,
> Krissa

How nice of her. This wasn't necessary. She didn't have to write.

. . . I could see your breath . . . my sweater hung to your knees. . . .

He and she had parted bitterly, without farewells or forgiveness. They had hurt each other almost beyond anything Quinn could now imagine. Why she was apologizing for her phone manner? It seemed so trivial.

But maybe that triviality was good, a sign that the pain was at last over, a sign that perhaps they could speak to each other without feeling as if they were balancing at the edge of the Grand Canyon, a breath away from toppling in.

If so, he could pick up the phone and call her. He didn't need some big excuse like her brother almost dying. They could just chat. *For fifteen years I've only heard about you through your mother.* Quinn had dutifully sent Peg French a card at Christmas and flowers on Mother's Day too. *I don't even like your mother.* Well, he probably shouldn't say that. *So I'm just calling to find out how you are from you yourself.*

That was all right. That was dignified and sensible. Fifteen years had been long enough. They could probably talk to one another like two normal human beings. At least over the phone.

He still had her phone number. He dialed the 612 area code, then the number. It was simple. He was right. This didn't need to be complicated or dramatic. Just a phone call between two old friends. A light boyish voice answered.

"Hello, this is Dr. Quinn Hunter. Is Mrs. Aarnesson available?" How strange to call her that.

"Just a second," the boy said. Then Quinn heard, "Mom, it's for you. It's some doctor."

He tried to imagine her coming to the phone, a grown woman, the mother of four, but all he could see was a seventeen-year-old girl getting off a plane, her hair blazing with coppery fire.

"Yes?" Her voice was clipped, worried.

"Krissa, it's Quinn."

"Quinn!" She was startled. "I'm sorry, I thought . . . What a nice surprise."

"And a relief, I hope. I heard myself announced as 'some doctor.' "

"Yes." Now there was a faint laugh in her voice. "I have three boys at hockey practice. I do not want to be hearing from strange doctors."

Quinn knew, surely even better than she did, exactly what ice hockey could do to a knee. "I just got your note, and I see," he suddenly heard himself say, "that my calendar puts me in Minneapolis right after the holidays." He hadn't planned on saying this. It wasn't true. Why was he saying it? Because the sound of her laughter, the memory of her hair, her eyes, was making everything complicated, everything desperately dramatic. It was all starting again, but it was already too late. He couldn't stop. "I wondered if I might see you."

Chapter Five

Q: In the first album, your lyrics, while intelligent, are rather cool, voices speaking from a disembodied universe. Everything after that is warmer and fuller, more rooted in the physical world. How do you explain that?
A: By blaming Danny. How else? [*Laughs.*] Danny and his sister are from northern Minnesota, and it gets staggeringly cold up there. They are used to letting nature organize their lives in a way that was new to me. Danny's sister, in particular, is keenly aware of the sensory world around her. She learns about something by interacting with it physically. She is almost incapable of reading something over your shoulder. She has to have her hands touching it before she can read it.

She also has exceptionally acute senses. She can walk in a room and smell the cucumbers in the salad. Two colors that look exactly the same to me, she can see a difference between. Her physical universe is a very rich place.

You can't associate closely with a person like that and not have it affect how you view the world

—Cameron Winkman, "Quinn Hunter," from *Today's Bards: Interviews with Rock Songwriters,* (New York: Vernon House Press, 1976), p. 94

PRINCETON, NEW JERSEY, NOVEMBER 1971

The mail cascaded through the slot in the door to Danny's dormitory suite, the individual envelopes skating across the pitted oak floor. The sound made Quinn look up, but neither he nor Danny stopped. How could anything in the mail be as interesting as the song they were writing together?

So the envelopes lay on the floor until frustration with one part of the melody made Danny restless. He plucked at one of the buttons hanging loose from the tufted back of the worn green sofa. He raked his fingers through his already wild black hair. He stood up and, humming the same four notes over and over, he paced around the room. At the door he bent over and scooped up the mail. He started flipping it, one envelope at a time, onto one of his suite-mate's desks, experimenting with the rhythm of the four notes.

Quinn had his eyes shut. He was listening, trying to follow Danny's experiments. Danny would, Quinn knew, figure this thing out. The trouble was that he didn't know when he had. Telling him had become Quinn's job.

Suddenly the humming stopped. Quinn looked up. Danny was ripping open a daffodil-yellow envelope. The rest of the mail was again on the floor at his feet; he must have dropped it.

Quinn folded his arms across the top of the guitar and watched in interest as Danny skimmed the letter, flipping through the three daffodil sheets quickly. Danny had never said anything about a girlfriend back home, but this was the sort of stationery a girl would use, and Danny was certainly reading it with the eagerness that one would have for a girlfriend's letter. When Danny was finished, Quinn raised his eyebrows inquiringly.

"My sister," Danny explained.

"Your sister?" Quinn was astonished. "You have a sister?"

Every August at the family camp in Maine, Quinn had slept in a long low attic designed to house dozens of brothers, sisters, and cousins. There were cots and bunks, and ropes were swagged across the ceiling so that blankets could be hung to separate the boys from the girls. But Quinn had slept there alone.

"Sure," Danny answered. "Didn't I mention her? Obviously, I didn't or you wouldn't be sitting there like a walleyed pike."

It was true that they had talked little about their families. Such things were merely *facts*. The music was what was important. But Quinn had sensed a solitariness in Danny that mirrored things he felt within himself. "I assumed you were an only child. I am, so I figured you were too."

"Well, I'm not," Danny answered. "I've got one sister. She's a year behind me."

"What's her name? What's she like?" This was intriguing, the idea that Danny had a sister. "May I see her picture?"

"You could if I had one, but I don't."

How could a person not have a picture of his sister? Quinn's parents had gotten a new portrait of themselves taken as a going-away gift for him, no doubt charging the photographer's fee and the sterling frame to his trust.

"Then tell me about her," Quinn said. "Where's she applying to school? Does she want to leave Minnesota?"

"You bet she does."

In fact that was what her letter was about. She was coming east for her college interviews in a couple of weeks. She would be flying into Newark airport, which was forty-five minutes away.

Quinn borrowed a car from an upperclassman, and he and Danny went to meet her.

Danny had repeatedly said that Krissa looked nothing like him, but as they were watching the line of passengers stream off the plane, Quinn was looking for a feminine version of his partner—a raven-haired beauty with parchment skin and flashing eyes. He was still looking for this creature when, from the corner of his eye, he saw Danny carelessly embracing a delicately built girl with titian-colored hair spilling over her shoulders and down her back.

She turned and Quinn stepped forward to put out his hand.

Except he couldn't move. For one glowing moment all laws of the physical universe ceased. Gravity, respiration, centripetal force, cellular division, were all suspended. Every being on earth paused, breathless, weightless, motionless, as Quinn Hunter looked down into a pair of honey-colored eyes.

And then, as if the cosmos needed to make up for that lost moment, everything started to spin, whirling at a fantasy speed.

This is it. She's the one.

They were on a carousel, riding dancing tigers, panels of lighted mirrors glittering with thousands of sparkling white lights, organ music lifting and swirling as the world spun by.

No. It's just that she's his sister, and you're so close to him. You're making too much of this.

She had high cheekbones and a narrow chin, her lips were soft and blossoming. Her coloring was warm—honey, sunshine, and ivory, peach rosebuds, and pale opals. Her skirt was long, swirling in a dark design of paisley and vines. She wore a full-sleeved, cream-colored blouse gathered in beneath a laced vest.

You're not making too much of this. You will love her until the stars fall.

She looked like a figure in a hand-tinted woodcut illustrating a medieval manuscript. Her hair should have been bound in gold cord, her arms full of lilies and myrtle, and he should have been her vassal, her knight.

Danny had his arm around her shoulders, a gesture less affectionate or protective than presenting. *Here she is, my sister.*

Quinn did not know much anthropology, but surely somewhere there was a culture where this happened. You met another young man. You liked him, he liked you, you worked well together, so he gave you his sister. Quinn wished he knew where the society was. They were at the airport. They could get on a plane and go there.

Every instinct urged him to abandon all rules of courtship and open his heart to her, speaking to her as he had never spoken before. *I felt this. I know you did too. Let's not pretend that we didn't.*

But Quinn was a WASP. Rules—all rules—were too entrenched in him for violation. He shook her hand and asked her if she had had a good flight.

"Yes, thank you." She had Danny's musical accent. "Yes, I did." Then she paused, a little breathless. "I mean, I guess it was good. It's the first time I've ever been on a plane so I don't have anything to compare it to, but we didn't crash or anything. I suppose that's good."

She too knew the rules of courtship. She was sophisticated enough to know that those rules required her to hide her interest in him, but she was not experienced enough to do it well. As they walked across the parking lot to the car, she kept looking at him every time she thought he wasn't watching.

Not watching? She would never again be able to do anything that he would not watch.

New Jersey's rolling farmlands were smaller, more intimate, than the vast sweep of Minnesota's prairie. The wooded grounds were lighter, more parklike, than the timber she knew. Quinn was glad to be the one showing her this older, more settled world.

Then they arrived at Princeton—majestic and mysterious, with its scrolled iron gates and the graceful, crenellated spires rising out of the trees.

They dropped off the borrowed car and walked back to Dodd Hall. Danny and Quinn wanted to play their new songs for her. So Quinn parted from brother and sister on the stairwell, bounding up to his suite to get his guitar. He hurried back, not wanting to waste a moment.

Danny had said that she might not be entirely sure about coming east to school. He had been badgering her, and she was getting tired of hearing about it from him. So, Danny proposed, maybe Quinn could try to get her to see how important this was.

Quinn had agreed. Of course he had. He and Danny were partners. Danny's responsibilities were his. And that had been before he had met her. Now he would do anything. To have her here ... to be on that carousel, running it slowly, learning the contours of each dancing animal ... their reins would be garlands of flowers; ribbons would flutter from the golden poles.

The door to Danny's suite was open. As he crossed the living room, he heard the voices behind the closed door to Danny's room. So as he always did when Danny was expecting him, he rapped lightly with one hand while simultaneously opening the door with his other.

Krissa was changing her clothes. Instantly Quinn turned his back, apologizing, but a vision had burned into the back of his eyes. The swirling carousel melted and from its dissolving frame rose a girl and her doe-like body, a soft band of flesh between the top of her bikini panties and the hem of a tank T-shirt, glowing and warm, inescapably alluring.

Quinn was sexually experienced. But his encounters had been typical adolescent sex, a bit on the chilly side, both parties more curious than aroused. He did not think of himself as an unusually warm-blooded animal, but as he stood outside the door of Danny's room, eyes shut, his head back against the wall, he was nearly fully erect.

In a moment Danny called out, "You can come back. We're all decent."

Quinn opened the door. Danny was grinning wickedly. Quinn ignored him, instead summoning up all those years of cotillions and junior tea dances in order to speak to Krissa. She was embarrassed. He kept his gaze focused steadily on her face. "I apologize. I should have knocked."

"You did knock," she said, a smile slowly coming to answer his. "You just didn't wait for an answer."

"It wouldn't have mattered," Danny told her. "I would have told him to come in. I'm so used to seeing you that I wouldn't have thought anything of it. And what's the big deal anyway? Now he knows you wear underwear, but he probably could have guessed that on his own if he cared to give the matter any thought."

Quinn imagined that this was a matter upon which he would give a great deal of thought.

She had changed from her swirling peasant garb to what she'd be wearing for her interview with the Admissions Office. It was a green wool dress. It had a white collar fastened with a little silver pin, and she looked faintly prim, almost like a Puritan. The Cossack maiden was now Priscilla Alden.

"Now I'm ready to hear these songs," she said.

This was the first time they had sung any of their compositions to anyone else. Krissa sat forward in the deep chair, her chin propped on her hands; she was listening.

Oh, Danny ... Danny boy ... this sister of yours, I like her, and she likes me.

Quinn could have played for her all day, all night, all year, but she had her interview to go to. So reluctantly they put down the guitar and walked her over to the Admissions Office to keep her appointment.

"Are you nervous?" Quinn asked.

She shook her head. "I might be for the ones tomorrow, but not this one. I don't really want to come here."

"You don't?" Princeton admitted women now, and Krissa had to be one of them. That was essential. Surely she understood that. "Why not?"

"I think I want to go to a women's college."

"A women's college?" Danny was walking on her other side. Quinn couldn't see his face, but he sounded surprised. "I didn't know that. What put that in your head?"

"I'm tired of hearing people talk about hunting and fishing."

"People at Princeton," Quinn spoke up immediately, "do not talk about hunting and fishing. That I can promise you."

"But the men still run the show, don't they?"

He had no answer for that; it was true. "If you're really stuck on this idea, don't believe what they tell you about Radcliffe and Holyoke." Quinn named two excellent women's colleges in Massachusetts, hours and hours from Princeton. "They're dreadful schools. Bryn Mawr and Barnard are the only places worth going to." Bryn Mawr was outside Philadelphia, Barnard was in New York—each was an easy train ride away.

"You'll have to go where they take you," Danny said flatly. "Don't count on being able to pick and choose."

They were at the Admissions Office now. Krissa wanted to go in alone, so they all stopped outside the old stone building, honey-colored with white trim.

Danny had his hands in his pockets. Quinn could now see his face. It was set, even a little grim. "You remember what we talked about last month?"

Krissa looked puzzled.

"Come on, you remember. That night at the filling station." Danny was impatient. "When I called you there."

Quinn had no idea what Danny was talking about.

"Oh." Krissa now remembered. "But *we* weren't talking about it. *You* were."

"But you're going to do it, aren't you?"

She shook her head. "You know the answer to that."

Danny exploded. "Goddamit, Krissa. Why the hell—"

Two people coming around the walk paused and stared. Danny lowered his voice, but he was still furious. Quinn had never seen him like this. "Use it," he hissed. "It's important."

"Nothing is that important," she said firmly. "I'm doing this my way."

"But what if your way ends up with you stuck on the Range?" His voice was growing loud again. Whatever he was talking about mattered the world to him. "What if—" He reached for her arm.

Her hand shot out. She grabbed his wrist before he could touch her. "You aren't planning on hitting me, are you?"

Hit her? Why had she gotten an idea like that? Danny wouldn't— Quinn couldn't even think it, it was so absurd.

She had her arm out straight. Her hold on Danny's wrist was so tight that his hand was turning red.

Danny mumbled something and pulled himself free. He turned away, and Krissa hurried up the stone steps, her green dress swirling about her knees.

It was a bright afternoon, warm for this late in the year. The grass on the building-ringed quadrangle was still green. People were out, sitting on the benches and under the trees.

Danny was working the toe of his boot into the little trench that edged the sidewalk.

Quinn knew Danny's music. There was anger in some of it. This outburst wasn't totally surprising.

But Krissa's challenge had been. Danny had been reaching for her arm, trying to stop her from going inside. It was a natural gesture. Why had she reacted like that?

Quinn spoke mildly. "That seemed like an odd thing for her to say."

"Actually it wasn't." Danny knew exactly what he was talking about. "Our dad is a Grade A bastard. He slapped me around a lot. Being hit is normal in our family."

Slapped? Being hit? Quinn could not have heard right. "Your father has actually hit you?" Quinn could not imagine his own father engaged in physical violence of any kind.

"All the time," Danny answered. "That's why it's so important to get her out of there. He hasn't hit her, and maybe he won't. But ever since I said I was going to leave home, there's been some weird shit going on."

Quinn froze, his mind suddenly filled with the image of Krissa as she had been when he had opened Danny's door too quickly, the curve of her waist, the sweet flesh of her bare arms, her bare legs. "When you say 'weird shit,' what precisely do you mean?"

"Oh, not *that*," Danny assured him. "And it probably won't sound like much, but after years of silence, of not saying a word to anyone, he's suddenly inflicting these long monologues on her. I can't explain it, but it's strange, his way of forcing her to do something. It makes our skin crawl ... maybe it is somehow sexual. Jesus, I wonder if that's why she wants to go to a girls' school."

"But a minute ago you ... you wouldn't have hit her." Quinn tried to keep it from sounding like a question.

"No, but I might have grabbed her too tight. I would have left bruises."

This happens. Quinn lay awake in his own suite that night. *It's not just something you only read about. It happens to people you care about.*

His parents had ignored him. They had robbed him. But they hadn't menaced him. He hadn't been in danger in his home. Krissa and Danny had been.

If he had had a younger sister, he would have taken care of her. He would have made sure she had partners at a dance, he would have gone to get her if her date had had too much to drink. Danny's sister needed protection of an altogether different order. And Quinn was prepared to provide it.

The next morning Danny had a class he didn't dare cut. So Quinn volunteered to get Krissa on the train for her interviews at the schools farther north. He rode the Dinky with her, the little two-car train that ran out to the Princeton Junction.

She was wearing her green dress again. Had she

really been a Puritan, the elders would have made her wear a white cap over that glorious hair.

He got straight to the point. "Your brother told me about your father."

"What did he go and do that for?" She was clearly annoyed. "It's not anyone's business."

"I want to help you."

"But nothing's happened," she protested. "Danny must have been exaggerating. You know him. He'll say anything." She was clearly determined to minimize this. "I can handle it."

He admired her pride. He turned sideways in the double seat and was facing her, one hand on the seat-back behind her shoulder. "I want you to go to Baltimore, spend the rest of the year with my parents."

"With your parents? Have you talked to them? What do they have to say about it?"

"They say they'd be glad to have you." Quinn had been prepared to lay it on the line with his parents when he had called this morning. *I pay the bills, I decide who lives here.* But he hadn't had to. They assented most agreeably, hardly even listening to his elaborate story about a friend's sister wanting to finish her senior year at an East Coast school. "They're very gracious people, and they'll let you go your own way. The house is big, you'll have complete privacy. The food's terrible," he added lightly, "but that will prepare you for college."

She shook her head, almost laughing. "You're really serious, aren't you? Danny said I wouldn't believe you, and I don't."

"I'm sorry, because I mean this. I'm very sincere."

"I know that ... and it's nice of you, but I'm going to be all right."

There was an iron-rock firmness in her voice. Danny had told him to expect that. "It's ideal," Danny had said when Quinn proposed the scheme, "but I can tell you now, she won't do it."

None of Quinn's notions about younger sisters had prepared him for this, a girl—a young woman—who didn't want to be protected, who wanted to take care of herself.

As they were waiting for the regular train, he spoke again. "About yesterday ... Danny wasn't going to hit you."

"I really wish you hadn't seen that."

"But I did. And surely you know he wouldn't have hurt you."

"No," she said simply. "No, I don't know that. But I do know if he had, he would want to kill himself."

Krissa did her interviews in Boston, then came back to Princeton for another night before flying out of Newark again. Then Quinn did not see her for another ten months.

If he had known that, he would have been wild, but he had assumed she would come out whenever she could, for Christmas and spring break, the big House Party weekends, times like that. But gradually he came to realize how unusual her interview trip had been. The French family didn't travel.

He wrote her, he called her. Both he and Danny were in touch with her all the time. To Danny's fierce relief she had gone home determined to get admitted into a good college. She wasn't going to tell anyone about the abuse in her home, but she was willing to do whatever else was necessary.

"She's going to do it," Danny exalted. "Her reasons may be all wrong, but she's doing the right thing."

"What do you mean, her reasons are all wrong?"

"Don't be modest," Danny scoffed. "She's decided to come because she has a crush on you."

"I don't see what's so wrong about that."

If she couldn't come east, then he would go west. At least that's what he had planned, but there simply wasn't time.

He and Danny had quickly realized that having a record contract within a year wasn't realistic. They had to get more performing experience, build a repertoire, establish an audience base. So they strong-armed Quinn's elderly trust officer into releasing money for better equipment and a used VW van to haul it in. Then they started on the club circuit in the college towns of the Mid-Atlantic and New England.

It was not glamorous. They drove as much as they sang—more than they sang. They hauled their own equipment, put up their own posters. They got shocks from faulty mikes. They slept in the van, parking it beneath a turnpike underpass, too exhausted to make it even to the next rest stop. They played in clubs that wouldn't allow original material. Sometimes they got paid; sometimes they worked for dinner and tips.

They treated college as their day job, how they kept themselves fed and housed until the music started to pay. That the music would start to pay they never doubted.

Quinn didn't have Danny's exceptional beauty, but he was golden and glowing, tanned, with thick hair that rumpled in the wind. His natural world was civilized and tame, yachting and tennis, champagne on the lawn, tea in the summerhouse, everything clean and open and neatly mown.

You can trust me, was the message of his bright hair and clear eyes. *You will have fun with me. We will be everything giddy and gallant, but I will not hurt you.*

And I might, flashed Danny's wild and dangerous beauty. Danny's power came from untamed nature, fierce blinding snowstorms and white-capped waves that crashed against rocky shores. His power came from anger repressed and then released, rivers of red-hot lava flooding down a mountainside. *No, you can't trust me . . . and that's where the fun is.*

Danny had nerve. He could do anything if he closed his eyes tight and did it quickly. Quinn had courage. He could assess a situation, weigh the odds, select a strategy, and then soldier on, however unlikely success might be. Establishing themselves as professionals took both.

They spent the summer in the Boston area, working

almost every night, sleeping in the back of the van, showering at friends' places. Then suddenly it was September and they were at the airport picking up Krissa.

She had been able to choose from several colleges, and she had chosen Bryn Mawr. Quinn was pleased. Bryn Mawr was close to Princeton. But he also honestly believed it was the right school for her. It was the least social of the Seven Sister colleges. Far fewer of its students wore green twill headbands and cotton turtlenecks printed with little Scottie dogs. Bryn Mawr valued self-reliance over country club credentials. Krissa had no credentials. But her self-reliance couldn't be questioned.

He knew now that the pulling magic he had felt on first seeing her was no accident, no trick arising from the way her hair fell across her shoulders. It was as if whoever had fashioned her had looked at his character and Danny's and had taken from each the traits that they did not share, then had embodied them in her.

She had Danny's elemental directness and the instinctive intelligence of people who live close to nature. But in place of Danny's blazing defiance, she had Quinn's steady determination. She and Quinn had held the same position in their families, the Perfect Child, the one who held it all together, the one who sustained the myth that this was a family at all.

Half of her was a mirror of her brother. Half of her was a mirror of himself.

How could he not love her?

As the fall semester began, things changed dramatically for Dodd Hall. Clubs, which last spring had booked them for Monday night, were now taking them on Fridays and Saturdays. Owners stopped trying to stiff them by giving them a check for only half the agreed amount.

Krissa was keeping their books for them. She had redesigned their poster. Whenever they were traveling, they checked in with her every day. So it made sense for her to take their phone messages for them, be their mail drop. They joked about having a secretary now, a manager, a booking agent. They played all their new songs for her; they discussed all their musical ideas with her. She never said much about the music, but organizing their thoughts for her, trying out different arrangements on her, was starting to feel essential to what they did. They couldn't imagine Dodd Hall without her. She was as much a part of it as they were.

He and Danny had such a tight schedule that visits to Byrn Mawr were always made en route to somewhere else. So it was always the three of them, and half the time they were talking business—Krissa checking the name of a club so she could letter the posters; Danny pulling crumpled receipts out of his pocket, imploring her to make sense of them.

But if they were sitting in a diner, she would sit next to Quinn instead of Danny, and sometimes he would lift his arm across the back of the seat. She would shift closer, her arm would brush against his side and he could feel her breathe. He would hold an umbrella over her in the rain. Her hair, curling madly in the damp, would spill over his arm and chest, and he would hear music in the wind.

But Danny was always with them, and Quinn kept telling himself that that was okay. How could he think of Danny as an obstacle, as a barrier to anything. *If Danny weren't here, I could put the moves on his sister.* No, Quinn couldn't think that. Danny was Danny.

It would all work out. Quinn was as sure of that as he was of the music. All three of them wanted the same things. Each side of their triangle had a diamond's strength—between Danny and Quinn was the music, between Danny and Krissa was the bond of blood, and Quinn and Krissa loved each other.

How could anything possibly go wrong?

Then one sleeting November night, giddy and wild, he and Danny shot over to Bryn Mawr, driving the weary van like maniacs, whooping and shouting, arriving at Pembroke West well past midnight. No one was manning the Bells desk that late. They pounded on the big glass door, rousing one of the women studying in the lounge beyond. She recognized them and let them in. Bryn Mawr had no rules restricting the presence of men in the dorms, so they dashed up to the third floor unescorted.

Danny banged on Krissa's door. "Open up, sister. Open up."

The door opened. "What are you doing here?" She was whispering, trying to shush her brother. She was wearing a quilted robe. The lace ruffles of her nightgown peeped out at the collar and cuffs. "Do you know what time it is? Are you out of your minds?"

"You bet." Danny couldn't be quiet. "Look at this." He held up a business card that a middle-aged man in a blue blazer had given them. "He's the A & R man with Presto Records. He came last night, and then brought back two more people tonight. They want to sign us."

"You're going to get signed?" Krissa's eyes were wide. She knew what this meant. "You're kidding. That's wonderful!"

Suddenly all three of them had their arms around one another, and they were back on the spinning carousel, riding the dancing tigers with the white lights twinkling and the hurdy-gurdy music spilling into the night.

"What's going on?" Krissa's suite mate, Brooke Shippen, pulled open the door to her room. Suites in Pembroke were designed for two women, each with her own small private bedroom. "Oh, Danny, Quinn . . . it's you. Oh, hi."

"Oh, hi," Danny teased. "You're talking to two major rock stars, and 'oh, hi' is all you can say?"

"At this hour, yes." But she pulled a robe over her Lanz nightgown, slipped her ever-present headband over her fair, straight hair, and joined in the noisy rejoicing. Danny and Quinn had had nothing to eat in more than twelve hours—this was constantly happening to them—and they devoured the box of Triscuits and half wedge of Jarlsberg cheese Brooke and Krissa had in their suite. When that was gone, Brooke and Danny went down to forage among the vending machines in the common room.

"Is this on the up-and-up?" Krissa asked Quinn as soon as the door was shut. "Who is this company? I've never heard of them."

"You've heard of Columbia, haven't you? It's the same outfit."

"Columbia?" She was impressed. Columbia Records had Dylan, Simon and Garfunkel, the Byrds, and Janis Joplin on their list. "You can't get any better than that."

"Surely that doesn't surprise you."

She laughed. "Do you have any idea how smug you sound?"

"I must be intolerable ... and I don't care."

She looked so wonderful, her fire-kissed hair curling over the shoulders of her blue-sprigged robe. He put out his hands, but then he found his arms closing around her and he was kissing her, not on her cheek, but with her head back against his arm, with her lips opening as his tongue brushed against them. She was fragrant, yielding. Her hands were on his arms, his shoulders, slipping over his sweater, the wool catching and pleating beneath her hands.

He pulled her closer, but her winter robe was quilted and padded. He could feel little of her golden curves. He eased back and touched the buttons of her robe. "Do you mind?" he whispered, already starting to ease the buttons free, the movement of his fingers quick and light.

She shook her head.

"It will just be this," he promised softly as the robe fell open and he slipped it down over her shoulders. "That's all. I won't ... I don't need to ..."

He was instantly aware of how little she had on beneath her nightgown and knew how pointless a

promise that had been. He couldn't imagine stopping.
Restraint was not possible. Not on a night like this,
not when he could feel the soft press of her breasts
against his chest, not when her back curved as it did,
not when her mouth tasted as it did. Even when he
heard Brooke and Danny's voices in the hall, he didn't
stop. He had waited too long for this.

The door rattled with a sharp knock.

The ruffle at the neck of her nightgown was white . . .

"Open up." It was the voice he knew better than
any other, his partner's voice.

The gown was held shut by tiny white buttons, cool
buttons, smooth buttons, buttons that would slip . . .

"We're back," Danny called out. "Bringing
victuals."

"Quinn . . ." This voice was soft in his ear. "Stop."

Krissa's throat rose and fell beneath his lips as she
murmured his name. Reluctantly he let go of her.

But before he did, he shifted his stance, bracing
himself, and with one hand tight and hard against the
base of her spine, pulled her against him. She gasped
and instinctively drew back, but for a moment, he held
her there. He wanted her to know. He would never
force this on her, but he needed her to know what it
was, what he had for her.

"I love you," he said and then let her go.

He scooped her robe off the floor and held it out
for her. Only then did he open the door just in time
to catch a little package of pretzels that fell from Danny's hand. It was the first time he had ever been sorry
to see his partner.

Danny had to have had some sense of what had
been happening behind that closed door, but he simply
came into the room and dropped his armful of peanut
butter crackers, Mars bars, and Cokes across Krissa's
desk. He hitched himself up to sit on the desktop.
Krissa and Brooke sat on the sofa. Quinn pulled out
one of the desk chairs.

He couldn't keep his eyes off Krissa. She hadn't
refastened the top button of her robe, and he kept

thinking about her and the buttons and the robe and the nightgown and all that they concealed.

She caught his eye. A faint blush colored her cheeks. Quickly she turned to speak to her brother. "So what happens next? Do you just go somewhere and make a record?"

"We want to hire a band first," Danny answered. For months now they had wanted a drum, keyboards, and a bass guitar. Two guitars and two voices were making them sound more folk than they wanted. But they hadn't been able to afford to pay other musicians a salary, and they didn't want to bring in other people as partners. The work, the risk, was theirs alone. "We also need to find a producer, someone who isn't going to want to use a synthesizer."

Quinn forced himself to stop looking at Krissa's buttons. "We don't have a deal yet," he reminded Danny. "Forget New York, forget the band, forget the music. The first thing we do is go to Baltimore and talk to lawyers."

"Lawyers?" Danny grimaced. "Why?"

"You had trouble trusting *me*," Quinn pointed out. "Surely you weren't planning on trusting a record company, were you?"

"Oh." Danny made a face and crossed his eyes, silently admitting that he had been wrong.

Some people would say, Quinn knew, that the disappearance of his trust fund was the deserved fate of inherited wealth. But now they were talking about money he and Danny were going to earn themselves. No one was taking any of that without his permission.

Brooke spoke. "My father's law firm has an office in California." She was a forthright and assured girl, attractive in a firm-jawed kind of way. From a good Philadelphia family, she was the sort of girl Quinn had known his whole life. She had been a good, good friend to Krissa, and Quinn liked her for it. "They have a couple of lawyers who work for entertainers. I know they do a lot of work for Neil Diamond."

"Neil *Diamond*?" Danny hooted.

Quinn ignored him. Neil Diamond had just signed a contract for four million dollars. It wouldn't hurt to talk to the people who were talking to him. "What time does your father get up?" he asked Brooke.

Early, was Brooke's answer. Her father was awake by five, in the office by seven. Quinn looked at his watch. It was three now. They only had two hours to wait.

William Garnett Shippen III, Brooke's father, had once been a young man himself, and he remembered his own impetuous ambition. He agreed to meet with Danny and Quinn that morning, and Dodd Hall's negotiations with Presto began.

It was mesmerizing, heady stuff. Not until they were driving back to Princeton late that afternoon did Quinn start thinking of Krissa again ... Krissa and the feel of her body within her nightgown. Then it was all he could think of.

He was a little surprised, even a bit uncomfortable, with his moment of sexual preening. He was not a person who measured his worth by the size of his erection. At least he hadn't been.

The minute he could get to a phone, he called her. She answered.

"Kissing you," he said without any other greeting, "was not an excess of the moment. It's something I've wanted to do for a long, long time."

"Oh, come on." Her voice was happy, teasing. "I'm just the embodiment of your lifelong fantasy—to have a sister."

"No," he said. "If I had a sister, she would be like Brooke. Go find her. Tell her I would be honored to have her for a sister. But you ... you I want for something else."

He wanted to ask her if she would have let him. *If Brooke and Danny hadn't come back, would you have let me make love to you?*

"If this deal goes through," he said instead, "we're

going to be busier than ever the next couple of months.
I don't know how often we'll get over to see you."

"We?" she asked.

"You know what I mean."

"Well, don't worry about being busy. I'm here to
get an education. Being a secretary, manager, and a
booking agent has been fun, but it's kind of getting in
the way."

Because Presto Records was a label bankrolled and
distributed by CBS Records, signing with them
seemed ideal. Presto had a reasonably small catalogue;
Dodd Hall would get more attention than they might
elsewhere. But behind this small label was the muscle
that also powered Columbia Records and their list.

So the deal with Presto went through with a two-
record contract and an advance, a recording budget,
and an option on their third album. Their lawyer, a
young associate of Brooke's father, introduced them
to Joel Feninberg who had worked with David Geffen,
the manager of Laura Nyro and Crosby, Stills, Nash
and Young. Joel was back in New York now, working
on his own, and Dodd Hall signed a management deal
with him. He knew everyone, and he helped them put
a band together. He had them audition Calhoun
Bates, a keyboard player, and Stan Rokowski, a drummer—two sessions players sick of studio work. Then
he urged them to hire Jingle Manetti.

Jingle was an enormously likable bass player whose
talent was right up there with the best, but a three-
hundred-dollar-a-day heroin habit had made him un-
employable. He claimed to be clean now. Joel believed him so Dodd Hall hired him. It was a smart
move. Rock critics who might otherwise have paid little attention to a pre-debut duo put a mental check-
mark next to Dodd Hall because Jingle was taking a
chance on them . . . and they on him.

All three band members were older than Danny
and Quinn. As sessions musicians, Stan and Calhoun
could play anything with anyone, and Jingle had

worked with the best of the best. In fact, in the first days of rehearsal, Danny and Quinn occasionally exchanged sick glances, intimidated by the experience of the people they had hired.

"*We* wrote the songs," Danny whispered to Quinn during a break, trying to bolster his confidence.

"True," Quinn agreed. "So we'd better not pretend we know more than they do. They'd see right through us."

"They probably already have."

"Then let's find out if they've got any good ideas."

Indeed, while the three band members were not as creative as Danny and Quinn, they knew their instruments, and rearranging the songs, opening them up for the drums and keyboards, proved around-the-clock exhilarating for everyone.

They were working out of a loft space in New York. This was clearly Danny and Quinn's last semester at Princeton. It was time to quit their day jobs. In his heart Quinn already had. He hadn't even taken the time to withdraw from his courses or arrange for a leave of absence. He was going to flunk out with gallantry and grace.

Danny was not so cavalier. He had worked hard to get into Princeton. He was determined to leave with a clean enough record so he could return. All fall he struggled to keep up with his classes, studying by flashlight in the van, charming their lawyer's secretary into typing his papers.

Late one Thursday night in December, Danny found that a professor had rescheduled an exam. He needed to be on campus the next day. He started cursing the minute he got the message.

"Come on," Quinn said. "Shut up and get your books. I'll drive you."

He figured that he would drop Danny off at Princeton and then head straight to Bryn Mawr.

As sophomores, the two lead singers of Dodd Hall no longer lived in the dormitory Dodd Hall. As soon as they got to Aughty Three where they lived now, Quinn tried to call Krissa. There was no answer in her suite. His foot tapping impatiently, he had the Bells desk try a couple of other women he knew on her floor. One of them told him that Brooke and Krissa had gone away for the weekend. They were off visiting a friend of Brooke's at Gettysburg College.

She was away for the weekend. So disappointed that he was almost irritated with her, Quinn knocked the phone to the floor. Danny looked up from his books.

"Gettysburg." Danny nodded approvingly when Quinn explained. "She'll like that."

Quinn made an exasperated noise. "I don't know why. If you've seen one battlefield, you've seen them all."

"Well, that's it." Danny was speaking more mildly than he usually did. "She hasn't seen any."

Quinn dropped onto his bed. Danny had a point. Quinn had grown up in a region crawling with Civil War battlefields. Minnesota wouldn't have a single one. But still . . .

Now what was he going to do with himself? He had been living on adrenaline and caffeine for weeks now, he could hardly kick back and mellow out all of a sudden, not without Krissa. There was no point in studying. He hadn't even bought the books for most of his courses. He'd been counting on spending the weekend with her. His one free weekend . . . why did she have to pick this one to go trace the lines of Confederate trenches?

He lay on the bed in foul-tempered silence until a knock on door roused him.

It was Tim Waxton who had been one of Quinn's suite mates in Dodd Hall last year. "Hunt . . . I heard you were here—"

No one in the band ever called Quinn "Hunt."

"I was looking for someone with your key." Wax acknowledged Danny with only a quick nod and a lifted hand. "Do you know where your studs are? I just swore to my mother that I had my rig together, but of course I don't."

Quinn swung his legs off the bed, went to his closet, and reached up to the top shelf. He handed Wax the box containing the studs and cufflinks belonging to the tucked formal shirt that he wore with his tux.

"Thanks. This is a life saver. My sister's got her ball tomorrow night," Wax continued, "and one of her escorts is bailing out on her. He claims he's come down with the flu. He's probably lying, but what can you do? So Mother's drafted me."

Many of the debutante balls required that each girl have two escorts, and the better they were, the better she looked. Being escorted by your brother was a defeat of the first order. Quinn knew all the rules for such events. They could be sort of fun, these weekends. Not like Dodd Hall, not like playing in front of an audience, not satisfying like that. But fun. And it would be something to do.

So Quinn spoke. "Would it upset your mother's plans if I tagged along?"

"That would be terrific." Wax clapped Quinn on the shoulder. He understood precisely what Quinn was offering to do. Quinn would be his sister's other escort. And he would do it right. None of Miss Waxman's friends would ever guess that Quinn had never seen her before and had no plans to ever see her again. "Mother'll be in heaven. To say nothing of my sister."

"Don't presume," Quinn cautioned. "She may hate me."

"She won't," Wax assured him. "She won't."

Quinn took his studs back and promised to be ready within the hour.

The door closed. Quinn took out his suitcase. After a moment, he heard Danny speak—

"Are you going to get wildly drunk and prong the deb?"

Such things had been known to happen after deb parties, but that was not Quinn's intention. "It would hardly seem consistent with doing her brother a favor."

"It's a real comfort," Danny drawled as he crumpled up a piece of paper and lobbed it in the trash, "to know that if my sister can't get an escort to her debut, that you'll go as a favor to me."

Krissa was not exactly on the debutante circuit. "This doesn't have anything to do with your sister."

"It doesn't?"

"No, it doesn't," Quinn said calmly. Danny got like this sometimes— honest, young working-class lad against jaded sophisticate, Class Struggle 101. "It's not about her. And it's not about you either. I'm not choosing sides. I wouldn't cancel a gig to do this, and you know it."

Danny gave a quick, reluctant nod. Yes, he knew that.

"So we're okay?" Quinn asked.

"Yes, we're okay."

"Good." Quinn reached into his closet and took out the black, zippered hanging bag he kept his tux in.

Danny spoke. "How come you never want to be alone with Krissa?"

Quinn dropped his tux on the bed and turned impatiently. "Didn't I just want to spent the whole weekend alone with her?"

"But why have you waited until now? Why haven't you ever told me to go lose myself for a couple of hours?"

"Now that's a charming thought." Quinn was getting irritated with this conversation. "I'm supposed to be trying to—as you so elegantly put it—'prong' your sister while you're cooling your heels in the hall? That doesn't exactly appeal to me, and I can't imagine it would to her either."

"Then we need to work something out."

"No, *we* don't." This was the first time Quinn remembered ever wanting Danny to shut up. "Whatever needs doing, I can do myself."

Years later Quinn came to understand this conversation. He loved Krissa and grew to love her even more. But his passion for her served Danny's purposes as well.

Danny had no reason to trust other people. His parents had consistently failed him. His father had abused him, his mother had allowed it to continue. Only Krissa had ever proved reliable.

He longed to trust Quinn and for the most part he did. But he could not trust Quinn's world. His nightmare was that some envoy from that world, a guy dressed in tennis whites, a girl with flowers pinned to her shoulder, would stroll by, and Quinn would look up and say, "Yes, I belong with you."

But if Krissa was at his side, Quinn would not go. She was the final cord by which Quinn was bound to Danny.

Danny was used to manipulating people. The tragedy of their lives was that he did not understand that in Quinn he had met the one person he did not need to manipulate, whom he could not manipulate.

Chapter Six

Explaining to her parents that she wanted to save the airfare, Krissa spent Christmas of her freshman year with Brooke's family in Philadelphia. Believing that they owed their parents no explanation whatsoever, Danny and Quinn cleaned out their dorm room, said good-bye to Princeton, and moved to New York, sending the masters of their first album to the recording company on Christmas Eve.

They asked Brooke and Krissa to come to New York for New Year's and then helped design the set of half-truths that was to be told the Shippens, Brooke's parents, about the visit. They were gifted young men, and it was a good story ... although a week later Mrs. Frank Rokowski of Queens, plumber's wife, rock drummer's mother, was perplexed by her mail. Who was Mrs. William Garnett Shippen III and why was she writing her a thank-you note?

Brooke and Krissa took the train into the city. As they came up from the platform into the main lobby of Grand Central Station, they could see people gathering to meet the arriving passengers. The crowd had formed itself into a loose semicircle, peering and peeking around one another, jostling, even pushing.

At the peak of the circle, in the best spot directly opposite the gate, was a small troop that no one was jostling. Everyone else had fallen back a step or so, giving these young men their own little stage.

Danny and Quinn were in the center, looking as

they always did. Danny, his black hair curling wildly from under the cuff of his stocking cap, wore a heavy wool lumberjack shirt and chopper's mitts. Quinn was in a navy down-filled parka, the white string from a ski-lift pass still dangling from the zipper pull. One of their companions was in full biker regalia, black leather, a helmet and goggles. Another had on a black-brimmed top hat with a band of wooden beads and a sweeping ostrich feather. There were beards and earrings, scarfs knotted low around ripped jeans. Shirts were tie-dyed, emblazoned with sequins and stars. They were men with presence and style, and Krissa was instantly enchanted with their flamboyance.

Quinn took her bag, then someone grabbed it from him. He was calling out names to her—Stan, the drummer, Jingle, the bass player, Calhoun, their organist, Pete, the sound engineer. Joe, he'd be on the road crew. Kevin, he was one of the technicians at the studio . . . Krissa lost track of who was who. Suddenly she was being swept through the station, a part of this glittering, laughing crew.

This was New York, jaded, self-confident Manhattan, but still people stopped as Dodd Hall passed by, people watched. No one knew who they were, but they were glowing, confident, energetic. Every step they took through this crowded train station, every shout of laughter was a challenge to other young people—"Aren't we grand? Aren't we enticing? Don't you wish you were with us?"

And it was a promise—"*You* deserve to be with us," they said to the kid buying a *Rolling Stone* at the newsstand, and to the part-time beauty college student filling in for her cousin at the snack bar. "Those people you are with, maybe they don't, but you, oh yes, *you,* you deserve to be with us." Vigor and ambition flashed off their studded leather. They knew they had an audience, and they glittered more brightly because of it.

Krissa was breathless, amazed, feeling dizzyingly lucky. She was a kid off the Range, her father was a miner. The girls she went to high school with were married, living in cramped trailers, about to have their first babies, and yet here she was, in New York City dancing on a velvety midnight cloud.

Over the next three years, it would come to seem normal to her to sweep through a vaulting lobby with a band of men far more famous and enthralling than the ones she was with now. But this was the first time, and the vitality, the starry incandescence of this moment, would never be repeated. No one in this little party was jaded, no one was sick of the crowds and the attention. Not even the older, more experienced ex-junkie Jingle. He had been here before, but he had never expected to be back, so his laugh rang the loudest of all.

Danny, Quinn, their organist Calhoun Bates, and an unspecified number of others were camping out in an unfinished loft on West 22nd Street, which the band had also been using as rehearsal space. Reached by a gated freight elevator, the loft was "illegal," not certified for residential occupation. As a result it had no kitchen; a coffeepot and a hot plate sat on the floor next to one of the electric outlets. There was a toilet and a sink but no bath; the men showered at the nearby "Y."

The space was only vaguely heated, so Brooke and Krissa spent most of the time wearing Quinn's sweaters and wrapping themselves in blankets, which, like the sheets and towels, were "on loan" from the housekeeping department of Princeton University. The weekend was a wonderful, unstructured swirl of comings and goings, wild talk, loud music, a fair amount of alcohol, but—in deference to Jingle and his former habit—no drugs.

She and Quinn were never alone. Except for the bathroom, the loft had no partitions or doors. But it didn't matter, at least not much. With so many people, all doing so many different things, and with there always being music, the two of them could bundle up in a corner, a blanket around their shoulders, talking in low voices, more intimate, more apart from things, than when it was them and Danny.

At night she could see the light stubble on Quinn's chin. In the morning she could smell the toothpaste on his breath. She felt the texture of his clothes—the melting chamois of his shirt, the thick tweed of his warm blazer. Danny and Quinn never bought clothes; they weren't about to waste Dodd Hall money on that. And with Danny you could tell, but Quinn's clothes grew more gloriously worn with each careless washing. Krissa loved them. She had never known truly well-made clothes until she had met Quinn and Brooke, and the craftsmanship in their garments enchanted her.

New Year's Day was white and wet. Danny started organizing an expedition to a restaurant. "But it's Afghani food. I don't think Krissa will like it," he said.

She had been reaching for her coat. She stopped, puzzled. Why would he say something like that? Since when had she been unwilling to try new foods? Food served in the homes on the Iron Range was enormously varied. At one point in history, thirty-three different ethnic groups had been working in the mines, each with its own food. Krissa had grown up eating sarma, potiça, and porketta roast. She loved interesting tastes and new smells.

There was some scheme going on here. Danny never did anything by accident. He always had a plan, a purpose. Krissa hung back, waiting to understand this one.

He was an irresistible ringmaster, getting his slightly hungover clowns into their coats and out of the door. As the loft's multilocked door closed behind the last of them, she understood this particular idea. Quinn was staying behind too. That was why ten people were being forced to brave sullen skies and damp snow, so she and Quinn could be alone. That was Danny's plan.

Her stomach turned. What were she and Quinn supposed to do now? Make love on the sofa that the men had found in an alley? Keep track of the time so they could be sure and be finished by the time everyone else got back? It was too sordid.

Quinn was over by the windows, leaning against the cold radiator, his hands in his pockets. "Don't be hard on him. He means well."

How had Quinn known what she was thinking? "The two of you ... you didn't talk about this, did you?" That would have been even worse. "You didn't plan it?"

How long shall I keep everyone away? Danny might have said. *How much time will you need?*

"No." Quinn stayed over by the radiator, for which she was thankful. "This was a surprise to me, too. But we don't have to take orders from him."

"Oh, Quinn," she sighed. She didn't want him thinking that she was uneasy about him, that she didn't trust him. "It's just that—"

"Hush up. You don't have to explain. I'll take you out for something weirder than Afghani food, but first I'm going to force you to listen to a new song."

Relieved and grateful, she sat down on the sagging sofa and watched him plug in his guitar. How did he get to be so *nice*? If he had tried to make love to her, she would almost certainly have let him. But she didn't know how she could have relaxed, how she could ever have enjoyed it.

She realized that he had started to play. She forced herself to pay attention.

"I've heard this," she said. "You were playing it this fall."

"You've heard the melody." He hadn't started singing yet. "My lyrics were never as strong as his music. I came up with something better. It's on the album. It may be our first single."

He started to repeat the intro, so Krissa had a moment for another question. "What's it called?"

" 'Cinnamon Starlight.' "

Then he began to sing, and as he sang it the first time, Krissa thought it one of the prettiest love songs she had ever heard. The rhymes were lovely—

"untold/marigold," "interlace/slightest grace." The images were spicy rich. Before she could speak, he began to sing it again, and as she listened to the lilting lines, a thought occurred to her, a dizzying, dazzling, arrogant thought that his eyes confirmed.

The song was about her.

His fingers were moving lightly over the guitar's frets. His voice warmed the glaring loft.

He was singing about her. She could scarcely breathe. He had written these beautiful words for her.

The song was over. The last notes faded, the sounds lingering for a moment in the corners of the room. Quinn set the guitar aside and put out his hand. "That's the song. Now I promised you something to eat. Shall we go?"

"No."

What difference did it make where they were as long as it was the two of them together? How could she have thought anything else mattered?

Quinn had been smiling—he knew how good his song was. He was looking at her, and suddenly his expression changed, his eyes, his shoulders growing intent. He took a step forward, and Krissa knew that in a moment his arms would come around her, and she'd feel the lean shape of his body against hers, and he'd be making love to her.

But she underestimated him. He touched his fingers to her face. "This would be the first time for you, wouldn't it?"

She nodded.

"Then not here. Not like this."

ST. PAUL, MINNESOTA, DECEMBER 1992

"All right, Coach . . . ah"—Krissa checked her clipboard—"Coach Wiley. We're ready for your team."

Coach Wiley had the littlest of the little, the age-six-and-under hockey players. Half of the team was going to have trouble getting out on the ice, and today

was only picture day. The kids had to get themselves
into a line and remain upright for a minute, a minute
and a half. Some weren't going to succeed. When they
fell, they were like little upended turtles. They had so
much equipment on that they couldn't get back up on
their own. They would struggle around on the ice until
one of the moms plucked them up.

Krissa always volunteered to do these things, help
with the team pictures, drive on school field trips, go
on the Cub Scout campouts. She loved being with
kids, all kids, not just her own. The little ones were
so sweet and earnest; the older ones so interesting in
their determined efforts to be grown-up and cool.

She helped Coach Wiley steer his munchkins out on
the ice. They got in line, Coach Wiley got into position, and Krissa and the other mom got out of the
way.

After Coach Wiley, Coach Myers's team had to be
gotten out onto the ice and lined up. "Okay, moms,"
the photographer called out, "you can get out of the
picture now."

"Don't you love it?" the other mother said to Krissa
as they moved off. " 'Okay, moms, you can get out of
the picture now,' " she imitated the photographer. "It
makes one feel so important."

Krissa laughed. "In college my boyfriend was in a
rock band. I spent my entire undergraduate career
getting out of other people's pictures."

"Oh, that's right," the other woman exclaimed. "I
had heard that about you. Dodd Hall ... you're the
Cinnamon-Haired Girl. That's incredible. I wanted to
ask you, what was it like? Do you see them anymore?"

"No, not really."

Krissa started counting the little preprinted envelopes the children had brought their picture money in.
Some families had ordered the "Mini-Memory Mate,"
the least expensive package, but plenty of others had
gone all the way up to the "Grandparents' Special."
Where did people get their money? Maybe if you had
one kid in one sport, you'd go for it all, but she had

four boys in about forty million sports and with registration and uniforms and equipment, you started to notice even the little things like picture money.

The lovely funny warmth of the afternoon was gone. And it wasn't because of the money. Krissa knew herself. She only fussed about money when there was something else she didn't want to think about.

And this time she knew what it was. Quinn was coming.

People knowing about Dodd Hall, she was used to that. *The Aarnesson boys' mom, she was the Girl with Cinnamon Hair*—that was one of the first things people moving into the neighborhood heard. Most people found it exciting, a little splash of glitter in the third row at the P.T.A. meeting. Or it was a rueful joke, a sign of how they were all aging—*My kids' den mother is Dodd Hall's Cinnamon-Haired Girl.* Only a few were annoyingly curious, but that usually said something about them. The emptier a person's life was, the more interested they were in hers. She never satisfied their curiosity. She never let her past as the Cinnamon-Haired Girl become something serious.

But now Quinn was coming.

Why? He said he would be in the Cities on business. Lots of people came to the Cities on business without seeing her. It made no sense for him to come.

She had been too stunned to even say, "Oh, it will be so good to see you." It *ought* to be good to see him. They ought to be able to have a cup of coffee and laugh about the old times, exchange a quick embrace, a kiss on the cheek, with nothing at stake.

But every time she thought about him coming here, she felt sick.

PITTSBURGH, PENNSYLVANIA, MARCH 1973

The second week in March—it was a date engraved on Danny and Quinn's hearts. Their first album would hit the stores and they would be in Pittsburgh, starting a tour to promote it. Of course they weren't the main act. They were opening for the record company's most prominent singer-songwriter. His fans were thoughtful and educated, and he attracted many women. Opening for him, Danny and Quinn thought, would be a great opportunity to build their audience.

Knowing that the crowd was there for the other singer's sensitive and dreamy introspection, Dodd Hall opened with a pair of wistful ballads, their aching sadness soaring on a carpet of perfect harmonies. But there was nothing milksoplike about the songs. The emotional stance was manly, two guys standing legs apart, shoulders back, braced to be hit by sensation and loss. A two-fisted melodic energy paced tigerlike behind the bars of these lovely melodies.

The cage restraining this beast came down a bar at a time. Danny and Quinn led their audience gradually into a more swelling sound, building intensity with each song until exploding into the celebrations of "Bridges Ice First" with Jingle's hard-rocking, blues-based bass line. The crowd surged to its feet, alive, electric, rocking. Danny and Quinn couldn't help a flash of triumph, Quinn's understated satisfaction anchoring Danny's dangerous blaze.

They gave a generous performance, inclusive and warmhearted. If one were judging by their later standards, much fault might be found. The lighting was terrible. They still weren't sure how much to relate to the band, and that awkwardness showed. But the energy of the show compensated for the flaws.

Krissa watched them from the wings at stage left. She knew their set as well as she knew her name. She had listened to days and days of rehearsal, to countless variations in the order of the playlist, but none of that had prepared her for the muscular vitality of this show.

As the final song came to an end, she moved forward, rubbing her arms. They were covered with goose bumps, and she felt as if she had been breathing starlight. In a moment Quinn would bound off the

stage, and she would be the first to greet him. He
would catch her in his arms, and she would tell him
how magnificent he was.

The final note crashed into the bursting wall of applause. Hands over their heads, Danny and Quinn acknowledged the roaring cheers and triumphant, the
sweeping lights flashing over them, they quit the stage.

Going off stage right.

Startled, disappointed, Krissa watched their backs
disappear into the darkness of the other side of the
stage. Roadies brushed past her, hurrying to shift the
equipment.

Oh, well, this was hardly the end of the world. She
wasn't a fan with only one chance to get an autograph.
She followed a cinderblock corridor down to a blue-
steel fire door. Beyond the door was square lobby
area. Krissa could hear the sounds of a noisy celebra-
tion. Two girls drifted out of an open door. Both were
exotically clad, one in layers of tie-dyed chiffon, her
beaded earrings swinging nearly to her collarbone.
The other was in a purple crocheted granny gown.
Through the loose open stitch, Krissa could see her
bikini underpants and her nipples. They were
groupies.

She peered into the hospitality room. Gathered
around a platter-laden buffet table were people she
knew. The band was there as was Petey, the road manager, Joel Feninberg, who had flown in for the show
as had LisaAnn Curruthers, the representative from
the booking agency. Beyond them she could see
Danny and Quinn. Sweat stains darkened the plaid of
Danny's shirt. Quinn had taken off his maroon
sweater, and the blue Oxford cloth shirt he had been
wearing underneath was also marked from his exer-
tion. They were standing next to each other, but each
was turned to face a reporter, answering questions as
the reporters scribbled notes. Both were lively and
animated, talking quickly. Danny was particularly exuberant, gesturing extravagantly as he spoke. He flung

one hand back wildly, clipping Quinn across the shoulder.

Quinn didn't stop talking; he didn't look away from his interviewer, but Krissa saw him bring up his elbow and poke Danny in the ribs. Danny retaliated, and the two of them, still concentrating on their respective interviewers, never looking at each other, traded jabs and pokes—a light blue elbow dueling with a plaid one. They were having such fun, two kids roughhousing.

"Oh, Krissa, you're here. Good." It was Petey, the road manager. "Quinn asked me to keep an eye out for you. He should be done in fifteen, twenty minutes. Do you want something to eat?"

"No, no," she heard herself say. "Actually, I don't want to interrupt. I know they're doing interviews."

Never before had she felt excluded. Never before had she felt that the bond between Danny and Quinn might be stronger than what either felt for her. But onstage tonight they were Lewis and Clark with a great adventure before them, the first overland route to the Pacific. Where did she fit into that? They were on stage, and she wasn't. "Will you tell them I've gone back to the hotel?"

She showered and put on her nightgown, a Juliet gown she had made, gathering up yards of light muslin into a band tied at her throat. The sheets were cool and smooth, and she opened her art history textbook, then leaned back against the pillows and thought about the groupies. What was it like to wear a dress that showed your underpants and nipples? What was it like to be so casual about sex that you could do it with almost anyone? Why had those girls come backstage? Were they there for the main act, or had they come for Dodd Hall? Had they wanted to meet, wanted to have sex with, Danny and Quinn?

She forced herself to study. The hands on her watch moved slowly. An hour, ninety minutes, two hours . . .

Then at last the knock came. It would be both of them, she had to be prepared for that. On tonight of all nights, why wouldn't they want to be together? She opened the door, determined not to be disappointed.

Quinn was leaning against the door frame, his maroon sweater still over his shoulder. The sweat that had marked his shirt and matted his hair had dried. She peered around him, up and down the hall. He was alone, absolutely alone.

He cantilevered himself away from the door frame. "I don't know why Petey let you get away. You were the one I wanted to see, not those other jerks."

Those "other jerks" were rock critics whose attention was essential to Dodd Hall's success. "What did you think?" he went on. "Were we bloody marvelous or what? Danny is amazing, isn't he? Did you hear him on 'Bridges'? Even I didn't know he could sing like that."

Quinn had been standing shoulder to shoulder with Danny during "Bridges Ice First," matching him note for note, breath for breath, on this rocking, hard-driving song about the dangers of making connections with other people. "Maybe he's not the only one who deserves praise. Now are you going to come in, or shall we spend the night in the hall, talking about my brother?"

"I always like talking about Danny," Quinn answered mildly, but he came in, letting the door fall shut behind him.

Since the night Presto had first expressed interest in Dodd Hall, she and Quinn had never been alone in a bedroom. But he came into the intimacy of her half-lit hotel room with ease and confidence, a person who had every right to be where he was.

And they both knew exactly why he was there on the night of his first big concert. Coyness was not possible. He had not come to talk, to find out what she thought of the concert. He was here to make love to her.

He opened his arms and she came to him, resting her hands on his shirt front, feeling the rise and fall of his breath behind the fabric. She remembered how he had been on stage, the flashing, masculine energy, a sexual vitality free of preening or posturing. Here he was—his body, his voice, reduced back to a human scale, here beneath her hands.

For the first time in her life, she felt apart from her body, as if it were something separate and distinct from the rest of her, as if it were indeed a prize he could earn.

And it's not something my brother has for you.

He was kissing her, his lips first firm, then soft and warm, warm and open. His caress was confident, purposeful and direct. He ran his hands down her back over her hips, pausing at the slight ridge caused by the elastic band of her panties. He traced the low-slung line of elastic as it curved around her body. She felt an intimate possessiveness flowing from his fingers. Her undergarments were his to know, his to touch, his to remove. He was a triumphant Olympian, a young warrior who, having staked a claim, having proven his worth, now came to take possession, to claim his prize.

There was so much fabric in her Juliet gown that his hands kept catching, the muslin wrinkling and pleating, interrupting the smooth glide of his explorations. She felt one hand at her thigh, crumpling the gown, searching for the hem, for the smooth feel of her leg underneath. His other hand came to her hair, tilting her head back, exposing the line of her satin throat. He bent his head lower, kissing her pulse. She winced at the scrap of his chin. It was well after midnight. He hadn't shaven since the morning before.

He drew back immediately. "Am I going too fast?" He took her hand and in a moment they were sitting side-by-side, thighs touching, hands clasped. "You need to tell me if I'm making a mistake. Am I taking too much for granted?"

"No, you're not." She brought a forgiving hand up to his face, smoothing it across his cheek, around his jaw, down to the smoother column of his throat. The light from the bedside lamp glowed against his warm skin, and his pulse beat steadily.

Somewhere inside him, beneath her fingers, was his upper trachea, and in the cavity of his larynx were his vocal cords, two pairs of folded membrane. Everyone had them, but his had been touched by magic, the sounds resonating from them were richer, more mellifluous than what came from everyone else's throats.

Of course, his voice wasn't just from his vocal cords. It was from the air he took into his body and what he did with that air. He was better than an alchemist. He took air and turned it into music. She leaned her cheek against his shoulder and let her hand search over his chest, seeking the power of the lungs he kept stowed safe behind his fortressed ribs.

"What are you doing?" he asked.

"Looking for your voice. Where does it come from?"

Beneath her cheek, her hand, she could feel him laugh. "If I showed you, you'd slap me."

"No, I wouldn't."

Her hand was still at his chest, lingering there. He trapped it against him, palm down, and then slowly guided it downward, gliding down his body. The muscled wall of his midruff curved in from his sternum. Through his shirt, she could feel his pliant diaphragm, the play of his lungs and his muscles, the quivering as they leaped to her touch. But as she felt the coarser, warmer denim of his jeans, he let go of her hand. He wasn't going to force her to touch him. But his breath was growing more rapid. She was encouraged by his pleasure.

And she was curious. She slid her hand down until the side of her palm rested against the hardness beneath his jeans. His breathing suddenly quickened, and emboldened she stroked all the way to the root. Then with her thumb and forefinger on either side of his width, she followed his outline back up, tracing the way it angled away from the jeans' zipper.

As always, her hands had a life of their own. Like

a blind person, touch was her surest sense. She learned through her hands. She had to touch in order to know. Had she only been arousing him with these caresses, she would have been more hesitant, more timid. But this was a quest for knowledge, the need to have questions answered, an instinct sometimes stronger than the sex drive.

His erection ended nearly at the waistband of his jeans, and he wore no belt. She slipped her fingers under the denim, easing up the elastic of his briefs, and touched the tip of his penis. It was hot, velvety, like nothing she had ever felt.

"Here, let me help you." Quinn unsnapped his jeans, his deft fingers working quickly. He unzipped the jeans, eased them down and open. As he did, he moved back across the bed, half-sitting against the pillows she had piled at the headboard. She sat facing him.

The hair on his lower body was darker than the gleaming, golden hair on his head, and her questing fingers noted, coarser. A blue-red vein ran up the strong shaft of his penis. She touched it. It was springy, full of life.

He was running his hands up her arms over her shoulders. "I thought I was the one who knew what to do."

She looked up from her studied scrutiny of his loins. "No, I don't have a clue ... and even now I can't imagine—"

"Imagine what? It actually going in?"

She nodded.

"I've imagined it enough for both of us. It does work, trust me." He slid his hand up her leg, beneath her gown, and pressed his palm against the crotch of her panties.

The faint pink stirrings inside her suddenly burst over the horizon, a glowing golden dawn. His hand felt so strong, so warm. The sensation was miraculous. Her breasts tingled, her tissues moistened. Then she felt a light tattoo, his fingers—his trained pianist's fingers—rippling over her, a waterfall of wonder. She gasped his name. It was wonderful, it was heaven, it wasn't enough. The moist silky fabric of her panties, the springy curls of her pubic hair were cobwebs and moss keeping him from what she needed.

She bent to kiss him, but he held her off, taking hold of her nightgown, lifting it over her head, leaving her nearly naked. Even in the heated, pillowy air of the hotel room, she shivered, her apricot-toned nipples puckering into blushing plum.

"Let's get you under the covers," Quinn said. He pulled back the blankets, holding them open for her. Then he unbuttoned two buttons on his shirt, and although it was a conventional open-front shirt, he pulled it off over his head as if it were a polo jersey. Then he stepped out of his jeans and briefs. Under the covers with her, he hooked the elastic of her panties and pulled them off too.

So this embrace was deliciously dark, deliciously open. Their bodies were hidden by the comforting weight of blankets. But within their twin cocoon, there was nothing between them. Her naked breast pressed against the light matting of hair on his naked chest. Her smooth legs tangled with the length of his. Just as he was powerfully aware of the high rounded mounds of her breasts, all she could think about was his penis, insistent and erect, pressing into her soft stomach.

Their mouths were exploring each other as they embraced, open and tasting. She could feel him everywhere, his lips, his hands cupping her breasts, running down her spine. His pace accelerated, he was fiercely aroused. Desire and curiosity impelled her. All this was new to her, all wonderful. Quinn pressed her back onto the sheet. A knowing hand on her inner thigh urged it up and open. Then he—no, no, not just "he," this was Quinn, glowing, gifted, Quinn—was between her legs. He pushed against her, penetrating.

She gasped sharply. It hurt.

He pulled back instantly although he had barely

opened her at all. "I'm hurting you. I don't want to hurt you."

The bedside lamp was still on, and Krissa could see the light stubble on his strong jaw, the pulse pounding at the side of his throat, the damp tendrils of golden hair at his forehead and neck. She didn't want this to stop. "But Quinn, isn't it always ... I mean, the first time, for a girl ..."

"Yes, but I don't want—" He stopped and was looking down at her—serious, intent, possessive. "I don't want it to be anyone else. Not as long as I am alive."

He wasn't cruel. He wasn't violent or brutal. Nor was he faint-hearted. A bedrock-deep determination ran through his character. To protect what he had, to acquire what he wanted, he would do what needed to be done.

And he did. He watched her steadily, supporting himself on his elbow so that his soothing hand was smoothing her hair. His eyes were passion-filled, but still gentle, wanting to assure her that this was an act of love.

She was tight. She felt as if her tissues were being pressed inward, curving back around on themselves, instead of blossoming forth, opening for him. The discomfort was acute.

But Quinn held steady, and her body eased at last. Like an unruly pupil giving way to a firm master, giving way not stubbornly and resentfully, but with secret relief at the restoration of the natural order of authority, she accepted his penetration.

He was fully encased in her. Her hands were on his back, his shoulders, and she could feel his deep soul-satisfied shudder. "This is what I dreamed of," he spoke low in her ear, "having you like this."

The idea thrilled her as well, the idea that they were joined, that she was giving him such pleasure. But in truth, it was only the idea that was enticing. The actual event was without physical magic. Discomfort had

driven away the silvery desire. Even when he began
to move, his pistoned grace did not restore it.

She loved him. She gloried in his pleasure. But a
part of her felt precisely as she had outside the backstage hospitality room earlier this evening, that he—
and Danny—were journeying on a bright road, leaving
her behind.

She supposed he would not neglect her afterward.
He would give her a turn. But it would be like being
a kid sister. The big boys climb the tree first, and
now that the tree house was all built, they give you a
obligatory boost up, and you too are in the tree, surrounded by the leafy branches, seeing the world from
on high. But you can't help thinking that it would
have been more fun to have been up here first.

Quinn was talking to her, touching her, even as she
was drawing nearer and nearer to a set of mysteries
of which she knew nothing. "Touch me," he said.

She didn't understand. She was touching him. Her
hands had been in his hair, at the small of his back,
even feeling his gluteal muscles tighten and release.

"No, down here." And he took her hand, bringing
it between their bodies to his erection.

Half in her, he was searingly hot, moist, viscous.
"That's you on me. That's a pledge." He sank into
her slowly, trapping her hand. "That there's no room
for doubt."

She could feel her own hand pressed against herself
by his weight. He eased back, put his hand where hers
had been and began again the little tattoing. Then a
vertical probing sought her clitoris.

Tingling ribbons shot through her, moon-kissed garlands that had nothing to do with being anyone's kid
sister—or any kind of sister at all. It was about your
pleasure being utterly necessary to a man, about him
not wanting to travel on this bright road unless you
are with him every step of the way.

The stars dancing through her gathered into one
ever tightening circle and burst open, skipping and
scattering in a spray of diamonds cast across the night

sky. Quinn too gasped and, his breathing ragged in her ear, shuddered with deepest pleasure.

As they lay together afterward, caught in some misty land of love and sleep, Krissa felt as close to him as she ever had to anyone, and she remembered the rest of the Lewis and Clark story.

The two explorers had not found Oregon on their own. They had had Sacajawea, a young Indian woman who had been their guide. They could not have done it without her.

Chapter Seven

A suspicion has been confirmed. We now know for certain—a significant number of people working as executives in our nation's recording industry are *deaf.* How else can you account for the pairing of that pre-eminent asshole, the *so* sensitive Stephen Grange, with Dodd Hall, a new rock band out of Princeton. The combination *looks* okay. Quinn Hunter's lyrics do have a singer-songwriter polish to them. But it *sounds* wrong, at least to those of us backward enough to think rock is still something we're suppose to listen to, rather than reflect upon and meditate to.

Whatever bozo wrote Dodd Hall's press kit calls them "folk rock," and indeed there's no doubt that these two can sing harmony like no one since the Everly Brothers, but Danny French's melodies and arrangements are retro-rock, drawing muscle from that clean, hard tradition.

Go to this concert, but leave early.

—Miles Adapter, "It's Enough To Make You Puke: Who's Touring This Spring," *Creem,* March 1973, p. 4.

One photograph, often reprinted, captured for Krissa the soaring magic of the next three years. Dodd Hall was playing at a state fair. The concert had just finished, and in the background of the photograph were the lights of the midway rides glittering over the shadows and shapes of the massed fans.

Krissa and Quinn were running from the stage, hand-in-hand, their feet hardly touching the ground. They were starry-eyed, laughing, running toward the carnival lights.

Quinn loved her. Night after night he was onstage, the audience listening to him, loving him, melting into him, and he stored that adoration, distilling it into warm, rich honey which he brought to her. With the sunlight dancing in diamond splashes, he loved her.

At night it was as if their bed were enchanted. Like a brass four-poster in a fairy tale, soaring through the night, it carried the two of them on a drifting, dreaming journey. They'd be kneeling in wonder, having tossed back the patchwork counterpane, looking down at the minature world below, the lighted church steeples, and the shadowy parks. Together they were floating alone in the magic world of the stars.

As the first tour crossed the East Coast, the lower Midwest, and then on to the West Coast, Krissa met up with the band nearly every weekend. On Wednesday or Thursday, Petey would call her with a schedule. A car and driver would meet her after her last class on Friday and take her to the airport. Another car would meet her at the other end of her flight, taking her to either the venue or the hotel. On Sunday evening, the routine would be repeated in reverse. She had a credit card with "Dodd Hall, Inc." on one line and her name on the next.

She loved staying in hotels. Every time she turned a key to open a new room, she felt a little thrill. What pleasant luxuries would be behind this door? Sometimes there was a lighted make-up mirror, sometimes the soaps and shampoo were tucked in a pretty basket. She always looked in the sewing kits, wondering what color of thread the hotel thought its guests would need.

She would buy a small bunch of flowers at the airport. She would bring scarves to drape the lamp-

shades. She would carry herbal tea bags and a little
hot pot in her suitcase, and within twenty minutes
of her arrival, Quinn's room would be fragrant with
blossoms and tea and warmed by soft, yellow pools of
shaded light.

With the second and third albums, greater success
came, and the rooms gave way to spacious suites. Krissa's makeshift college-girl tricks turned into the arrangements of an experienced, accomplished hotel
resident. Promoters were by then sending flower arrangements to the suites. Krissa would rip the arrangements apart, thinking them too stiff. She would phone
housekeeping for more vases and would arrange the
flowers in simple, graceful bouquets, putting them on
the nightstands, the bathroom vanity. She would tip
the bellman to rearrange the furniture. She would call
room service, and ignoring the menu, ask them to send
up platters of finger sandwiches and cheese, bowls of
strawberries and grapes, and a tea trolley with a silver
urn of steaming water.

She understood Quinn's childhood, how empty of
love it had been. Any hint of warmth or nurturing
mesmerized him, and she was good at both. He would
open his arms, gathering her in, whispering into her
coppery, scented hair that she was magical, a sorcer-
ess, an enchantress.

This was what she had longed for during her last
year on the Range, to be creating this kind of beauty.
She couldn't sing or write or paint. Her palette was
perfumed rooms, soft flowers, and curving teacups
warm to the touch. Quinn wrote song after song paying tribute to her gifts, to the Girl with Cinnamon
Hair.

It wasn't only Quinn who needed her. Danny did
too. They would have stood up on stage and played
their music for free. What they wanted to be paid for
were the other twenty-two hours in every day. It
wasn't that life on the road was hard. No, mining was
hard. Life on the road was just boring.

They would land at an airport and take a taxi to

the hotel. There they would sit for interviews. A limo would take them to the venue for the sound check; the limo would take them back to the hotel. Then the limo again, the meet-and-greet in the dressing rooms before the show and then more faces to meet and greet afterward and perhaps another interview. Out to back fence to sign some autographs. Then the limo back to the hotel. That was their day, typed up on a schedule which was slipped under the room door each morning.

They were stuck on planes, trapped in hotel rooms. There was no variety, no fresh air, no exercise. Desperate, they would try to talk to the venue people, the groupies, the reporters, anyone just for some change. After the first year, all those people, in city after city, started to seem alike. It was enough to make even Quinn want to lob a Sony out of a twenty-story hotel window just to see what would happen.

Of course, there were parties—catered affairs given by the local promoter, room parties for members of the traveling entourage only, and in big cities, visits to the local club scene. But when everyone around you encourages you to think only of yourself, to talk only about yourself, every day starts to feel the same.

They never knew where they were. Krissa always did, and she was certainly not going to be within an hour of San Simeon and miss the Hearst Castle. It was easy to make the arrangements. Petey always had a phone number that would bring around a limousine in twenty minutes. She would drag Danny and Quinn out into the sunshine. They would tour art museums and historic buildings with her.

They were cultured men; they appreciated art and history. As much as they loved their traveling ministrel show, they missed Princeton's intellectual life. On the road people only talked about music; no one read anything but reviews.

Except Krissa. During the week she lived in a lettered world. She was reading Trollope and Herodotus.

She was studying genetics and psychology. Quinn and Danny drank up her knowledge.

Krissa would sit backstage during the sound check, working on her art history papers, and as soon as Danny and Quinn were free, they would grab her outline, commenting, criticizing, even though they had never seen any of the paintings she was writing about. They would steal her books. Even her economics textbooks were more interesting than the clouds outside one more airplane window.

Because they needed her, Krissa was absolute queen wherever she went, different from any other woman. In every town was a community of round-eyed girls who knew what hotels the rock bands stayed in. These girls would walk along the corridors listening for the sound of a guitar. They would knock on the door. "Are you with Dodd Hall? Can you tell me where Danny French's room is?"

They were the groupies, and Krissa loved the way they dressed. They swirled tattered lace tablecloths around their winsome bodies. They tied scarves around their breasts, braided necklaces in their hair. They wore drooping feathers and flea-market beaded velvets. They were gorgeous, junky, and sexy.

Krissa knew that she was supposed to feel a sisterly solidarity with all women—Bryn Mawr made a big point of that—and she wanted to, she truly did, but with the groupies, she couldn't.

How could anyone have sex so casually? How could anyone have so little sense of her own rights? The goals of these young women seemed paltry to Krissa. Yes, it was exciting to be backstage during a concert, to be invited to the parties, to travel with the band for a week. But for young women to scheme and connive for that, for them to think the reward would be satisfying enough to justify their obsessive efforts ... it left Krissa chilled, heartsick.

All groupies are not created equal. The men had their hierarchies from the lowly roadie up to the princely lead vocalists, and so too we had ours. At the bottom were the pathetic, little drug puppies who climbed into the parked buses and gave blow jobs to the roadies with everyone watching. Higher up were the girls who only had sex with musicians, and above them were the grand rock courtesans who accepted tribute only from the megastars.

At the hierarchy's peak were the wives and the long-term girlfriends. They got their positions from the commitment they inspired. That was the ultimate—to live in his house, to have your own credit card on the band's account, to—even though none of us understood this at the time—be able to trust him for something other than regular injections of semen. I was in awe of the women who had achieved that. What did they have that I didn't?

One thing I was innocent of—one of the *few* things I was innocent of—was treating the wives like they were the enemy. Other girls did. When a band came to town, two groupies would rush up to the wife, offering to take her to the latest boutiques, the shopping places too new for any of the drivers to know about. With the wife out of the picture, two other girls would move in on her man. Or a girl might come on very strong to a musician in front of his wife or girlfriend. The girlfriend would get mad at him, they would fight, and the groupie would have her chance.

If the other members of the band didn't like someone's girlfriend, she was an isolated target. Her man couldn't protect her all the time—he did, after all, have other things on his mind. If the rest of the organization didn't care about what happened to her, things would happen to her.

One person who particularly intimidated me was the pretty, warm-smiling girlfriend of Quinn Hunter. She went to some fancy, woman's college. What a trip that must have been—spending the week at some prim college and the weekend in the loony, junked-up world of rock-and-roll.

I don't think she ever appreciated how secure her position was. She was also Danny French's sister, and the whole Dodd Hall organization was behind her. No one tried to get the band pissed off at the Cinnamon-Haired Girl. It wouldn't have been possible.

—Kitty Satin, *Inside Satin: A Rock Groupie in the Age of Disco* (New York: New American Library, 1986), p. 36.

Chapter Eight

Among the musical guests most popular with the original *Saturday Night Live* cast was the rock duo Dodd Hall, who initially appeared on the fourth show (November 1, 1975), the first one to be hosted by Candice Bergen. Cool and unflappable, the two singers slid smoothly into the prevailing backstage mania. Although they had little relish for slapstick, they had dry wits with a strong sense of the absurd. Even though at this point they were far better known than any of the Not Ready for Prime Time Players, they didn't act like stars; they knew that whoever owned the ball made the rules.

French and Hunter also knew a tremendous amount about blues music. As Ackroyd and Belushi became avid blues fans over the next few seasons, Quinn Hunter's personal record collection was a treasure trove, and Dodd Hall often joined the all-night jam sessions at Belushi and Ackroyd's hangout, the dark, grimy Blues Bar near Canal Street.

Kip Campbell, *Cheeseburger, Cheeseburger: The Rise and Fall of Saturday Night Live* (New York: Viking, 1991), p. 89.

NEW YORK CITY, JULY 1975

The line outside the restaurant was long, snaking along West 23rd Street. People were being told that they might have to wait ninety minutes, perhaps two hours. Some recoiled, and shaking their heads, moved off; there were plenty of little restaurants in Chelsea, they'd find another one. Other people nodded acceptingly and went down the sidewalk to the line's end. The evening air was warm and filled with light sounds, soft laughter and low, intimate conversations.

Across from the restaurant, a lone figure came up out of the subway, a lean man clad in jeans and a dark T-shirt. He stepped off the curb, pausing for traffic to break. The spreading white-yellow beam of the street lamp shone against his black hair. The people on line stirred, nudging each other, gesturing, whispering, "It's him . . . look, there he is."

The willowy actress who supported herself working as a hostess for the restaurant saw him too. She stepped inside the restaurant, said a quick word to the manager, and then came back outside, adjusting the scooped neck of her leotard and tightening the sash on her skirt.

Inside the restaurant, two busboys abandoned their other duties to clean a suddenly vacated table; the manager hurried to help. And no more than five minutes after coming up from the subway, Danny French was sliding into a tweed-covered banquette.

Krissa finished serving coffee to Table Eight and gave Table Twelve their check. Only then did she, the one member of the restaurant staff not scurrying to attend Danny, come over to his table. She looked down at him dryly. "Denise—she's one of the other waitresses—her brother showed up tonight too. He came to steal her tips."

Danny grinned, the fine, clean lines of his narrow features lighting up with his twinkling smile. "Then things could be worse. I may be a rathole as siblings go, but I'm not here to cadge a twenty. Now sit down. I need to talk to you."

Krissa was in the middle of her shift; outside was a mass of hungry potential customers. Everyone was rushing, this was no time for a waitress to sit down and chat, but Krissa did. The other waitresses were already moving in to cover her tables.

Danny, Quinn, and the rest of the Dodd Hall family were spending six months in New York working on their fourth album. They had given up the lease on the seedy loft on West 22nd and were renting a much better one in the flower district on West 26th, using it for offices and rehearsal space.

Krissa had come to the city to spend the summer before her senior year. She and Quinn were living in a high-ceilinged apartment which he had sublet in Chelsea. It was one floor of a newly renovated brownstone. The owner was a classical musician on tour in the Orient, and he had filled the rooms with hanging plants and track lights, rosewood furniture and Haitian cotton upholstery. The kitchen was equipped with exotic spices and heavy Copco pots which gathered the heat from the stove and held it steadily. It was a home, the first Quinn and Krissa had ever shared.

She loved it. She loved living with Quinn, preparing meals for him, doing the dishes with him. She loved shopping in all the little markets on Ninth Avenue. She bought bread and meat from the Italians, flowers and produce from the Koreans, and coffee from the Greeks. She loved the people Danny and Quinn knew, artists, writers, actors, and other musicians. Dodd Hall was part of a hip crowd, young and countercultural, all with names instantly recognizable to readers of *New York* magazine.

But as much as she liked everything about this life, she had, within a week, found a job at this restaurant just a block or so away from the brownstone.

When she told him about the job, Quinn was silent for a long moment, his foot tapping. He clearly did not like the idea. "I thought the point of this summer was for us to be together."

"It is," she agreed ... although he was not entirely correct. The *point* of the summer was for Dodd Hall to make a new album. A by-product of that goal was that she and Quinn could be together. "But my scholarship grant has a line for summer earnings, and I intend to earn that."

For a month last winter Dodd Hall had had all three albums on the *Billboard* chart at the same time. Danny and Quinn were making staggering amounts of money. Both were supporting their parents, and Quinn wanted to support Krissa as well. He wanted to pay for every pencil, every tissue, every teabag that she used.

"No," she had told him. "I want to do something on my own. I want to meet people on my own."

The restaurant manager had hired her without knowing who she was. He was simply pleased to have someone on the staff who was not an aspiring actress. Then on Krissa's first night at work, the gang from the loft ambled over for their supper break, Danny and Quinn, Jingle, Stan, and Calhoun, the new producer, and assorted assistants and other friendly faces. The next night Danny and Quinn were jamming with some other musicians, and they brought them to the restaurant. Word spread, and within a week, the place had acquired a reputation. It was instantly chic and trendy, the place to see any musicians in town for the summer.

The dazzled management issued orders: Do anything for "the guys," as Danny and Quinn were known. If that meant letting Krissa sit down for thirty minutes during the busiest dinner hour, so be it. In return, she willingly covered for other waitresses when auditions came up.

She was not surprised to see Danny here alone on this evening. On the least excuse, he popped on the subway and moved about the city. He adored being recognized. He was, she knew, having a grand time this summer, conducting lively affairs with three women: an actress who had a bit part on Broadway; a comedienne; and a crackerjack editor, one of Random House's rising stars. All three women knew about each other and at some cost to their self-esteem, accepted the non-exclusivity of Danny's affections.

Krissa looked across the table at his impish grin, grateful to be his sister, relieved to be *only* his sister. "What's up?" she asked.

He got right to the point. "What's Quinn told you about the new songs?"

"That the bar-band tunes are great fun . . . although half your fans may hate them."

"What about the others? Have you heard them?"

"No, but he's talked about them."

Once they had been released from the isolated spaceship of a traveling rock band, Danny and Quinn found themselves hungry for new musical challenges. Even before he had found a place to live for the summer, Danny wrote six hard-rocking, bar-band tunes, exuberant and energetic. The matching party-hard lyrics had come easily to Quinn. The songs were charged with a school's-out, Friday-quittin'-time exuberance, and both men were pleased with them.

Following that, Danny, now acquainted with the actress, the comedienne, and the editor, composed half a dozen more melodies, these much more sinewy than anything he had done before. He already knew that the arrangements would feature fiercer bass lines and punchier drums. The melodies were full of controlled anger and restrained violence, and above all, they were full of sex, physical love in unabashed nakedness.

Quinn did not feel that sex was his natural subject. His lyrics were often charged with strong undercurrents of sexual tension, but he had always linked physical desire to other longings. He had never written openly about sex.

But he was not about to be outgunned by Danny. So he spent three days reading seventeenth-century poetry—John Donne and Ben Jonson, Robert Herrick and the Cavalier poets. If these guys in wigs and funny pants could write about sex with bright-edged authority, he decided at the end of this reading orgy, then so could he. He closed his eyes and leaped.

For a week he sat upright at a desk just as if he were a junior accountant at Peat, Marwick. He worked nearly around the clock, living on coffee, drafting and revising, meticulously refining his meter, crafting and tightening his images. Such sustained concentration hadn't been possible on the road, and he drove himself.

The resulting lyrics, although no one in the rock community noticed, owed much to their seventeenth-century forebearers. The language was polished and robust, the rhythms were frank and colloquial. The tone ranged from high-spirited eroticism to a troubled ripeness.

These were not sweet songs, but nor were they cynical. However menacing, sex always had meaning. Quinn wasn't writing about a back-of-the-bus blow job, a junked-up, underage groupie going down on an uncaring roadie. He was writing about a man and a woman on a rocky ledge high above a swift-rivered gorge where a single gesture, a touch of a hand to a cheek, becomes a moment of blood-pounding surrender demanding life-defying trust. A touch could become a blow, a caress a push, and far, far below at the end of a terrifying fall, lies a rushing, rock-studded river. Yet not to touch is another death, the doom of a patient spider spinning a slow suffocation.

The images were strong, almost violent. The intimacy was oppressive, a man loving a woman so intensely, so passionately that courtliness and tenderness seemed lifeless etiquette.

He finally rose from his desk, the lyrics completed. Krissa was at work so he set off to find Danny, tramping across Seventh Avenue, his shoulders hunched, his hands jammed deep in his pockets, feeling more and more distant from the songs with each step that he took. He couldn't explain it, but there was something primitive about them, something atavistic, culturally, even genetically remote about the songs. He wasn't going to be able to sing them. He may have been a lead singer in a rock band for the last few years, but he had lived in his parents' elegant, repressed home for the eighteen that had come before that. He wasn't going to be able to do anything with the songs except hand them to Danny. An iron-riveted gate had slammed into place, locking the songs on one side and himself on the other.

This was 1975. The traditional ways that men had of distinguishing themselves from women were suspect. Conventionally masculine behavior had been branded as pointless posturing or savage machismo resulting in the degradation of women and the burning of Vietnamese villages. Men were supposed to be as sensitive and as emotionally responsive as women.

You weren't supposed to be competitive; you weren't supposed to be protective. Manly vitality, physical courage, brutish strength ... those weren't things to be glorified. But Quinn had been on a journey into the mysterious jungle of a man's psyche and this was what he had discovered.

Leslie and Deb, the Dodd Hall organization's two secretaries, were at their desks in the outer office of the loft. A couple of other people were milling about, draped across the worn leather sofas or perched on carved arms of chairs—the Dodd Hall offices were furnished with the comfortable, battered grandeur of a long-established fraternity house.

Behind the offices, Dodd Hall had installed a rehearsal studio. The band didn't record here, but they saved themselves tens of thousands of dollars on each album by working out ideas here before going into the recording studio. Recording studios billed by the hour. You got charged even if you were only sitting around fighting or waiting for a couple of tardy band members.

While Quinn had cloistered himself to write the new lyrics, Danny and the rest had been working on the bar-band tunes. They were, Quinn saw, playing out of position, something that they tried whenever they were feeling stuck. Danny was behind the drum kit, Jingle had taken over lead guitar, Calhoun was on bass, and thin-voiced Stan was singing. It sounded horrible, but they often got fresh ideas out of it. Quinn wasn't very interested in the bar-band songs right now. He needed to show the new lyrics to Danny, and to Danny alone.

Jingle, with his long experience of rock bands, took one look at Quinn's face and got the message. "I'm on break," the bass player announced, leaning his guitar against one of the amps. "And I think everyone who doesn't own stock is too."

Although strong-minded men themselves, Stan and Calhoun usually let Jingle speak for them within the organization. They respected his judgment and figured it was in all their interest to have the back-up band speak with one voice. If Jingle thought Danny and Quinn, the two shareholders in Dodd Hall, Inc. needed to be alone, Stan and Calhoun weren't going to question him.

Danny stayed on the stool behind Stan's drums. As soon as the others were gone, Quinn pulled the song lyrics from his pocket. "Here they are. They're great, but I'm not singing them."

He went over to the window to give Danny a chance to read them. Danny looked at the first one. Quinn began to pace. Danny went through the songs once, then twice.

He had the papers spread out across the drum heads. His face was almost expressionless but his foot was tapping. He was singing the songs in his head, and it was as Quinn had dreaded. Danny loved them.

"This isn't smut, Quinn." His voice was mild. "It's pretty potent, but it's not smut."

"I know that." Quinn jerked at his shirt collar impatiently. Flat-out dirt, lyrics about cocks and cunts, he could sing if there was ever a reason to do so. "My ancestors did not spent nine hundred years civilizing and repressing Western society for me to sing this." He grabbed the lyrics to "Magnets of Fire" off the head of the tenor drum. "Is this any way for a civilized person to behave?"

Danny started to read the lyrics again.

"You see what that's about, don't you?" Quinn continued. "Unpack that metaphor and you've got a guy who's mighty close to violence. Violence with the woman he loves."

"He's not going to do it," Danny argued. "He's not going to hurt her, and she knows it."

"I don't care. I'm not going to glorify that kind of brutishness."

"But it's not about violence." Danny continued to defend the song. "It's about physical strength, it's about liking to be strong, liking to know you have power. What's so horrible about that?"

"Well, to start with, that kind of thinking got us into Vietnam."

Danny had no answer to that. "I still think we can sing them."

"I don't."

Later that night Quinn told Krissa about the scene in the loft, but beyond assuring her that none of the songs had any of the images associated with the Cinnamon-Haired Girl, he refused to show her the lyrics themselves.

She was surprised. "If you're embarrassed with *me* . . ."

"Exactly. If I don't want you to see them, how am I supposed to feel about a couple million strangers?"

"But you showed them to Danny."

He looked at her blankly. "That's different."

It was? How? Did he trust Danny more than he trusted her, did he feel closer to Danny than he did to her?

Apparently so.

Now, a day later Danny was at the restaurant to talk to her about the songs. "They're really great," he was saying. "Absolutely the best things he's ever done, but he's spooked by them. He took a look at the hairy beast inside him, and he hates the idea that it's there. He's overcivilized."

Krissa could see Danny's point. Quinn did have a hunter's purpose and stamina, a warrior's intensity and cunning, but he had let them loose only on twentieth-century battlefields. He could hold firm while negotiating a contract; he could command attention whenever he walked on a stage. Evolution had favored those who, like him, combined physical strength with intellectual resourcefulness, but to speak of evolution instantly evoked a primitive, brutish world with which Quinn felt no connection.

"But he says that you have no problem with the songs," Krissa said to Danny. "Is it just that you're crazy and he's not?"

"Undoubtedly that's part of it," Danny agreed easily. "But don't forget"—he held his arms out away from his chest—"this scrawny body has taken blows in defense of women and children. That was my male initiation ritual. Quinn's probably had something to do with new golf clubs."

Krissa was still peeved at Quinn's keeping the lyrics from her. This talk of male initiation rituals did not help. "I don't know why you are talking to me about this."

"Because you've got to help him. I could talk myself blue in the face, and it won't make a hoot of difference. You're the only one who can reach him."

"Is it so necessary that he be 'reached?' Isn't this his right, not to sing these songs?"

Danny and Quinn had a pact, she knew, that they would never record or perform a song unless they both believed in it. Either one had veto power, and there was no right to appeal, no outside arbiter.

"Of course it is," Danny again agreed. "But you read them."

He pulled some much-folded papers out of his pocket. The sheets were Xerox copies, but still in Quinn's handwriting.

Krissa smoothed the creases out of the paper. This was strange, having Danny handing her the lyrics. Quinn had always sung new Dodd Hall songs to her. But Quinn wasn't singing these songs.

Slowly she read them. Without music, she had to

approach them as poetry rather than lyrics. And it was hard, here in the restaurant with all the noise of dishes and forks and talking, to concentrate. At first it was just words, words that didn't mean anything, but then the words gathered into pictures, images, and suddenly they were all alive, the meaning of the songs pricking her arms, racing down her spine.

Growing up on the Range, she knew how quickly the northwestern sky could darken with howling winds. Even in the twentieth century, tumultuous forces can grip a family, isolating them as surely as the dark stony ignorance of a cave. A family's survival, even today, can depend on a man having resourceful courage and an almost beastlike strength.

The man in these songs—a woman could trust him. Yes, he was mysterious, but he was powerful. The primitive man strong enough to kidnap a woman from her family is strong enough to provide for her. These were the instincts of this man, protective, even dynastic.

Yet the woman had power. In these lyrics, love was a desperately risky proposition with stakes second only to salvation. Krissa had always believed in Quinn's love, but only by reading these lines did she fully understand what that love meant. When he had given it to her, he had given her the weapon with which, if she so chose, she could kill him.

"They're incredible, aren't they?" She heard Danny's voice.

She nodded. "I can't believe he wrote them. They're so unlike him."

Although there were moments . . . at night, in bed, when his breathing was fast and harsh, when she was so aware of his strength and power.

"So you'll help him? He's running scared, and he hates being a coward."

"I don't know how I could help." She still wished that Quinn had shown the songs to her.

"Of course, you do," Danny answered confidently. "The one time he must be closest to this side of him-

self is during sex ... and probably right before he
comes."

"Danny!"

"Make him talk about it then. Stop him, don't let
him come until he talks about it."

Krissa may have known her brother for her entire
life but he could still shock her. "Are you out of your
mind? Do you honestly expect me to—" She stood
up. "I am not going to listen to this."

She was outraged. *During sex ... and probably right
before he comes....* She couldn't believe Danny had
said that to her. True, it had been exactly what she
had been thinking, but to have your *brother* talk that
way, to know that he was thinking about your sex
life, not just in general outline, but down to details of
erections, penetration, and orgasm, that was repellent.
And not only was he thinking about it, he had a place
for it in one of his schemes.

He had done this once before. *My dad is a little
strange. He beats my brother. He's weird around me.
Please admit me to your college.* It was the same
ploy—take something private, secret, and use it to get
something.

She hadn't done it on her college applications, and
she wasn't going to do it now. Yes, Quinn was a public
figure, and yes, he did write songs that were intimately
revelatory. But you had to drawn the line somewhere,
and here Krissa drew it. What happened between her
and Quinn in bed had nothing to do with Danny; it
had nothing to do with Dodd Hall. Everything else in
their lives was Dodd Hall. Surely this was private. She
would not be her brother's puppet.

But within a day she knew that Danny had been
speaking the truth. Quinn was tormented. Fiercely
proud of the quality of the lyrics, he was simultaneously attracted and repelled by their primitive vision
of love. Unable to resolve the conflict, he felt like a
failure. She wanted to help him.

And—if she were going to be strictly honest with

herself—she loved it that she was the only one who could help him.

Danny would have known that. He would remember how eagerly she had helped him with his homework. He would know it was because she had longed to feel needed and important. He had learned how to manipulate her, how to control her.

It made her furious.

But it also grieved her soul to see Quinn troubled.

So that night, as he was poised over her, his weight on his arms, about to enter her—in this most intimate of moments, she did exactly what her brother had told her to do.

In the morning Quinn took the lyrics back to Danny and said that they could get to work. Then he wrote one more song, "Self-Chosen Snares," which became the title track for the new album. He borrowed that phrase from a sixteenth-century poet, Sir Phillip Sidney. In the poem the speaker rails against physical desire, finding it distracting, ensnaring. Quinn took the opposite stance. Despite all the pressures on a man in this day and age, despite being blamed for the oppression of women, he, while willing to admit fault, was not going to apologize for feeling desire.

Chapter Nine

Just when they were on the verge of getting boring, Dodd Hall has released the astonishing *Self-Chosen Snares*. Although the average Dodd Hall fan is a white guy who can't dance ...

—Joel McLease, "*Self-Chosen Snares*: Dodd Hall" (review), *Rolling Stone*, November 1975, p. 84.

Self-Chosen Snares shot into the Top Ten and stayed there month in, month out, for more than a year. It never made number one, but in the long run it sold far many more units than the various disco albums that rose higher but faded faster.

The white guys who couldn't dance loved it because, by and large, those guys secretly wished that they could dance. The album spoke to their deepest anxiety—that because they were smart, they were dweebs, weenies. Intelligence could be combined with manly vigor, *Self-Chosen Snares* asserted, and Dodd Hall fans loved that message. Women bought the album too, responding to its fierce, but intelligent sexuality. Danny, who liked confrontation in any form whatsoever, wanted to release the provocatively ambiguous "Magnets of Fire," as a single, but everyone else with any voice in the decision thought that a hideous idea. So potentially offended listeners at least heard the song within the context of the whole album.

Dodd Hall's *Self-Chosen Snares* tour—what a glory that was.

After all I had been through during the summer of

1975, I had at last sworn off heroin addicts. It finally penetrated my jeweled headbands and feathered toques that there's something limited about a guy so junked up that he nods off in mid-thrust.

Any sensible girl might have gotten a job behind the Sears and Roebuck's costume jewelry counter, but your road-weary Miss Kitty instead joined the Dodd Hall camp followers. It wasn't an easy place to pick up a plane ticket, there wasn't a prayer of getting on the payroll no matter *what* you were willing to do (and there were some pretty big "what's" in that outfit), but you could get a seat on the roadie bus and be surrounded by men who were—and this was a big change for some of us—wide awake.

The critics used a lot of big words to talk about that album, "atavistic," "Jungian." All I knew was that those guys plugged their guitars into raw masculine exuberance. They were their own power station. How we loved them that year, their music, their glamor, their fame, their cocks. Onstage, Danny French and Quinn Hunter sang side-by-side, shoulders back, like two mountaineers climbing higher and higher toward musical ecstasy, their only link to safety being the rope knotted between them.

Backstage the quintessential Quinn remained true to his Cinnamon Haired Girl, but during this tour Miss Kitty finally added the delectable Danny to her "Inside Satin" list.

—Kitty Satin, *Inside Satin: A Rock Groupie in the Age of Disco* (New York: New American Library, 1986), p. 176.

BOSTON, MASSACHUSETTS, NOVEMBER 1975

With the lights it was easily ten to fifteen degrees hotter onstage than anywhere else in the arena. Stan and Calhoun could signal to have the lights off the drums and the keyboards. Jingle could step into the shadows for occasional relief. But Danny and Quinn couldn't. They were out in the amber and rose heat for every minute of every show. From the wings, Krissa could see the sweat gleaming on their faces, on the columns of their throats, on their chests under the open *V's* of their shirts.

Everything about the *Self-Chosen Snares* tour was bigger, wilder, crazier. Playing in larger venues, Dodd Hall needed more equipment, more personnel to manage the equipment, and still more personnel to manage the personnel. Life on the road was a swirling galaxy of music and madness, a caravan of rock-and-roll gypsies always in peril of blasting themselves straight out of orbit.

From the wings Krissa could see the first three or four rows of the audience, their vibrant, upturned faces, shouting, and their raised arms. Behind them was a pulsing black mass. Twenty thousand people ... it was an unbelievable number. You could bring every man, woman, and child from the largest town on the Range and you still would have a quarter of the seats unfilled.

The band crashed to a finish with a new arrangement of "Bridges Ice First." The audience was on its feet, pounding, roaring, as Danny and Quinn backed offstage, fists over their heads, acknowledging the applause, bidding farewell.

The wings were crowded with people: the promoter's friends, the venue people, the venue people's friends, Dodd Hall's guests, the guests' guests, all the travelers on this spaceship of glitter and feathers. Danny and Quinn were instantly surrounded, hands wanting to touch them, voices calling out their names. Quinn pushed his way through the clamor and the chaos, looking for her. She stepped forward, and at the sight of her, others moved back. Everyone knew who she was, knew that she was this spaceship's queen.

His arms closed around her, sweaty and hard, crushing her ribs, lifting her off her feet. "Where were you? I missed you."

"My flight was—" Her flight had been a nightmare.

O'Hare was fogged in, nothing was getting in or out of Chicago, and that always messed up the system for the whole nation, even the Philadelphia to Boston flights. She had waited two hours for her plane and then had sat on the runway for another hour. And this was still the early part of the tour. Come January, Dodd Hall would be playing the West Coast. She'd be trying to get from Philadelphia to Seattle in high-blizzard season.

But Quinn didn't need to hear about that. He had just brought twenty thousand people to their feet, he and Danny had transported them from scholarly New England to a starry planet where Dionysius reigned, governing their kingdom through rituals of excess and splendor. What was a grounded plane compared to that?

"I saw almost all the show," she said instead. "You were marvelous, both of you, all of you, everyone."

"Did you like it? Isn't it great? What'd you think of the lighting? Isn't it finally right?" He was still breathing hard. Krissa could feel his chest heave against her breasts and feel his breath ruffle her hair. "Come on, let's get out of here."

He seized her hand and pulled her out of the crowd. Laughing, running, he opened a door. They were tripping on the metal treads of a narrow staircase, dashing down an empty hallway. It was a wild, dancing chase. He came to another door, and shouldering it open, he turned as it slammed behind them, catching her in his arms. It was his dressing room, and they were alone.

"God, but I missed you." His hands were all over her, her shoulders, her back, her breasts, her legs, every touch fervid and urgent. She could taste the salt on his skin, hear his breathing in her ear, feel the sweat beneath his shirt, but she wasn't keeping up with him. She couldn't. It was happening so fast. It was like watching the show, the band is always a step ahead of you, pulling you along, carrying you in their powerful, cresting wake. She felt his hands on her legs, her thighs. He must have lifted her skirt. Even the denim of his jeans was sweat-stiffened, she could feel their dampness pressing into her legs. He hooked the elastic band of her panties and as he slipped them off, he lifted her, pressing her back, and she was sitting on the dressing table, naked beneath her skirt.

He was kissing her, his head bending and turning, and over the sound of his breathing she heard the rasp of his zipper, and his hands, hot and firm, cupped her from behind, pulling her forward as he surged inward, his eyes squeezing tight at the luxurious relief her body provided.

He was taking her, screwing her, fucking her in his dressing room.

The room was long and narrow, harshly lit. The mirror was cold against her back. Quinn's leather bomber jacket hung from a hanger on the back of the door. The book he had been reading was open, face-down on a chair. It was science fiction; he didn't usually read science fiction.

He pulled her tighter, the movement of his hips was driving, thrusting. She loathed it. Everything that he was doing, every breath, every motion, seemed coarse and swinish. His belt buckle scrapped against the soft flesh of her inner thigh. She was glad her back was to the mirror. It was bad enough to live through this. What if she had to watch?

She loved him. She laced her fingers through his thick hair trying to feel something, but she couldn't. This wasn't making love. It was barely even normal human copulation. This was part of the performance, the natural inevitable end to his show. That's what all the energy, the music, the audience's insistent pounding had been about—sex. He couldn't have sex with them, so instead he was having it with her. She was a substitute for them, a useful receptacle.

His breath caught, and he climaxed, collapsing against her for a moment. Then he pulled back, his eyes glowing, and his hand came in between their bodies, his tapering fingers searching through the dampness of her pubic hair. She pushed him away. She

would have almost preferred him to order her to her
knees to scrub the floor; at least she could have done
that. Orgasm was out of the question.

"Later?" he asked.

"Later," she agreed. What else could she say?

He kissed her, did up his pants, and then he was
back on duty, back to being Dodd Hall, greeting
guests, signing autographs, posing for pictures, the
usual post-show, dressing room mingling and chit-chat
while she stood here, his semen seeping out onto the
crotch of her underpants.

Was this why she had left class early? Was this why
she had sat in an airport for hours? Why she had
missed a wine-and-cheese party for all art history ma-
jors? So Quinn could have someone to have sex with?

The wine-and-cheese party at the college would
have had jug wines poured into little plastic cups.
There would be cubes of yellow and white cheese.
One of the faculty wives might have made a hot arti-
choke dip. Here at the concert, the backstage hospitality room would have rich, deeply veined Roqueforts
and massive Stiltons. But so what? She would rather
be at school.

She didn't blame Quinn. Yes, he was having fun,
meeting these people, luxuriating in their attention
and praise, but he wasn't being self-indulgent. This
was part of his job. The road was full of distant, impossible rockers, little spoiled brats out to get petty
revenge on the grown-up world. Not Dodd Hall.
Quinn Hunter had been born a grown-up, and he set
the tone for the rest.

The dressing room grew crowded. Someone stepped
back, jostling her, stepping on her foot. Whoever did
it didn't turn, didn't apologize.

She wasn't a child. She wasn't a groupie. She didn't
have to wait here. She could go back to the hotel,
take a shower, and study. She had two papers due
next week. She really had a lot of work to do.

She tried to catch Quinn's eye, but he was too intent. He always concentrated on whomever he was

talking to; he made them feel important. That's why he was good at this. She circled around him, coming up behind where he was sitting, and laid her hand on his shoulder. She bent to whisper in his ear. Only she, Danny, and Petey, the road manager, had the right to do that.

He had his hand covering hers before she could speak. "Don't go," he said softly, looking back up at her. His hand was warm, the pressure on hers firm. "Please. I'll be done in ten minutes."

He felt guilty. She could at least credit him for that. He must have guessed that she hadn't liked what had happened. He got to his feet, and within fifteen minutes he nearly had the room cleared. As the last people were leaving, Petey came in, bringing three others.

"Quinn, Krissa, I'd like you to meet—" he rattled off some names. They were people from a radio station. Quinn, although it was the last thing he wanted to do, stepped forward and shook their hands.

"This is really wonderful of you," one of them said. "We can't tell you how much this is going to help."

"Ah ... that's great," Quinn answered. "I'm glad I can do it."

He had absolutely no idea what he was talking about. Krissa could tell, although she didn't think the radio station people could.

"A Christmas present drive for needy children," Petey said smoothly, seeming to address the radio people. "That's the sort of thing Quinn is always happy to support. A P.S.A. and the appearance tomorrow, that's the least we can do."

Clearly he was reminding Quinn that he had agreed to tape a public service announcement and make an appearance for charity. And Quinn had forgotten about it. He was not going to be able to come back to the hotel with her.

How could she blame him? He and Danny needed such energy for the concerts. They didn't try to remember all the details of their schedule. They knew that Petey or someone else would get them where they needed to be.

He turned to her immediately. "Will you come with me? We could go together."

But that would be more standing around, more waiting while people clustered around him, talked to him. He had told her about all those hours he had spent on the sofa of his mother's living room, watching his parents drinking their cocktails and talk to each other. Didn't he remember what that had been like?

"No." She hoped she didn't sound petulant. "I haven't unpacked or anything. But I'll wait up."

"I feel like I have to go." He was speaking softly.

Of course he did. She knew that. He honored his commitments. She loved that about him. She touched his face. "It's okay, Quinn, really it is."

Back at the hotel she took a bath and ordered herself something to eat from room service. She put on a robe and settled down to work. She was writing a paper on the sculpturer Augustus Saint-Gaudens. Tomorrow she would go to Boston Common to look at Saint-Gaudens's memorial to Robert Gould Shaw, a young uppercrust Bostonian who had died in the Civil War while leading black troops. She would have liked to have written about his Lincoln in Chicago, but Dodd Hall wouldn't be in the Midwest until next month and the paper was due before then. Every tour she looked at their schedule and planned her art history papers around the museums they'd be near.

Everyone thought it was so amazing that she was doing all this traveling and still staying in college. Why didn't she take a leave of absence? Why didn't she just quit? Her future was set, wasn't it?

But Bryn Mawr was the one thing in her life that was not Dodd Hall. Studying for a test gave her a reason not to go to one more tedious sound check. Writing a term paper was her excuse for not listening to Quinn tell a reporter the exact same thing he had told some other reporter two nights before. Her books gave her a purpose, a reason to think of her own time

as something valuable. *I'll meet up with you later, just
as soon as I finish this chapter.* Everyone respected
that. No one pressured her not to study. That was part
of the code of the Dodd Hall traveling ministrel show,
that Krissa's studying was important.

That's why she had insisted on working at the restaurant last summer. So she would have her own
schedule, her own obligations.

But this was her last year in school. What would
happen when she no longer had to study? What then
would be important about her? Just the fact that
Quinn loved her, that's all. What would she do while
Quinn gave his interviews, visited radio stations, stood
in front of an empty hall, saying "This is mike number
one, this is mike number one." She would wait, that's
what. She would wait.

She made some notes about Saint-Gaudens's life;
then her dinner came. She went on working while
poking at her chicken. She was deeply absorbed when
she heard a sound at the door.

But it was a knock, not a key, and the baritone
voice speaking her name was Danny's, not Quinn's.

Danny had not gone with Quinn to tape the P.S.A.
Nor would he go tomorrow to wrap a few toys in
Christmas paper. This was the biggest difference between them. Danny did not do charitable benefits and
fundraising events. Raised in a very public-spirited tradition, Quinn supported charities whenever he could.
Danny, still the product of his father's isolated,
working-class home, was suspicious. In his heart he
believed that the best dolls and biggest trucks gathered in this toy drive would end up in the overstuffed
closets of bankers' kids.

Krissa knew that Quinn minded Danny's attitude.
His appearances and private donations helped, but the
way a rock band could really help a charity was to
play benefit concerts, and without Danny's coopera-
tion Dodd Hall couldn't do that.

Danny greeted her carelessly and, without waiting
for an invitation, came into the room. He went straight

for the table she had been using as a desk, picked up a chicken leg, and started to eat it while looking through her notes. He was getting her papers greasy. She hated that.

"These don't make any sense," he complained. "Your notes used to be clearer than this."

"I used to have more time."

That wasn't it. She had found herself in the last year or so making her notes more and more cryptic precisely so Danny and Quinn wouldn't understand them. She was tired of them piggybacking on her education. It could be such a nightmare. She would have blocked out exactly what she was going to read on a plane trip, then she would get on the plane, open her book bag, and find that Danny or Quinn had taken the book she needed. Not only did she have to twiddle her thumbs all the way home, but she had to spend Sunday evening scrounging around the dorm for another copy of the book.

They would go through the outlines of her papers, tossing off all kinds of bright ideas. The ideas would be so cleverly worded, they would sound so fresh and different, that she would have to stop and rethink her whole argument to see if they made any sense. They usually didn't. It was frustrating and time consuming.

She knew that they relied on her for intellectual stimulation, that she kept them from turning into brain-dead rockers, and she felt guilty about resenting it. But resent it she did.

He must have sensed her irritation for he dropped her papers apologetically. "Petey says you got in late. Did you hear much of the concert? Did you know that we put 'Cinnamon Starlight' back in?"

"No." "Cinnamon Starlight"—the first song Quinn had written about her—was her favorite Dodd Hall song. She was sorry she had missed it. "Did the crowd like it?"

"Sure. They always like it when you do your old ones."

"Old ones?" Krissa had to laugh. "Danny, you guys have only had a contract for three years."

"Three years is a lifetime in this business. And sometimes I do feel like my life didn't start until I met what's-his-name."

The room service tray had come draped in linen, the salt and pepper in tiny silver shakers. The room was full of flowers, autumnal arrangements in bronze and golds with willow branches and dried grasses. "The Range does seem like a long way away," Krissa acknowledged. There was nowhere in their hometown to buy cut flowers. People grew their own in the summer, but in the winter you did without.

"Sometimes it does," Danny agreed. He picked up another piece of chicken and looked at her as he took a bite. The light from the lamp shone behind him, turning the curls of his wild black hair into a halo. "But I think about the mines every day."

"I know you do." Those deep noisy pits full of blasting and dust—in some secret spot of his heart he still dreaded ending up down there, poking rocks back onto a conveyor belt.

"Quinn doesn't get it. It's the one thing about me he doesn't understand."

"How could he? You can't blame him for that."

"I know, but it does make me glad you're around. You keep me square with my past. I was the one who wanted 'Cinnamon Starlight' back in."

"I don't follow you. How is that song about being square with your past?"

"It isn't, you dope. It's about you. Haven't you ever wondered what I'm doing when Quinn is up there, singing about how much he loves you? I'm plenty weird and all, but even I'm not going to sing a passionate love song about my little sister."

"You could sing it to your guitar."

He instantly started humming "You'll Never Walk Alone," the song he had had to sing to his guitar during those high school graduation ceremonies. It was nice, them having this kind of knowledge about each other. No one else knew this about him. She supposed in every person there were bits of you that you shared only with the people you had been a child with.

"I can do things like that with the other 'Cinnamon' songs," he told her, "but with that one—it's so important to Quinn that it is about you, that it seems disloyal not to get as close to him as I can on it."

He wiped his hand on his jeans and for a brief instant laid his palm to her cheek. "So next time we do it, don't listen to him. Listen to me, and maybe you'll hear a little of the gratitude I actually do feel. If it weren't for you, I'd still be on the Range."

Krissa could feel the tears smarting in her eyes.

"Let's not get all misty about it," he said briskly. He had had enough sincerity. He took another bite of chicken and sauntered across the room to turn the TV on. Changing the channel, he found two test patterns and one commercial. He stepped back from the set, waiting for the commercial to finish. "Oh, look," he exclaimed a moment later. "It's *Singin' In The Rain*. Damn, I wish it were *Carousel*. I could harmonize to 'My Boy Bill.'"

For some reason Quinn had not been given a suite that night, but a conventional room with two double beds. The room was not very well laid out. The television could only be seen from one of the beds. Krissa pulled the pillows out from under the spread and settled comfortably against the pillows. Danny moved one of the straight chairs up, but it wasn't comfortable. After a minute he grabbed the pillows off the other bed, and sticking them behind his head, stretched out next to her. They watched the movie in friendly silence. During the commercials, he talked about the music and the dancing.

Debbie Reynolds and Gene Kelly were in the midst of their final fight when the door to the room opened and Quinn came in. He was wearing a casual shirt, a long-sleeved chamois flannel in a hunter green, but he had knotted a dark, blunt-ended knit tie under the

collar. Now the knot was loosened and the top button
on his shirt was unfastened. He looked rumpled and
weary.

"Don't get up," he said to Krissa. "What are we
watching?"

She told him.

"Oh," he brightened. "I like that." He motioned
for Krissa to scoot over closer to Danny.

She did. He reached across her and captured one
of Danny's pillows and stuffed it behind his head. The
bed was a double, small for three people. Krissa's leg
was against Quinn's leg, her arm was resting against
Danny's arm. On screen Jean Hagen was getting ready
to fake her song.

Krissa turned her head to look up at Quinn. The
motion send her hair sweeping across Danny's shoulder; she felt him brush it off. She liked it when Quinn
wore dark colors. They made his hair glow as if it
were reflecting firelight. But he did look tired tonight.

"What's wrong?" she asked.

"The radio station—it was a mob scene."

She understood. He had been told that taping the
promos would be quiet and quick, one deejay and one
engineer at midnight. But half the station's employees
had appeared, bringing their friends, all wanting to
meet Dodd Hall. There had not been a moment for
him to step in the shadows.

But he had chosen to be famous, he and Danny had
worked hard for it. So he wasn't tense or resentful,
just tired. Krissa could feel in him the relaxed ease of
energy well spent.

Debbie Reynolds began to sing.

Danny and Quinn responded instantly. Music, any
music, called to them, and their physical beings sang
in answer. Quinn was tightening his knee cap, clench-
ing and unclenching the muscles of his thigh. Danny
drummed his fingers on his chest. Both were keeping
perfect time. The beat in Quinn's leg and in Danny's
arm moved against her in complete accord as if they
were coming from a single source. She closed her eyes

and let the warmth of their bodies encircle hers, their love of music caressing her. She felt massaged, dreamy. Her body grew lanquid. She was floating, drifting, vanishing.

Vanishing. Krissa jerked awake, icy cold. What was happening? Was she disappearing? Becoming nothing more than the field through which Danny and Quinn's forces passed? And lying here like this, equally close to both their bodies. For God's sake, Danny was her *brother.*

She was suddenly suspicious of all the great things he had said to her this evening, about appreciating all she had done for him. Yes, he had meant them, but why had he chosen tonight? Did he sense how discontented she was with Quinn? They always knew things like that about each other. Was this his way of keeping her roped in?

She scrambled out of bed, sickened.

This is wrong, she wanted to shriek. *I can't do this anymore. Leave me alone.*

Quinn was on his feet, having knocked a pillow to the floor in his haste to rise. Danny was at the end of the bed, leaning forward pantherlike, his open shirt falling from his chest. They would have moved in unison, two gunfighters pivoting to flatten themselves on either side of a slowly opening saloon door; two pairs of hands grappling under fire to hoist one flag. This is how they worked, in partnership, in silent union.

They were worried. Danny's dark brows were low, his forehead troubled. Quinn was reaching out a hand to her. They were watching her intently. When she didn't speak, they automatically, inevitably, glanced at each other.

What happened? Is she okay?

I don't know.

Their wordless dialogue was complete.

Krissa shut her eyes. Even in their concern for her, they did not look like normal men. It was something in the confident set of their shoulders, in the texture of their skin. It was as if they were wired differently from other people, wired to emit light, not simply reflect it. Time and again Krissa had seen people who did not recognize them be drawn to them, unable to take their eyes off them, knowing immediately one thing about them—that they were stars.

She sighed. How could you say no to people like that? How could you stand up for yourself . . . especially when you had no idea what there was to stand up for?

Chapter Ten

So I asked Quinn to put his foot on the coffee table. He did so. "A little to the left," I asked, standard photographer's talk. "A little more. Let your knee fall naturally."

He complied, but over his shoulder, he sent an amused glance at his partner.

"Ah, yes," Danny mused, mocking, making a window with his hands to frame the shot, "the famous inseam shot. Photographers love our inseams. Forget our faces, let's just get those inseams in there. We are changing our name to the Mighty Inseams. The weight of the world balances on these two inseams."

I think men, all men, photograph better when they are erect. They feel better when they know the meat is working.

I photographed Dodd Hall several times, and they were always professional about such matters. They weren't junkies so it was easy enough to talk them into the appropriate state. But they knew it was business and didn't expect anything afterwards.

—Livia Smith, *Rock's Eye: Ten Years Behind the Camera and on the Circuit* (New York: Ariel Books, 1988), p. 67.

KANSAS CITY, MISSOURI, DECEMBER 1975

It was snowing. Quinn dropped his head back against the seatback and looked out the window of the airplane. The air was thick, but the flakes were melting as soon as they hit the dark pavement. The plane had pulled back from the gate fifteen minutes ago, but nothing had happened since.

The shows in Kansas City had gone great, but they had had a down day afterward, and Quinn had gotten restless and bored. It was a bitch. They never had down days on the weekends when Krissa was around. They always fell midweek. So the day had drifted away, and here they were on another plane, he and Danny sitting side by side in the first class cabin.

Petey was up by the galley, talking to one of the stewardesses. She picked up the telephone to speak to the pilot. A minute later Petey came down the aisle. He stopped at Danny and Quinn's row and squatted down. He spoke in a low voice. "They say we might be here a while. Do you want me to try and get you guys off the plane?"

That would mean the airline wheeling up a set of stairs to the plane, escorting Danny and Quinn back to the terminal under umbrellas, and then explaining to the other passengers why they couldn't deplane. It was the sort of fuss Quinn loathed. "No, don't bother," he told Pete. "There's no need."

"And we'd still have to wait," Danny added. He used to like having a rock-star fuss made about him, but even he had had enough of it. "We might as well do it here."

Petey nodded. He had probably known that they would refuse. Quinn went back to looking out the window. It was still snowing.

In a minute he heard Danny. "Did you know that Kansas City has an art museum with a super Oriental collection?"

Quinn looked at him. He was reading some sort of local entertainment publication. "Nope."

"The Nelson Art Gallery." He turned the page. "And the Truman Library. It's really close. I would have liked to have seen that."

Quinn would have too.

"I didn't do a damn thing today," Danny went on. "We should have done that."

Yes, they should have. "Why are you reading that now?" Quinn asked. He could hear himself; he sounded like a cross child. "This would have been useful yesterday."

"I didn't see it yesterday . . . but it wouldn't have made any difference."

He was right. Getting themselves to a museum, doing anything that didn't have to do with the tour, they couldn't seem to manage that without Krissa. Quinn knew that Danny was thinking the same thing.

"Maybe we should hire someone to force us to have a good time." Quinn was only half-joking. "A Minister of Cultural Affairs, a Director of Fun and Games."

"It wouldn't work." Danny stuffed the magazine back in the seat pocket. "They'd suggest something, and we'd say that we were too tired or that it sounded boring, and they'd believe us. Krissa's the only one who stands up to us."

That was true. When Krissa decided that she knew what was best for them, she didn't listen to objections from anyone, including them. It almost seemed that days like today were her fault, for not being here.

School was important to her, he knew that. But here he and Danny had this megabuck payroll riding on their shoulders. It was hard sometimes to get worked up about the due dates on her papers. Surely her turning a paper in late wasn't the same as if he and Danny missed a gig. They had contracts, some of them with killer penalty clauses.

"We need to have her on the payroll," Danny groused.

They both felt this way. Every other rock band on a record company-sponsored tour put half their friends on the payroll as assistants. It meant they never made any money on the road, but they were happy. So why couldn't Dodd Hall list Krissa as an assistant?

Because she wouldn't let them. "Not while I'm in school," she always said.

Of course Quinn didn't really want her as an assistant on the payroll, he wanted her on his tax return as his wife. But her answer to that had been the same. "Not while I'm in school."

School, school, school. He was getting sick of hearing about it. She had her whole life to go to school. Why was she so set on doing it now?

The concerts down in Texas put both of them back into good humor again, and then halfway through the one on Friday, Krissa appeared.

Last month she had stopped using her Planned Parenthood-supplied birth control pills. She had lots of reasons—two and a half years was long enough to take hormones like that; it was unnecessary to have daily protection when they were only together on weekends, etc. etc.

All that was probably true, but she wasn't, Quinn knew, telling the truth. She had really quit because of the night they had had sex in his dressing room right after the show. She hadn't liked it, and so by quitting the pill she was making such encounters more difficult.

That irritated him. He had apologized to her for what had happened, he had promised that it wouldn't happen again. Didn't she trust him? She should know that he would keep his word.

Of course there was no denying that he wanted it. Sometimes he'd come off the stage, charged up and ablaze, and among the crowd of roadies and hangers-ons and people trying to look cool, there she would be. He would want her right then, not two hours later in the discreet silence of a hotel room, but then.

Danny came offstage racingly urgent too. It was impossible for the two of them to perform together and not know this about the other, that your partner had the same salty thrill surging through his body that was surging through yours. And Danny was, Quinn knew, getting those appetites attended to. Catherine Barge,

Kitty Satin, Andrea Dana, the grandest ladies of the rock world, swept into his dressing room.

Twenty minutes later Danny would show up at the post-concert party with one of those ladies at his side. He would be relaxed in postcoital ease while Quinn would still have every nerve ajangle. It almost made him envy Danny ... but not really, of course not. Quinn wouldn't trade anything for loving Krissa, but sometimes, there was such tension in the show ... well, he could understand why other guys stopped trying to be faithful. He wasn't going to. He was a Hunter, and Hunter men were faithful to their wives even when they weren't their wives yet.

When she had told him about quitting the pill, he had, as a gentleman should, offered to start using a condom. But she had already had herself fitted for a diaphragm.

At first, it made no difference. She was sensible and discreet. Then he realized that he could feel it. Not during intercourse, he was entirely unaware of it then, but beforehand if she were lying in a certain way. His fingers were long, and he could touch the rim. She was warm and softly pebbled inside, her vaginal walls rich, waving muscles. The diaphragm was a slick synthetic barrier, a smooth dead dome of rubber capping her cervix, preventing him from reaching her. He was sending pulsing points of life into her, only to have them crash uselessly or be strangled in the thick, white spermicidal cream.

Protection, precaution—these were the euphemisms for birth control. He hated the words. Why did he and Krissa have to take precautions against each other? Why did she have to protect herself from him?

That night when they were in bed together, he reached across her to turn on the lamp. She was lying on her back, her rich hair gleaming against the hotel's white pillows. He loved her hair, the color of it, the smell of it, the entangling, entwining enchantment of it. She was magic, the earth's magic—marigolds and woodlands, warm winds blowing moonlit clouds. It was as if no other woman had lived before her. She was Eve.

He reached for her wrist and started to unbuckle her watch.

She was curious. "What are you doing?"

"Taking off your watch."

She probably could have guessed that on her own. He laid the watch on the nightstand, the two pieces of the leather strap arching away from the watch's flat face. Then he brushed aside her hair, searching for her ear.

She had pierced ears. A little friction nut behind each soft earlobe held the jade stud in place. Carefully, having never done anything like this before, he pried the fastener off. She held very still.

"I'm not hurting you, am I?" he asked.

"No."

Slowly he slid the earring's prong from the little hole in her ear. He kissed her ear, tracing its delicate shell with his tongue. Then he fitted out the two pieces of earring back together and laid it next to her watch. Lightly touching her jaw, he turned her head so that he could reach her other ear. He took that earring out, kissed that ear.

"Is this what you wanted?" Her voice was half-smiling, half-breathless. This might be strange, but she liked it. "For me to be as God made me, to be wearing nothing at all?"

"But you're still wearing something." And he kissed her again, knowing that she didn't understand what he meant.

He went on kissing her, her mouth, her throat, her breasts. He knew her, he knew what she liked, and soon she was trembling, her body moist. She was embracing him, but when she tried to do more, when she tried to please him, he stopped her. Tonight they were doing it his way.

He went on, caressing her, kissing her, arousing her, one hand splayed out warm and firm on her stomach. Then at last, he moved that hand downward, curving his hand over her, slipping his forefinger inside her. He touched the diaphragm.

He whispered to her, "Let me take this out."

"Quinn!" She was startled. "No, that's crazy. It's—"

He smothered her words with another kiss. He ran his free hand up her arm, over her body and breasts, still kissing her, still touching the diaphragm.

She twisted her head free. "Quinn, what are you thinking of?"

Of union. Of completeness. Of having her need him as much as he needed her. "We don't need this. Let it just be you and me."

He could take of her. That's what so much of *Self-Chosen Snares* was about, being strong enough to face anything for a woman, using your stamina and vigor, not to dominate her, but to provide for her.

"Quinn . . . no . . . don't."

He could feel her struggle, but her voice was soft, her body heated. He murmured his desire close against her fragrant skin, his lips on her breast, the curve of her waist, waiting for her to speak again, waiting for her to say "no" again. But she didn't, and she was no longer fighting him.

He raised himself on one elbow, and as he started to dislodge the device, he watched her, he wanted to see the knowledge in her eyes, the knowledge of what he was about to do, about to give her. She would be Leda, Europa, and he, godlike, possessing, claiming, impregnating.

Her eyes were dark and yearning, troubled . . . and resigned.

Resigned.

Oh, God. This was just like everything else about their lives, something she was doing for him, something she was putting up with for him.

So he didn't do it.

Everything was over in a matter of moments. Even with the diaphragm snugly in place, Quinn climaxed almost instantly and she followed a moment or so later. He stayed with her for a silent minute, then rolled away.

"Sorry about that," he said as soon as he could breathe again. "I always said these songs would turn me into a mad rapist someday."

"Don't joke, Quinn." She was sitting up. "We have to talk about this. You weren't serious, were you?"

No, no, of course not ... "It's just that I need you so badly." And it wasn't just him. Danny needed her too.

"But this isn't the answer to that. If anything had happened, I'd hardly be able to travel anymore."

She was right. He knew that. Neither one of them were using the word, but they had been risking a pregnancy. Pregnancy and a child ... he hadn't been thinking about that, about an actual baby with diapers and bottles and all. He'd only been thinking about her being dependent on him, with her choices taken away from her.

The least he could do was admit it. "I was trying to trap you. To the extent that I was thinking—which wasn't much—I was trying to force you into marrying me now."

"Oh, Quinn," she sighed. "You know that we'll get married as soon as I graduate. You know that. Why can't you trust me until then?"

He should. Surely she was the most trustworthy of women. But she wasn't graduating until May, and Dodd Hall was touring every minute between now and then. If only she could be with them ...

So many people depended on him. He and Danny had so much to do, and all they needed was her. She kept them sane, she kept them honest, she kept their feet on their ground.

His parents would have renounced everything for one another. His father had sold the family business so that he would have more time with his mother. Quinn couldn't help it, but that's what he wanted, for Krissa to drop everything and coming running to him. He wanted to be all that she would ever need.

But he wasn't. She believed that she needed to be in school.

"Don't you know how much I hate this?" Her voice was anguished. "I know you guys want me to quit school, and sometimes I wonder if I'm being selfish"—

Quinn sometimes wondered that too.

—"But I can't. Danny and I started this thing back on the Range, and I feel like I've got to finish it."

"But this is what Danny wants too." Quinn could hear the urgency in his voice. "In his own way he needs you as much as I do. You're the only one who knows what the Range is all about and the mines and how far you've both come, and he needs someone around who knows about that."

She was shaking her head. "He doesn't trust me either. He doesn't want to lose control of me. As long as I am in love with you, he still controls me."

That sounded horrible, and Quinn wanted to tell her that she was wrong, that she was crazy. But she wasn't.

What a mess this was. The three of them were so close, it was all so confused.

She spoke again. "I know this isn't a great time to bring this up, but have you thought about next semester, about your schedule?"

No, he hadn't. When he was in the middle of a tour, Quinn thought only of each day. You had to give your all at every single concert, night after night. You couldn't distract yourself, thinking about what lay ahead. "I guess we're going to the West Coast after Christmas, aren't we? And then in March we go to Europe."

That he was sure of. This would be Dodd Hall's first major European tour.

"That's right," she said, "and those are all long flights, with the time changes and customs, it's going to be impossible. I can't be flying back and forth every weekend."

No, no, she couldn't. He hadn't thought about it, but of course she couldn't. "What will you do? You'll have to take a leave of absence. There's no other way."

"No," he heard her say. "No, I'm staying at school. I won't be coming to Europe ... or to California. Not at all, not even for weekends."

Not coming at all? He couldn't have heard her right. Not coming?

Dark shutters slammed shut, blocking out the light. He could feel his mind drawing in, becoming a narrow, windowless corridor. At the end of the corridor was one thing, the absolute necessity of her being with him.

She was talking about how hard the travel would be. He knew all that. That's why she would have to leave school.

"But, Krissa, you can't. We need you. Nothing will be right without you."

"This is my last semester. I've got to study for Comps."

"Comps?" What was she talking about? Oh, yes. Bryn Mawr seniors had to take grueling comprehensive exams. "I know, I know. The timing's terrible for you, I can't help that, but please understand. You'll be able to go back next fall."

"But Brooke won't be there. I won't—"

"Brooke?" Why was Brooke so important? Did Brooke matter more to her than he did? "Krissa, you have got to understand—"

"Maybe *you* could understand for a change." And now she sounded mad. "Out of four years, can't I have one normal semester? Don't I deserve that?"

"Yes, yes, of course, but ..." Everything she was saying was right. Of course, it was. But still it was all ending up wrong. The conclusion was entirely unacceptable. "You can't do this. You just can't." He didn't know what else to say.

"Yes, I can."

Quinn Hunter does not want to talk about the end of his romance with French's sister who is now living in Minnesota, married to someone else, but he does so manfully. He isn't coy. He knows that when you've written the songs he has, you can't refuse to talk about your life. It's part of the job.

He sits quietly, one arm hooked over the back of the sofa, waiting for the question. Dressed in jeans and a Brooks Brothers white shirt, open at the neck, he is a remarkably attractive man, remarkable also for his cool poise, his cool elegant gestures, his cool restrained speech, all this coolness in contrast to the fierce passion that he has felt and written about.

The question is obvious. How could any woman leave *you*?

He smiles, shaking his head. Gallantly he accepts all responsibility for the breakup. "When you're on the road, your life is narrow, and it's easy to resent it when a woman wants to broaden hers in a way that isn't, at the moment, possible for you."

So is theirs one more retelling of the impossibility of loving in the limelight?

No, he answers. It has its own twist. "Although I'm an only child, I never felt like the front and center of family life."

French interrupts with a comment on Hunter's parents, which Hunter asks the reporter not to print.

"Then Danny and I started singing together, and I met his sister. Suddenly I had everything. It seemed like at last it was my turn. For years and years I had watched my parents lead a life that satisfied them enormously, and now I had that too."

Hunter is articulate and thoughtful. "So when that was threatened, I reacted with this powerful desperation, this blind urgency that came screaming out of childhood. I felt like I would have done anything to keep her. I put tremendous pressure on her. But there was only one thing I needed to do—let her be on her own for a while, and I was simply incapable of it. I really left her with no alternative."

The question is directed to French, the partner of one, the brother of the other. How does he feel?

He shrugs. "He's being too easy on her. She could have held on."

—Judith Leach, "The Thinking Woman's Hunks," *Washington Post*, July 10, 1977, Sec. C. p. 1.

AUSTIN, TEXAS, DECEMBER 1975

Friday night Krissa had told Quinn that she wasn't
going to meet up with Dodd Hall in Europe. She spent
most of the show Saturday night in his dressing room.
She didn't want to hear Dodd Hall sing "Cinnamon
Starlight." She wanted to study. She clung to her
books as if they were a life raft. What would she be
doing this time next year? Needlepoint? Drugs? For
a moment she could imagine herself hating Quinn.

She kept track of the time while she worked. She
was beginning to close up her books, when she heard
someone at the door. It was too early for the show to
be over. Quinn couldn't be—and it wasn't Quinn. It
was Danny.

He slammed the door behind him and locked it.

This was Quinn's dressing room. He couldn't lock
Quinn out. "Danny, this is Quinn's—"

"I know that," he snapped, turning to face her. He
was angry. "I know where I am. What I don't know
is what the hell you did to him."

She froze. Danny had been impatient with her before, irritated, exasperated, but never angry. "I beg
your pardon?"

"You know what I'm talking about. You and Quinn.
Look at your watch. We're done, encore and every-
thing. Since when did we ever play such a short set?
What happened between the two of you?"

"I don't see that it's any—"

"Don't tell me it's none of my business," he
snapped. "He wanted to get off the stage tonight. He
couldn't wait until it was over."

"Oh." Krissa sat down. She hadn't wanted that.

"He says you are unhappy. Good Lord, we can't go
out and do a half-assed job because *you* are unhappy."

That made her mad. What had happened to the *Oh,
Krissa, I'm so grateful. Oh, Krissa, I couldn't have
made it off the Range without you?*

She glared at him. "Don't I have a right to be unhappy?" It felt good to be angry like this. She had

been sick and miserable all day. The anger was cleansing, cathartic. "Are you and he the only ones with any rights?"

"Rights?" Danny hooted. "This isn't some little college-girl romance you've got going here. You know how much is at stake here. You know how fragile this is. What if people had hated *Snares*? They could have—it was a big risk. Or what if they hate the next album? What if there isn't a next album? It could all be over tomorrow, and you and me, sister, we'd be back on the Range before the year was out."

"That's ridiculous." Krissa knew that this was his secret fear, but Chris Oberlin's investments had Danny and Quinn set for life. "And maybe being back on the Range doesn't sound so bad to me."

"You'd like to be married to some guy who only cares about whether or not you've got supper on the table on time?" Danny hadn't sounded this sarcastic since they were kids. "Is that what you want?"

How would it be different from what she had now? "You know, Danny, you may be this rock-and-roll sex god, but at heart you're still a Ranger. You've never left. Your body's left, but your mind . . . you're still stuck there."

There was a knock on the door.

"What do you mean? Stuck there?" Danny jerked his fingers through his hair. This hit his most vulnerable spot "How dare you say that? You can't mean—"

"I mean every word." She was glad she'd found a way to hurt him. "You say you're above it all, above the boats and the chain saws and the guns, but the bottom line is that you still think like a Ranger. I'm just here for Quinn to use. I'm here to get supper on the table on time. That's the Range, Danny. I'm a girl, he's a boy, so he's more important."

"It has nothing to do with what sex he is." Danny kicked one of the chrome legs supporting the counter under the mirror. "It's that a whole lot of money is riding on his shoulders every morning that he gets up. The receipts from this concert, from one concert on one night, are more than Dad makes in a decade. And yes, that makes him important."

The knocking persisted.

"Oh, so that's it, is it? The money?" Her voice was sarcastic too. "Who'd have thought to see you turning into a capitalist? My brother, the robber baron."

Danny glared at her. He had no answer to that, and he hated not having an answer. He spun and jerked open the door. Quinn was standing there, his hand raised to knock again. "It's your dressing room," Danny snarled at him. "Why didn't you use the key?"

"What's wrong?" Quinn stepped forward, ready to play peacemaker. "You two are fighting. What are you fighting about?"

"Don't get in the middle of this, Quinn," Krissa warned. "This is between Danny and me."

Danny scoffed. "You wouldn't be saying that if you thought he would be on your side. He and I agree here."

"Yes, but at least he knows that he's wrong, and you don't. He knows he's Custer. He knows he's at the Alamo."

Danny shot her another fierce look. "Custer wasn't at the Alamo."

"I know *that*. I didn't say he was. I was talking about two different things, Custer at Little Big Horn, and . . . those guys at the Alamo, whoever they were."

"Davy Crockett," Danny snapped. "Davy Crockett bought it at the Alamo." Then suddenly he started to laugh. "Can't we be the Confederacy too? Or Dunkirk?"

"Not Dunkirk." Now Krissa was laughing too. Danny didn't believe that Quinn was important because he made a lot of money. Danny believed that Quinn was important because he was making Danny happy. "They got away at Dunkirk. You can't get out of this one."

"Krissa . . . Danny . . ." Quinn was very concerned.

"Oh, wipe that look off your face," Danny told him.

"This is nothing. You should have heard us fight as kids."

"We did not fight as kids," Krissa argued calmly. "You didn't pay enough attention to me to fight."

"That's probably true." He doubled up a fist and lightly, affectionately, cuffed her on the arm. Then he grew serious. "But don't forget what I said. Whether you like it or not, you're as much a part of this as we are, and we can't afford a weak link." He paused on his way out to punch Quinn on the shoulder too.

The door closed behind him. The room was silent for a moment. "Do you want to tell me what that was about?" Quinn asked.

"I called him a robber baron."

"Danny?" Quinn was amused in spite of himself. "A robber baron? How did you get there? He's a complete socialist."

"I didn't say that I was right, did I?"

Quinn shook his head and started to unbutton his sweat-stained shirt. He grew serious. "I did a lousy job tonight."

"I know. That's why Danny was in here—to blame me for it."

"Blame you? He shouldn't have done that."

"Why not?" she returned. "You and I both do."

Danny wouldn't let up on her. He badgered her unceasingly about her decision to stop traveling. She was, he said, as much a part of the Dodd Hall organization as Jingle or Petey; she should expect to make some sacrifices. Look at all the groups who had fallen apart while their popularity was still high. She didn't want that to happen to them, did she?

"Oh, come on," she scoffed. "You and Quinn? Nothing's going to happen to the two of you." They weren't going to be as comfortable without her, but they'd still be together.

"You don't know that. We've always had you. Why take the risk?" Danny ran an impatient hand through his already wild black hair. "People's jobs depend on us. You can't screw around with that."

Danny went on and on, making the entire Christmas break a nightmare. Half the time she was furious at him for putting such pressure on her; the rest of the time she wavered, wondering if perhaps he was right. Had she allowed them to need her? Even encouraged them to? Did she have the right to simply turn her back when everything stopped being easy?

But it was only for four months. They were big boys. Couldn't they survive for four months without her?

For his part, Quinn said nothing. He was in the unhappy position of believing that she had the right to stay home and at the same time, feeling utterly unable to live with that. He and Danny were men. They could not believe that with something as important as this, they weren't going to get their own way.

Chapter Eleven

It turned out to be a joke. You couldn't suddenly decide in the winter of your senior year to have a normal college life. It was too late. Everyone knew who Krissa was, but she had no close friends except Brooke. She belonged to no organizations, she had no allegiances. Of course, any of the theater productions would have been happy to cast Dodd Hall's girlfriend in a part. The political crowd would have loved to have her on the podium of their rallies, speaking for Dodd Hall. But it had to do with Dodd Hall. Had she not had cinnamon-colored hair, no one would have cared.

She felt like an idiot. This was like the worst stereotype from the fifties. It was against everything Bryn Mawr stood for. Women came to Bryn Mawr to get an education, not to find husbands. But that's all she had done in college—find Mr. Right. Yes, Mr. Right was wealthy and talented, devoted and passionate, but that didn't change the fact that there was nothing in her life except him.

He and Danny would not leave her alone. Nearly every day one of them called her. She would be sitting in the lounge, finally feeling like she was having a conversation with other women in which Dodd Hall didn't matter, and Brooke would stick her head in the room. "The phone's for you, Krissa. It's your brother."

And everyone always knew who her brother was.

Everyone knew that she was going off to talk to Dodd Hall. It was exciting, it was glamorous. She wasn't like the rest of them ... even though that was what she longed for.

She used to love it, being so close to the center of Dodd Hall's fame. She loved being the Cinnamon-Haired Girl ... the look on people's faces when they learned that she had inspired the Cinnamon songs, the curiosity, the awe. She had adored it. No longer. *No, that's not me. That's a character he has created. I'm not that. I'm—*

Well, that was the problem. She didn't know who she was.

"You aren't going to believe this." Danny's foul temper vibrated through the phone line. "Quinn thinks we ought to take voice lessons. Voice lessons, us? Can you imagine?"

"Some would say," Krissa acknowledged, "that the two of you already know how to sing."

"No, no, it's not that." Danny clearly felt so quarrelsome that he didn't even want her agreeing with him. "Of course, we know how to sing. This is to strengthen our voices so we don't get polyps and growths and stuff like that."

"That certainly makes sense."

"But rock and roll isn't supposed to make sense. It's supposed to be out on the edge. We're supposed to be taking risks. Sure, every note could be our last. That's what it is all about. This isn't dinner theater."

Then a day, an hour, a couple of minutes later, it would be Quinn's turn.

"This is physical," he said. "The writing of the songs—that's all in our heads, but performing, we use our bodies. We need to think of ourselves as athletes. We've got to stay in shape."

Danny and Quinn were bickering. Krissa was baffled. They so rarely disagreed. And there was no reason for this disagreement. She could easily imagine each taking the other side. Danny being for a vocal coach, and Quinn against it. For all his bad-boy posturing, Danny was a realist. He did what had to be done. He was the one who had sung "My Boy Bill" to get into Princeton. Quinn hadn't. Quinn was, at heart, the more romantic of the pair. He could afford to be.

Clearly they were just disagreeing for the sake of disagreeing.

Then they disagreed on how they should work with translators in Europe. Krissa could not figure out what the problem was, much less which side each of them was on.

Concerned, she called Petey Williamson, Dodd Hall's extremely sensible road manager.

"Oh, it's nothing," he told her. "I've been on more tours than all three of you put together. Fighting is standard operating procedure. It's normal, it's essential."

"But not with Danny and Quinn. They've never fought before."

"No," he admitted. "I guess they miss you."

Thanks, Petey, thanks a lot. This was just what she needed to hear, that she was the cause of this.

The question of playing benefit concerts came up again, whether or not they should play without pay in concerts designed to raise money for worthy causes. They had never agreed about this, but it hadn't really been a problem before. Quinn had done what he could on his own. Danny hadn't. They accepted that about each other. But now they were fighting about it.

"This is for an orphanage," Quinn protested to Krissa after apologizing for waking her up. He had gotten confused about the time change. "An orphanage! How can you say no to kids who don't have homes or parents?"

Krissa couldn't have. "Why are you upset now?" she asked. "You guys have been over this before."

"Because this is a foreign country," Quinn answered. "Because we're guests here, guests who are making all kinds of money. We should show our gratitude."

Again Krissa called Petey. He was as puzzled as she. He could not say why this particular benefit should have set Quinn off. "It was such a routine request. We get a couple like this a week. And it's not like the institution is in big trouble. Frankly, I think that the people were more interested in meeting the guys than they were in actually expecting any help."

Two hours later Danny was on the phone. "I suppose Quinn's told you that I'm turning into our resident Ugly American."

"He did not say that." Krissa was no longer trying to mediate these quarrels. She was just trying to survive them.

"I guess this is what you meant about me still thinking like a Ranger."

"No, that wasn't what I meant."

But Danny's self-accusation had some merit. His socioeconomic class probably was a factor here. Certainly the Rolling Stones, raised in middle-class homes, played plenty of benefits while the working-class Beatles almost never had.

"Well, you should have meant it," Danny told her. "I know there's a real 'shirt off your back' mentality on the Range, but that's for family, for people you know, not the unwashed masses—"

Krissa stopped listening.

She thought about all the women through history who had supported creative men—Milton's daughters, who had read to him after he had lost his sight, Countess Tolstoy, who kept the family fed while the novelist was giving away all their possessions, and of course, Dorothy Wordsworth, sister of the poet, William. Krissa felt a kinship for Dorothy Wordsworth; she too had had two men on her hands, her brother and his friend, the poet Samuel Taylor Coleridge.

Yes, and what had happened to that threesome? Dorothy had a breakdown from which she never recovered, and the two poets had been estranged for years and years. They had gotten into that trouble without Dorothy being in love with her brother's friend as Krissa was.

She grew pale. She had trouble concentrating. She was sleeping too much. She tensed every time the phone rang.

She used to love it when Quinn called. She'd curl up, tucking the phone close between her ear and chin, basking in his attention, the warmth of his voice. Now she wished the two of them would leave her alone. The phone receiver felt slick and damp whenever she lifted it to her ear. It was like they needed her to be thinking about Dodd Hall every minute of every day. Why were they so afraid to let her be on her own? She felt smothered, controlled.

Brooke tried to take some of the burden off her, encouraging Danny and Quinn to talk to her instead of Krissa. But it did no good. Neither man would take his complaint to anyone but Krissa.

She understood. Danny and Quinn weren't mad at each other. They were mad at her. That's how it was. That night in Texas when she and Danny had fought in Quinn's dressing room, they hadn't been angry with each other. They had both been angry with Quinn. The three of them all needed the other two so much that when one was angry at a second one, it felt safer, less threatening to turn the anger on the third, who was not involved.

How twisted it all was. Powerful cords bound them together, cords woven out of Danny and Quinn's talent, Quinn and Krissa's love, Danny and Krissa's childhood. But it was no longer working. They could no longer fly together. Yoked together, they were bound to crash, falling into the sea like Icarus, not even breaking apart on impact, but still together as the sea closed over, drowning them.

BONN, WEST GERMANY, MARCH 1976

"Okay, fellas, that should do it."

The sound check was over. Quinn looked at his

watch. It was four o'clock. Could he call Krissa? What time was it for her? He was having trouble keeping things like that straight. "Hey, Petey." He shielded his eyes from the stage lights, scanning the empty rows of seats for their road manager. "Does anyone know what time it is on the East Coast?"

"I'm here." Petey was crossing the narrow wood boards of the stage. He came closer. "I need to talk to you two alone."

Danny was still at the mike. "What's up?"

Petey gestured for Quinn to move closer. "Krissa called me this afternoon, and she—"

"Krissa called *you*? Is something wrong?" Quinn didn't like the look on Petey's face. "She's okay, isn't she? I'll talk to her. Where's the nearest phone?" He was already moving away, calling out, "Hey, where's the phone? Does anyone know where the phones are?"

"Hold it a minute." It was Petey. "Before you rush off, would you let me finish?"

This was Petey's talking-to-the-spoiled-brats tone. Quinn stopped. "Okay. I'm listening."

"She's asked me to ask the two of you to leave her alone for a while. She doesn't want you to call her."

"Not call her? That's crazy." Quinn didn't care if he sounded like a spoiled brat. "You aren't serious, are you?"

"I'm not likely to make something like this up, am I?"

No, Quinn had to admit silently, heavily. No, Petey wouldn't. Dodd Hall tours ran smoothly. All reservations were always in place, cars were always where they needed to be, everything worked and everything made money, and that was in large measure because of Petey.

Petey wouldn't be lying ... but Krissa, how could she not want to hear from them?

"You guys have really gone overboard." Petey was blunt. "If your manager's not around to tell you when you're fucking up, then it's my job. Listen to me, you've fucked up here big time. Neither of you have let up on her for an instant, you've put her in the middle of everything, and you've worn her out."

Quinn shifted uneasily. Petey would not speak these words lightly. He had the longest temper of any human Quinn had ever met.

"One of you she could handle," Petey added. "But not both."

Quinn looked at Danny. Danny was pushing around a mike wire with his foot, lifting it, straightening it with his toe. It was a little kid's gesture, what you do when the grown-ups are yelling at you.

Slowly Danny lifted his head and looked at Quinn. His eyes were fierce, resentful. "She's my sister."

"But she's my— she loves me."

They were blaming each other. When anything else had gone wrong, when planes had been late, when tapes had been erased, when one had a sore throat, it was a mutual problem. This was different.

"So she may." Danny was being sarcastic. "But correct me if I'm wrong—isn't her name still French? And whose is that, yours or mine?"

That was a low blow. "If I had anything to say about it, that wouldn't be her name."

"Isn't that the point? That she isn't letting you have anything to say about it?"

"Stop it," Petey ordered. "That's the last thing she'd want, the two of you fighting over who's got first claim on making her miserable. Right now neither of you do."

Danny kicked the mike stand and stalked offstage. Quinn stormed off the other side, mad at Krissa, mad at Danny, and furious with himself.

This was really nuts, this business of trying to work with Danny and be in love with his sister at the same time. No, it wasn't nuts, it was just difficult. All along he had pretended that it was the greatest thing on earth, him having such strong ties to both of them . . . and goddamn it, it *should* work. It should be the greatest thing on earth. If Danny weren't so . . . so Danny.

But Danny was Danny. And maybe it wasn't Dan-

ny's fault, but Quinn's for . . . well, he didn't know for
what exactly, but it probably was.

He couldn't even think straight about this.

He needed to talk to her, just the two of them, away
from Danny and all the Dodd Hall hurly-burly. That
was the answer. Cancel a couple of concerts, fly back
home, and sit down with her. That's what his father
would have done.

Yes, Reed Hunter would have dropped everything
and flown home. The promoters would have been outraged, the fans would have been disappointed, the
tour as a whole would end up in the red, but Reed
Hunter would have gone.

Quinn did not.

ITASCA COUNTY, MINNESOTA, MARCH 1976

Krissa decided to go home for spring break. Danny
and Quinn were expecting her to meet up with them
in Italy, but she couldn't. She was sure that if she
went, they would never let her leave. *We love you . . .
we need you.* It wouldn't let up.

She was almost in despair. She had refused to travel
with them, so they had called her every day. She had
refused to take her calls, so Quinn was writing her
every day.

He didn't understand. His letters made that clear.
He thought all their problems would be solved the
minute that she graduated. They would be married,
they would never be apart. It sounded perfect to him.

And a living nightmare to her. His needs, his schedule, his work would control everything about her life.
That's how her mother had lived. Quinn was a far
kinder, saner man than her father, but his life wasn't,
and so it ended up the same way.

At times she wanted to stand up for her rights. *If
you want to be with me, you'll have to do what I want
to do. You'll have to quit Dodd Hall and organize your
life around me. I will not organize mine around yours.*

Except that she didn't have a clue as to what she wanted to do. She had majored in art history. Did she want to go to graduate school, work in a museum, teach? She didn't know. She had spent nearly four years at one of the best women's colleges in the nation, and she had done nothing but follow a man around. She hated herself for it.

Her mother picked her up at the bus station in a new powder-blue Lincoln that Danny had paid for and drove her to the new all-brick split-level that Danny had also paid for. Krissa had seen the new house—she had been up to the Range for a week last summer to help her parents move, although her mother didn't trust her to do much more than pack the everyday dishes. But she hadn't seen the new car, so she admired it, even though she could tell from the look on her mother's face that she was commenting on all the wrong things.

"So what are you going to do with yourself this week?" Peg asked her as she pulled out of the parking space.

Do with herself? Krissa had come home because she had no idea what she was going to do for the rest of her life. She hadn't given a moment's thought to what she would do this week.

Her mother went on. "I've got some sewing for you to do if you don't have other plans."

Sewing. Krissa used to sew all the time. She had stopped during her last year in high school because Danny had told her she was wasting her time; colleges didn't care whether women could sew. But she had loved it the neat line of stitching flashing under the pressure foot, a seam springing flat when you clipped the curve. Time disappeared when you sewed. It was you and your hands and your work, each seam an accomplishment, something you could finish, something you could do right. "I'd love to," she told her mother.

"I've got material for curtains for the laundry room and Danny's room. I would like to get Danny's room done, I do want it to look nice for him. But the fabric was expensive, Krissa, very expensive." Peg French pursed her lips and glanced worriedly in her driving mirror. "So I don't know . . ."

Krissa might be having her share of self-doubts, but one thing she knew for sure—she could sew. And her mother knew it.

"I'll be careful, Mom."

"Well . . . all right," her mother said grudgingly. "But do remember—it's for Danny's room."

Which, to Krissa's mind, lowered the stakes to zero. Danny had not been back to the Range since the day he had left for college. He had never seen the new, all-brick split-level, and as far as Krissa knew, he had no plans to do so. It wasn't the goodness of his heart that made him support his parents. It was his revenge. *You don't make any money, Dad. I do.*

So the care with which Krissa measured the windows the next morning and did her calculations wasn't for Danny. It was for herself. Here was something simple, something she knew she could do and do well. Her mother hovered over her. "You will pull a thread, won't you? That fabric cost the earth."

"Yes, Mother."

"And pull it all the way first. I don't hold with this business of pulling and cutting a few inches at a time."

"Yes, Mother."

"Oh, leave her be." Ed French shook his newspaper impatiently. "She can cut a straight line."

"Now, now, Ed." Peg's voice was high-pitched. "You don't know anything about making curtains."

All day Peg fussed endlessly, snapping off lights, straightening newspapers, asking Ed if he wanted more coffee, a pillow, the channel changed. He rarely answered her. He seemed more withdrawn and moody than ever. His moodiness left Peg agitated. Ed French had once controlled his son through physical abuse; he had controlled his daughter through those long monologues. Now he controlled his wife with his angry sullenness.

Just as Krissa finished pinning the first set of seams, her mother decided that she should use a ballpoint needle. "It wouldn't hurt," Krissa agreed, although she didn't think it would matter.

"Then you'll have to run into Hibbing," Peg announced. "I don't have any."

Hibbing was forty minutes away. But it would be, Krissa knew, faster to drive into town than it would be to debate the issue with her mother.

It had snowed the night before. The packed drifts along the shoulders of the plowed roads sparkled, and the yawning, rust-red pits of the abandoned mines were silent and white. March was still winter on the Range. The beauty was familiar—slender-trunked trees and ice-crusted lakes.

She found that she loved being in the fabric store. She drifted around the racks, imagining a rainbow of possibilities. She touched the fabrics, admired the trim, and, as always, was mesmerized by the array of color in the banked spools of thread.

She should not have gone to Bryn Mawr. It had not been the right school for her. Her greatest gifts were her sure, instinctive taste and her deft hands. Her abilities would have been best developed had she been able to study the decorative arts, had she taken courses in the history and theory of costume, had she been able to explore the practical and the feminine. But the Bryn Mawr art history department was classical and conservative. You studied the work of dead white men. Going away to school had, of course, been the right thing to do, but she had chosen the school simply because it had been close to Quinn. Intellectually, she had done herself a disservice.

She looked up from the fabric racks and saw that it had started to snow again. She bought the needles and hurried out to the car. Dropping her purse on the seat, she turned the key in the ignition. The radio came on automatically. A rich sound filled the cushioned car—two knowing baritone voices. Danny and Quinn ... "Cinnamon Starlight."

She snapped off the radio. She had not come home to hear about cinnamon.

Dear God ... what was she going to do? She dropped her head against the steering wheel, feeling sick and miserable. When Quinn had first sung that song to her, she had been so happy, so sure that he was all she would ever need. She had made all her decisions based on that, and now she had run out of choices. Everywhere she turned, every path she could see, had two figures already on it, ahead of her, turning back to make sure she was following. If she wasn't, they would drag her along. Danny and Quinn would never let her go. There was no escape from them.

She took a breath, then tried again to start the car.

She had flooded it. Now what was she supposed to do? Hold the gas pedal all the way down or tap it sharply and release it? She didn't know with this car.

She heard a light rap on the car window, and she saw the shape of a man's heavy parka. Snow blurred the glass, and she tried to unroll the window to see who it was, but the car had automatic windows. It took her a moment to figure out that she needed to turn the key to ACC before the windows would work. At last she got the window down. Jerry Aarnesson was outside, waiting patiently. She had not seen him since high school.

He bent down so that his face was level with hers. "Need some help?" he asked.

"Yes, this car of my mother's, it's too fancy for me."

"It's just flooded. Scoot over and let's see what we can do."

Krissa moved her purse and slid across the front seat. Jerry got in.

He was a big man, tall and muscular. He filled her mother's rich-lady car with simple, masculine size. As he turned the ignition key, flicking it with a light touch, Krissa could see the muscles in his leg bunch and contact as he tapped the gas pedal. The car started instantly. He listened to it idle for a moment, not racing it as she would have done, just listening to it as if it were saying something he understood.

"There you go. You should be in business now." He glanced over his shoulder. "Your mother keeps the scraper in the trunk?"

"Probably." Peg French, the perfectionist, the compulsive cleaner, would not keep her window scraper on the back seat.

Without removing the ignition key, Jerry deftly unhooked the trunk key from the ring. He got out of the car. Krissa slid back across the driver's seat and watched him through the windshield as he wielded the brush end of the scraper in long, sweeping strokes.

Quinn couldn't do things like this for her anymore. He would end up signing autographs while the snow piled up, coating the windshield. He didn't like it that the simplest gallantry was forbidden to him, that he couldn't even get her coat from a restaurant cloakroom for her, but he couldn't.

Jerry put the scraper back in the trunk. He came around to the driver's window to return the key. He bent down to speak to her.

"You shouldn't have any more trouble, but I'll follow you home just in case."

"Thank you, but really, I'm sure it will be fine."

"We're on the same road. It's no big deal." He turned away, then stopped and bent down again. Krissa unrolled the window again. "I have a litter of puppies at home if you want to stop. They are nice little things."

"Puppies?" How sweet that sounded. Krissa liked little things—puppies, kittens, babies. In college or on the road you never saw any. "Yes, I'd like that."

So when they reached his property on Levering Lake, she slowed to let him pass her and then followed his truck up the drive to the little house he had been building when she was in high school.

She parked and went in with him. It was a small, simple house, entered through a galley kitchen. Lined up parallel with the kitchen were two bedrooms separated by a little bath. These—the kitchen, the bath, the bedrooms—felt like afterthoughts. The single large room in the front of the house was what counted.

That room was pine-paneled and the entire east wall was a bank of windows facing the white, frozen lake. A stone fireplace dominated one of the side walls. Across from it was a beautiful piece of cabinetry work, a glass-fronted gun case where Jerry kept his rifles and his shotgun. The furniture was in earth tones— browns and sands. An overstuffed chair was positioned in front of the TV, and the magazine rack next to it was filled with hunting and fishing magazines.

Krissa had stayed with Quinn's parents twice. Their home was beautiful, large and airy with a wide center hall and a curving staircase. The rooms were full of chintzes and china, needlepoint pillows and eighteenth-century prints. Krissa had admired it, but she hadn't been comfortable. It was all so unfamiliar.

But this room, Jerry's room, she understood. A sportsman lived here. When he had laid the stone for the fireplace, he had been dreaming of the day when he would kill a sixteen-point buck and he could mount the head over the mantel. The beer mugs now arrayed along the mantel he had collected while he had been in the Navy. The TEAC stereo components with the big reel-to-reel tape deck he had brought back from the Orient. All the pipes and the wiring, much of the lumber and the shingles, he would have gotten from the mines.

The "five-finger discount" it was called. A man should steal his day's wages. Whatever fit in your lunch pail was fair game; the challenge was getting out the bigger items. Garages all over the Range were full of stuff stolen from the mines, things that no one would ever use. But taking them was part of the sport, a working man's way of asserting himself.

She knew that this would have offended Quinn. He would never steal from anyone, even from something as distant and impersonal as the corporations that owned the mines. But it didn't offend her. This was familiar, this was how she had grown up. It may have seemed like she had been with Dodd Hall for a lifetime, but she hadn't. The bulk of her lifetime had been spent here, on the Range.

"This is a nice place," she said to Jerry. "You must be proud of it."

"Well, yes." Clearly he was very proud of it. "But it's not like your folks' place. That brick is something else." Few houses on the Range were brick. Brick was expensive. He shook his head. "Your brother's done well for himself."

"Yes, he has." Krissa didn't want to talk about Danny. "Now where are those puppies? Why don't I smell them?"

Jerry laughed. "Because you're looking at an old Navy man. That's one thing the military teaches you, how to be clean."

He brought their box out of one of the bedrooms. There were six of them: little Brittany spaniels with a soft, blurred look to them. Krissa scooped one up. It was tiny and warm. She kissed its head, then cuddled it in her arm, stroking its little chin with her fingertips.

"Will they be hunters?" she asked.

He nodded. "The obedience dogs, you've got to take them into the Cities to sell. People around here want hunting dogs."

Krissa knew that. She was glad she did. She was glad she remembered the ways of the Range. She ran a finger down the center of the puppy's little head. She could feel its skull underneath the warm fur.

She heard Jerry speak. "You've been living some kind of life, I hear."

She looked up. He was on the floor opposite her. He was leaning back on his elbows, his tall, muscled frame stretched out. He had a broad Nordic face with flat, high cheekbones and a rounded jaw. His eyes were pale, a clear blue, and his hair was almost platinum.

"I have," she answered. "But I think I'm done with it."

She meant to go on. *For a while. I think I'm done with it for a while.* But she didn't.

"So things didn't work out with that fellow, the one that sings with your brother?"

"No," she said. "No, they didn't."

What was she saying? Things weren't over with Quinn. Why was she saying that they were? She just needed a little time off, time to think about herself for a change.

But how easy it was to talk as if everything was over. It felt right, as comfortable and familiar as this room.

"Are you pretty cut up about it?" he asked.

"No," she said. "I'm relieved." The puppy was asleep now. It looked so sweet and trusting.

She didn't want to talk about herself. But she didn't feel like she could ask him anything. He was so much older than she was. You didn't ask your father's friends a personal question . . . at least Krissa wouldn't have if her father had had any friends.

So they talked about the dogs and the things that were happening on the Range. It was easy enough to keep the conversation going. They knew all the same people.

After a while they gathered up the puppies and took them back to their mother. Jerry put a frozen pizza in the oven and while it heated, they watched the news on TV. Krissa called her mother and said that she had run into some high school friends. She didn't know why she was lying, what she thought she had to hide, but she lied anyway.

"I build a sauna last summer," he said after they had eaten. "You want to take one? My sisters have left some bathing suits here."

Krissa paused. Saunas . . . taking off your clothes . . . that could be about sex. She wanted this evening to be about puppies and the network news, not about sex.

But it wouldn't be. This man was ten years older than she was. He wasn't thinking of her in that way.

Saunas weren't about sex around here. They were part of the culture, how you got clean.

"That sounds great."

The sauna was a small, slant-roofed outbuilding across from the garage that he had been building the one evening she had been here during high school. The structure was divided into a small changing room and the sauna itself. Both were floored and paneled with cedar, the narrow fragrant boards fitting together perfectly. Two long benches ran along the wall of the sauna, arranged like steps, one low, one high. A protective railing surrounded the wood-burning stove, and everything felt clean, woodsy, and beautifully built. Krissa loved fine workmanship; it spoke to something within her. That night in high school she had been drawn to Jerry's craftsmanship. Now she was again.

He slid another log into the stove, latching the cast-iron door. His hands were broad palmed and blunt fingered, a working-man's hands. But they were gifted hands.

"Did you build your gun cabinet?" She wished she had looked at it more closely.

He nodded as he poured water on the rocks heating on the stove. Steam hissed upward. Krissa drew a breath, and she could feel the warmth fill her lungs.

She lay down on the lower bench, her head on a folded towel. She could feel her forehead, her arms, her legs moisten first with the steam from the rocks, then with her own sweat. She couldn't write songs like Danny and Quinn, she couldn't bring an audience to its feet. She was more like the man who had built this sauna. She could work with her hands. She had sacrificed that part of herself to Dodd Hall.

Her body grew soft and heavy as the heat eased into her. She closed her eyes and turned her body over to the heat. It drove the tension from her muscles, the thoughts from her brain. There was nothing but her body and the heat. The waves of steam lapped over her. She couldn't think. She didn't need to think. The world was hot and dark and simple, so wonderfully simple.

A little bell tinged. Jerry pushed open the door to the changing room and the slap of cold air awakened her. Then he pulled open the outer door, and this air was truly icy. Krissa dashed outside, dropped to the ground, rolling herself into a deep drift of snow. The frosted air opened her lungs, crackled through her whole being, lifting her into airy, icy lightness.

"You ready for more?" Jerry called.

"Of course." Krissa scrambled up. Barefoot, bare-legged, bare-armed, she ran through the snow into the sauna's womblike warmth.

They did it again and again, ten minutes in the sauna, then the icy plunge into the snow.

She rubbed her fingers across her chest. The outer layer of dead skin beaded up into tiny gray cylinders that felt gritty under her fingertips. The old Finns used to beat themselves with pine boughs, but Jerry had some long-handled, natural-bristle brushes, and they scrubbed and scrubbed themselves. Her body felt smooth and fresh, and very, very clean. She didn't know when she had felt so clean. And that night back at her parents' new home, she slept more soundly than she had in years.

Jerry took her ice fishing the next day, and they went to the curling rink after supper. He introduced her to his friends, people also in their early thirties, but married long enough so that their kids were twelve or thirteen and could be left home alone. They were open-hearted, friendly people. Of course they all knew who Danny was, but none of them asked her about Dodd Hall. No one needed to know what life with a rock band was "really like." It was so far outside their range of reference that they didn't care.

If Krissa had been an outsider, they would have been polite and careful with her, but she wasn't. She was from the Range. She was Ed and Peg French's daughter. Nothing she had done over the last four

years could change that. They welcomed her to join
in their fun, and they knew how to have fun.

Of course, the fun was all that Danny had been so
desperate to avoid, the loud-voiced good cheer, the
unending talk about hunting and fishing, cars and
boats, the protracted efforts to pin down a date or a
fact. But Krissa didn't mind. She loved being outside
all day, ice skating or sledding until she was exhausted
and then taking long, steaming saunas at Jerry's.

Her mother was shakingly angry with her. "How
can you? How can you be gallivanting around like
this? What would Quinn say?"

"This has nothing to do with him."

That felt true. Quinn seemed far away. The Krissa
that he loved, the "Cinnamon Starlight" girl, she too
seemed far away, remote and unreal. Reality was this
world of pine boughs laden with snow and long, laughing card games and gambling with piles of pennies.
This was the world of her childhood.

Except that it was nothing like her childhood. This
was what her childhood should have been like. The
French family had not been a part of the warm and
generous community that was the Range at its best.
Ed French had isolated his family. But now at last his
daughter was getting it right, she was having her turn.

Jerry was an easy person to be with. He seemed
straightforward and uncomplicated, neither moody nor
needy. He did not have Quinn's courtly manners, but
he looked after her comfort in a rough, woodsy way.

"There now," he would say, starting his truck on a
cold night and holding his hand up to the defrost vent,
checking on the engine's warmth. "We'll have you
toasty in no time."

Or one night they stepped into the vestibule of a
bar, and two men were shoving each other, about to
fight. Jerry had encircled her with a protective arm
and hurried her past the trouble. "You don't need to
be a part of that."

The calm air of authority that Danny and Quinn
got from their talent and their success, Jerry got from

his size. He was almost always the tallest and strongest man in the room. He didn't preen or pose, he didn't even seem to think about it. It was just a part of him, something that had probably been true since his earliest adolescence. Silently he accepted the responsibilities attendant upon strength. He was always one of the first to get up when someone came in a bar and said a car was stuck in the snow. He automatically walked first through unbroken snow. Breaking a path was easy for him. He occasionally lifted Krissa over a snowbank, swinging her as easily as if she were a small child.

The questions about the place of masculine energies in contemporary culture that had troubled Quinn before the recording of *Self-Chosen Snares* didn't confuse Jerry. He was a man, responsible for taking care of women simply because he was bigger than they were.

In the covered shell on the back of his pickup, he carried blankets, flashlights and a compass, extra batteries and extra fuel, a shovel, flares, sand, even some food and cans of Sterno. If a person were to be stranded on a cold Minnesota night, she could, Krissa thought, do far worse than Jerry Aarnesson. He could keep a woman—a family—warm and dry.

On her last night they took saunas again, and when they were back inside dressed and warm, he switched on the TV. When he sat down, he was closer to her than he had before. After a moment, he put his arm around her.

He had touched her before, but it was always part of doing something else, getting her over a snowbank or through a crowded room. This was different. And in another moment, he turned her face up to his. She had never kissed a man with a mustache before and it felt strange, a little ticklish, but not bad.

Then he kissed her again. Because she was so used to kissing Quinn, she automatically opened her mouth when his touched hers, even though he hadn't tried to deepen the kiss.

Encouraged, he brushed one hand across the front of her sweater. When she didn't object, he slipped his hand under the hem of the sweater, pulled her turtle-neck free from the waistband of her jeans, and moved his hand upward, closing it over the soft flesh of her bare breast.

His hand was bigger than Quinn's. That was what she thought of first. His fingers were not longer, but they were wider, his palm was broader and deeper, the texture of his skin rougher.

And his touch was different. Quinn's was erotic, arousing. Jerry's was assessing. He cupped her breast, letting its weight rest in his hand. His thumb explored the upper circumference, measuring its girth.

At first she didn't like it. It felt too disengaged, this hand on her breast. It was like he was a perspective buyer at a slave market, feeling the dark breasts of the women for sale. But as his thumb and forefinger curved around her nipple, she understood. He was a tactile man. This was how he understood things—by touching them. Perhaps this was not a caress, but there was nothing calculating or disengaged about it. He was following his instinct to explore weight, shape, and texture. She was like that herself. A warm comfort spread outward from his touch.

His other hand came slowly down her body, and she knew that in a moment it would be between her legs, exploring there with the same deliberate weight. She heard him speak. "This is okay, isn't it?"

His hand was already there, resting solidly against the seam that curved inward from the zipper of her jeans. She had seen that hand pass over a sanded board, assessing the finish quickly, confidently. He would lean forward as he worked, blowing the dust off the wood with his breath.

"You want to, don't you?" she whispered back.

"Now that's one dumb question." He stood and effortlessly scooped her up and carried her to the bedroom. It was neat, the bed crisply made, the clothes stored away. The Navy taught a man to take care of himself. That's what she needed: a man who could take care of himself.

Don't think. This will be all right if you just don't think.

She would never escape from Danny and Quinn until she had someplace to run to. And surely this is what her life would have been like if she had had different parents and a different brother. The Range was her heritage. This miner's burly body was her destiny. This wasn't about sex. It was about going back to what she was, how she had been raised.

It doesn't matter that he doesn't feel like Quinn, that his hair is too light, his shoulders too broad, his arms too thick. Don't let that matter.

She was safe here with him, warm and safe and clean. He would never demand too much of her. *Just don't think.*

In the years that followed, Krissa came to understand that it was too simple to say that Jerry was a father figure for her, a refuge from Danny and Quinn's needy intensity. That was certainly true. But what she did that night also resulted from the whole system of her family—a pattern that she, Danny, and her parents had been trapped in since the time she had been born.

Danny had been a fitful, restless, colicky baby. She, born a little more than ten months later, had been quiet and easy. That had been the pattern. Danny was the bad child, and Krissa the good one. The conviction was so deeply woven into the family that even when Danny was being a model soul in high school, Ed and Peg still responded to him as the difficult one, the temperamental one.

But with the success of Dodd Hall, the powder-blue Cadillac, the all-brick home, things changed. Danny became the good child, the one Peg needed to have pretty curtains for.

So what role did that leave Krissa? If Danny was the good child, what could she be but the bad one? If he was soaring, what choice did she have but to bury herself?

Chapter Twelve

AMSTERDAM, MAY 1976

The interviews were over. The last photographer was packing up his equipment. The last reporter was shaking hands. The reporter would have liked to stay. He would have liked to have hung out with the boys, schmoozed with them, become their friend. But Danny and Quinn were stretching, switching off the mental tape players that coughed up the answers to the questions that people had been asking them for years and years now. This late in the tour they gave up trying to say anything different.

"Everything go okay?" Petey peered around the door that led to one of the suite's bedrooms. None of the management staff was ever with Danny or Quinn during interviews. A point was made of that. They weren't your everyday, junked-up rock idiots who couldn't be let off the leash.

Gradually the room began to fill with familiar faces. Dodd Hall always laid out a nice spread for reporters; coffee, pastries, and fruit in the morning, sandwiches in the afternoon. The buffet was never ostentatious. Caviar, out-of-season raspberries, and other flashy delicacies, those were for the disco crowd. But the offerings were generous, and there was always plenty left over for the assorted mongrels from the Dodd Hall traveling kennel who descended afterward to clean up the platters.

The room filled up quickly today. There were easily fifteen guys crowding into room that had once felt spacious. Tom, the head roadie, was on the phone. Jingle was on the floor, plucking at an acoustic guitar; his head was curved down over the body of the instrument so he could hear it over the noise. Quinn sat quietly in an upholstered chair, one leg hooked over the arm, his foot swinging. This was the lull in the day, and he had learned to make use of it. He let all his thoughts turn into a rusty orange liquid. There was a tap in his body. He turned on the tap and the orange liquid drained out, leaving him relaxed and mellow. In a couple of hours the energy would start to build, the surging tide of electricity that would crest the minute he stepped onstage.

The second phone range. Petey moved to answer it just as Stan sat down on the floor next to Quinn's feet and—for God only knew what reason—started trying to balance a beer on Quinn's foot.

"Hold still, mate," Stan said. "This will never work if you keep twitching."

Quinn promised to oblige.

He did not know what made him look up just then, but he did, holding his foot still, glancing idly across the room.

Petey had given the phone to Danny. Danny was greeting whoever had called. Then suddenly his face went blank, dead, and he turned his back to the room.

Danny turning his back . . . Danny who never locked his door, who did not believe in privacy . . . Danny had gone pale and turned his back.

Quinn was on his feet, Stan's beer bubbling out of the can onto the carpet. He caught Petey's eye, and with a quick, silent jerk of his head, ordered everyone from the room.

Petey snapped his fingers and made a herding gesture toward the door. Everyone obeyed. In a moment, the room was quiet. Empty glasses and half-filled plates lay on the tables, the sandwiches with big crescent-shaped bites out of them. A dark, wet circle marked the carpet around Stan's beer can.

Quinn waited until Danny looked around. Then he

spread his hands, offering to leave as well. Danny shook his head. "It's Krissa," he mouthed.

Krissa? Quinn put out his hand for the phone. She was graduating from Bryn Mawr tomorrow. Quinn wished like hell he could be there. But he couldn't. So at dawn dozens and dozens of roses would be delivered to her dorm. A caterer would bring breakfast, enough for everyone on her floor. And then, perhaps as early as next week, she'd be on a plane, and they would never be separated again.

Why was she calling Danny, not him? He nudged Danny on the arm, wanting the phone.

Danny hardly noticed. "I can't believe it," he was saying into the phone. "How could you do something like that?"

Danny's voice was rough and impatient. He was clearly very upset. What had Krissa done? What could they be talking about?

"What do you mean you don't want to discuss it?" Danny demanded. He was now sounding angry. "You've got to tell Quinn . . ."

Tell Quinn what?

"He's standing right here. Come on." Danny's voice was almost brutal. "You owe him that. Here he is." Danny thrust the receiver toward Quinn.

"Danny, *no*!" Quinn could hear her, even though he hadn't touched the phone. "Please don't make me. I can't."

The anguish in her voice was excruciating. Quinn grabbed the phone. "Krissa, love, tell me, whatever it is, tell me, I'll make it right."

He heard a gasp, almost a sob, and then a sharp click. She had hung up. He couldn't believe it. What was going on?

"Did she hang up? Did she hang up?" Danny demanded. Quinn had never seen him this angry. "Goddamn her. How could she be so stupid? Of all the people who want to stab us in the back, I thought we could trust her. It just makes you want to—"

"Stop it," Quinn ordered. Krissa stab them in the

back? That was absurd. "Stop ranting like a maniac and tell me what happened.

"What happened? What happened? My darling baby sister, the love of your life, the one person I thought we could count on, she up and married someone else yesterday."

What? Krissa, married? *Married?* Yesterday?

"She skipped graduation. She finished the work, she'll get her degree, but she didn't go to the ceremonies. She got married instead. To Jerry Aarnesson. A goddamn Ranger. Do you believe it, she married a Ranger?"

Quinn could barely speak. "Married? My God, why?"

Danny shrugged, his face as hard and angry and bitter as his voice. "Why does anyone get married? She's having a baby in December, early December."

The room blurred. Quinn rubbed his hand over his eyes. Danny was still there. "What are you saying?"

"That it's over. That it was a waste of time. After all we went through, after all that she and I did to get out of that goddamn place"—suddenly the anger drained out of Danny's voice and it was thick and choked—"she's going to end up with a life exactly like Mother's."

Krissa was married. The words were like some dense scientific principle. Each word was linguistically familiar; he knew what each meant, but strung together, none of them made sense.

"She's pregnant?"

It wasn't possible. January, February, March ... It couldn't be true. She couldn't be having a baby in December. To be pregnant she would have had to—

She would have had to have had sex with someone else.

Some man—and all Quinn knew of him was his name, Jerry Something, God, he didn't even know his name—this man had had sex with Krissa. He had put his erect penis into her without protecting her, without letting her protect herself. Quinn's thoughts lashed out, hoary and explicit. And now inside her, some little jellylike being, half her and half this guy whose name Quinn didn't know, was growing.

Flashing, fiery waves of pain sheered through him. How could this be happening?

His shoulders were braced, his back a tight knot of muscle, a sailor tied to the mast, waiting for the captain to pull back his arm, for the black whip to come whistling through the salt air, slashing him open to the bone. That would be better than this.

Krissa. He couldn't think about it anymore. He'd die if he did.

But how could he think of anything else? He cleared his throat. "Who is he? What does he do for a living?"

"This is the Range, Quinn. What do you think he does?" Danny spit out the question. "He's in the mines. He's a mechanic."

The mines—this was what Danny had always dreaded, ending up in the mines. And now Krissa had married a miner.

Married. "We have to get her out of this. I'm going up there. Now. Today." This was more important than any concert. "Are you coming?"

Danny was sitting on the arm of the sofa, staring down at his feet. He was shaking his head. "I don't think either of us should go. Not calling until after she was married was a sign. She didn't want to be rescued."

"But—"

"But nothing. She's not stupid. She had options. She could have had an abortion. Or if she couldn't stomach that, she must have known that we would have seen her through." Danny raked his hand through his hair. "The real bitch is that she couldn't come to me. She's mad at you, she wants to get back at you, so she does this incredibly stupid thing, but coming to me for help is like coming to you, and she couldn't."

Quinn thought he would hit Danny. No, he couldn't,

he agreed with him. He would do both, hit him and agree with him. "If you're blaming me . . ."

"You bet I'm blaming you," Danny snapped back. Then he stopped. "No, shit, I'm blaming myself." He rubbed his hands over his face. "The two of you . . . it's my fault. I was always there. I couldn't keep out. I don't know . . . it just seemed so important that you be together."

It was important. It had been the most important thing in the world, maybe even more important than Dodd Hall. No, he couldn't say that because you couldn't divide things up like that. She was Dodd Hall.

"Oh, lord, don't blame yourself," he muttered to Danny. "It had to be something I did." Although he didn't know what . . .

Danny groaned and got up. "It's a waste to try to figure out who did what. We're not like two normal separate people."

No, they weren't. That's what Jingle always said about them, put a coin in one and you got a dial tone out of the other.

They were facing each other. Danny's dark eyes glinted. Quinn's were distant and troubled. "So there's nothing we can do?" The voice was Quinn's.

"No." Danny's answer was slow. "No, she doesn't want to have anything to do with us."

They had had setbacks before. Climbing this far hadn't been easy. They were a rock band in a time of sequins and disco. But always before there had been something to do: sing louder, write tighter, hustle harder. Every time they had knuckled down and done it together.

Now there was nothing they could do.

"Maybe we are being impossibly arrogant." Danny slung his arm around Quinn's shoulder, a rare gesture of affection. "Maybe she just fell flat out, head over heels, impossibly in love with him."

"Oh, great. That makes me feel lots better."

But Quinn reached back and gripped Danny's shoulder.

*   *   *

After the band broke up, the Amsterdam concert that Dodd Hall played that night became a legend. It was utterly unlike any other in tone and in set list. No one ever called it the act's best show—it was too atypical for that—but it was the one written about the most.

Before the concert each night, the band gathered for a few moments backstage to talk about the set. None of them could stand doing the same thing night after night. Of course, they had to play their big hits, but their show was long enough that they could try out some of the new stuff or cover a song or two of someone else's without the audience feeling cheated.

Quinn had spent what had remained of the afternoon alone, and he was last to join the others. The incandescent force that always gripped him before a performance hadn't come tonight. He was empty. He had nothing to give the audience. He was physically dematerialized. He felt he didn't even have a body to sing with. But he would go out there. It was his job.

Danny and the band were at the far end of a concrete-floored open area just beyond the dressing rooms. Quinn crossed toward them slowly. At the sound of his footsteps, everyone turned.

There was an instant silence. Faces, familiar faces, were looking at him—Jingle, Stan, and Calhoun, they all knew.

Quinn couldn't stand what he saw on their faces, the pity for him and the grief for her. Stan and Jingle were from working-class homes. They, more than he, understood the rock-hard pit Krissa had thrown herself into.

He looked down at their hands. They all had musicians' hands—deft, long-fingered, light of touch, with leathery calluses. Calhoun kept his watch on. Jingle had sweatbands around his wrists. Otherwise, their hands were bare, ready to go out and do their version of a day's work.

He wondered what a mechanic's hands looked like.

Everyone was waiting for him to speak. He couldn't.

So Danny did. "It's your call, Quinn. Do you want to be brave and stoic, or do you want to wallow in it?"

Quinn had been raised to be brave and stoic, to rise over the pain. He could see the months unfolding ahead of him. That's what he would do, suffer quietly, mourning Krissa in quiet dignity. That was what was right, that's what was expected of a Hunter.

"Fuck it," he said suddenly. "Tonight let's wallow." This was what he had to give to the audience, his pain.

Danny clapped him on the shoulder. " 'Heartbreak Hotel'? You start?"

"Okay, but you'd better be ready with 'My Boy Bill' in case I fall apart."

They had never performed "Heartbreak Hotel," the old Elvis Presley hit, but they had played around with it in rehearsal. Danny had staged a theatrical opening, singing it himself because he was the one who liked theatrics. Quinn had never sung the opening, but having heard Danny sing something was as good as having sung it himself.

They took the stage in the dark, Stan mounting his platform, Calhoun curving over his keyboards. A spotlight picked up a spot on the stage: an empty mike, a wooden floor.

The crowd become quiet, startled by the single light. Just before they grew restless again, Quinn stepped into the spot and simply, elegaically, with no instrumental accompaniment, began to sing. It was a lament, a grieving lullaby, nothing like Elvis's original. At the chorus, Danny's voice joined his from the dark, a ghostly unseen harmony, the song's stated death wish becoming a shivering possibility. A slow, tingling keyboard, almost unnoticable at first, supported the voices and gradually the lights rose.

They sang songs that night that they would never sing again. They sang other group's hits, focusing on darkness and anger. They sang old folk songs like "On Top of Old Smokey," mining that song, not for its grief, but for its bitter blaming. "You might have courted too slow, but the fault was really hers. A false-hearted lover will send you to the grave."

The anger built. Even the party-hard tunes off the first side of *Self-Chosen Snares* became angry anthems. You partied to escape. They crashed to a finish with a second version of "Heartbreak Hotel," and this time the words shimmered with rage. This girl had made them care about her. By what right, how dare she, how dare any woman, do that?

As they broke for the wings afterward, tightened, almost cleansed by their anger, a sea of hands was waiting for them, touching them, telling that they were the greatest, that the concert had been the greatest, that—

"Fine." Quinn pushed through the mass. "That's great." When the dressing room door slammed behind Danny and him, leaving them alone, he spoke. "They'd better be happy with this one. I don't know what town we're in, but when I find out, I'm never coming back again."

And he didn't.

ST. PAUL, JUNE 1990

"Hello, I'm Krissa Aarnesson. This is my husband Jerry. We live next door."

"Ben Zagursky." Their new neighbor, a pleasant, if momentarily harrassed-looking man, put out his hand. "Lynn is around here somewhere." A moving van was parked at the curb and two movers were carefully an gling a sofa down the ramp. "I don't think we left her behind ... although I suppose it's possible."

Krissa smiled. "We won't keep you." If the new people had been moving themselves, Jerry and the twins would have stayed to help unload the truck, but with professionals doing the work, the Aarnessons would only be in the way. "We'd like to have you over for supper tonight. What time would be good for you?"

"Oh . . ." Ben was hesitant. "I don't know."

"We're not talking about anything fancy," Jerry assured him. "Just a quiet family meal."

"Well, it won't be quiet," Krissa amended, "not with our boys."

Ben suddenly smiled, and Krissa thought that it might be nice having him live next door. "Okay then. We'd love to come."

"Great," Jerry said. "Now let us take your kids off your hands. We'll keep them next door, and we'll see you tonight."

"You'll watch our kids?" Ben marveled. "Where did you people drop from? Heaven?"

"Close," Jerry answered. "We're from the Mesabi Iron Range."

The economy of the Range collapsed in the late seventies. Foreign competition ate into the demand for American steel. That cut off the need for iron ore. The mines shut down, people were laid off, stores closed, the lines for free government cheese were a block long. Rangers lost their boats, their cars, and finally their houses. Eventually unemployment in some of the mining communities would run as high as ninety percent.

Jerry lost his job in 1979. On his own, he might have clung snail-like to the little house he had built, losing everything he owned one piece at a time, but Krissa, however shell-shocked she had been during the first year of their marriage, had recovered her energy and her initiative. They moved to the Cities and Jerry found work on the sales force of a lawn mower manufacturer. It was a good place for him. He was a straightforward and likeable enough guy that sales came naturally, and he certainly knew machinery. It did keep him on the road. He was gone at least four days a week, but in truth, the separation didn't bother either him or Krissa.

They bought a house in Ramsey Hill, a grand old neighborhood, now terribly dilapidated. They did all the work on their deteriorating house themselves. For years and years, they lived without interior walls and with gaping holes in the floor, that ran from the attic to the cellar. For four months one year, Krissa had had to do the dishes in the bathtub because that and the toilet were the only places in the house with running water. For a year, the furnace had been hooked up in the dining room, a hulking gray beast with ducts snaking across the floor.

Most of the houses in the neighborhood were being restored, and Krissa and Jerry's was the focus of neighborhood life. They had the open, hospitable manners of Rangers. People were always welcome to drop in on the Aarnessons. You never had to wait for an invitation, call first, or even make up an excuse as to why you were on their doorstep. Krissa always had a pot of coffee on, and their house was the center for many noisy gatherings of people talking about furnaces and plaster.

But over the years as the houses were finished, the neighborhood changed. Some people finished their restorations and turned their attention to their careers. Far more found that their marriages could not survive the strains of rehabbing. They divorced and sold out.

The new people were different. Buying a house in Ramsey Hill was no longer a risk. It was just expensive, even rather chic. When Garrison Keillor started making good money from his *Prairie Home Companion* show, he moved to Ramsey Hill. Lawyers, investment bankers, stockbrokers, all the yuppies, moved in. They were well-educated, goal oriented, complicated, occasionally high-strung, and Krissa liked them.

Jerry did not. He was by no means an unintelligent man, but he lacked intellectual curiosity. He was practical, happy to explore new ways of doing things. Anything more abstract—politics, history, or art—didn't interest him. He didn't understand these new people.

Why were they so driven? Why couldn't they relax and have a good time?

So Krissa knew that on this June evening there would be a moment during dinner with their new neighbors when the guests would be frozen into awkward silence. She herself would make a wonderful impression. She was a Bryn Mawr graduate, a mother active in her children's school, she had her own business, she was one of them. But her husband . . . he was a decade older than her, he hadn't been to college, he had been in the military. He was different. He didn't fit in. They wouldn't know what to say.

Krissa would not be mortified by this silence. She had long since gotten over her anger, the rage she had felt for Jerry because he was not Quinn. She accepted him, she valued him for what he could do, did not fault him for what he could not. There was no intimacy in their marriage, few common interests or joys, no emotional satisfaction, but Krissa had long since stopped expecting any of that. He was a good father to their boys. That was enough for her. She could stay married to him forever.

But sometimes she had to wonder—would he be able to stay married to her? He missed the Range, and he knew that people around here thought that he was this strange liability strung around Krissa's neck, that he was a leftover from some lesser life. No man likes to be thought of that way, especially a Ranger.

Chapter Thirteen

Quinn was wearing a business suit. In the last five months, since learning of Krissa's marriage, he had sought anonymity more than usual, and he had discovered that a charcoal vest, a white shirt, and a dark tie did the trick. Dodd Hall fans, as repelled as they would be by the label "narrow-minded," simply did not look at businessmen.

Riding the Metroliner train down to Baltimore, he was seated in the first-class section along with the other businessmen, but his frame of mind was more suited to the students in the back cars. Like any self-respecting undergraduate, he was so bloody mad at his parents he could hardly see straight.

This weekend was their twenty-fifth wedding anniversary, and they were giving themselves a big party at the club. If you wanted to get technical about it— and there were times when Quinn did want to get this technical—he was giving this party since he now paid nearly all their bills.

It wasn't the money that was irritating him now— well, it wasn't entirely the money. He dredged up his feelings about supporting them only when he was pissed off about something else. What bothered him was that all summer, the entire time that they had been planning this party, they had automatically assumed that he was going to be able to come. It never occurred to them to ask him, to check the date with

him, to do anything but twitter away about the menu
and flower arrangements.

He did have a few obligations in life. Dodd Hall
had returned from Europe to begin a massive stadium
tour. For all his parents knew, he might have been
scheduled to sing to 57,000 people in Yankee Stadium
on this particular night.

But what was so truly, beyond-all-enduring irritating
was that he could come. Jingle's younger brother was
getting married this weekend, and he had asked Jingle
to be his best man. Jingle's junkie days had devastated
his family, and so six months ago Jingle had told the
Dodd Hall organization that nothing was going to stop
him from standing up with his brother. Everyone had
respected that, no one wanted to work with another
bass player so the night had been kept open, and
Quinn was free to go to Baltimore.

His parents met him at the train station. His mother
had a new car, another one of her indistinguishable
Country Squire station wagons. Why she thought she
needed a station wagon was beyond him. She did not
haul around the junior tennis team any more, she did
not carry twenty-three tulip-and-ivy centerpieces to
hospital benefit luncheons. But she thought she did.
That, Quinn supposed, was the point.

He sat alone in the backseat as if they were all
setting out to get his back-to-school clothes. He listened to his parents talk excitedly about the party. No
one had cancelled. The tables were ever so lovely.
And the musicians, they were so happy with the musicians. They had been worried when nice Mr. Noble
retired, but the club had found new people and they
were good, quite good.

How nice. His parents had found a musician. What
was in the backseat of their station wagon? Chopped
pimento loaf?

What a hypocrite he was. What would he have done
if his parents had asked Dodd Hall to play for their
sedately planned dinner dance?

Well, gosh, Mom, we'd love to. We've got thirty-four

people and three forty-eight-foot semitrailer trucks crammed with equipment. The big amps weigh a thousand pounds each. What's a good time for the rigging call?

He had gotten up and dressed like a vice-president of Standard Oil because he hadn't wanted anyone to pay attention to him, and here these two people were cooperating beautifully, ignoring him as no one else ever could, and he wanted to choke them for it.

Of course, everything irritated him now. Every day he struggled to hold on to his mild good manners. It had started with Krissa's desertion. He knew he shouldn't blame her, he knew he shouldn't think that this rasping grayness was her fault . . . but he did.

The minute he got home, Quinn excused himself and went back to the kitchen to see Jewel. She rapidly dried her hands on her apron and thrilled to see him, held open her arms.

"Welcome home, my boy." She embraced him and then stepped back. "Let me take a look at you. Don't you look handsome? I'm so proud of you." She patted him on the shoulders. "And that last concert of yours, I *liked* that one."

In August, Dodd Hall had played R.F.K. stadium in Washington, D.C. Quinn had sent Jewel a couple dozen free tickets and had dispatched a herd of limousines to bring her family in from Baltimore. He smiled at her, his exasperation with his parents easing. Jewel was in his corner. She and Danny were the two people he could trust. "Not bad for a bunch of white guys?"

"No, indeed. Not bad at all."

"I owe it all to you," he said.

"No, you don't. Now about your friend, that Danny boy, how is he?"

"He's fine. Crazy as ever, but fine."

"And what about yourself? You look too thin. Is no one feeding you properly?"

"I'm fine too. Really I am."

This was a lie. He was not fine. Jewel was right, he was not eating much, but the real problem was that he wasn't writing. He had not written a line, not a single one, since Amsterdam when he had learned about Krissa's marriage.

Why the hell had she done it?

She was the one he was really angry with, not his parents. That's why he couldn't write. There was nothing inside him except this anger.

"I'm waiting for a song called 'Fried Cinnamon,' " Danny had joked early on. "Or 'Cinnamon Crisp.' " Danny alone knew how angry Quinn was.

"No. I'm not going to write about her."

It was a matter of honor. Everyone—the media, the fans, everyone—knew what had happened, and they were all waiting for the next album. They expected Quinn to spill out his hurt and grief for their listening pleasure. But he only had anger, and he wasn't going to expose Krissa to that.

It did come out in his performance. Ever since the Amsterdam concert, there had been a new level of passion in his voice. Even he was surprised by what he was capable of. He used to have a gesture, a little slice of the hand visible to no one but Danny, that he used to tell Danny to restrain himself, that he was building emotion faster than the crowd could follow. Now Danny was using that gesture to signal to him.

Jewel pushed him down into one of the kitchen chairs. "It's that pretty girl, isn't it? She broke your heart, didn't she? I liked her."

Quinn didn't answer.

"She's in Minnesota, isn't she? How is she doing?"

"I don't really know. We only hear from her mother." Then he reported the most recent, most unbelievable news from Minnesota. "Her mother says she's going to have twins."

Having twins was an involuntary act, Quinn knew that. But somehow the fact that she was having two children made her betrayal seem even worse than if she were having only one.

"Twins? And her husband's in the mines?" Jewel

shook her head. "Does he have a trade or is he one of the laborers?"

"I honestly don't know." Quinn supposed that Jewel knew a whole lot more about wage earners that he did. "He's a mechanic. Is that what you mean?"

"Yes, but twins are still hard. I hope she's got lots of family to help out. Some white people don't keep up with their families, you know."

This Quinn did know the answer to. Danny had told him that the Aarnesson family was full of generous, warm-hearted people. They would help her. But to tell Jewel that would require him to say the words "Krissa's husband." He couldn't do that.

The kitchen door swung open. It was his mother. "Quinn, darling, do come here. We have our wedding album out. I know you'll want to see the pictures."

Quinn kissed Jewel and followed his mother to the front of the house. The tea table in the living room was covered with memorabilia; menus from cruises, the lace handkerchief his mother had carried at her wedding, his own blue-beaded baby bracelet. There was the ribbon his mother had been wearing the night she had met his father. There was the glove she had worn the night he had proposed. From the first moment of their meeting, his parents had viewed their relationship as something that needed to be enshrined.

Quinn flicked through the collection, letting his parents tell him what everything was. His mother was noting the history of each dried corsage and each matchbook in a small leather-bound book. "That way you'll always know," she told him.

Was that what he was supposed to do in his old age, look through the debris of their romance? Well, why not? What else would he have to do if he couldn't write anymore?

He started paging through his father's Princeton yearbook. That irritated him less. Something fluttered to the ground, a piece of paper landing with its blank side up. Quinn picked it up. The side facing him felt a little coarse; the reverse was glossy and slick. He turned it over. It was a flat, unused wrapper for Tulip Chocolate. Quinn had seen pictures of it in old ads, but he had never seen one of the actual wrappers.

It was exquisite. His great-great-great-grandfather had commissioned the design in 1898, and it had never been altered. Art Nouveau vines scrolled and flowed around the fluid script letters. The tulips were in the rich, clear colors that Louis Tiffany was then using in his stained glass, cobalt, emerald, ruby.

Quinn didn't remember his grandfather, the last one in the family to have made the chocolate. Bradford Hunter had died when Quinn was an infant, and shortly thereafter Reed had sold the factory and the rights to the product. As far as Quinn knew, he had never tasted a Tulip Chocolate bar. When people talked to him about it, remembering its sweet, rich scent, he felt like the crown prince of a country that no longer existed.

He traced the lettering on the label, then turned to his mother. "Can I have this?"

She leaned over to see what it was. "Of course, dear. Of course, you can."

What if he had asked for that fading pink ribbon? Would she have given it to him? *Oh, Quinn, darling, it means so much to me.* This label she had given away without a thought or a pang. It meant nothing to either of his parents.

But Tulip Chocolate had meant so much to so many people, a fragrant memory from childhood. Quinn looked across the antique-filled room to his father, seemingly the most civilized of men. This was the king to whom Quinn was prince. But he was a bankrupt king, and nothing that Quinn could do would change that. No money Quinn had made as a musician, no territories that he might conquer, no Grail, no Golden Fleece that he might capture, could ever restore the lost ancestral lands. Tulip Chocolate was gone. His father was Edward VIII. He had renounced his heritage and his duty for the sake of the woman he loved.

No wonder the son was so unable to face the loss

and betrayal of the woman he had loved. Loss and betrayal were his partriarchal legacy.

Quinn had planned to get through his parents' party by drinking heavily. Instead he remained stone sober. Glass after glass of golden champagne was pressed into his hand; he set each aside untasted.

He did his princely duty, dancing every dance, choosing his partners among his mother's generation rather than his own. And when at last he was back home, sitting at the desk where he had done his schoolboy homework, he took out the Tulip Chocolate label, and for the first time since learning of Krissa's marriage, he began working on a lyric.

It was about loss, but not private loss, not loss of a romantic love. This was public loss, the lost innocence of a country at war few believed in, the loss of Roose velt, Churchill, and Kennedy—of a king young men could believe in. It was about hungering to live with a tradition one could value, about longing to pay heed to customs that one could respect. It was called "My Grandfather's Chocolates."

In the last stanza the grandson's regret and bitterness blazed into anger, fury at the generation who squandered their traditions. And as Quinn worked and reworked those lines, he knew that he was coming as close as he could to writing about Krissa.

Technically Danny and Quinn shared an apartment in Chelsea on a block near the brownstone where Quinn and Krissa had lived during that magic summer of recording *Self-Chosen Snares*. But it was more a place to store their belongings than a residence. Housing was so tight in New York that the Dodd Hall organization frequently lent the apartment to young musicians starting out, so whenever Danny and Quinn were in New York on break from the tour, they had to stay in hotels.

As a result Quinn didn't know where Danny would be on a Sunday when they didn't have to catch a plane until Monday. There would be no reason for him to have gone to the loft where Dodd Hall, Inc. had its offices and rehearsal space. With Quinn not writing, there wasn't anything new to rehearse. But it was the only place Quinn could think of to go, so he went straight there from the train station. The outer office was empty and more or less neat, but the door to the large studio was ajar, and Quinn heard voices. He went in.

Some kind of meeting was breaking up. The circle of chairs suggested that—even the piano bench had been pulled into service. There were ten or twelve people milling about. It was an odd group. The women were in painter's pants or embroidered peasant blouses; they had none of the flash and trash glitter of rock groupies. The men were mostly bearded and wearing scholarly wire-rimmed glasses. There was a Catholic priest. Quinn knew none of them except Danny. It was strange, Danny knowing this many people that he didn't.

They were leaving, and Danny made no move to introduce any of them. So Quinn did nothing as they filed out, except nod respectfully to the priest. Surely a priest had better things to do on Sunday then meet with Danny French.

"Who were they?" he asked Danny as soon as they were alone.

"No one you know."

That was obvious. But of course Danny owed him no explanations. The Dodd Hall office, much like the fraternity house lounge it resembled, was like a quasi-public space to everyone in the organization. Anyone could use it for anything.

And Quinn didn't care about the meeting. His own joy in this new lyric, his own fierce pride, would not be complete until Danny had seen it. He had already been thinking about trying to get permission to use the Tulip Chocolate label for the cover of the next album.

He handed Danny the lyric.

"What's this?" Danny asked.

Most Dodd Hall songs started with the music, but Quinn did occasionally write a lyric first. "It's a song. We are a songwriting team, remember?"

"You wouldn't know it by the last six months, would you?"

Clearly Danny wasn't in the best of moods. These lyrics would jolt him out of it. Quinn was sure of it. "Aren't you going to look at them?"

"Sure, sure." Danny dropped his eyes to the paper. He read it. He didn't say a word. He read it again.

His silence didn't bother Quinn. Quinn hadn't expected him to say anything, not at first. Danny never did.

What was unsettling, what was unnerving, was his stillness. He wasn't simply silent, he was also still. His feet weren't tapping out a melody that he was starting to hear in his brain, his head wasn't nodding to some aural pattern that only he could hear. He was absolutely still. He had read Quinn's lyric, the first thing Quinn had written in nearly half a year, and he wasn't hearing even the softest whisper of a melody.

He looked up and shrugged. "It's great, but you already know that."

"I do," Quinn agreed. His voice was cautious. "So what's the problem?"

"I can't relate to it. Come on, I can't write music for that, and even if I could, I couldn't get up on a stage and sing it."

"What?" Quinn could not believe this. "Why not?"

"Listen, I'm sorry," Danny went on, not sounding the least apologetic. "But come on, losing the family business? I'm not exactly from a long line of entrepeneurs. My people didn't put other people out of work; they were the ones getting put."

He had a point, but the song was about a lot more than that, and they were things Danny understood. He had no idols, no leaders he admired; he felt betrayed even by Bob Dylan. Surely he could overcome the bit of capitalism in the song to connect with every-thing else it was about.

"I'm sorry," Danny said again and held out the lyric.

Quinn refused to take it. This was the first song he had written in five months. Danny couldn't hand it back to him. "Why don't you think about it? Give it your best shot?"

"Okay." Danny folded up the paper and stuffed it in his shirt pocket. "But I don't know how good my best shot is. I'm not the one who grew up on a tennis court."

Tennis? What did tennis have to do with anything? Quinn stared at his partner in sudden fury. Here he had killed himself to be able to sing *Self-Chosen Snares,* and Danny wasn't even going to try on this one. What a shit he was. That was it, he was just being a shit.

At least Krissa would be able to make Danny do it, just as she had made Quinn work on *Self-Chosen Snares.* Now it was Danny's turn. Quinn would go talk to her right now, ask her to get Danny to see how important this was to him, how this song was the most personal thing he had written except the ones about her. She would make Danny—

No.

He couldn't talk to Krissa. She was out of this. She wasn't waiting for him in the brownstone. She was back in Minnesota, a miner's wife, pregnant with twins.

He and Danny sat together on the plane down to Atlanta. They were the last ones to board, and every-one else had automatically left a row for them to sit together. But they hardly spoke.

Halfway through the flight, Danny started drum-ming a beat on his armrest. He was hearing something in his head. Quinn watched those long, light fingers rap out a rhythm. It could be something for "My Grandfather's Chocolates." The meter would work.

But it could also be something else altogether. Quinn was not going to ask. Right now he did not want to speak to Danny. He would sing with him, but he wasn't going to talk to him.

What had made their friendship work for these five long years? Quinn had thought about the question a lot. He had even tried to write about it, but he couldn't do it without making them sound gay, which they were not.

Among a certain type of creative men, there was a history of strong, if difficult friendships. From Wordsworth and Coleridge to John Belushi and Dan Ackroyd, these were creative friendships with bonds deeper, stronger than the shared creativity. " 'Tis better to have loved and lost/Than never loved at all"—Tennyson had written that about a male friend, his sister's fiancé.

Strong male partnerships permeated the world of rock and roll. Mick Jagger and Keith Richards, the Glimmer Twins of the Rolling Stones, had known each other since they were four. Even Johnny Rotten and Sid Vicious of the Sex Pistols seemed to be two halves—one cerebral, one physical—of the same rather unpleasant person.

Danny and Quinn respected each other's gifts, but lots of people admired one another without feeling as if they were twins separated at birth. Certainly at first, the two of them had also been in awe of each other, each secretly wanting to be the other. But with success, maturity, and increased self-assurance, that had faded. Quinn would not have been Danny for anything on earth.

But nor would he have lost Danny's friendship for anything on earth. Sometimes when they were singing harmony together, standing close so that they could hear each other over the crowd and the guitars, Quinn could feel a difference in the side of his body that was next to Danny. It was open and the nerve endings, like tendrils of ivy, had stretched across the space between the two of them and had stitched together so that they became one.

But as he sat next to his silent partner now, he wondered if the totality of their friendship was over-whelming them. Sometimes it seemed like the two of them had been trapped in the same room for too long and they had breathed all the oxygen. They were bricked up behind the same wall, all hope of rescue gone, suffocation was inevitable, and only one question remained—which one would breathe the last breath?

They needed fresh air. They needed it desperately, but Quinn did not know how they were going to get it without Krissa. How was Dodd Hall going to survive without her?

Krissa went into labor several weeks before her due date. Although Quinn did not hear about it until the next day, the night that her children were born was the first time since meeting her that he had sex with someone else.

It was Election Day. The *Self-Chosen Snares* tour was at last drawing to an end. They had been on the road for more than a year, and the album—bless its heart—had stayed with them every step of the way, remaining on *Billboard's* Top Ten month after month. They had released five singles off it, all of them had done well. But it was time to move on. Stan, their drummer, had terrible tendonitis. He needed surgery again. And Danny and Quinn needed to get to work on the next album, their fifth. They had already missed the contractual deadline for it.

Danny had indeed written a superb melody for "My Grandfather's Chocolates," but he was still refusing to record or perform it. A year ago Quinn had been looking forward to recording this new album, thinking that by then his life would be in order. He and Krissa would be married, they'd have a home of their own, she wouldn't be busing dirty dishes in a restaurant. Instead he found himself urging Danny and Joel to extend the tour yet another time so he wouldn't have to go back to New York by himself. But that was out of the question. They were all too tired, and Stan was popping painkillers, soaking his hands and wrists in hot water before every show, and icing them for an hour afterward.

There was a room party back at the hotel. It was the usual, noisy crowded affair; Quinn did his duty and then went into one of the bedrooms where a couple of people were watching the election returns. Whatever interest anybody had in politics had faded since the end of the war and Watergate. As far as Quinn knew, none of them had voted. He didn't even know if he was registered anywhere. But it was nice to sit in this half-darkened room, watching the anchormen and their big red-and-blue maps of the states.

As the hour got later, the others drifted away. Jingle, the last one to leave, switched off the TV. Quinn nodded to each of them, but didn't rouse himself. He was too weary to get up and go find his room. Maybe if he just sat here a while longer . . .

Then he realized that Jingle hadn't been the last one to leave. There was still a girl here, curled up at Quinn's feet, her cheek resting against his knee. He had talked to her earlier in the evening. She seemed nice, but he didn't remember her name. He looked down at her; he thought she might be asleep. He leaned his head back against the sofa. The weight of her head against his leg was soothing. He wasn't going to disturb her if she was asleep. He had been sleeping so badly the last month that he hated the thought of waking someone else up.

But she wasn't asleep. A moment after he had dropped his head back, he felt a fingertip on the inside of his knee, lightly following the inseam of his jeans, tracing up one leg, then down the other. Then again. He raised his head to look at her, but she was bent over him, and all he could see of her was the rippling length of her straight, fair hair.

Her hand was now open against his inner thigh, and

she was lightly massaging him there. It was almost more comforting than arousing. He leaned his head back again and let her go on stroking him. It seemed a sweet kindness, a woman solacing a weary man. After a while he noticed that the back of his hand was against her breast, and idly he turned his palm, feeling her round, soft weight naked beneath her gauzy shirt. But even that seemed like too much work and his hand fell away.

She was touching him directly now, the same slow leisured massaging up and down the front of his jeans. She leaned forward and laid her mouth on him. Through the denim he could feel her breath, warm and damp. A delicious heaviness settled over him, and soon that was all he wanted, for this to go on and on. He didn't need it to accelerate, to quicken into climax. He simply wanted this warmth to continue.

His erection was straining against his jeans and she had her hands on the buckle of his belt. He forced himself to lift one heavy hand and touch her hair. "You don't have to do this," he said.

"No, no." Her voice was soft, her accent lightly Southern. "I want to."

She freed him from his jeans. The air in the room was cool against his exposed flesh, but the chill was instantly replaced by the warmth of her hand and then the light flick of her tongue. She traced a wet, silvery line around the rimmed head of his penis and then came the luxuriant wonder of a mouth closing around him, taking him in.

She was a little hesitant. She didn't seem to know entirely what she was doing, but it didn't matter. It had been so long for him, and this felt so very good. His muscles churned and tightened, he touched her hair again, signaling for her to move away if she didn't want him to come in her mouth. She shook her head; she did want it. His eyes squeezed shut, and he came.

Satiated, he sagged back against the sofa, a warm wave of physical ease flooding over him. He felt more at peace than he had in months and months. The girl slipped back down to the floor, again resting her cheek against his knee.

He took a breath and sat up. Taking her by the shoulders, he lifted her to face him. She was pretty with brown doe-like eyes.

"Thank you," he said quietly.

Her lips tightened, and she looked as if she might cry. She hadn't expected him to be grateful. He was a rock star, after all. He had opportunities like this almost hourly.

"Do you want me to . . ." He gestured down toward her.

"No," she said. "No, that's okay."

It wasn't fair, it wasn't right, but he was glad she wasn't expecting anything of him. It was the last thing in the world he felt like doing.

He never fully understood these girls. Was it enough for them that he was a singer with a rock-and-roll band? Was that a good enough reason to do this for someone who didn't know your name?

He touched her cheek. "You are really very kind." He supposed that was an odd thing to say, but that was how it felt, that she had been kind. She had brought him peace, succor. "Is there anything I can do for you? Is there anything you need?"

She shook her head. "I just feel so bad for you. You still miss her, don't you?"

The fans all knew what had happened. He nodded, unable to speak.

She stood up. "They say you haven't been sleeping. Will you be able to now?"

"Yes, because of you."

"That's what I wanted." Then she was gone without him having asked her name.

That was the year Jimmy Carter was running against Gerald Ford. By the time George Bush ran against Michael Dukakis, Quinn was a different man, a practicing physician and a dedicated citizen who, knowing that he was going to be out of town for that election, had dutifully filed an absentee ballot.

He was attending a medical meeting in Dallas and came back to his room following the dinner. He turned on the TV as he loosened his tie.

And there she was, the girl whose name he had never known. A woman now, she was anchoring Dallas's local election coverage. Her once flowing blond hair was chin-length and neatly coiffed in the usual female television journalist hairdo, softly bouffant, lifting away from her ears to expose simple gold earrings. Her doe-like eyes were crisp and alert, but perhaps because it was again Election Night, Quinn recognized her immediately.

He had to sit through forty-five minutes of alternating local and national coverage before he heard her name, Paula Kessler. And the next morning, fifty cut lilies were delivered to the station with a card. "Twelve years is too long to owe a debt, but I only learned your name last night. Quinn Hunter."

She called him at his office in Washington the next day, laughing and pleased, overwhelmed that he had remembered the incident, much less recognized her. The next time she and her husband were in Washington, he took them both out to dinner. Their marriage was solid and her husband knew of the occasional misspent moments of her youth. She was exactly what you would want a Dodd Hall fan to grow up to be.

From then on Quinn sent her flowers on every election. A savvy florist in Dallas alerted him to state primaries, school board elections, even the annual elections of the professional organizations she belonged to. It was turning into quite an expensive joke, but he didn't care. He still did not feel as though he had repaid her for her kindness.

INTERSTATE HIGHWAY 35, MINNESOTA,
LABOR DAY, 1990

Krissa waited to speak until they had gotten on the
interstate at Moose Lake. Dusk was darkening the
open road that lead south from the Range to the
Cities, and the van was quiet. Patrick and Adam had
fallen asleep in the middle seat. In the rear, the twins
were plugged into their Walkman, a dual adapter splitting into two sets of headphones, which isolated them
from anything their parents might say.

Jerry was driving easily, effortlessly. He loved to
drive. On the road he felt free.

Krissa spoke. "Your mother says you were talking
to the people at the mines about a job."

She wasn't entirely surprised that he wanted to
move back to the Range. He felt more and more alien
in the Cities. He loved the time they spent visiting
their families, the hunting, the fishing, the male com-
radery. They had lived in the Cities for ten years,
which was as long as he had been in the military.
Perhaps this would be a pattern for his life—ten years
off the Range, ten years on.

"The Range is a good place for kids to grow up,"
he answered.

"Not for Patrick."

Patrick, their youngest, had a learning disability. He
was starting kindergarten tomorrow, but Krissa had
noticed his difficulties more than a year before. She
had had him tested, and he was already working with
private tutors and special materials.

Jerry thought that she was pushing the boy. They
should accept him as he was. He was a big kid. He
could always make a living. But Krissa was not going
to let one of her boys stake his future on the strength
of his back. She was not going to have him grow up
on the Range.

And there was nothing for her on the Range, no
opportunities. She couldn't start another upholstery
business. When a sofa wore out up there, when the

arms frayed and the cushions got stained, people bought a throw from the Sears catalogue. Here in the Cities, Krissa worked only for designers, and they sent her their most difficult projects. She worked with gorgeous, fragile fabrics. Their beauty delighted her. She would never even see fabrics like that on the Range, much less handle and shape them.

And there was more than her business. She didn't want to leave her house, her neighbors, the University Club pool where all the kids hung out in the summer, the Quality Trash Book Club reading group she belonged to, the stores she shopped in—she would give that up for the boys, but not for Jerry.

He could go back to the Range if he liked, but he was going to have to go alone.

The first week of school was always a nightmare. The boys brought home thick packets telling Krissa about gym clothes and art smocks, about soccer sign-up and scouts, about the new resource teachers, the improved testing service. She had to give permission for field trips, sign up to be room mother, offer to help in the classroom. The boys had new friends, new teachers, a new bus driver. Adam claimed that none of his friends had sat with him at lunch. Brian reported that he had the worst math teacher he could have gotten. Poor little Patrick thought his teacher's neck looked like a turkey.

"I mean, there's all this skin, Mom. Just hanging down in folds. It jiggles when she talks. It jiggles. I can't look at it. I can't. Will you go talk to her, Mom? Please."

Krissa could not imagine what she would say.

Other mothers kept calling her. The ones new to the school were full of questions; the others were trying to add something to Krissa's already overwhelming schedule—would she volunteer to do Junior Great Books? It was a fourteen-week commitment, but only one hour and one lunch period a week, nothing much really . . . Oh, and there was two full days of training you had to take first.

The boys' friends were calling to talk about their new classes, new bus routes, and turkey-necked teachers. The phone rang and rang all afternoon. "I am not home," Krissa finally announced when it rang for the millionth time. "I cannot take any calls. I am dead."

"Okay, I'll tell them that." Curt's eyes twinkled as he picked up the phone, and for a glittering moment, this blond Scandinavian-boned boy looked far too much like his Uncle Danny for his mother's taste.

He answered and a moment later, covered the receiver, handing it to her, saying "I don't know who it is, but I think you should take it."

Krissa laid down her pen and came to the phone.

"Hello," a pleasant woman's voice said, "I am looking for Krissa French Aarnesson."

"This is she," Krissa answered. No wonder Curt had passed the call on. No one ever called her Krissa *French* Aarnesson.

"My name is Mary Ellen Sciora. I'm a producer with *The Oprah Winfrey Show* here in Chicago, and"—

So Danny was going to be on *Oprah*. He was getting almost as much publicity as a homeless activist as he had gotten in Dodd Hall. Krissa got calls like this a couple times a year, people writing articles on Danny, wanting background on him.

—"we're doing a show on women who were the inspiration for some of the important rock stars of the sixties and seventies. It's going to be a fun show, very upbeat, and—"

"Wait a minute," Krissa interrupted. "You want me to be on *Oprah*?"

"Yes, yes, we do. The show would not be complete without Dodd Hall's Cinnamon-Haired Girl."

"*Me?* You want me to talk about Dodd Hall?"

"Oprah thinks it will be a great show. It won't be anything lurid. As I said, the focus will be very positive, very—"

"I'm sorry, but I do not want to do this. I *really* do not want to do this."

Three days ago she had told her husband that she liked her house more than she liked him. This was not the time to do *The Oprah Winfrey Show*.

"We'll fly you to Chicago. We'll pay all your expenses. You'll be seen by millions of people."

That was supposed to convince her, being seen by millions of people? "I really don't think so."

The woman paused and in a moment spoke more gently. "We occasionally do have guests who address some very painful issues, and they find it very therapeutic to be open about their difficulties."

Open? Telling millions of people about how she had felt, how she had felt so swallowed, so unsure, that she had had to betray her brother and his partner? That wasn't open. That was nuts.

Therapeutic? Krissa could imagine. She would be sitting on the dais in the line of chairs, examining everyone's clothes, mentally changing their shoe colors, generally minding her own business, when Oprah would say, "Welcome to the show," and Krissa would start crying. And crying. She wouldn't stop. Ever. They would have to replace the carpets afterward. No, they would never be able to film in that studio again. The subflooring would have warped.

Or worse, truly worse, Oprah would say, "Welcome to the show," and Krissa would tell her everything, everything, and then start to cry.

So tell us, Krissa—I can call you Krissa?—what was it like to have those beautiful songs written for you? What was it like to be the Girl with Cinnamon Hair?

It was wonderful, it was awful. She wasn't me, but that's what he thought I was, and that's what I wanted to be, but I didn't really. I wanted to be myself, but I didn't know who that was.

What happened? What went wrong?

Nothing. Everything. We were so young. That's what's wrong with being a rock star. You're so young when you do it. You start out there in a place you ought to end up.

Quinn Hunter ... what is he really like?

He was wonderful and he was a mess. He needed so much and didn't think he had the right to need anything at all. He loved me and he loved my brother. He wanted to be a gypsy, a vagabond, singing songs with my brother. He wanted to be the All-American Dad, stable and reliable, taking care of everything, taking care of me. He wanted to love me as consumingly as his father loved his mother. He wanted to be nothing like his father at all.

Was it true love?

And that was when the crying would start.

The voice on the phone continued. "You would be helping so many other people. We get so many letters from women who have unresolved issues—"

"I am sorry," Krissa said into the phone again. "I simply can't do it." If she said one more word, if she tried to explain, Krissa would start to cry right here in the middle of this kitchen. Oprah could afford to replace her subflooring; Krissa could not.

Wasn't it bad enough that sometimes she would be driving a van full of kids and hockey equipment and she would turn on the radio and hear those two voices, and the boys, the hockey sticks, the skates would fade and she'd be twenty again?

Wasn't it bad enough that her husband would rather go fishing than live with her?

"I don't mean to upset you." The woman sounded very nice and warm. She was probably as nice and warm as Oprah. They were probably all nice and warm there. That's what made them so dangerous. "Would you like to talk about it?"

"I just can't do it. I ..." Krissa floundered. "I have all these school forms to fill out."

Chapter Fourteen

Jerry had worked all winter. In the old pick-and-shovel days, the mines had closed during the months of bitter cold. It had been rich ore they'd been mining back then. You could take it straight from the ground and load it into railroad cars for shipping. But that rich ore was gone. World War II had pretty much used it up. Now the industry was processing the lower-grade taconite, ore that was trapped in hard rock. These rocks had to be crushed and ground so that the iron could be released. Such work could be done indoors, and some of the new big shovels were built so that they could operate down in the pits year-round without freezing up.

It was good to have winter wages. There was an uneasy feeling across the Range, a lot of talk about a recession and foreign competition. The taconite boom had brought prosperity, but now it looked like the good times were coming to an end, and the bad times would be dark indeed.

Krissa and Jerry were living in the little house he had built. The stone fireplace was still imposing, the gun cabinet, the sauna, and the bookcases were still beautifully crafted, but the place was small for four people even when—especially when—two of them were infant twins.

For months after the babies had been born, Krissa had felt like she was swimming in a dark fog, a pale copy of herself, all shadows and hormones. By the time the boys were six weeks old, she couldn't remember not having had them. At three months they were on a semi-predictable schedule, and she felt as if she might be able to come up for air . . . although she was not sure she wanted to. She had thrown herself into a deep, dark hole, and perhaps it was easier if she did not look up into the light.

Danny hadn't seen her babies yet. Nothing he had done had ever hurt her more. One thought had gotten her through the final swollen month of her pregnancy, that after the babies were born, Danny would come to see them. When he saw them, she would be herself again. He would help her make sense of the life she had so blindly chosen.

But he hadn't come. She had at first tried to excuse him. Dodd Hall was still on tour when they were born. Then they immediately started to work on the new album. By Christmas she had run out of excuses. Quinn always went to Baltimore for Christmas; Danny could have come to the Range then, but he hadn't. She had named her firstborn after him, Brian Daniel, but Danny hadn't come. He had forsaken her.

But she had her babies. They were irridescent bundles of perfection, their frog-shaped little tummies rising and falling with their sweet, milk-scented breath, their powerful cheeks sucking and gulping, their beautiful soft hands curling about her finger. Sometimes she would sit in Jerry's big chair with one sleeping child in each arm and know that this was why God had put her on earth, for these babies.

She had collapsed under Danny and Quinn's smothering need of her. Here she was again with two more males needing her. Danny and Quinn had made jokes about being identical twins separated at birth, and these two babies really were identical twins, but caring for them was fitting and right. She did need to be needed. She did need to be loved. Surely raising children was a better way to satisfy those cravings than chasing around a pair of rock stars.

One afternoon in April she was cleaning vegetables

at the kitchen sink. She did not like this kitchen. It had been designed by a man. It had no dishwasher, no window over the sink. If you were standing at the sink when the back door opened, the towel rack clipped you in the back.

Which it did.

"Oh, I'm sorry," Jerry said, peering around the door. "I didn't know you were there."

He always said that. "What are you doing home?" Krissa glanced at her watch. It was the middle of the afternoon. Then she saw his face; it was solemn, full of bad news. "What is it? What's wrong?"

"It's your dad, honey." Closing the door, Jerry took her arm. His broad shoulders filled the kitchen's narrow galley. "There was an accident at the mines ... an explosion, dynamite. Your dad, he's dead."

Dead. Krissa stared at him. Her father, dead? That wasn't possible. She'd been standing here just a minute ago, peeling a carrot, the long orange scraping curling through the slot in the peeling knife. People didn't die while you were peeling carrots.

"Dynamite ... but they're so careful."

It was a stupid thing to say, but it was all she could think of.

"I know," Jerry murmured. "And no one knows why he was there."

That was right. Her father hadn't died. He was on light duty. He wouldn't have been near a blasting site. So he hadn't died. Jerry was playing a trick on her.

No, no, he wasn't. Of course, he wasn't.

"Come get your coat," he said. "We need to go tell your mom. Mr. Olaf and Mr. Barnling"—these were men from the mining company—"were going to go. I said you and I should go first."

"But the babies—they're sleeping ... I can't—" She couldn't think clearly.

"My mother's out in the truck. I picked her up on the way. She'll stay with them."

He stepped back outside and signaled to his mother. In a moment Mrs. Aarnesson was inside, kissing

Krissa, telling her not to worry about the babies, to go to her mother.

They turned up the drive to the French's new house just as one of the garage doors was smoothly rising on its automatic tracks. Peg's gleaming blue Lincoln backed out, then stopped, blocked by Jerry's truck. Krissa got out as quickly as she could, hurrying over to the Lincoln.

Peg lowered the window. "Krissa, what are you doing here?" She was irritated. She didn't like having her plans changed. "The truck's in my way. You're going to make me late."

"We need to talk to you, Peg." Jerry was close enough in age to his mother-in-law that he used her first name. "Why don't you come inside?"

"Didn't you hear me? I'm going to be late."

Jerry opened the car door and let out his hand. "Please, Peg, come in."

Peg pulled the door shut. "What's wrong with you? Whatever you've got to tell me, you can tell me here."

"Really, Mother, please come inside."

"Don't be telling me what to do. I think I know what's best."

Jerry looked at Krissa silently, questioningly. She shrugged. What choice did they have? So bent over the open window of Peg's car, they told her that she was a widow. "There's been an accident at the mines," Krissa said. "Dad's been hurt . . . he's been killed."

Peg French glared at her. "Now, Krissa, don't talk that way. You know better. It's not—"

"It's true," Jerry interrupted. "He's dead. Mr. Olaf and Mr. Barnling are on their way now."

Peg was staring at the padded steering wheel. Then suddenly she shoved the car into gear. "Mr. Olaf and Mr. Barnling—we can't have people like that coming to the house, not with the state the closets are in."

"The closets?" Jerry couldn't help himself. "The *closets*?"

But he was speaking to the air. The Lincoln had shot into the garage. Krissa and Jerry followed it on foot, having to duck their heads and hurry so that the garage door wouldn't close on top of them.

Peg was inside, hanging up her coat. "Krissa, you make some coffee, and I'll get started on the front closet. No, no, I'd better make the coffee. You'll never get it right."

Jerry was looking bewildered, but Krissa understood. Cleaning and being critical were her mother's two most familiar activities. They had gotten her through every other ordeal of her life. They would serve her well again. Krissa was not going to interfere. She went into the living room to start finding Danny.

He made it to town within twenty-four hours. By then all the cogs and flywheels of the mining community had been set in motion. People knew what to do when someone died, and they were doing it.

Knowing of Danny's wealth, the funeral director was sparing no expense. The casket was solid walnut with genuine bronze fittings. Why would any funeral home on the Range have stocked such an expensive coffin? Maybe they had flown it up from the Cities just for this. Krissa started to protest.

Her mother cut her off. "Nothing's too good for your father."

Krissa had to leave the room. Her father had been a selfish, angry man. He had hit his son, he had used his moods to control his wife, who was, in turn, angry about being so controlled.

He had probably been mentally ill. Those moods of his might have been clinical depression. If so, Krissa knew that she ought to be more forgiving. But she couldn't be right now, especially as she began seeing puzzled looks on people's faces as they heard the details of the accident. "That's mighty peculiar," was all anyone said, but Krissa guessed what they were thinking. This was no simple accident, something union and management could blame each other for. Ed French had no business near that site . . . unless he was committing suicide.

Even in dying he's found a way to torture us.

These were not thoughts Krissa could share with her husband. Jerry dwelt in the world of the straight-forward. He would not understand her anger and ambivalence. He was being the stalwart son-in-law, taking care of all the arrangements, making everything easier, everything except her emotions.

So when the back door to her house swung open and her brother's arms were closing around her, relief flooded through her, warm and comforting. Here was someone she could tell everything to. Any cold and bitter anger she felt, Danny would feel even more intensely.

She rested her cheek against his lean chest, drawing peace and strength as she never could from her husband's brawnier frame. Jerry was so tall, his chest so deep barreled. Danny was more compact, more—

More like Quinn.

Suddenly sick, Krissa pulled away. Was she that desperate that she would cling to her brother's body because he was built like Quinn?

Yes, she was that desperate.

She spoke quickly. "You haven't seen Mother, have you?"

Jerry had picked Danny up at the little one-room airport that served Hibbing and Chisholm. They had stopped here before going on to the new house.

"No. How is she?"

"I have no idea," Krissa answered honestly. "She's somewhere in outer space. She comes down to earth only to criticize me. I can't do anything right."

"And it will get a whole lot worse." Danny was, as always, blunt and realistic. "God knows what she'll do with herself now that she doesn't have him to fuss over. But tell me about yourself. How are you?"

"Fine," Krissa lied. "Do you want to see Brian and Curt? They're sleeping, but if we're quiet—"

Danny waved a hand. "Don't wake them up for me. I didn't ask about them. I asked about you."

Oh.

Don't ask that. Ask about them. They're such perfect

miracles, the two of them. That's what everyone else asks about—them, not me.

"So how are you?" he repeated.

She couldn't answer. Her throat was swollen, her eyes were raw and stinging. She felt as if she had been crying for hours and hours, but she had hardly cried at all.

"You look awfully thin ... at least in most places." Suddenly he was speaking lightly as if hoping that would make it easier for her. He stepped back and eyed her chest. "I know you're my sister and I'm not supposed to notice, but I think I would have remembered those ..."

"Stop it." Krissa knew that he was trying to be funny, but she was nursing the twins and she hated the way she looked. *Look at my children. Don't look at me.*

"I'm sorry ... I'm just worried about you."

Krissa pushed her hair off her face. "Mother's still so mad at me that she can hardly stand to be near me or the babies."

"Well, I have moments of being rip-roaringly pissed off too." He glanced back over his shoulder through the window in the kitchen door. Jerry was in the yard, unloading something from the truck. "You left a lot of crap on my plate when you dumped Quinn."

How easily he spoke that name. Danny would have been with him this morning, just a few hours ago. It was almost unimaginable to her that Quinn still existed, that he was still walking around in the world, speaking to people, meeting them ... and so utterly lost to her.

Here was her chance. Anything she told Danny he would repeat. Here was her chance to explain, to tell Quinn that she still loved him.

I'm sorry, I'm so hideously sorry, but I did my best to explain to you, to try to figure out how to breathe while I was with you, but you wouldn't let me, you wouldn't leave me alone.

But that was still blaming, finding fault. This wasn't

Quinn's fault; it was her own. She had done this to herself.

Danny spoke again, his voice coming from somewhere far outside the narrow walls of her life. "He's not coming until Thursday morning. He'll go straight to the church. Otherwise we'll be mobbed."

"He? Who are you talking about?" Krissa felt her hand at her throat. "You don't mean Quinn, do you? He's not coming here, is he?"

"Of course."

"Danny, no."

Quinn coming here. Seeing him, remembering how it had been, how close they had been, and what she had thrown away.

And having him see her, so distracted and confused, her breasts so swollen and hard, her face and wrists all bones. No.

She had never asked her brother for anything, not money, not time, not even loyalty. She had spurned every offer of financial assistance he had made since her marriage. But now . . . she would beg.

"Danny, please, for all that you hold dear, please keep Quinn from coming."

"I can't." Danny slowly shook his head. "I'm sorry. I can't. He always thinks he has to do the right thing. He's got to come for Mother's sake. You know how she feels about him."

Oh yes, Krissa knew that. How she knew. Not a week went by when Peg French didn't say it, her tone flat and accusatory, "You could have had Quinn."

Tell Quinn that for once he can't do the right thing. Tell him not to come.

But Danny wasn't going to do that. Appealing to all that he held dear was pointless . . . the dearest thing of all to him was Quinn.

"Look," Danny went on, "it's not going to be easy on him, seeing you either. He's a wreck, Krissa. Nobody knows it except me, but it's the truth. He didn't write for six months."

"But there's a new album." It was due to be released in a week or so. "He wrote that, didn't he?"

"Haven't you heard it yet?"

"No." How could she have? No one had sent her an advance copy.

She dreaded this album. If Quinn was angry with her, this would be how he expressed it. What was the punishment for faithless women? Being stoned, burnt, entombed . . . her punishment would be to listen to this album.

"You may not like it," Danny said bluntly. He again glanced through the window to where Krissa's husband was working. "It's about Jerry."

"About Jerry?" Krissa was astonished, horrified. "How could it be about Jerry? He doesn't know Jerry."

"Well, it's not about him per se," Danny admitted. "But guys like him, blue-collar wage earners. God knows what our fans are going to think. The voices are all from the working class."

"But how . . . what does Quinn know about working people?"

"I would have said nothing, but we got into a fight about a song about his grandfather that I said was capitalist and elitist. So I guess he did what writers do, research. He went around to bars and docks, listening to people. I think he wanted to know why you'd marry a working man, but he really did get it right. There's a lot of anger in the songs, basic working-class frustration and anger. I can't imagine what your average Dodd Hall fan is going to see in them."

Quinn writing about working-class anger? Krissa could feel a knot twisting in her stomach. "It's me he's angry with, isn't it?"

Danny jammed his hands in his pockets, but he didn't lie to her. "Yes."

She was sick. "Is there anything I can do?"

"Nope. You took yourself out of this. But look on the bright side. We got some terrific songs out of it."

The door opened. It was Jerry. "Why don't you put

some coffee on?" he said to Krissa. "I met with Reverend Nilsson this morning. Here's a list of some things that we need to think about. Maybe it'll be better if we go over it before we see your mother."

Krissa had already made coffee. She poured it out, then took Jerry's list. His handwriting was roundish and unformed. It made him look stupid.

She shouldn't think that. Jerry wasn't stupid. He simply didn't have the occasion to write very often. He couldn't help it that he wasn't Danny or Quinn. And wasn't that what she had wanted from him, that he not be Danny or Quinn?

"Music" was at the top of the list. She turned to Danny. "Are you going to sing?"

"Me, sing?" His eyes flashed. "Me and my 'goddam guitar'? You think Dad's going to start liking me more just because he's dead? I don't think so. Anyway, Dodd Hall has enough problems with bootleg tapes as it is. I don't want anyone circulating a tape of the two of us singing at my father's funeral. But I'll call the organist if you want."

"Good deal," Jerry said. "What about pallbearers?"

Krissa and Danny exchanged glances. Their father hadn't had any friends.

"You want me to ask my dad to round up some people?" Jerry continued. "Men from the union?"

No, indeed, Jerry was not a stupid man. He was a man who made things simple so that they could get done. Krissa handed the list back to Jerry. He could make the rest of the decisions. Danny didn't care, and Peg would object regardless of what they did.

Then Brian woke up, and his cry woke up Curt. Krissa was back on duty. Danny kissed her and went off to see their mother. Krissa didn't see him again until the viewing at the funeral home that evening.

When he had come to her house, he had been dressed as always in worn jeans and a flannel shirt. She wouldn't have been surprised to see him dressed like that at the funeral home. He wore those clothes on stage, in meetings, during photography sessions.

Why not at his father's funeral? But he was in a beautifully tailored, three-piece charcoal suit with a white shirt and a somber navy tie. A discreet pair of gold cufflinks glinted at his wrists. The jacket settled smoothly across his shoulders, the trouser cuffs broke perfectly at his gleaming wing-tip shoes. If he had had normal hair, he would have looked like an elegant, young stockbroker.

It was the first thing her mother said to her. "Doesn't Danny look nice?"

Yes, he did. Krissa picked up his hand and twisted around the white cuff of his shirt so that she could look at a cufflink. It was monogrammed. *Q.R.H.* Quinn Reed Hunter.

"That's Quinn's suit, isn't it?" she whispered.

"God, yes," he said in normal tones. He didn't care who knew. "You don't think I'd own a thing like this, do you?"

"How did he talk you into wearing it?"

Danny grinned. "He has his ways."

Krissa knew that. Oh, how she knew that.

Danny was the local curiosity, the most important person to have come out of the town. Many of the people at the funeral home this evening had come not to pay their respects to Ed French, but to see his son. They needed to know that he remembered them. They needed him to give credence to the stories they had been telling. *I taught Danny French in the fourth grade ... Danny French went to our church....*

He had wanted to stay either in a motel in Hibbing—their hometown didn't have one—or with Krissa and Jerry. But Peg wouldn't hear of it. She couldn't have people knowing that he slept on his sister's sofa.

"She's driving me nuts," Danny whispered to Krissa as the viewing was breaking up. "She's suddenly started to like me. I don't get it. Can I borrow a car? I've got to spend the night in Hibbing."

"Don't you dare," Krissa ordered. "She'd make it out to be my fault if you do, and I'll never hear the end of it. You can do it. Just be grateful they're not still in the old house."

"Oh, okay. But how am I going to get there? Town was starting to fill up when we came. She'll make me drive, and you know everyone will notice that silly car of hers. I'll get mobbed."

"I'll ask Jerry's dad to take you." The Aarnessons were still there. Krissa was family now, and they were standing by her. "And he probably has some kind of hat you can wear."

Danny had been right. Town was unusually crowded. There was a line of three unfamiliar cars waiting ahead of them at the stop sign. There were four more cars at the filling station, again cars that Krissa and Jerry didn't recognize. Several knots of young strangers were standing along Main Street.

"Who are all these people?" Jerry asked. "What are they doing here?"

"They've heard that Danny's in town."

There was a light rap on the window. A long-haired girl in granny glasses was peering at them. Jerry rolled down the window.

"Excuse me, mister," she said politely, "do you know where Danny French lives?"

Jerry shot a glance at Krissa. She gave him a quick shake of her head. "Can't help you there," he said to the girl. "Sorry . . . but what would you do if you found him?"

The fan looked puzzled. Why would anyone ask such a silly question? "Get his autograph. Talk to him."

"What about?" Jerry asked.

He was honestly curious, having no experience with glowing-eyed fans. But Krissa knew all about them. You couldn't question their dreams. It wasn't fair. She touched Jerry's arm, stopping him. He understood and wished the girl luck.

"This is some family I married into," he said as he drove on. "Now I see why your folks have an unlisted number. Will all these people be at the funeral tomorrow?''

"More. Lots more." The Dodd Hall circus followed Danny everywhere.

Krissa had forgotten what it was like. When you were famous, you moved inside a little bubble created by security people, back doors, and VIP lounges. Outside the bubble were the fans, sometimes hordes of them. Everywhere you walked, people were looking at you. You learned to forget about them, to walk through an airport carrying on a conversation without noticing that half the people who saw you stopped and tried to listen.

The next morning there were cars parked all along both sides of the road leading to the church. Someone had parked on Mrs. Barnling's marigold bed and she was furious.

A limousine came to pick up Jerry and Krissa, then went on to get Danny and Peg. Someone from Dodd Hall must have been driven up from the Cities. There were no limos on the Range. The funeral directors used regular black Cadillacs.

A large crowd of people had gathered outside the church, but the sidewalk was clear. Petey Williamson was waiting under the little portico. He sprinted out to the limousine and slid inside. He murmured a word or two to Mrs. French, kissed Krissa, and shook Jerry's hand, looking at him curiously. So this was the guy Krissa had left Quinn for.

Krissa knew that this would be the first of many such looks. Everyone from Dodd Hall would wonder about Jerry.

"Things are in good shape," Petey reported. "Quinn's been here for an hour, and he spent most of the time out here with the people. He talked to them about this being a funeral and promised he'd come out again if they'd leave you folks alone."

Danny stepped out of the limousine and nodded to the crowd. He touched a few hands, then quickly walked into the church. Jerry gave his arm to Mrs. French. Krissa and Petey followed.

The minister was waiting for them in the vestibule. He greeted them with a few low words and then gestured for them to go into the sanctuary. Mrs. French was still holding Jerry's arm.

Krissa didn't know if her mother even noticed that she was walking with her son-in-law, not her son, but it seemed grimly fitting. When Peg French had so long denied Danny the support and protection he had once needed, what right did she have to turn to him now? So brother and sister were left to walk in together. Danny put out his arm for her, something he had never done.

But this was what it would have been like, he and she alone in the quiet vestibule of a crowded church, him offering his arm to escort her down the aisle, this was what it would have been like if she had married Quinn.

She slipped her hand in the crook of his arm. Beneath her fingertips was the soft cashmere of Quinn's suit. They stepped into the sanctuary, and suddenly she could feel the cool weight of a beaded satin gown. Lilies of the valley and peach roses cascaded over her hand. The church was filtered by the screen of her ivory veil.

Then someone coughed, and she was herself again, a nursing mother in a homemade black dress.

The church was full. But she instantly caught sight of a gleaming golden head. It was Quinn. Cowardly, she looked down at the floor as Danny guided her past that pew.

After the service there was a lunch in the church social hall, organized by the Rebekkah Circle to which Jerry's mother belonged. All the Dodd Hall people came up to talk to Krissa, but they were as awkward as if the funeral had been for her. What do you say to a person who has buried herself? It seems a little silly to talk about the weather.

But it was better than having to face Quinn and his anger. He was still outside signing autographs.

Her mother-in-law pressed her to eat. One sister-in-law called the other sister-in-law so she could report to Krissa that the babies were fine. What kind, kind women they were. She didn't know what she would have done without them. But they were no replacement for Brooke. She could talk to Brooke. Brooke had understood her.

That's what she needed, a friend who understood her, who could listen to her sorrow and confusion. No, she needed someone who could help her take care of newborn twins. Brooke couldn't have done that.

Then she heard someone speak her name.

Not someone. This was a voice she would know anywhere.

She turned. She couldn't lift her head. She couldn't look at him. The white vee of his shirt was in front of her. His vest, his coat, were navy. His tie was a deep, dark burgundy.

"I thought you were outside," she said.

"Danny came out and relieved me."

"I suppose that's easier for him than this."

"It was for me too."

She forced herself to look up. She tried to keep it all separate—the burnished gleam of his hair, the clean strong line of his jaw—so that she was only looking at parts of him, not really him.

Don't be a coward. Look at him. He is entitled to be angry. You must endure it. Look him in the eye.

His eyes were the color of ashes, soft, feathery light ashes.

Ashes smudged everything with soot. You couldn't be near ashes and not get them on your hands and your clothes. But the ashes in Quinn's eyes were the cinders of sorrow, not hate or anger. He wasn't angry with her. He didn't hate her.

She had to say it; she couldn't pretend to know. "Danny says you were still angry with me?" It was a question.

"I was. Until three hours ago I was."

"What happened?"

"I came to the Range. Danny's always said I should come here, that I would never understand either of you until I did. I drove by your house. I wanted to see where you live. There were clothes on the line, diapers and baby clothes. There was smoke in the chimney. You were home."

And you sat at the end of the drive for a long, long time. She could feel in her own body what had happened to him, how as he had looked at her little house and the clothes on the line, his anger had dissolved. The anger had been giving him life and force for all these months, and suddenly it had vanished, leaving him empty.

She wanted to touch him. What a comfort it would be to lay her hands on his cheek, to touch his shoulder, feel his arm around her. Just for a moment, just to have the memory. Petey and Jingle had kissed her, why not Quinn?

Because she loved him.

She pressed her hands to her eyes. It was all right to cry. This was a funeral. You could cry at a funeral.

"Krissa, please . . ." His voice was low. "Don't cry. It's not fair."

No, it wasn't fair. He would be powerless if she broke down. He couldn't put his arm around her, he couldn't find a quiet spot to comfort her. He could only ask someone to find Jerry.

She took a breath and looked up.

He had his hands in his pockets. He never put his hands in his pockets when he was wearing a suit; it was some antiquarian notion of his father's. But he was breaking the precept now, and Krissa knew why. It was the only way he could keep from touching her.

He cleared his throat. "Is there anything I can do for you?"

People had been asking that for three days. They had been talking about arranging for the obituary and making a Jell-o salad.

Quinn was asking something else.

Take me out of here. I made the most disastrous mistake. Save me . . . save us from what I've done.

But she had her sons now. She would never leave them. *Then come with me. Come with me and see my children, my two petal-soft babies. Come with me and for a moment we can pretend that they are yours too.*

Jerry loved Brian and Curt. He was glad that they were boys. He was pleased that they were healthy; he was proud that there were two of them. But he didn't marvel at them as Krissa did. To her they were miracles, sweet treasures of divine light. That they would grow, that they would learn to walk and to read, seemed incomprehensibly wondrous to her.

She had tried to say that to Jerry. He had looked at her blankly. "All kids grow up. It's what they do."

There would be, she knew, a level of joy and wonder that she would always feel toward these children that she could not share with their father.

She could have shared it with Quinn. If she hadn't been so weak, if only she had been able to hold on . . .

"Krissa, I—"

She looked fully at him and saw the truth of what Danny had said. His glowing good looks hid it. He was a wreck. His eyes usually so clear and warm were distant and troubled.

"What is it, Quinn?"

"Nothing. Never mind."

He was right. Between them there was nothing, and they were going to have to learn not to mind.

Chapter Fifteen

So it was sixteen years. Sixteen years passed before they saw each other again. Dodd Hall broke up. Quinn went to medical school. Jerry lost his job and the Aarnessons moved to the Cities. Quinn had his own practice. Krissa and Jerry got divorced. They knew these facts about one another, but they never met.

Until now. Krissa was standing at the end of the Blue Concourse at the Minneapolis-St. Paul International Airport, waiting to meet Quinn's plane. After sixteen years.

She was a wreck. No, she wasn't. She didn't fall apart. It wasn't like her. She was the Aarnesson boys' mom. She ran bake sales, she planned class parties, she checked homework. She was straightforward, she was organized, she was practical. She could do anything. How could she be a wreck?

But her palms were moist, her stomach was twisting. The air was so heavy, she couldn't seem to fill her lungs.

This was crazy. She shouldn't be feeling like this. Nothing was at stake here. So what if Quinn thought she looked horrible? So what if he thought she was a boring housewife? What difference did it make? Who cared what he thought?

She did. Oh God, she did. She wanted him to think that she was beautiful, fascinating, mesmerizing. That her life was perfect, that she was everything he had ever written about and more.

She hated feeling this way. She hated wanting that from him. What if she left? What if she just walked out and went home and didn't answer her phone for the rest of her life?

She looked back down the concourse. A moment ago it had been empty. Now two, three men were hurrying up, dark-suited businessmen carrying attaché cases and garment bags. Quinn was not one of them.

Why was he coming? Why was he doing this to her? He said he had business in town. So? That didn't mean he had to come see her, did it?

The next wave of passengers came in a mass, a wall of people extending the width of the corridor. They were all a blur, barely even shapes of individual men and women. Suddenly there was one, lean-figured, elegantly built, with a white shirt and a navy blazer: Quinn.

Sixteen years, and still her eye went instantly to him. *Dear God, please don't let it all start again. Don't let me feel anything for him.*

Was that what she was worried about? Yes. That he would speak once and she would suddenly be twenty-one again, desperately in love with him, seeing him at her father's funeral, aching to apologize and explain, yearning to be with him. All that pain. She couldn't face that pain again.

It was too late to run. And there was no need. She could do this. She wasn't a girl anymore. She was a woman.

She stepped forward to meet him. "Quinn. How nice to see you."

That was all wrong. It was stupid, too formal, cold.

"Krissa."

There were a few faint lines at the corners of his eyes. His hair was a little warmer, a little darker.

"Did you have a nice flight?"

"It was uneventful."

We didn't touch. Everybody kisses each other these

days. You go to someone's house for dinner, and you kiss host and hostess both coming and going.

This man had written the Cinnamon songs for her, and he hadn't even shaken her hand.

"Do we need to go to the baggage claim? Did you check anything?"

"No," he said, gesturing to his carry-on bag. "This is it. Are you sure I can't rent a car?"

"No, no, there's no reason to do that."

How was she going to endure this? The awful politeness. This wasn't her. She was never like this. They started across the airport.

"I don't suppose you have this kind of weather out in Washington."

"No, our winters are usually mild."

They were talking about the weather, she and Quinn, the weather.

They were at her van. She opened the tailgate. He lifted his suitcase in. They came around to the front He got in the passenger side, she the driver's side.

Look at him. Make yourself look at him. You aren't going to fall in love just by looking at him.

She couldn't stand this anymore. She had to speak. "I'm sorry, Quinn. All this chit-chat, it isn't like me. But if I say anything, anything at all, I'll be twenty-one again, wanting to drop to my knees and beg you to forgive me."

"Forgive you?" He sounded startled, and now she did look at him. His head was turned toward her, the clean, open lines of his face were drawn and puzzled. "No, no. It's the other way around. I was the one ... I made it impossible for you." His voice grew more definite. "I drove you away. I've known that almost since the beginning. It was all my fault. I have never blamed you. You have to believe that."

His eyes were warm and urgent, their smoky gray depths speaking to her. She answered, "I betrayed you."

"It wasn't like that. We both know it wasn't like that. I was so selfish. I couldn't see—"

She interrupted. She could see where this was going, each of them trying to blame themselves, wrapping themselves in guilt and pain. "We have to stop this. Rehashing the past like this, there's no point. It won't accomplish anything. It just makes all the pain come back."

He had been leaning toward her. He sat back. "You're right." He sounded rueful. "Sitting on the plane, I swore I won't do this, that I wouldn't ask for your forgiveness, that I wouldn't make my guilt your problem. How long has it been, how long did I keep that resolve, five minutes?"

She had to smile. So there were things about this meeting that he had been dreading too. That made her feel better, closer to being herself again. "Actually the walk across the airport had to have taken three hours. That's how it felt to me."

His laugh was low. She had forgotten what a nice laugh he had, how it could be soft, yet still rich and masculine. Maybe this wouldn't be so bad. After all, he wasn't even spending the night at the house. He was just coming for dinner. Maybe they would be able to laugh a little bit. Isn't that what a woman ought to be able to do with her old boyfriend? Have dinner, laugh a little bit, and then say good-bye? What could be so hard about that?

On the drive home he asked about the boys. "Your twins, they must be sixteen by now."

She nodded and told him that Adam was twelve and Patrick seven. "Adam is the most complicated, the most sensitive. And Patrick ... well, being the youngest is hard, and he is a competitive kid."

"And the twins, they're identical?"

"Physically." It felt good to talk about the boys. She could feel herself soften and warm. "But their personalities are different."

Brian, the older by ten minutes, was the more polished, the more outgoing. In any situation he spoke first. "I wouldn't be surprised if he ended up a politician."

If he did, Curt would be his campaign manager. Although quieter, Curt was no pale copy of his brother. He was more subtle, more of a thinker. He could organize, plan, execute. Brian spoke first, Curt spoke last.

They were off the expressway now, coming up the steep hill that rounded the University Club. "We're almost home," she said. "This is our neighborhood."

Quinn looked out the window. Some of the houses along Summit Avenue were mansions from the Gilded Age. Others were like Krissa's, sprawlingly comfortable Victorian homes with wide porches and old trees. "This is really nice." He sounded a little surprised.

"I suppose my mother makes it sound like I'm on food stamps."

"She does her best."

Krissa looked across the car. His voice had been dry, but his eyes were laughing. "I can't wait for you to meet my kids. I hope they're all home."

They were. Through the open door of the mudroom that lay between the kitchen and the garage, Krissa could see the four of them with their shining hair and broad-shouldered builds. They were in their usual after-school dishevelment—Patrick had no laces in his shoes, Adam's shirt was half tucked, Brian was at the sink, scrubbing something off the leg of his pants, and Curt was reaching under his sweater to scratch his back. But they were all there, her four-man starting rotation, her offensive line, her palace guard. How proud she was of them.

She introduced them to Quinn. The twins stepped forward, offering to shake his hand. They were nearly as tall as he was.

Each of them was, on his own, an attractive kid, but side-by-side, with their attractiveness mirrored and doubled, they were a striking pair indeed. Their bright hair was neatly trimmed; their eyes were alert, their faces were clear and lightly wind burnt.

At twelve, Adam knew that he couldn't live up to his older brothers' assured performance, so he mumbled a word or two of greeting in Quinn's direction without looking up from his math homework. Seven-year-old Patrick chirped a "Hi" and, his chin in his hands, watched Quinn with an air of bright-eyed curiosity. Mom's visitor was almost as neat as a new kind of dead bug.

Quinn greeted each. Then there was a moment of awkwardness. As poised as the twins were, they had no idea what to say next. Krissa supposed that she needed to ask her usual, boring questions about homework, but before she could speak, Quinn did. "So what sports do you guys play?"

That was not a good question. What sports *don't* you guys play would have had a more manageable answer. But Adam leaped in, using this as a chance to redeem the ground he had lost to his brothers by his mumbled greeting. Quinn answered, not with a polite "how nice," but with a very informed-sounding question about the composition of the league. Within moments all four boys were talking, interrupting each other. Suddenly the kitchen was full of guy-talk: positions, league-strength, speed versus quickness, injuries. Adam pivoted on his stool. Brian and Curt hitched themselves up on the counters. Curt was drumming his heels against the base cabinet. Quinn was leaning back against the wall oven. Krissa hadn't had a chance to even ask him to sit down.

"No, that's not what's in the latest literature," he was saying. "The worst injuries happen when . . ."

The boys were in heaven. They had probably expected Uncle Danny who thought track and cross-country were the same, and if they weren't, why the hell not?

And Krissa herself was glowingly gratified. Quinn liked her kids.

She worked on dinner, letting their talk go on for almost half an hour, and she was sorry to break it up. But these were kids who had to get exercise every day. They had already gone thirty minutes without fighting; she was on borrowed time. "You guys got the rest of the ice off the driveway, didn't you? Why don't you go shoot some hoops?" She smiled meaningfully at Brian. This was not an idle suggestion.

He knew an order when he heard it. He stood up, and the others followed him, trooping off to the mudroom for their coats.

"Isn't it a little chilly for outdoor basketball?" Quinn asked.

Krissa glanced at the thermometer outside the kitchen window. It was ten above zero and the sun was setting. It would get colder by the minute. "They play ice hockey. They're used to the cold."

Patrick came back into the kitchen struggling with the sleeve of his parka. "Can you come with us?" he asked Quinn. "Curt's got a great jump shot. You should see it, you really should."

Patrick had the eyes of a seven-year-old, sweet and trusting. You had to be of stern stuff to resist their plea. "Sure," Quinn said slipping off the tall stool he had been sitting on. "I'd be glad to."

That sounded like a lie.

Krissa had seen Quinn extricate himself from quite awkward situations. "We won't trouble you to come any farther," he would say to a junior promo man who wouldn't leave Danny and him alone. "I can't imagine why that would be interesting," he would say to a prying reporter asking overly personal questions.

So she fully expected him to come back inside soon. He was not—at least as far as she knew—a hockey player; he was not used to this kind of cold. But instead it was Curt who came dashing through the kitchen a few minutes later. "Quinn wears the same size shoe we do," he called out over his shoulder as he bounded up the back stairs.

And five minutes later Quinn himself was back in the kitchen, this time following Brian. "Quinn's going to borrow one of our sweat suits, Mom."

"If we have time before dinner," Quinn added, as

if he were one of the boys' friends, polite enough to ask permission. His face was red from the cold, but everything about him was glowing. He was a man coming to life at the feel of a ball in his hands.

"It's okay, isn't it, Mom?" Brian, too, was flushed and excited. This was really great.

"Of course, it is."

She turned down the oven and let the basketball game go on. But eventually she had to call out to them. It was a school night, and the boys did have homework. At dinner, five of the six people at the table talked about college basketball, a topic not dear to Krissa's heart. They went on talking when they were done eating, Quinn sitting back from the table, and the boys all turned toward him. Patrick was on his knees in his chair, leaning across the table, propped up on his elbows.

Krissa was losing sight of the fact that this was Quinn sitting here at her dining room table. Quinn Hunter, the man she had loved, the man who had written the Cinnamon songs for her. He was someone who had come for the boys.

If Oprah ever called again, she was going on the show. The world needed to know about this. *Yes, Oprah, he seemed glad enough to see me, but then he met my kids, and I vanished.*

And you didn't like that? Oprah would ask.

No, it was wonderful, I loved it.

But it was a school night. Krissa regretted it, but she had to get the boys moving. "Just clear the table, guys," she said. "I'll do the rest."

The boys groaned, but stood up, piling their dishes. They knew they were lucky to be escaping the rest of dish duty. Quinn, too, started to rise but then sat back down when he saw that she was not moving.

"At this point in the evening," she said, "we divide by age, not sex. You do not have to go to your room and do your homework."

He thanked her.

"Would you like some coffee?"

"If it's decaf."

Patrick stuck his head in the dining room. "Do I have piano tomorrow, Mom?"

"Yes, and you've got to practice."

Patrick groaned. He had been dealt a difficult hand in life. He had a learning disability. Somewhere in his brain one wire was crossed with another, and *d's* and *b's* looked alike to him. He could not keep a column of numbers straight, he could not tie his shoes.

Balancing his disability was his athletic skill. He was, in a very athletic family, the finest athlete. This little boy was both fast and quick, he could jump, he could skate, he could swim, he could dive. His ball-handling skills were excellent, his concentration unshakeable. Sports was how he kept up with his big brothers, what he based his self-esteem on.

Piano playing, like anything that involved finger placement, was nightmarishly difficult for him, and Krissa always sat at the piano with him. Even though Quinn was here, she was not going to make Patrick practice alone.

She was about to make her excuses to Quinn when he spoke. "Do you take piano lessons?" he asked Patrick. "So do I."

"You do?" Patrick and Krissa spoke simultaneously. They were both amazed.

"But you're a grown-up," Patrick marveled. "Who makes you practice?"

"Nobody. And some weeks I don't," Quinn admitted. "Then I'm unhappy at the lesson. Why don't you come show me what you're playing?"

Krissa stared at the two of them as they crossed the dining room toward the library, a little room tucked in behind the front hall. Quinn taking piano lessons, that seemed very strange. It made her wonder about what the rest of his life was like, where he lived, what kind of relationships he had. The whole evening he had been talking to the boys; she hadn't learned anything about him.

She heard Patrick speak in his usual solemn way. "I'm not very good at it."

"You're just starting." Quinn's voice had the hearty tones of a consoling adult.

"No," said Patrick. "I have a learning disability. I'm not stupid or anything, but some things are harder for me than they are for other people."

This was what Krissa had told him to say when other kids teased him for the trouble he had lacing up his skates. It muted the children a little and paralyzed all adults into silence. Indeed Krissa did not hear Quinn say another word.

The practicing started. A few minutes later Krissa got up from the table and peeked into the library. Quinn, who understandably did not have a clue how to help a learning-disabled child play the piano, was sitting quietly next to Patrick on the bench. He was turned slightly toward him, one hand resting on the piano bench behind the boy. His expression didn't vary even when Patrick skipped a line of the music.

Patrick stopped. "Did I play that line?"

"No, you didn't," Quinn said. His voice was neither blaming nor pitying. He was simply stating a fact. It was the perfect way to deal with Patrick. It had taken Krissa years to learn that; Quinn had picked it up in five minutes.

But he was a doctor. She kept forgetting that. He would know how to talk to people.

She couldn't imagine it, him in a white coat seeing patients or in green surgical scrubs performing operations. What was he like? Probably confident and articulate, as good with his patients as he was with the boys.

What did this man have to do with the Quinn she had known?

He was speaking to Patrick. "Is this what your disability makes you do?"

Patrick nodded. "Sometimes Mom holds this marker up to the page."

Quinn took the long strip of red plastic and held it

up to the music. A minute later Krissa heard Patrick say, "You're better at this than Mom."

She stood in the doorway for quite a while, watching Quinn's hand move down the page of music, wondering about him. In fact, she was still there when Patrick's timer went off.

As usual he stopped playing in mid-measure. He hopped up from the bench. "Now do you want to come up to my room and help me with my homework?"

He was talking to Quinn. Krissa stepped forward. She was ready to have a turn with Quinn. "No, Pat. You do homework like always, and I'll check it when you're done. Now, Quinn, are you ready for that coffee?"

"If it's no trouble."

He followed her out to the kitchen. "You've got nice boys," he said.

"Thank you." She liked hearing him say that. "It was good of you to sit down with Patrick. He doesn't like to practice. You saw how he quit the minute the timer went off."

"I set a timer when I practice too."

Krissa had been getting out the coffee cups. She looked over at him over her shoulder. "You do?"

"Otherwise I would never stop."

That made sense. "Someday maybe my children will feel that way about something besides hockey and television." She heard a knock on the side door. "Add talking on the phone to that list," she added as she crossed the kitchen. Among the neighborhood families with teenagers and only one phone line, adults who wanted to speak to one another often had to turn up in person.

It was, as Krissa expected, her neighbor Ben Zagursky. "Your line was busy," he said as he crossed the threshold. "And—"

Ben saw Quinn over Krissa's shoulder. He had to be surprised. The only men who were ever in Krissa's kitchen were Cub Scout dads. "Oh, Kris, I'm sorry. Am I interrupting something?"

"No, not at all," Krissa answered. "I'd like you to meet an old friend of mine, Quinn Hunter, visiting from Washington D.C. Quinn, this is my neighbor Ben Zagursky."

Quinn came around the kitchen's center island and put out his hand. "Hello, Ben. It's nice to meet you."

The men shook hands. Ben was looking a little puzzled. "It was Hunter, right? Quinn—"

Ben stopped. His eyes widened. Krissa could see what was happening. He knew who Quinn was.

She looked at Quinn. This must happen to him all the time. His expression was pleasant, approachable.

Ben looked uneasy for a moment. What were you to say when the guy hanging out in your neighbor's kitchen turns out to be Dodd Hall? But Ben was a vice-president at Cargill Industries. He was not without resources. He cleared his throat and spoke smoothly. "I certainly have enjoyed your stories."

It took Krissa a moment to understand what he had said. "Stories?" She had expected him to say songs. "Stories? What are you taking about?"

Quinn looked amused, and Ben explained. "He writes short stories for *The New Yorker*."

She stared at Quinn. She hadn't known that.

"It's only one or two a year," he said, sounding like he was apologizing ... although heaven only knew what he would be apologizing for.

"Why didn't I know that?" How could she not know this about him? It was important. Yes, he had become a doctor, but he was still playing the piano, still writing.

"I don't get *The New Yorker*." That was all she could think to say.

"Good for you," Quinn said instantly. "Getting *The New Yorker* can turn into your life's work. I don't know anyone who isn't at least six weeks behind. If you're caught up on *The New Yorker*, you don't have enough to do."

"What are the stories like?"

"Flat," said Quinn.

"Great," said Ben.

"Who am I supposed to believe?"

"Me," said Ben.

"Me," said Quinn.

"Are they first person?" she asked. Quinn's songs had been like that, a specific character speaking of his own situation.

Quinn nodded. "But they're nothing like the songs."

"Yes, they are," Ben countered. "Why don't you collect them and put them out in a book? I'd buy it."

"I don't need the money, I don't need the attention ... which is an excuse to keep me from deciding how I feel about them. I'm not entirely proud of them. But can't we talk about something besides my literary shortcomings?"

"No one was calling them shortcomings except you," Krissa pointed out, but she let the subject drop, knowing that in the very near future she would be standing over the Xerox machine at the library copying *The New Yorker*. "Coffee, Ben? It's made."

"Thanks, but no. We still haven't had dinner yet. But tomorrow's already shaping up to be a disaster. Could one of the twins pick up Katie at the day-care center at five-thirty and then drop her off at Susan Maxwell's?"

Krissa turned to look at the massive wall calendar that hung between the doors to the mudroom and the kitchen bathroom. She never told other people that the boys would do something. That was the boys' decision, but she could often tell them when they couldn't.

As was the case tomorrow. "They've got hockey practice until five, and at five-fifteen, one of them has to pick up Patrick's carpool." When the twins had turned sixteen, Jerry had bought them a used Chevy. He paid for the insurance and one tank of gas a week on the condition that they drive their mother's carpools and run her errands. "They have to take three other kids home. They'll never get done by five-thirty."

"What about if I left my car?" Ben suggested. "Then the one who isn't driving the carpool could—"

"No," Krissa interrupted. Ben drove a Mercedes that cost more than she and Jerry had originally paid for the house. Brian and Curt were careful drivers. Nonetheless she wasn't going to let them drive such an expensive car. "But I'm wildly flattered that you'd think of trusting them with it."

"That shows you how desperate I am ... but if I trust them with my kids, why shouldn't I trust them with my car?"

"I could go get her." Adam, Krissa's twelve-year-old, appeared at the foot of the back stairs. "I could walk over and then take her to Mrs. Maxwell's."

"Isn't it too far?" Ben asked.

"Not for me. You could leave the stroller for her."

"Well, then okay. It would be a big help."

Krissa reached in a drawer and handed Ben a pen. Familiar with the ways of the family, he went over to the calendar and wrote down everything Adam would need to know, where he was to be, what he would need to take with him.

"Your boys baby-sit?" Quinn asked while Ben was going over the information with Adam.

"My boys do anything for a buck. They don't get allowances. Adam knows the smell of desperation. There's going to be good money in this job."

Ben gave Krissa the pen back. "That's one less thing to worry about. Now if Patrick could skip school and take a few meetings, I'd be in great shape." He turned to Quinn. "Is this alien chaos or do you have a family?"

Quinn shook his head. "I feel like I'm on a wildlife preserve."

"That's because you've only been here one night," Krissa remarked. "Come for the weekend and you'll see that we're really our own all-sports network. Now, Adam, if you've finished your homework you can go practice. Ben, if you don't want coffee, what about a glass of wine?"

"The kind you buy?" He was smiling. "No, thank you."

The two men exchanged polite farewells, and a brief gust of cold air spurted into the kitchen as Ben opened the door. Krissa turned back to Quinn. "Do you still take your coffee black?"

"Do people call you 'Kris' now?"

"Only Ben. Do you use cream or sugar?"

"He has a crush on you, doesn't he?"

Krissa set down the coffeepot. "What?"

"It's true, isn't it?"

She was nearly speechless. Ben had been in the kitchen for five minutes, tops. "How on earth did you know?"

"The way he looked at you ... I don't know. This may be one thing I have a strong antenna about, people being in love with you."

All the uneasy feelings Krissa had had at the airport were coming back. "Being in love—that's much too strong. That's not what it is."

Ben's wife, Lynn, was a residential realtor. She usually worked on weekend afternoons, and often Krissa and Ben would join forces, taking the kids sledding or out to one of the lakes. On cold winter afternoons they would pile into Krissa's kitchen. Her cookies would be homemade, and she would have fresh cream to whip for the cocoa. The kitchen would be fragrant with a slowly simmering casserole of lamb, white beans, and rosemary. Ben would know that he and his kids would be phoning for a pizza, and Ben would far prefer the lamb and rosemary ... and Krissa herself.

"I don't really think it's about romance," she said to Quinn. "It's nostalgia for the way he grew up. His politics are in good order. He's proud that his wife works. He admires her ambitions, but he can't completely accept the consequences of that. That she's not really a homemaker, that the kids are in day-care and there's never any food in the icebox. He has this image of me as the last of the stay-at-home moms. He wants it for his kids as much as for himself."

This was not the whole truth. Ben did want her for himself. He admired her as a woman.

And she encouraged him. She didn't tease him or flirt with him, but she did allow him to preserve his image of her. He wanted to think of her as strong enough to discipline her children, feminine enough to want everything, including herself, to be lovely. All that was true. She was strong; she did treasure warmth and comfort, beauty and ritual.

But she did worry. She worried about money, about the roof and taxes. She worried constantly about the boys. How much allowance should be made for Patrick's disability, for Adam's high-strung disposition? If something were wrong with the twins, would they tell her? Or would they keep it between themselves until it was too late for her to help?

But she never shared any of her worries with Ben ... even though he longed for her to. She preferred to let him keep his perfect image of her, maintaining it at the expense of genuine friendship.

She knew what incredible folly his dream of her was—how it was beyond folly—how it was danger, risking the stability of two families. But she couldn't help herself. Working at home as she did, sometimes there were days when he was the only adult she spoke to. He was interested in her. He wanted to know what she thought, what she had been doing.

And the temptation of that, the temptation posed by someone—another adult—who wants to hear from you, who values your words and your thoughts ... any lonely woman could understand the temptation of that.

Krissa didn't like to think of herself as lonely, but ...

"The wife and kids at home—it's a powerful American myth," Quinn said. "I'm certainly not above its appeal. But you work."

"I know, but people don't really notice, because I work at home and because I get up so early I can do much of it when everyone else is asleep. I never work on the boys' time. I lead the Cub Scouts, I go along on all the field trips. I bake cupcakes for every stupid school party. Does that seem like enough reason to fall in love with me?"

"I don't know," Quinn answered. "I've never had one of your cupcakes."

"If you're being metaphoric"—she felt defensive— "then Ben hasn't either. He wouldn't do anything to jeopardize his family life."

"I didn't mean it that way."

"I don't want you thinking I'm having an affair with my neighbor's husband." She was still bristling.

"Do you love him?" he asked.

She didn't want to answer too quickly, she didn't want to be protesting too much. But she knew the truth. She didn't love Ben.

She loved her children, and despite all the twists and kinks of the bonds binding them, she loved her brother. But love a man as a partner, an equal, a friend?

She could hardly remember what that felt like.

She picked up the coffee tray; still a little on edge. Patrick's father-hungry eyes ... Ben ... why was Quinn seeing all the cracks in her life?

She carried the tray out to the living room, a long, sweeping room that ran along the side of the house. It was a warm, frothy room, spilling over with tartans and tapestries, cushion after cushion filling chairs, paisley patterned shawls flung over the table tops. She had spent very little money furnishing it. The fabrics in here were seconds and bolt ends designers she worked for had given her. The furniture was yard-sale wicker she had spray painted navy and hunter green. Almost everyone admired the room.

But when she was feeling bad about something else, she noticed how wrong the shape of the lamps were and how one table was too high, another too low. Even painted dark colors, wicker felt all wrong when it was below zero outside.

There had been something strange about this whole

evening. It had been too easy. Quinn had slipped into the family routine effortlessly. And he was not a person who knew a lot about families. Had he been so engrossed in the boys because he was avoiding something else?

She was too old to torment herself with this sort of thing. She was going to ask. "Quinn, why are you here?"

And suddenly, sickeningly, she knew the answer to that—Danny. He was here because of Danny.

Her brother's name hadn't come up once during the whole evening. Not once. But wasn't what had happened between Danny and Quinn the important story? She and Quinn hadn't broken up in front of 20,000 people, a sold-out concert at Madison Square garden. She and Quinn hadn't had to record part of an album singing to taped tracks of each other's voices because they refused to be in a studio together.

He hasn't come here for me. He's here for Danny.

It was a bitter thought. Even after all this time, it hurt.

But there was no pretending it away. "You're here because of Danny, aren't you?"

She didn't remember having poured the coffee, but she must have because they were sitting on the sofa and Quinn had a cup in his hand. He leaned forward and set it down on the coffee table. The green-bordered saucer clicked lightly against the polished wood.

He started to talk, explaining that Danny wanted to sell the rights to the Dodd Hall songs for use in commercials—soft drinks, cars, athletic shoes. He spoke neutrally, but it didn't take much sense to know that he hated the idea, that he truly loathed it. He wouldn't be here otherwise.

"And you'd rather slit your throat," she said when he was done.

His lips tightened. He was relieved to be understood. "Yes. I hate it when I hear someone else's songs used that way. And my own—I can't stand the thought. Can't you hear it, 'My Grandfather's Chocolates' being used to sell some overpriced candy bar?"

And the Cinnamon songs. Tell me you would mind selling them. "Then say no. You own half of everything. Danny can't do anything without your consent."

"He doesn't make that easy. He wants to use the money for a shelter for women with children. What's more important—my white male elitist emotional history or hungry women and children having a dry place to sleep? I'm supposed to 'just say no' to that?"

"Danny can put other people in the wrong every time, Quinn. That's his specialty, finding hooks other people can't get off of. But you've never let any of his antics get to you before." Then she realized that she had no way of knowing whether or not that was true. "Or have you?"

"No, I haven't. When he first started giving away all his money, Chris wanted me to do something, and I could honestly say that I didn't care. But that was a long time ago, when I was still so angry. Then that idiotic hunger strike of his forced me to admit that I still have some feelings for him, some pretty powerful ones."

Krissa wasn't sure what to say. "Danny is not a good person to have powerful feelings about."

"If he died, I would want to sing at his funeral."

"Oh, Quinn . . ."

"I know, I know. It would have been a zoo, the worst sort of media circus, and my being there would have only made everything that much crazier, but I would have done it."

All evening long Quinn had seemed like this normal well-adjusted guy. Maybe he was a little obsessive about playing the piano, but everyone was entitled to a few quirks.

This—what Krissa was hearing in his voice—was not a little quirk. There was real pain in his voice, knots of isolation and regret. He went on. "So I want to propose an alternative to selling the rights to the songs. That would be a concert. We could sell the broadcast rights, release a live album. He could have all the money for—"

"Wait a minute." Krissa almost spilled her coffee. "A concert? A *reunion* concert? The two of you?" This was beyond unhappiness, beyond isolation and regret. Quinn had gone stark-raving mad. Right here in her living room. "Are you out of your mind?"

"Yes, but so is he. Now listen, it makes some sense. I'm not talking about anything permanent, it would simply be one concert, one—"

"But you hate each other."

"Hated," he corrected. "Fifteen years is a long time. I can't hate for that long. Don't you think people would come? To hear Dodd Hall sing 'My Grandfather's Chocolates'?"

"Yes, of course. It would be . . ." She couldn't think of what to compare it to. But a lot of people, a lot, would pay absurd amounts of money to be at such a concert.

"So will you call Danny for me?"

Krissa blinked. She was to call Danny? How had they gotten there?

She didn't like this. She didn't understand why Quinn wanted to do such a concert, and long experience as a mother had made her leery of schemes she didn't understand. Things that began "Just do this, Mom," usually did not end up well.

But she wasn't Quinn's mother. His bad ideas were not her responsibility. She stood up. The downstairs phone was in the kitchen. "Reaching Danny is always hit or miss, and it can take him as long as a week to call me back."

Danny, however, was his usual unpredictable self. The one time she didn't want to talk to him, he was sitting right there in the shelter office and took her call immediately.

"What do you want?" he barked into the phone.

Danny could sometimes be exasperatingly cold, even brutal. Half his time was spent trying to keep all the rival factions of homeless activists working together, and he didn't have enough tact left over for anything else. Krissa had tried to learn not to mind.

She was direct. "Quinn Hunter is here, and—"

"Quinn? *Quinn?*" Danny was shocked.

She had his attention. She didn't always. "Yes, and he—"

"Dr. Knee? So Dr. Knee is with you? Did he tell you what a jerk he's being about the song rights?"

Dr. Knee? How in character this all was. Both of them had a raw sore that was fifteen years old. Quinn was hiding the pain of his by acting as normal as possible; Danny was hiding his by jeering. "He did say that he didn't want to sell them for commercials," Krissa said patiently. "But he had another idea for raising money."

"Oh?" Danny had to be interested. Raising money was the most important part of his work.

"He's willing to do a concert with you, a reunion concert—"

"A concert. Him and me?"

"Yes, he said that you could sell—"

"I'm not singing that shit with that shithead."

The boys had left the dishes on the kitchen counter. That wasn't like them. Then Krissa remembered; she had said she'd clean up the rest. "That sounds pretty final," she said to Danny.

"Who has that kind of time?" he demanded. "I haven't exactly been coddling my voice for the last ten years here. Can you see me, going to take voice lessons, waiting in the hall with all the budding operetta stars?"

Krissa could see Danny doing anything he felt like doing. But she wasn't going to argue with him. She had done her part. This wasn't her mess to clean up.

Now Danny was having to explain his outburst to the other people sitting around the shelter office. So Krissa cut in with a farewell and went back out to the living room. Quinn stood up.

"He's not interested," she said.

Quinn's expression didn't change. "Did he give a reason?"

"Not really. He said something about not wanting to take the time to get his voice back in shape, but I don't imagine that was the real issue."

"Did he say anything else?"

"As a matter of fact, he did." And Krissa repeated, word for word, Danny's inelegant remark about Quinn and their music.

Quinn let out a sharp, quick laugh. "That sounds like him . . . and it gets me off the hook."

"Does it? You could—"

Krissa stopped herself. She had been about to suggest that Quinn call Chris Oberlin, the one person he and Danny both still trusted. But she thought this was a terrible idea. She wasn't going to encourage it.

She heard some footsteps. It was the twins.

Brian spoke first. "So, Quinn"—this had a very rehearsed quality to it, at least it did to Krissa's ear—"Mom said you were staying downtown. Can we run you over?"

The rehearsal paid off. You would have never guessed that Brian had had his driver's license for only two and a half months.

"That would be good of you." Quinn stood up. "I'm ready any time you are."

This was clearly important to Brian and Curt. They wanted to show Quinn that they could drive, that they could give people lifts and drop them places. So Krissa kept her mouth shut. She didn't even tell the twins that it was nice of them to offer. They wouldn't want Quinn thinking of them as people who still wanted their mother's praise . . . although of course they did.

She put on her coat and walked outside with them. Curt was putting Quinn's bag in the trunk; Brian was already warming up the car.

She and Quinn stood on the sidewalk for a moment. They were underneath a streetlamp and his breath was a little white cloud in the air. "Thank you for agreeing to go with them so easily," she said. "For not making a fuss about taking a cab. It's important to them."

"I gathered that."

He was kind and sensitive. He had always been. "You still miss Danny, don't you?"

He nodded. "Sometimes it seems like my punishment for what I did to you."

His eyes were flat and stoic. He had run a long way to escape this pain, finishing college, going to medical school, doing a residency, starting a practice, but the marathon was over and the pain was still here.

That was so sad, but what could she do? She had other responsibilities now. She had her children. She remembered how she had been during her last days with Dodd Hall, how weak and desperate she had become, how incapable she had been of standing up for herself. She couldn't let that happen again.

I'm sorry, Quinn. I'm so terribly sorry. But the two of us, it's just too late. I can't help you.

So she said good-bye and stepped back from the car.

She slept little that night, and finally got up and went down to her basement workshop. Sometime after five she came upstairs for more coffee. She heard a knock on the side door.

It would be Ben. He was an early riser. She suddenly felt awkward. She wished Quinn hadn't seen how complicated things were. She didn't like anyone knowing. She thought about not answering the door. Ben would think she was still in the basement, the sound of her heavy sewing machine blocking out his knock. If he really needed to talk to her, he would phone.

No. Ben was her neighbor. She wasn't going to let Dodd Hall ruin that for her. She hurried to open the door. "Come in, come in." She was talking too fast. "Do you want some coffee?

He handed her her newspaper. The slick plastic bag

it had come in was cold. "Your guest has left?" he asked.

Her *guest*? Ben didn't usually speak so formally. "Yes, of course. He was just here for dinner."

"What brought him here?"

"I'm not really sure. Just this and that." She didn't want to talk about Quinn.

She poured Ben a cup of coffee. He took the mug from her.

"So you're the 'Cinnamon-Haired Girl'?"

Krissa could feel her hands rising, lifting to push her hair off her face. She clenched her fists, forcing herself not to touch her hair. "Surely you knew that. Everyone does."

"I didn't."

You would have if you or your wife ever did anything for the P.T.A. or if you ever volunteered to sort the gift wrap the kids sold as a fund-raiser. You would have heard about it if you ever drove on a school field trip. You could afford to drive. An extra tank of gas doesn't mean anything to you. It does to me.

What was she thinking about? This wasn't about Ben and his wife not doing their share. It wasn't about how much more money they had than she did. She only fretted about money when she was upset about something else.

He was still speaking. "I think that at some level I knew. A couple of months ago I heard one of the Cinnamon songs on the radio, and I instantly thought of you. It's really incredible, how all the Cinnamon songs describe you, your warmth, the way you love beautiful things, your generosity—"

Krissa did not want to hear this. That she had been the Cinnamon-Haired Girl was supposed to be amusing, something people smiled about. That was the rule. Everyone understood that.

Ben shouldn't be talking like this, as if it were something that still mattered. He was close to saying things that should never be said between the two of them, things that would lead to terrible trouble. He was breaking the rules.

This wouldn't have happened if Quinn had stayed away.

Apparently Ben had told other people that Quinn had been in town, and suddenly that was all Krissa was hearing about—Dodd Hall, Quinn Hunter, the Cinnamon-Haired Girl. She wanted to scream. The tidy little package she had kept her past in had been ripped open. People were curious, intensely so, and they weren't hiding it anymore. They weren't letting her make the rules. She had lost control.

I try not to control my kids too much. I let them trash their rooms. I let them spend the money they earn as they want. I'm not my mother. I'm not Danny. I can let go.

But I had wanted to control this, my past. And I can't.

Once again Dodd Hall was too much for her.

One night, long after her children had gone to bed, Krissa came downstairs and sat cross-legged on the floor in front of the old turntable Jerry had brought back from the Far East. She did something she never did anymore. She played the six Dodd Hall albums.

She listened to the beautiful Cinnamon songs, the songs he had written about her, the feelings he had had for her. She could no longer imagine being loved that much.

She listened to the power of *Self-Chosen Snares*. He couldn't have sung those songs without her. Having her in his bed made him able to sing those songs.

She listened to the angry songs of the fifth album and the tales of parting and loss in the last one. This was what she had done to him.

And she cried. Long, long into the night, Krissa cried. This was the man she had sent away, the man she wouldn't help.

Was she punishing him?

No, no. She was glad she had married Jerry. He wasn't the right husband for her, but had she married a different man, she would have had different children and that was unimaginable.

Why don't you help him? Doesn't he deserve it?

Yes, oh, God yes, he did. She ached for him to be happy.

How could she turn her back on him? She had held out for a week, but no longer. She couldn't resist. What would it be like to be loved that way again?

Chapter Sixteen

What we, everyone of my in-between generation, had to unify us during that summer and all of 1978 was Dodd Hall's final album, appropriately titled *The Last Piece of Chocolate*. That wistful opening riff swelling into stateliness, the measured grandeur of quiet suffering . . . even now I weep.

And how typical of my fragmented, disjointed generation that we should love this album. As passion filled as it is, it's not really there. It never was. The best song, "My Grandfather's Chocolates," was recorded after Danny French and Quinn Hunter had sworn that they would never speak to each other again. They each came into the studio separately and sang their beautiful harmonies to tapes of the other's voice.

—Brian DeWitt, *Lost Mirth* (Seattle: Fog Mountain Press, 1990), p. 165.

"He smiled at the wrong time."

—The only public comment made by Quinn Hunter about the breakup of Dodd Hall.

PLAYBOY: Did you smile at the wrong time?
FRENCH: I don't know what you are talking about.
PLAYBOY: Did you smile at the wrong time?
FRENCH: Yes.

—Tom Maddox, "Playboy Interview: Danny French," *Playboy*, August 1990, p. 109.

WASHINGTON, D.C., JANUARY 1993

Quinn got back from Minnesota late on Friday night. Saturday morning he was up early, meeting three friends for their weekly tennis match. Then he had calls to make, mail to deal with, a few errands to run. In the evening he had a date, dinner and a tasting of Australian wines with a woman he had known for a year or so.

Halfway through the day he stopped dead. He wasn't going to be able to go through with this.

He knew a lot about pain. His patients always had it. Those who handled the pain the best had learned to think about something else. But there was a level of pain you couldn't distract yourself from, and there was nothing to do but wait these times out. That was what he knew was ahead for him the rest of the weekend, waiting until the bright images of Krissa faded enough so that he would be able to think of something else.

After the Madison Square Garden concert, the last time he had spoken to Danny, Quinn could have continued with a musical career. The record company would have signed him to a solo deal; other songwriters wanted to work with him. A Broadway production needing to replace its leading man called. There were inquiries from Hollywood about screen tests.

But Quinn was not interested. Music was Danny, and he was bitterly angry with Danny, too angry to even grieve for Dodd Hall. He was determined to do something that had nothing to do with Danny. He was going to reclaim the life he would have had if he had never met Danny. The final Dodd Hall album was released in June; the following September he enrolled at Johns Hopkins, an excellent university in Baltimore.

He had been a lit major during his year at Princeton, and he was looking forward to his humanities courses. But they proved to be disasters. He couldn't get away from being Dodd Hall. The discussion sections were led by graduate students, young men and women who idolized Quinn's lyrics. They couldn't grade his papers. All the other students would get long, helpful comments on their papers; his were returned with an *A* and a "Nicely Done" on top. He couldn't speak in class. His voice instantly choked off all other discussion. Who was going to be so presumptuous as to agree or disagree with the bard of his generation? Everyone was always looking to see what he did first. When a teacher asked a question, people glanced at him. Did he want to answer? If he came up to a coffee shop's door at the same time as someone else, the other student fell back, letting him go first. He knew that he was always watched. He had to take the lead; no one gave him any choice. It gave him considerable sympathy for the Prince of Wales.

There was one refuge from his special status—science courses. When you sat down with someone as a lab partner, you had to develop a working relationship, even if your partner was six years older and ten million dollars richer. Because Hopkins's medical school was one of the best in the nation, the college was full of pale-faced premeds who felt like they were on a desperate treadmill; one *B*, they feared, would keep them out of med school. They didn't care who Quinn Hunter was; they just wanted their *A*'s.

Quinn had no natural aptitude for science. He had to work very hard, and even so, he was never near the top of the class. Both the hard work and the anonymity suited him exactly.

It was a long dark tunnel from which he saw no reason to exit. He had stayed at Hopkins for medical school, choosing surgery because he enjoyed working with his hands, something he had learned from Krissa. He had become an orthopedist because he liked the leisured meticulousness of working on a knee. Each operation was a performance. He strove to make each move neat, efficient, elegant. How he held a needle, where he placed the stitches, all that was part of the art. A well-trained operating room team moved in graceful choreography, each dancer knowing his part of the dance. Like priests, they had purified themselves beforehand. The operating table was an altar; the operating room a stage.

There were far worse fates for ex-rockers.

He was proud of his practice. He was not a gifted

doctor, but hard work and unwavering determination had made him an excellent one.

He and his two partners maintained offices near the Georgetown University Hospitals, and he lived in Burleith, the neighborhood right above Georgetown. It was a pleasant, unpretentious place with trees and narrow row houses. It was not fashionable; it had no grand mansions or walled gardens. But Quinn liked it well enough that he had never bothered to move, even though his house was so small that when he bought his piano, he had had to give away all his living room furniture.

He had a balanced, varied life in Washington. He had a piano teacher and season tickets to the National Symphony and the Folger Theater. He belonged to a squash club, a tennis club, and a church. He gave away pianos through his own foundation and sat on the boards of several other charities. Sure, there were occasional moments of pain, flashes of emptiness, desperate gnawing regret, but they didn't come often. He honestly believed he could live out his life on the course now set.

Then he had seen Krissa again, and the regret churned and swelled. She had children and a basket of bright lemons and red apples on her kitchen counter. He could have had that. He wanted it. He wanted his hall to be brightened with glowing leaves in the autumn, and at Christmas for his mantel to be draped with holly branches and magnolia leaves. Brass vases filled with marigolds, a basketball hoop in the drive, kids with bikes and dental bills, noise and joy, all that could have been his ... if he hadn't driven her away.

He sent her flowers and a brief note thanking her for her hospitality. He would have done that for anyone. He would do no more.

Had she been anyone else, he would have done all that he could to win her. It would have been the most glorious of courtings, breathing joy back into his life. But she was the Cinnamon-Haired Girl. He had wooed her already, doing all that he could. And it had been too much and all wrong.

He knew what she had been thinking when she had said good-bye. She wasn't going to give him a chance to hurt her again. He couldn't blame her.

At the end of the week he got a letter from her, again forwarded to his office from the hospital.

Dear Quinn,

The flowers—they're beautiful. Thank you so much. Irises and tulips, this house is not used to such loveliness in the winter. You didn't have to do it, but of course I adore them.

It was good to see you. I didn't make this clear—it wasn't clear to me—but I do want us to keep in touch. I don't want another sixteen years of silence. I want us to be friends. I shall pester you with Christmas cards and school pictures. I shall call you when one of the boys hurts his knee. You will have to take Patrick and his grubby little friends out to lunch when he comes to Washington for his sixth-grade trip. That won't be for four years so you have time to prepare yourself.

My mother will hate it. She loves gloating over the miraculous things you've done with your life. On the whole, I'd rather hear about them from you.

As ever,
Krissa

Thirty seconds later he was on the phone, and ten days later he was again at the Twin Cities airport.

She was waiting beyond the security check. Her hair glowed coppery against her black sweater, and her narrow chin gave an air of sweetness to her face. He leaned forward to kiss her cheek, and when he stepped back, he was holding her hands.

Surely he wasn't already in love with her again. It

couldn't possibly be happening this quickly, could it? Yet he felt lightheaded, spinning through an inky night lit by radiant stars. Or maybe he was on stage again, and the stars were the flickering fires of the cigarette lighters which fans were holding aloft.

This was insane. He wasn't singing anymore. He was a doctor; doctors don't feel this way.

Her hands were slender and warm in his. "We're out of our minds, aren't we?"

"Oh, God, yes." She was sighing, laughing. "It feels like the stupidest thing I've ever done. All week I've alternated between feeling like I'm on top of the world and like I'm about to step into an abyss."

"That's the problem with being on top of the world." He was laughing too. "The only way to go is down."

He felt a flame catch. A rolling wave of soft gray smoke surged upward. He knew the sensation—he had written about it. It was the most basic of instincts, it was desire.

He didn't know when last he had felt so alive. He was awake to everything, the click of heels on the airport's tiled floor, the swirling smells of cologne and coffee, the stir of warm air forced from the heating ducts. The sights, smells, and sensations of a physical universe sprang to life, honoring the flesh.

"We really are crazy." Her voice was low. "We're asking for trouble."

"I know. I know."

Her hands were warm in his, the pulse in her throat beat softly, her breasts rose beneath the soft, dark sweater.

Slowly he pulled on her hands, bringing her to him. But he kept his arms straight so that their clasped hands were low between their bodies, keeping them apart. *Yes, we are out of our minds. But I don't care.*

He bent his head to hers. This was no social kiss. His mouth was open when it touched hers. The kiss was firm and knowing, denying nothing.

Do you remember the time I seized your hand and

we ran and I locked the door to my dressing room and
lifted you onto the counter? I could do that again. Now.
This instant.

He took her arm as they crossed the parking lot.
Her quilted, down-filled coat was so bulky he could
feel nothing of her. He buckled his seatbelt low across
his hips and turned to watch her drive.

She had thrown her coat into the backseat. As she
reached forward to put the keys in the ignition, the
deep vee neck of her dark sweater gapped a bit and
he could see the first rise of her breast and a narrow
edging of ivory lace.

His parents were not wrong about everything. He
could envision the kind of evening they were having,
drinks in front of the fire, comfortable chairs, a long,
long talk, just the two of them. It sounded perfect, but
the twins' car was parked at the curb of her house
and before she had even turned off the van, the door
between the house and the garage popped open. Patrick was in the doorway, wriggling with excitement.

"I heard you drive up," the boy exclaimed. His eyes
were bright; he was happy. "This is really great. Are
you going to stay all weekend? Will you come to my
game? Mom says we couldn't bug you about it, but I
know you'll want to come, won't you?"

As greetings went, this was not a bad one. "Of
course I'll come. I'd love to."

"I knew it. See, Mom"—he turned to Krissa—"I
told you he'd want to come. I told you."

"I'm glad I was wrong," she said patiently.

Patrick disappeared. Inside the scarlet-trimmed
mudroom Quinn took off his coat and hung up Krissa's for her. "You don't have to protect me from your
kids. I can take care of myself."

The kitchen smelled of something rich and meaty.
Krissa opened the oven and pulled out the rack. She
lifted the lid of a casserole dish and the smell was
instantly richer. Patrick was sitting at the kitchen
table, entering arithmetic problems onto graph paper.
Quinn supposed that he needed to do that to keep his

columns straight. He watched Patrick copy another problem.

Halfway through it, Patrick looked up. "Oh, Mom, I forgot to tell you. My ear hurts."

Krissa closed the oven and glanced at the clock, a quick look of irritation flashing across her face.

"I'm sorry." Patrick looked worried.

"Oh, sweetie, it's not your fault," Krissa consoled him. "Run get the otoscope."

An otoscope was the instrument doctors used to examine ears. It was not a part of the usual family first-aid kit. Quinn wasn't sure that he had one in his office.

In a moment Patrick was back. Quinn watched with interest as Krissa kissed him and bending her knees, inserted the instrument in his ear and looked at it, quick and professional. She glanced up at the clock again. It was after five-thirty. Her pediatrician's office must be closed.

Suddenly Quinn caught her eyeing him with a dawning expression that he knew well. Usually he saw it when people realized that this anonymous Dr. Hunter was really Quinn Dodd Hall. Well, Krissa knew all about him being Quinn Dodd Hall. She was remembering that he was a doctor.

"Can you write prescriptions in Minnesota?"

"I don't think so, not legally."

"I didn't ask if you could do it legally. I just asked if you could do it."

"If it's not for a narcotic, most pharmacists would be understanding."

"Great. It's for Patrick, *double A, R, N, E, double S, O, N*. Amoxicillan 250, 150 cc's, one teaspoon three times a day."

He frowned and held out his hand for the otoscope. He sat down on one of the high stools and drew Patrick to stand between his legs. He ruffled the boy's thick, light hair, then looked in his left ear, then his right, then back in his left.

"The left one's red all right."

"So you'll do it?" Krissa asked.

He shook his head. "I haven't looked in an ear since I was a resident. And I never see kids his age in my practice. They don't start injuring their knees until high school. I'm not comfortable prescribing for children."

"Well, I am. Trust me. My old doctor let me do this all the time."

He had to smile. "And I don't suppose it's occurred to you why the new ones won't?"

"Certainly. They're so scared of law suits that they can't practice. Quinn . . . please."

He was sorry, but he wasn't going against his medical judgment, not even for her.

Then he thought about her neighbor Ben, the married guy next door who was almost in love with her. Ben couldn't have an easy time of it. He must want to help her, make her life easier, but there wasn't a thing he could do. His hands were tied. Quinn's were not.

He moved Patrick aside and went over to the phone. He dialed a number. Then when the little tone sounded, he entered the numbers of his credit card. A woman answered.

"Suzanne, this is Quinn Hunter. I'm sorry to bother you on a Friday night, but is Frank available?"

Frank Owls was a pediatrician in Washington. He and Quinn had been residents together and now occasionally played squash. Frank came on the line. "Hi, Quinn. What's up?"

"I'm in Minnesota and I'm being held hostage by a woman with an otoscope and a seven-year-old son who has a slightly inflamed ear. She wants 150 cc's of Amoxicillan 250. Shall I give it to her?"

"Does he have tubes?" Frank asked.

Quinn relayed the question to Krissa, who shook her head.

"How much do you trust the mother?" Frank asked. "How many children does she have?"

"To the end of the earth and four. This one is her youngest."

"Oh, good heavens," Frank exclaimed. "Why are you wasting my time? Any woman with four children and half a brain knows all there is to know about ear infections."

Quinn thanked Frank, hung up, and pulled a prescription pad from his blazer pocket. He uncapped his pen and began to write.

"That was a pediatrician?" Krissa asked.

Quinn nodded. "He says that raising four children teaches a person more medicine than I seem to know."

She grinned triumphantly, and as he handed her the prescription, she patted him on the head. "You're a dream date, Quinn. Friday night antibiotics. What more could a girl want?"

He put his hand to the curve of her waist. But before he could do anything else, a clattering racket burst down the back stairway. "Hey, Quinn. When did you get here?"

It was one of the twins. Quinn dropped his hand. You might be able to get away with a few gropes in front of a seven-year-old, but not in front of a sixteen-year-old. "Five minutes ago," he said to the boy. "How are you, whichever one you are?"

"I'm Curt, and I'm fine."

Krissa held up the prescription. "Would you mind running this over to the drugstore and waiting for it?"

"I'd better come too," Quinn added. "We might have to do some talking to get this filled."

But the pharmacist filled it readily. Curt was a pleasant companion. Quinn enjoyed his youthful self-assurance. When boys his age came into Quinn's office, they had been injured and had awakened from a young male's glossy sense of his own indestructability. Curt still felt invulnerable. He wasn't arrogant, he wasn't a brat, he simply liked being himself more than he might in a couple of years.

All four boys were home for dinner. "Tomorrow,"

Krissa told him as he helped carry things out to the table, "you are taking me out to dinner. Just me. You aren't inviting them."

"That sounds fine."

"And it will be incredibly expensive."

"That sounds even better."

After dinner, she again brought coffee out to the living room. The boys were either upstairs or in the back half of the house so the adults at least had the illusion of privacy.

She handed him a cup. "I'm not going to sleep with you, Quinn."

He couldn't quite bring himself to say that that sounded fine. "I didn't expect you to."

"It isn't that I don't want to. I do. I'm surprised at how much. At the airport it was such a shock ... I haven't thought of myself that way in years."

So he wasn't the only one coming back to life. "Is it that you don't want the boys to know?" He had dated women with children before.

She nodded. "Brian's been going with a girl for a year now, and they aren't having sex ... At least, I'm pretty sure they aren't. Both her mother and I really want them to wait, and if—"

"Wait a minute," Quinn had to interrupt. "You talked to his girlfriend's mother about this? People's *mothers* discuss this?"

"Of course."

He was horrified. "She called you on the phone and you talked about whether or not the kids were having sex?"

"Actually, I called her." Krissa was laughing. "Whose side are you on here, Quinn?"

"Brian's. One hundred percent, no question about it, Brian's. I can't tell him from Curt, but I am on his side."

"He'll appreciate that."

"I don't plan for him to know. So you think if you hop in bed with me, that will seem to give him permission to hop in bed with his girlfriend?"

She nodded. "Does that seem strange?"

"No, it makes sense. Do the boys ever go visit their father? Do you ever have a weekend on your own?"

"Not during hockey season. And the rest of the time they split up. Two go, and two stay home. Jerry's place is so small that if they all go, they have to stay with my mother which isn't a great arrangement. And it's good for Brian and Curt to be apart."

"Then we won't worry about it for a while. We'll just watch hockey together. That's got to be better than sex."

What happened after "Not Far Enough From Home" in Hartford? Danny, you went back and started banging your head on the drum platform, and Quinn, you sat down on the stage and buried your face in your hands.

D.F.: We do have moments of superb onstage presence, don't we?

Q.H.: We were telling everyone to go home and smash their records.

You record a song when you first get to know it. I suppose it's a little like having sex with someone the first time you meet her. It can be great, it may never be better than that, but more likely as you get to know her, things will improve.

That happens to us all the time. We record a song and then go out on the road and play it for an audience a hundred times and then we finally figure out what it's really about. In that incident you're referring to, we'd been playing around with tempos—

D.F.: If you just want to hear the record note for note, stay home. Don't come to the concert.

Q.H.: And that night, the song suddenly worked as it never had before. So a year too late, we were ready to record it.

Are you saying that you'd like to do a live album?

D.F.: No, he's saying that women should keep away from us. We're lousy one-night stands.

—Andrea Rush Wilchost, "The *Rolling Stone* Interview: Danny French and Quinn Hunter," February 7, 1977, p. 45.

LEXINGTON, KENTUCKY, JULY 1976

A pounding on his hotel door woke Quinn. He ran a hand over his face and groaned. This was not supposed to happen. Dodd Hall traveled with a security crew, he and Danny used pseudonyms, the list of room numbers was tightly controlled, all of that necessary so that a person could get some sleep.

The pounding continued, "Come on, Quinn. Open up. It's me."

It was Danny. Quinn pulled on some jeans and fumbled with the locks on the door. Danny charged past him. "What's going on?" Quinn asked, slipping the chain back on the door, still a little groggy.

Danny had stopped in the center of the room. He started to speak, then went over to the windows. "You know that young lady I was with this evening?"

"No. I didn't see her." Danny's occasional tomcatting was not anything Quinn wanted to witness.

"Good." Danny was pacing in front of the windows, nervous, agitated. "Because she was not a lady."

Quinn was awake now. "Not a lady as in she was a tart, a strumpet, a fallen angel, a person of questionable virtue—or not a lady as in she wasn't female?"

"The latter. Although"—Danny raked a hand through his hair—"I don't suppose she has the highest moral character."

"How did you find out?" Quinn asked. "What did you do?"

"What did I *do*?" Danny was outraged. "What do you think I did? I stopped. I tried to be nice. I took her arm very gallantly and escorted her out the door. It was hard not to think of her as a woman even though I knew that she had this boner under her skirt."

"I don't know much about it," Quinn offered, "but on some level somewhere, she probably is female."

"Not where it counts." Danny jerked at the drapes.

"Aren't you making a pretty big deal of this?" Danny had not been exactly fastidious this summer.

"Even if she had gone down on you, would it have been the end of the world?"

"What would you have done?" Danny demanded. "Would you be this philosophical if it had happened to you?"

Things like this did not happen to Quinn. "Yes, I'd be extremely philosophical . . . in the middle of a six-hour, scalding shower."

PLAYBOY: When you look back to your Dodd Hall days, what personally do you feel the worst about?

FRENCH: The opening guitar riff in "Wayward Slopes." It stinks.

PLAYBOY: I said personally.

FRENCH: Personally? Not musically? I guess it would have to be the girls . . . the women. There was a period of about six months on the road—it was after my sister got married—when the women were all faceless to me. I was using them. I know that's what they came for, but I didn't have to encourage them in their weakness and confusion.

When I started studying Biblical texts, I think that was the first thing that genuinely hit home, the role of the women. Women were so essential to Christ's work especially during His last days. They could do much of what they did because they were politically invisible. No one was watching them. Their invisibility gave them power. It made me think about all these women on the road, how invisible they were to me, even though what they were desperately trying for was visibility. It's a sad commentary on our society that some women believe that fucking a rock star will make them able to see themselves.

You can't let people be invisible. It's not right. And it's politically dangerous.

PLAYBOY: Do you have relationships with any individual women?

FRENCH: My sister.

PLAYBOY: What's that relationship like?

FRENCH: A one-way street. She does it all. I don't do anything for her. I should, but I don't. I don't know what's going on in her life. I don't know what worries her, what scares her. She wants this real bourgeois life for her kids, and I don't understand that.

But isn't there a point at which a person can say, "hold it." Stop judging me by personal relationships—which in my case are lousy to nonexistent—and judge me by my work, which has, I believe, had an impact. What's important here?

—Tom Maddox, "*Playboy* Interview: Danny French," *Playboy,* August 1990, p. 106.

Chapter Seventeen

Krissa could feel herself melting. Quinn was coming every weekend when he wasn't on call, and he made those weekends leisurely, luxurious, and above all, easy. She didn't have to plan anything; she didn't have to pack anything. Restaurant reservations, theater tickets, flowers, simply appeared. For the first time she could remember, someone was taking care of her.

Quinn thought her life was difficult. That was crazy. Difficult? She knew difficult. Doing diapers for twins when you didn't have a dryer, that was difficult. Washing dishes in the bathtub because that was the only working faucet in the entire house, that was difficult. Putting a pair of four-year-olds and a newborn in snowsuits day after freezing day, that was difficult. Having two sullen adolescents interested only in skateboarding and heavy metal music, that was difficult.

But her house was now finished. She had a garage right off her kitchen. She could warm up her car every day without even putting her coat on. She had a washer and dryer in the mudroom; she could change a load of laundry in less time than it took onions to brown. Everyone in the house could dress himself; everyone could go to the bathroom by himself; and two of them could even drive.

Had Quinn shown up when her life was truly difficult, she would not have had time to see him.

But even if things were not as difficult as they had once been, she was a single mother with four boys and little money. She had to run a tight ship. But now, with Quinn around, she found herself preaching less to the boys, indulging them a little more. She'd call for a pizza when she didn't feel like cooking. She didn't fuss at Quinn when he bought the boys Lacrosse sticks and then cross-country skis. She thanked him graciously when he gave her a pair of butter-soft, lined leather gloves that probably cost what she spent on a week's groceries. She was even less compulsive about her own work. Normally if she had an extra fifteen minutes before meeting Patrick's bus, she would dash down to her workroom to install a zipper in a seat cushion. Now she would fix some tea in a delicate violet-garlanded pot and as she would watch the steaming amber liquid arch out of the graceful spout, she would think about how happy she was.

Everyone liked Quinn. She and Jerry had always been invited to all the large parties in the neighborhood, but now she and Quinn were being included in the intimate dinners for four or six couples. He was developing his own friends, certain men whom he always chatted with at hockey games, whom he sought out at parties. He fit in so easily that it sometimes seemed as if he had been here forever.

The boys liked him too. How they might have reacted if she had started to date in a more conventional fashion, Krissa did not know. But Quinn was someone they had heard about their whole lives. They had seen his pictures, they knew his voice. He came to their hockey games, he shot baskets with them. He helped Patrick practice the piano. He was not a threat to their family life; he was part of it.

The boys were learning from him: learning how a man moves, how he thinks, feels, speaks. They were aware of the muscles in his arms, the cleft in his chin, the veins in his neck. What was masculine in their blood responded to what was masculine in his. He was a man, independent and confident, what they longed to be.

Krissa had not wanted her boys to feel, as did some

sons of single mothers, that their job in life was to grow up and rescue her. So she made them work hard now. They did the dishes, took the garbage out, and did the yard work. They changed light bulbs, they replaced the washers in the faucets. But it was work for the family. She never expected them to do anything for her personally.

But Quinn had grown up seeing his mother attended to, and he had been taught his first lessons of gentlemanly courtesy on her. Now he unconsciously shared those lessons with Krissa's sons. "As long as you're getting up," he would say to someone about to catapult himself out of a chair, "why don't you see if your mother would like another cup of coffee?"

The boy in question would blink, peer at Krissa's cup, then at her. "Yes, yes, I would," she would answer whether she wanted one or not. "That would be very nice of you."

Why don't you pop out and start your mother's car? ... I think there is another bag of groceries in the car ... could one of you ...

In Krissa's world, a mother was the family pack mule, the chuckwagon, the traffic cop. Her father had never once done anything for her mother's comfort. In Quinn's world, however, motherhood was a position of honor.

Krissa was not complaining.

In her heart she knew that the loveliness of these weekends did not have a secure footing. Quinn was doing everything for her. She was doing nothing for him. He would not speak of his needs; he would not allow her to think of them. It was like their Dodd Hall days again, only this time it was her turn. She was the important one.

Things could not endure being out of balance for long, she knew that. But this business of having someone put her first at all times was such a marvel to Krissa. It was like being nestled in the deepest down quilt; she couldn't stir herself to worry.

And she knew that there was something else she

ought to be worrying about—she and Quinn never spoke about Danny. They never even mentioned his name.

Danny, on the other hand, could not stop talking about Quinn. Chance comments from the boys had made it clear to him how regularly Quinn was visiting. Danny immediately started calling Krissa more, although she noticed he never called her on weekends when Quinn might be in the house.

"So was Dr. Knee there this weekend?" he demanded one Monday in February. "Why does he keep coming back? What does he want?"

He was clearly trying to control her again. She spoke patiently. "This has nothing to do with you, Danny."

"What's he doing? Reliving the past? What's wrong with his life now that he has to go back?"

"He can hardly be reliving the past." She was still calm. "We spend the whole weekend at hockey games."

"Maybe it's not your mutual past. He's probably doing the childhood thing again. His mother is such a chilly bitch; now he has this perfect mother and all those great brothers who he can—"

Danny could be exactly like a two-year-old. Krissa knew two-year-olds. The important thing was not to let yourself get drawn down to their level. "Danny, be quiet."

Danny stopped. "Was I out of line? Oh, God, I'm sorry. It's just that everyone is going crazy around here. They've got the stupidest, stupidest health inspectors on our backs. It is so frustrating, I'm going nuts."

Danny had been like this since the end of the hunger strike. He was feeling fettered, caged, easily frustrated.

I'm going nuts.

"Danny." Krissa suddenly felt worried . . . urgently so. "Are you okay?"

"No, of course I'm not okay. This city is absurd.
They'd rather have people starve or eat out of the
garbage than consume a single morsel prepared in a
noncommercial kitchen. Why don't you ask Dr. Knee
to let us sell the rights to just one song? That would
more than pay for a new kitchen."

"Forget kitchens for a moment. How are you?"

"I just told you. I'm—" He stopped. "Oh, if you
mean *that*, I guess I'm okay."

Yes, she had meant that.

ITASCA COUNTY, MINNESOTA, APRIL 1977

Danny had to leave the day after their father's funeral.
The release date for the new album was a week away;
the tour to promote it was to begin then.

"It's the only nice thing Dad's ever done for me,"
Danny joked as he handed Krissa his coat. He had
stopped by Jerry's little house to see her again before
leaving. "Dying this week instead of next. This isn't
convenient, but next week would have cost big bucks."

"You would have cancelled a concert to come?"
Dodd Hall had never yet cancelled a gig. They had
played on borrowed equipment when one of their
trucks had gotten lost; they had stood onstage with
hundred-and-one degree fevers. They had always
shown up.

Danny shrugged. "Probably. Quinn would have
made me."

Quinn. She had seen him at the funeral yesterday.
His eyes had been tired, full of ashes. She hadn't slept
all night, thinking about him.

Brian and Curt were lined up on the floor, strapped
in their infant seats. Danny squatted down in front of
them and returned their round-eyed gaze for a moment, then rose. "I don't know anything about
babies."

It was, she supposed, an apology. She wasn't going
to accept it. She loved him, he was her brother, but

he should have come see the babies when they were born. He had been wrong. "Would you like some coffee?"

"That would be great."

He followed her into the narrow kitchen and waited as she poured out the coffee. He was wearing his familiar plaid-wool shirt and well-worn jeans. He had a stocking cap pulled low over his silky black curls.

He took one of the mugs. "Jingle and Petey said that at the funeral yesterday they told you about that stupid chocolate song."

Apparently after not being able to write for almost six months, Quinn had come forth with a deeply felt lyric about his family. "My Grandfather's Chocolates" the song was called. Although he had written it last fall, it had not been included on the new album. Danny was refusing to sing it.

"They didn't exactly call it stupid," Krissa answered. "They say it's a wonderful song, the best thing Quinn's ever written."

"My music for it is pretty good too. I hope they said that."

"They did. So what's the problem?"

Danny shrugged. "I just can't relate to it. All this stuff about his father selling the family business. What does that have to do with me?"

On the surface nothing. But Danny was never one to cling to surfaces. "You sang 'You'll Never Walk Alone' to your guitar, didn't you?"

"Yes, and I almost had to whore myself on 'My Boy Bill.' Is that what you're suggesting?"

"No, of course not. But why don't you—"

Krissa stopped. It wasn't right, that Danny wasn't willing to try to connect with the lyric, especially since Quinn had struggled so hard to sing *Self-Chosen Snares*. It wasn't right, but it also wasn't any of her business. Saving Danny and Quinn from themselves wasn't her job anymore.

"I suppose you think I'm being a shit," he challenged her.

"It's not my place to think anything about it."

He frowned and glared at her, exasperated. He wanted her to get involved. That's why he had brought this up. He was trying to suck her back in. He wanted her to force him into singing the song; he knew that that was the right thing to do, but he wanted to be able to blame it on her. *I'm just doing this for Quinn's girlfriend,* he could say.

But she wasn't Quinn's girlfriend any more. *It's too late, Danny. It's over. I'm not a part of Dodd Hall anymore.* She had her sons, this small house, a husband. This was her life.

The exasperation drained out of his eyes. He understood what her silence meant.

He turned his back, not wanting her to see what he was feeling. He picked up the little pottery cup in which she kept the matches she used to light the burners on the stove. He rattled the matches for a moment; they were wooden and blue-tipped. Then he set the cup back down. "Did Dad commit suicide?"

No one had said that word aloud. No one else had the nerve. Krissa glanced over her shoulder. Both of the babies had fallen asleep. "The mine's calling it an accident."

"But there was no reason for him to be near the blasting, was there?"

"Probably not."

Danny pulled off his stocking cap and ran his hand through his black hair. "You know, don't you, that when I say he was crazy, I mean it. I'm not just talking. I really do think he was mentally ill."

"I don't know much about it, but it does seem possible."

"Does it ever worry you, that it—whatever it was he had—that it might be hereditary?"

Krissa drew back. "No, never." She hadn't given that a moment's thought. True, this hadn't been the cheeriest year of her life, but any sadness she felt seemed justified. "Do you?"

He nodded. "Sometimes, yes. Depression does run

in families. Can't you feel it sometimes, that just around the corner is this big blackness waiting for us?"

No. She had never felt that way.

"I don't want to end up like him." Danny was still speaking. "I really don't."

It was a dreadful thought. "But your life is much better than his. You're successful. You have money and power, all the things he was so angry about not having."

"But does that make any difference?" Danny argued. "If this is an inherited condition or if it's a disease like cancer, it might not matter two hoots what your life is like. It's still going to get you."

He really meant this. He believed that this might happen to him.

"People can get help, you know. Drugs, psychiatrists, things like that."

He looked at her. "Can you imagine Dad going to a shrink?"

He had a point. On the Range you took care of your problems yourself. Going on welfare, visiting a psychiatrist, were pretty much the same: a sign of weakness.

He went on. "Nor can I see myself going."

That too was unanswerable.

"So I want us to make a pact," he said. "If you see me or if I see you starting to be like Dad, then whoever sees the problem tells the other that it is time to check in somewhere for treatment, and that one will go. No questions, no arguments, you just go. I would go on your word that I needed help, and you'd go on mine. Would you agree to that?"

"Yes, but I've already done the craziest thing I'll ever do."

"Don't be glib. I'm serious."

He was. Every line of his face was set and solemn. His beauty, usually so wild and daring, so full of mercurial passions, now had the look of a Grecian statue, one expression locked forever in pale marble. "Of course, I will, Danny. Of course."

"Will you shake hands on it?"

His hand was extended to her. It seemed so strange. As far as she could remember, they had never shaken hands. When did you ever have occasion to shake your brother's hand?

When he thought he might be going crazy. Krissa put hers in his, feeling his light, strong clasp around her fingers.

The cover of *Self-Chosen Snares* had been shot after shot of Danny and Quinn's hands pressed together, photographed from every angle. The lighting had picked out the difference in their colorings—Danny's pale skin against Quinn's golden tan—but all else had underscored the similarity, that these two hands were shaped exactly the same.

"Why are you asking me?" she said. "Why not Quinn? He's the one who is with you all the time. He'd see it first."

Danny let go of her. "Because you're my sister. However unfortunate a lot that is, you're stuck with it for life."

The Colony is supposedly a democracy with everyone, the floor managers, the team leaders, and the other staff members, having an equal voice. But some animals are more equal than others. Danny French is the leader; everyone knows it. No one can recall an important decision that has not had his approval. Many bonds link the members of the Colony, people who have chosen to live and work at a homeless shelter. One of the strongest of those bonds is their admiration of French.

He embodies all the contradictions of the leadership myth. He is surrounded by people. Yet he seems profoundly solitary. One cannot question the deep warmth he feels for the people the Colony cares for, the genuine spiritual love. This is most clear when he deals with the people whom society calls mentally ill. "God may speak to them in a different voice than He uses when He speaks to you and me," French says, his dark eyes riveted on his listener's face. "Who are we to say that the Voice we hear is more authentic? And how do you know that suddenly one day you won't start hearing a different one, too?"

—Maggie Copnick, "Mitch Snyder's Heirs: Homeless Activists in the Nineties," *Airways InFlight Magazine,* March 1991, p. 32.

Chapter Eighteen

Quinn tried to keep Krissa from coming out to the airport every Friday. He didn't want her to bother, he could take a cab or rent a car. But she liked meeting him. She would leave her car at valet parking, a luxury that she used and let him pay for, and then would go to the World Club, the airline's lounge for frequent travelers, another luxury she was letting him pay for. The receptionist knew her; they would chat for a moment or two. Then Krissa would make herself a cup of tea at the large silver urn.

It was a comforting luxury to sit in this quiet, well-ordered lounge, surrounded by quiet, dark-suited businessmen, sipping tea from a quiet, well-designed china cup. It was a magically peaceful time for her, a time for transition. These moments in the lounge were a ceremonial threshold, a gateway at which the Den Mother, the Hockey Mom, the Upholsterer all had to step aside. Only the Woman could cross into the enchanted lands beyond. Then she would hear the whisper of the club door opening and the low murmur of the receptionist greeting Quinn. He would sign his name at the register, lay down his pen, and then turn, looking for her.

He never did more than take her hand and kiss her cheek. This was a lounge for businessmen; there was a credit-card phone on every slate-topped end table. But he always did take her hand and kiss her cheek, and sometimes when he would step back, he would be breathing as if he had been running.

If there was time, he sat down and they had a drink together, sharing their news, their thoughts, before they submerged themselves in the crashing tide of the boys' lives.

One Friday in March, Quinn's plane was late enough that Krissa could feel the magic fading. She was changing back into Den Mother again. She grew tense about the time passing. At home she was recovering a sofa and wing chair in a very difficult plaid. The fabric stretched and she was having to pin the seams at almost every inch to keep the plaid matched. She should have brought the small pillow covers with her; she could have pinned them here.

At last the receptionist told her that Quinn's plane was about to land. She went out to the concourse to meet him directly. She could see him walking up the long corridor from the arrival gates. He was moving more slowly than usual. She wished he would hurry up. The boys would be starving by now. No, they wouldn't be. They would have each eaten about five boxes of crackers, and that would be the end of any hope of a nutritious dinner.

Quinn looked weary and drawn. It must have been a difficult flight. She put her arms around him. His embrace was perfunctory, without strength. She stepped back. This was more than the result of a difficult flight.

He doesn't want to be here.

The thought seared through her. Quinn wished he hadn't come. He wanted to be home with his own bed, his own piano, his own company. He wanted to be alone.

She knew how he felt. She knew exactly how he felt. She remembered all those times when the thought of getting on another plane had sickened her, when she had longed to stay home even though home had been a dorm room. That was how Quinn felt now.

So why did you come?

For the same reason she had always gone. Because he had said he would. Quinn kept his promises. He fulfilled his obligations.

She had become an obligation.

A sudden flash of impatience cut through her worry. Yes, she and the boys might have expected too much of him. They might have dragged him to too many noisy hockey games. They might not have allowed him any solitude, but he was at fault too. He should have spoken earlier. "These are my needs. Here is what I must do for myself." Why had he waited until he felt trapped?

No, no. It was her fault too. In her heart she had known that this would happen, that even he could not go on denying that he needed anything from anyone.

In the glass-enclosed waiting area of the valet garage, she turned over her parking chit. There would be a brief wait for the car. She had to do something. She had to help him. Otherwise she might never see him again. She excused herself and went over to the bank of phones to call home.

Patrick answered. Krissa was sorry. She would like to be talking to one of the older boys, but she wasn't going to let Patrick know that.

"Quinn has a headache," she said. "Could you lay a fire in his room? Don't light it, just lay it and be sure there's enough wood."

That wouldn't be enough. Making him comfortable wouldn't be enough. He would sit in the wing chair for a half an hour, staring at the flames, but then he would feel guilty, a man not meeting his obligations, and the guilt would drive him back downstairs, still unhappy, still withdrawn.

She couldn't lock him in, could she? She looked across the little waiting room. He was facing away from her, standing quietly, staring out at the parked cars, his hands clasped behind his back like the Prince of Wales. His hands gleamed with a healthy light against the dark wool of his coat. They were still a musician's hands, long-fingered and deft.

Hands. There was nothing Krissa believed in more than the restorative powers of working with your hands, your mind working through your senses, as you watched something change or grow, the accomplishment bringing satisfaction and peace. She knew he now got that from performing surgery. It wouldn't surprise her if he had been in the operating room little this week, if he had instead spent his time in meetings, consultations, and conferences.

She turned back to the phone, speaking to Patrick in a rush. "Do you remember that model, the old Model A car that was too hard for you guys?" Actually all models were too hard for Patrick. "It's on the upper shelf of Adam's closet. Would you lay it out on the table in the guest room and be sure that everything's there? You might ask Curt to check it over."

Their ride home was quiet. She stopped at the liquor store. She knew that Quinn disliked the quality of her liquor. Every weekend he walked over to Selby Avenue with one of the boys and bought a bottle of wine at the little gourmet shop. She now gestured to him to come in with her. She got a cart. "You choose," she told him. "You're paying."

Now was not the time for silly financial pride.

And for the first time since he had arrived, she saw a bit of a smile. "I thought you would never ask."

She expected him to buy Scotch and cognac, the only two things besides beer and wine that she had seen him drink. But he bought everything— gin, vermouth, rum, and vodka. He found the task peaceful and relaxing. He also bought olives, maraschino cherries, and nuts—cans of cashews, packages of smoked almonds, jars of macadamia nuts. Krissa never bought nuts for snacks. They were too expensive, and the boys went through them too fast.

At home she left the garage door open and urged Quinn to bring his suitcase back outside and enter the house through the front door. At this time of day the boys would be in the back of the house. If they saw Quinn, he would be ensnared. His sense of obligation to them would be a steel trap, its glittering teeth biting his leg to the bone.

But the front hall was quiet, peacefully welcoming. The green leaves of the silk fig tree stirred lightly in the warm current from the heating duct; the dark oak floor shone with the dull lustre of oil soap, and a deep border of rough ivory lace circled the cloth covering the pedestaled table that sat in the curve of the staircase.

The boys' affection for Quinn was evident in the amount of wood they had carried upstairs to the guest room and the care with which they had laid the fire. Curt's talent for organization was apparent in the way the model was laid out. All the little tools were neatly arranged. There were Q-Tips, paper towels, and a fresh tube of glue. The reading lamp from Brian's room had been set on the table; it was already plugged in. Krissa felt a little rush of pride at the completeness of their arrangements.

"The boys were stuck on this model and wondered if you could take a look at it," she said to Quinn as she knelt down to light the fire.

"Of course," he murmured. Another obligation.

Downstairs she was instantly greeted with Brian asking if Quinn felt any better and Patrick exclaiming, "Mom, Mom, Curt took some glue from the basement." The boys were forbidden to take any of Krissa's professional supplies. Patrick wasn't tattling; he was marveling at Curt having the courage to flaunt a family rule, knowing that he would be caught.

Curt hooked his thumbs through the belt loops of his jeans. "You can ground me if you like," he drawled. He knew that he had been right to trust his own judgment over his mother's rules. This was an important step. He was becoming a man.

Krissa looked at the four of them standing there, their hair rumpled and shining, their shirts untucked, their shoes half-tied. Adam was eating a bowl of cereal. Patrick was cleaning out the peanut butter jar with his finger. "I love you guys," she said. "I really do."

"Oh, come on, Mom." Adam made a face. He was afraid she was going to get mushy. "We know that."

Which was, she supposed, the right answer. She, Danny, and Quinn hadn't known that as kids; none of them had been sure that they were loved. Her boys were.

Adam was the one person in the family capable of being quiet, so she sent him upstairs with a drink for Quinn. Forty-five minutes later, she took up something to eat: black bean pesto, cold vinegar chicken, and dilled cucumber.

He was at the table, his white shirt open at the neck, his tie loosened. His hair was longer than usual, its golden ends starting to curl. Whatever had happened to him this week must have included a cancelled hair cut. His sleeves were rolled up, and he was muttering to himself, holding up two pieces of the car. She watched him for a moment. He was a tidy worker. He checked the fit first. Then he dotted on the glue, perfect little dots neat and evenly spaced, tiny white polka dots on the thin edge of the dark plastic. The work was absorbing, consciousness draining without the pressure or high stakes of surgery. He might not be happy, but he was not unhappy either.

Quinn finished the model at four A.M. Krissa had come in at two before she went to bed, bringing some coffee and a plate of cookies. She had put more wood on the fire.

"I'm not being a very good guest," he had apologized.

"What makes you think you are a guest?"

When the car was done, he dropped into bed, not waking until early in the afternoon. He showered and went down the back stairs that led to the kitchen. Noise and warmth rose up the narrow stairwell, fol-

lowed by the most mesmerizing Oriental smells, star
anise, ginger, and soy.

Patrick was unloading the dishwasher. Adam was
sitting on one of the tall stools looking at the sports
page of the paper. Krissa was at the stove, a white
butcher apron tied close around her slender form. She
was lifting the lid of a pot, and steam surged up, enveloping her with a halo of spicy mist, and she blurred
for a moment. It was as though he was looking
through her, beyond her, into a luminous dream, a
shimmering, otherworldly ideal of womanhood, a Pla-
tonic vision of all that the feminine ought to be.

Then she smiled. The mist dissolved, and she was
something far more precious than any of Plato's ideals.
She was herself . . . and he loved her.

It had been a horrible week at the hospital. Equipment problems had forced the cancellation of two
days' surgical schedule. One of the obstetricians on
staff was in the middle of an ugly malpractice trial,
and that made all the doctors tense and edgy. At
home Quinn was working on a story which he hated,
and that always brought him down until he could get
it right.

He had wanted to stay home, wrestle with the story,
practice the piano—Krissa's piano was so horrible he
couldn't stand to play it—and just be alone.

What a mistake that would have been. If he had
stayed home, he would still be feeling as dissatisfied
with the story and just as frustrated about the cancelled operations. Krissa's home had restored him. She
had brought him peace just as she had done during
Dodd Hall.

"Oh, Quinn, great." Patrick dropped a handful of
forks into the silverware drawer and dashed across the
kitchen. "Mom said we couldn't wake you up, but I
knew you wouldn't want to miss Brian and Curt's
game. It's their divisional play-off game."

Quinn rumpled his hair. "I wouldn't miss it for the
world." He looked over the boy's head at Krissa. *This
has nothing to do with cinnamon. This is the present.*

This is now. And I love you. "Do I have time to get something to eat?"

The high school hockey championship was a big deal in Minnesota, and Quinn joined wholeheartedly in the cheering as the twins' team squeaked by their heavily favored opposition, thus earning the right to compete in the state meet.

"Why are you cheering?" Krissa had whispered to him furiously, only half-teasing. "If they had lost, I wouldn't have to watch any more hockey until next November."

Brian's girlfriend, Pam, joined the family for dinner. She was a pretty blond girl, a little shy around Quinn, carefully calling him "Mr. Hunter." That sounded odd to his ears. He was "Quinn" to his friends, "Dr. Hunter" to everyone else. This "Mr. Hunter" was a new fellow.

Which wasn't an entirely bad idea.

After dinner, Brian and Pam went out, and the other three boys walked over to the video store to rent a movie. Quinn went to the cabinet where Krissa kept her liquor and took out the cognac he had bought on Friday. He carried some glasses out to the living room. He poured himself a drink, swirled the cognac in his glass, savoring its rich smell, and leaned back, his eyes closed, utterly relaxed. In a moment, he heard Krissa's soft footsteps, smelled the soft spice of her fragrance, felt her soft weight settling into the cushion next to him.

He opened his eyes. She was wearing a thick white fisherman's knit sweater and her hair was twisted up on top of her head. Ringlets and wisps escaped, gathering around her face like a soft halo. "I was pretty arrogant, wasn't I? Thinking I could drag myself in here and fool everyone about how I was feeling."

She was smiling. "Someday you'll figure out that we aren't all like your parents, that we are paying attention to you."

"Let's not talk about them." He sat up. The boys

wouldn't be home for at least fifteen minutes. He moved to put his arm around her. "Let's talk about you, about how wonderful you are."

She batted his hand aside. "No, let's not. We aren't done talking about you. You haven't figured out family life yet. It may not be possible to have sex in this house—although I suppose Brian will figure out a way soon enough—but it is possible to find quiet if you need it. Watch Adam, he's the best at it. Or just put your foot down. I know speaking up isn't natural to you, but—"

No, it wasn't. He had spoken once before, he had said what he needed, and what had happened? Take a leave of absence from school, he had said. Come to Europe with us. I need you.

He had asked and he had lost her. How could he possibly take that risk again?

The Aarnesson family phone rang unceasingly on Sundays. The way girls called boys these days—even Adam had been getting calls for two years—startled Krissa, and she took the phone off the hook during supper Sunday nights. It made for a charming and restful family meal, with the twins bolting their food and glaring at their brothers wanting them to hurry up. Patrick, who at seven got few calls, relished his moment of power and on Sunday nights ate a multi-course dinner with leisured elegance.

But when she answered the phone on Sunday afternoon, the voice on the other end was deep and male. "Hello, I am trying to reach Dr. Hunter. Is he available?"

Quinn had not gotten a single call while here. She stepped into the library where he was sitting on the floor, leaning back against the sofa, watching a basketball game on TV with the boys. He nodded when she told him that the call was for him. Easily, unself-consciously, he levered himself up and backed into the kitchen, his eyes on the screen. In the doorway, he took the phone from her and tucked it under his ear, still watching the game. "Quinn Hunter here . . . hello, David, what's up?"

One of the doctors he practiced with was named David. Krissa supposed that he was calling about a patient, and she turned back to the leeks she had been cleaning. She had just picked up her knife when she heard a sharp hiss.

"You don't mean it," Quinn was saying. "When did it happen? . . . How?"

The blood had drained from his face. Someone must have died.

"I don't believe it," he said. Then he said it again. "I just don't believe it."

He had never lost a patient. He had told her that. People didn't die from knee surgery. They didn't always feel better, but they didn't die. What could have happened? She was at his side, her hand on his arm.

"Yes, yes," he was saying into the phone. He must not have heard her. "I'll be back as soon as I can. I'll go straight to Baltimore."

Baltimore? Why Baltimore? He practiced in Washington.

"Good-bye . . . I'll let you know . . . good-bye." The call was over. Quinn moved the phone away from his ear and stared at it blankly.

"Quinn, what is it?" she repeated the question. "Is it one of your parents?" His parents lived in Baltimore.

"It's both of them. They were in a car accident. They're dead."

Krissa's hand went to her heart. "Oh, Quinn . . ."

"They'd gone to the club after church. They always do. It was raining, and on the way home, the car—"

He stopped and tilted his head back, looking up at the kitchen cabinets, but she knew his eyes weren't focusing on anything. "Who would have thought? I mean, here Danny is trying to kill himself on a regular basis, and it's them . . . I thought they would survive us all. They seemed indestructible." He drew his hand across his eyes and gave his head a quick shake as if he were trying to wake up. "I've got to go straight to

Baltimore. I need to change my reservation." He
started to dial the phone. He put the receiver to his
ear and then looked puzzled.

He had not hung up between calls. Krissa took the
phone from him. "I'll call," she said. "You go—"

"And I'll need a car, so—" He stopped again and
put his hand across his eyes again. "Krissa, please
come with me. Please."

Go with him? To Baltimore? Her heart stopped.
How could she? She couldn't leave the boys on two
hours' notice. If she had a day or so, she could work
it out. They could stay with friends, she could come
tomorrow night, she could be there for the funeral.

But that wasn't what Quinn needed. He needed her
to walk in the door of his parents' empty house with
him. And he had asked her to. She hadn't gone to
Europe with him when he asked her to. Now she
couldn't go to Baltimore either.

She was heartsick. "Quinn, I can't. I can't leave the
boys. I can come tomorrow as soon as I get them
organized. I will come out tomorrow."

"Oh." He looked at her blankly. "But that's what
I meant, all of you."

All of you. Krissa shut her eyes, unable to speak.
Relief flooded through her, welling into every vein.
He wanted the boys too. He didn't just want her, he
wanted them. That had been his first thought, all of
them.

"I'll go tell them," she said.

The boys stared at her. How could Quinn's parents
be dead? It had never occurred to them that he even
had parents. But when they learned that they were
going to miss school, that they were going to get on
an airplane and fly to Baltimore . . . well, Krissa hoped
that if the Good Lord was watching, He understood
boys because hers were delighted. Quinn's parents'
dying was, without a doubt, the best thing that had
ever happened to them.

She began issuing orders. Curt was to take the
phone up to the guest room where Quinn was packing

and make whatever plane and car reservations were needed. Brian was to pack for both of them. Adam was to go next door, tell Ben and Lynn what had happened and ask them to call the schools in the morning. Then he could use their phone to find someone to take care of the dog. Patrick was to empty all the garbage and put out a note for the milkman.

Quickly she packed for herself and Patrick. Then she went into the guest room to check on Quinn and Curt. Quinn immediately started praising Curt, how organized and efficient he was, how he had remembered that they would need to rent a car with six seatbelts.

Krissa knew all this about Curt. "Where are we going to be staying? Your parents' house?"

"We might as well."

"Then are there any neighbors we can call? We should let someone know we're coming." And when he looked blank, she went on. "Quinn, trust me, you don't want to walk in the house and see coffee cups leftover from their breakfast."

That's what her mother had had to face, a washer full of wet laundry belonging to a man who was already dead.

"I'm sure someone will call Jewel," Quinn said. "You remember her. She's our maid. She'll get everything ready."

"Does she know what 'us' entails? That you're appearing with five other people? You should call her."

"You're right, you're right." He reached for the phone, then stopped. "This doesn't seem real. I think about going home and I see them there. Of course they'll be there. How can they not be there?"

"It's all right, Quinn. It's natural at first, not to be able to accept it."

"I just can't imagine them dying."

No. Krissa couldn't either. From everything Quinn had ever said about them, they sounded like overpoweringly selfish people. Why would they ever do something in their disinterest such as dying?

The father in Springsteen's "My Hometown" is a tender man, able to express affection through the gesture of rumpling the child's hair. He encourages independence, sending the proud, excited child to buy a newspaper on his own. He offers instruction; from the safety of his father's lap, the boy learns to steer a car—the car of course being symbolic of an adult's ability to control his own destiny.

But larger forces, economic and political, castrate the father's legacy. The hometown is bankrupt. When the singer repeats his father's gestures with his own son, he knows he is participating in a meaningless ritual.

"My Grandfather's Chocolates," written by Quinn Hunter, the lyricist for the band Dodd Hall, is less grim about society and more bitter about the individuals in it. Hunter comes from a heritage of socioeconomic power and he does see people able to make choices. They can control their destinies. The bitterness in the song comes because the father in it makes the wrong choices. He has forsaken his responsibilities. He is an elusive figure both to his son and to the economic life of his community.

The song has two central images, the bright-leafed cocoa trees and the chocolate bar left out to melt in the summer sun. At first we think that the father is showing the boy through the grove of trees. By the end of the song we have to question that assumption. Apparently the boy is alone, looking at a book with pictures of trees.

The child feels great guilt about the melted chocolate, but again we find our assumption is incorrect. It is the father who left the bar there. Turning to accept what is presumably a drink, he laid the chocolate, a gift for his son, down on the white porch railing and forgot about it.

The recording history of this song leaves as acrid a taste as scorched chocolate. Danny French, Hunter's partner in Dodd Hall, refused to sing it, and the song became a major factor in their breakup—a split the bitterness of which can perhaps been seen as "real-life" evidence of the emotional difficulties faced by men when they have been raised in a father-less landscape.

—Joan P. Malcolm, " 'Father, I Want To Kill You': Paternal Images in Contemporary Rock Lyrics," *Popular Culture Quarterly*, 3 (1989), p. 18.

Chapter Nineteen

When she had first seen it nearly twenty years ago, the Hunters' house had taken Krissa's breath away. It did again.

She was no longer impressed by the size. She was now used to the large houses of Ramsey Hill, and her own house was bigger than the Hunters'. Nor was she awed by the beauty of the neighborhood, whose sloping green lawns and deep shade trees gave the homes a more restful feel than the briskness of Ramsey Hill.

What was marvelous about this house was its authenticity. It was all real. The sideboards, the breakfronts, the tea tables, and the chests were superlative pieces, adorned with fine veneer and detailed inlay work. Many of them, Quinn told her later, had passed down through his family, having been made in Baltimore. Nineteenth-century Baltimore craftsmen had drawn inspiration from Philadelphia, so their work had more rigor and heft than what had been made in New York at the time.

Except for the seats on the dining room chairs, no two pieces of upholstered furniture were covered with the same fabric because, Krissa realized, none of them had ever been reupholstered at the same time. Barbara Hunter did not redecorate; redecorating was too *nouveau*. When something became intolerably shabby, Mrs. Hunter had had it redone, choosing a crewel, a dot, a stripe, a flame stitch in the colors already in the room. The various fabrics all blended together in graceful compromise.

The house made sense. The little tassels hanging from the keys of the bowfront glass vitrines weren't ornamental; they were there to keep the keys from getting lost. The inviting pile of books and spill of notecards on the open secretary was not an artfully purchased, carefully arranged collection. They were part of the Hunters' daily lives.

This look was the goal of many designers Krissa worked for. That's why they had her do crazy things like upholster a sofa with the wrong side of the fabric out. They wanted the fabric to look faded, the house lived in. That was absurd. The way to make a house look lived in was to live in it; the traditional decor of the Hunters' house came because the Hunters had had tradition.

Jewel was waiting for them in the kitchen. She was a wiry black woman perhaps in her late fifties, although it was very hard to tell. She hugged Quinn and greeted Krissa warmly, claiming to remember her well. "You sure did break that boy's heart."

"I know," Krissa agreed. She didn't mind Jewel saying that. At least someone in this house had been on his side. "But I'm here now."

"That's true," Jewel conceded, and the two women exchanged a look. *We will help him through this.*

The kitchen was quite different from the rooms in the front of the house. Everything about it was worn and inefficient. The narrow wooden cabinets dated from the thirties, Krissa guessed, and the stove and refrigerator had probably been bought during Quinn's childhood. There was no microwave or trash compactor. The table was chipped enamel.

In all the restored houses of Ramsey Hill, the kitchens were where the most money had been spent. They were beautiful and convenient, with brass hardware and hand-painted tiles. It was where the family lived. Not here. In this house, the family had lived in the formal rooms. The kitchen was for the maid.

As Quinn had predicted, Jewel had indeed sent someone to the grocery store, and her ideas of how to feed four boys coincided exactly with the ideas of those four boys themselves. There were two-liter bottles of Coke and Pepsi, pillowy bags of potato chips, plain and crab-flavored; Oreos and Fig Newtons; pulverized, processed, nitrate-filled lunch meats, and spongy, white bread—all the gorgeous junk food that was never served in their own home.

While the boys stormed their way through these provisions, Quinn and Krissa sat down with Jewel, who knew a lot more about how things were done than Quinn did. Today was Sunday. The funeral would be on Wednesday. There did not need to be an event at the funeral home Tuesday night, but people would expect to come back to the house after the services.

Tomorrow Quinn would need to put a notice in the paper, visit the funeral home, meet with the minister, talk to the cemetery people. Krissa and Jewel would hold down things at home, answering the phone and getting ready for perhaps as many as eighty people to come to the house afterward.

A lumpy mattress in the principal guest room left Krissa sleeping even less than her usual five hours, but she was happy to be up early to plan how to entertain in someone else's home. She went through the dining room and the pantry, opening all the cabinets and drawers to see what the Hunters had.

Everything was the answer. Clearly they entertained a lot. There were boxes and boxes of glasses, red wine glasses, white wine glasses, old-fashioned glasses, and cocktail glasses. There were sixty-nine glass luncheon plates and almost as many glass dessert plates. There were three large coffee urns for brewing coffee in the kitchen, two beautiful silver services for pouring it in the dining room. There were chafing dishes and platters, a superb collection of antique glass bowls in ruby, cobalt, and pine. There were hand-painted china plates, cookie baskets, and candy dishes.

Krissa found herself planning the menu around the

serving dishes. A pale green dip, either avocado or spinach, would gleam in the emerald bowl. Chocolate petit-fours would pick up the brown flecks on the spray of lilies that decorated the large oval platter. The bride's basket of silver and cranberry glass would be piled with snowy meringues. As she lined the dishes up on the dining room table, she knew that she was being as disrespectful as her children. The Hunters hadn't died so that she could play with their dishes.

> *For many blue-collar kids, rock music seems like the only ticket out. Was that true for you?*
>
> No. I was certainly blue collar. My sister and I grew up on the Mesabi Iron Range in northern Minnesota. My father was killed from a blast in the mines. But I was already at Princeton when Dodd Hall started. That's about as far off the Range as you can get.
>
> If we want to talk about rock as a ticket out, it's my former partner, Mr.—excuse me—*Dr.* Hunter we should be talking about. He didn't have the economic repression that the rest of us struggled with, but emotional repression. He came from this lockjaw Establishment family. There was no authenticity, no passion, no honesty. Writing rock songs got him somewhere honest.
>
> Rock and roll is about taking risks, about being willing to risk everything. But then you get so famous, you have so much money, you don't want to lose it. So you get scared of risks. There was a point in 1978, when he and I couldn't stand each other anymore, when we just couldn't breathe together. He's the one who had the nerve to chuck it, not me. He may be an asshole doctor now, but there was a moment, during that one last concert, when he came closer than anyone in our generation to the real defiance that should be behind rock and roll. He didn't self-destruct; he just took a stand.
>
> Why are we talking about this? It's boring. It's history.

—Dennis Eugenen, "The *Rolling Stone* Interview: Danny French," *Rolling Stone*, May 1992, p. 42.

For next three days Quinn was like a man sleep-walking. That was the only way Krissa could describe it. He did everything he was supposed to do. He sent a notice to the paper, met with the minister, and made arrangements at the cemetery. He never seemed over-whelmed by the amount to be done or frustrated at the many details. He never grew depressed or angry. In fact he never reflected any emotion. It wasn't Quinn who was systematically undertaking a son's final duties. It was a robot, a zombie. Quinn had put himself into emotional cold storage.

He never went anywhere without at least one of the boys. Curt did his homework in the car while Quinn was in the funeral home. Brian pushed a cart around the liquor store. Patrick played one of the church pi-anos while Quinn met with the minister. Monday eve-ning he took all four to his favorite place for cheese steaks. Tuesday they went for crab cakes. He showed them where Memorial Stadium had been, he drove them to the new baseball field at Camden Yards. He played father . . . so that he wouldn't have to think about having been a son.

After the funeral on Wednesday, Krissa watched as he greeted his parents' friends, shaking their hands, accepting condolences, gesturing them toward the bar. He had arranged to have a suit brought up from his home in Washington, and it was a jewel of men's ap-parel. Made of the softest wool in the darkest gray, it fit him beautifully, the vest gathering his shirt close to his lean chest, the jacket gliding across his shoulders, the trousers breaking perfectly. He had threaded the gold chain of his grandfather's pocket watch through a buttonhole in his vest, and the engraved gold of his cufflinks occasionally glinted from beneath the ele-gantly rolled hem of his sleeve. He looked splendid, a man with a great tailor and no inner life whatsoever.

What was going to wake him up? After everyone had left, he took the boys out for pizza.

She and Jewel stayed home to clean up. It was the kind of work Krissa loved, handling beautiful things, handwashing all the silver and china in fresh, hot suds, drying them with the linen towels that she had found stored in the base of the breakfront. The towels were old, deliciously soft and free of lint. Each was labeled in scrolling hand-embroidered letters of now faded blue thread. Scrupulously Krissa used the "china" towel for the china, the "silver" for the silver, the "crystal" for the crystal, and time and again she heard herself asking Jewel where something went.

What did it matter? So what if the Gorham silver was in the place usually given to the Reed and Barton? Barbara Hunter was never going to look for them again. This gathering had been the house's final song. Never again would these dishes be used on these tables.

But still it felt important to Krissa, a tribute one woman ought to pay to another. You put her belongings back in their place. You used her towels as she would have wanted them to be used. Her being dead didn't change that.

Quinn wasn't the only one who had been determined not to reflect or feel anything these last few days. Krissa realized now why she had insisted on preparing all the food herself, even though Jewel and Quinn had urged her to call his mother's usual caterer. As long as she was cooking and measuring and calculating portion sizes, she could hide from the pain of two unexpected, unnecessary deaths. This was what she always did, kept busy so she wouldn't have to feel. When she would see other women sitting at the edge of the baby pool, happy with their husbands, she would plan bike-trip birthday parties and Cub Scout cookouts, and she would be so busy that she wouldn't have to think about the fact that she had nothing to say to her husband.

But now, surrounded by the soothing grace of these beautiful objects, she let the door open a little. She had only met Barbara Hunter twice. She didn't understand her. She probably wouldn't have respected her if she had. But Barbara Hunter was another woman and she was Quinn's mother. Therefore she was important.

And Krissa grieved her death.

The house was not quiet until well after midnight. After the pizza, Quinn had taken the boys to a video arcade where he showered them with tokens as if he were riding on a Mardi Gras float. So their day had consisted of rigidly correct behavior at the funeral followed by overweening indulgence, and they were wild.

When they were at last all settled, Brian, Curt, and Patrick asleep, and the more wakeful Adam with a book in front of him, Krissa went down the hall and knocked on Quinn's door. He called out for her to come in.

His room was still that of a prep-school boy. The *World Book Encyclopedia* was on the shelves, the volumes pushed back to make room for the lacrosse and tennis trophies. On the desk was a picture of him and some friends on a boat, then a bigger picture of just the boat. There was nothing to indicate that this glowing-haired boy had grown up to lead one of the most influential rock bands of the seventies and then had become a surgeon.

Krissa had often wondered what he was like as a doctor, what it would be like to be his patient. The touch of his hands would be deft and professional, his manner unhurried and assured. He did not wear a white coat in his office, he had told her, just one of his quiet ties knotted over one of his elegant, understated shirts.

"Do you turn back the cuffs?" she had asked, curious as to what it would be like to have his knowing and trained hands on her body, searching for information about what was hidden beneath the skin. Onstage he and Danny had always rolled up their sleeves. For such leanly built men, they both had powerful forearms.

"I have to," he had answered her question about his sleeves. "I wash my hands so much. I should break down and buy some shirts that don't have French cuffs, but I can't bring myself to."

So the Quinn Hunter patient would sit on his examining table, feeling those sensitive fingers probing her knee while watching the tightening of the clean strong muscles in his forearms.

"Do you ever go to bed with any of your patients?" she had asked, only half-joking.

"My God, no. Never."

At the moment he was sitting up in the bed, his chest bare and a pad of paper lying on the blankets. The bedside lamp was on and the dusting of hair on his chest gleamed as the light caught the lean, trimly muscular lines of his arms. He moved over and patted the space next to him.

She sat down. "What are you doing?"

"I'm supposed to be making lists, but I find myself working on that story that was tormenting me last week. I don't have it with me so I'm writing out what I remember."

"Is that productive? Recopying it from memory?"

"No," he said simply. "Not in the least." He put the paper on the nightstand. "Thank you for all your help today. People couldn't stop talking about the food. It was wonderful."

"Did you eat any of it?"

He paused. "I don't remember. I don't seem to be operating at full steam here."

"You looked pretty enough."

He made a face. Krissa knew that he dressed well—and she thought he dressed better than any man she knew—not because he was vain, but because he was strongly sensuous. He liked the feel of well-cut, well-made clothes. Only marginally did he care what he looked like in them.

"I don't think it has sunk in," he said, "that they are dead. Whenever I couldn't remember someone's name this afternoon, I started looking for Mother. Yesterday, when I was trying to figure out how much liquor we'd need, I'd want to ask Dad who always knows things like that."

He was still using the present tense when he spoke of them. "It didn't really hit me either," she said. "Not until I was putting away your mother's silver."

"Did you put it away? I meant to tell you to pack up any of it that you might want and take it home with you. You like things like that, don't you?"

She adored them. But she wasn't going to take any of it.

Before she could say so, he went on. "Look at this." He reached for the nightstand again. From the little pile of keys and change he had emptied from his pockets, he took a small manila envelope, the kind with a clasped opening across the narrow edge. "The funeral director gave me Mother's jewelry back." He opened the envelope and shook the contents into his hand, tilting it toward the lamp.

Starry light burst from his palm, sparkling from the diamonds set in a pair of earrings, a pendant, and an engagement ring. The glittering gold chain from the pendant spilled down over the side of his browned hand, slithering down his wrist.

"There are four stones here," he said. "All about a carat to a carat and a half. I was thinking that each of the boys could take one, and then when they got engaged, they'd have the stones and wouldn't have to—"

"Quinn, no. You can't give the boys diamonds."

"Why not? What else am I going to do with them?"

They should go to family. "I don't know. But you can't give them to the boys."

"Would you at least take the pearls? You don't have any, do you? I've never seen you wear them."

Krissa did have "pearls." They were fake, so horribly fake that they deserved only to be called white beads.

"Buy me a string for my birthday if you must," she told him, "but don't give me your mother's. That's not right."

"Then what is right? What am I going to do with all this stuff?" For the first time since he had learned of his parents' death, he sounded exasperated. He was at last feeling something. "I don't know, maybe Danny's right. Maybe I should sell everything and give all the money to the homeless."

"Don't do anything for a while," she advised. "Decide right now that you aren't going to make any decisions about the house and the personal property for six months." It was hard to know what he ought to do. It seemed like a tragedy to break up this lovely collection of possessions, but he said he lived in the tiniest of houses. He had no need for more furniture and dishes. "Why don't you pay Jewel to take care of the house for six more months and not worry until then? Don't even think about it?"

"Okay, but what's going to change in six months?" He flipped the chain back into his palm and funneled the jewelry into the envelope. He did up the clasp. "If I put these in the safety deposit box tomorrow, they'll probably never see the light of day again. The Johns Hopkins Endowment Association will have to figure out what to do with them after I die."

That did seem like a shame.

Quinn wanted her sons to have his mother's diamonds. Krissa watched as he laid the envelope back on the nightstand. Each diamond made a little bump in the stiff manilla paper. He knew that such things ought to go to family. Was that what he was saying, that he thought of her children as his family?

They had not spoken of the future, and this was not the way to do it. They couldn't rely on symbols, his giving family heirlooms to her sons. They needed to be open and clear. But this was not the time to do it, not when he was exhausted and numb.

Krissa too was tired, but she was no longer numb. She had let herself grieve for his parents, and she knew why she had been able to—because she loved him.

When he had first come to see her, she had been

terrified, thinking of him as a magnet of fire that she would be powerless to resist. And so he had been. But the flames of loving him were not consuming her, turning her into the weightless gray ash that she had been so many years ago. Now she was warm and alive. The flames were orange-gold and she was dancing.

She could now answer her question. What would wake him up? What would make him able to face his parents' death? This would. Her love. She leaned forward and kissed him.

For a moment he didn't understand. But she let her lips linger on his, soft and open. She felt him stir. One hand came to her shoulder. The other slipped around her waist, and when she broke the kiss to look at him, she saw the cool gray blankness in his eyes begin to churn. He was becoming himself again.

With joy she kissed him again, a deep, warm kiss, vibrantly sexual, pulsing with life. The world dissolved into a dizzying whirl. Everything was mist and fog, smoke and wind, everything except the certainty and the knowingness of this kiss.

He drew back. "What about the boys?" he whispered.

She shook her head. "They won't roam around a strange house."

She now understood why she had been unwilling to sleep with him before. It did have to do with Brian and his girlfriend, Pam, but not with the example that Krissa was setting for them, but with the example they were setting for her.

Brian and Pam were not sure how committed they were to each other. Sex was frighteningly new to them, dizzingly important. Had her child not been at this stage, Krissa might have been able to sleep with a man without committing herself to him, without the stakes seeming as high as they seemed for Brian. But her decision had taken on all the consequences of Brian, and like Brian, she had not been sure of her commitment.

She was now. She loved Quinn. She had loved once before in her life, and it had been him she had loved.

She might love a third time, but only if it was again him. As long as he lived ... no, as long as she lived, for why should his death change this? As long as she lived, she might feel warmly about other men, she might sleep with some of them, but this love was Quinn's alone.

But as limitless, as bountiful, as was her love, there was a limit to her commitment. She would love him until she died, but she would not uproot her children for him. She would not take them from their home, their school, and above all, their father. She would not take them any farther from their father so that she could be with the man she loved.

The knowledge of this limit, the absolute certainty of it, brought peace. And although the rules of courtship demanded silence—for he had said nothing yet of love—she spoke, telling him all she thought and felt. In the past he had always been the one to speak. Starry images were his gift. She could not wreath her words with cinnamon-scented garlands. She could only speak simply. "I will never feel this way about any other man."

She did not worry about his response. He did not need to love her for her to love him; he only needed to be him. But she also knew that he did love her, that his silence sprang from their past. His love had once been a burden that she could not carry.

She went on. "I know you have not asked. I don't know if you want to or will, but I must tell you." No enticement of passion or devotion would ever lure her to take her sons out of Minnesota. "As much as I love you, my first duty is to them."

He moved over and held open the covers. She slipped in next to him, feeling against her breast and her legs, the warmth of his bare chest and the soft weight of his sweatpants. She was disappointed. She had assumed he was nude. Below the knotted waiststring of his sweatpants was a tantalizing pressure.

She ran her hands down his chest, unknotted the string, and loosened the waistband, sliding the pants down over his lean hips. The pants caught on his erection. He lifted them free, his hands tightening and closing over hers.

"No, no." His voice was low in her ear. "Don't try to be fair. Don't worry about me. Be selfish. Let me please you."

That sounded like heaven. Krissa lay back, burrowing luxuriously into the depths of the bed, stretching her arms up over her head, leaving her body open to him to do whatever he chose.

He brought his hands up to her face, his fingertips lighting on her cheekbones. A rippling wave of sensation danced across the softly padded bone; she couldn't imagine how human fingers produced such sensation. The little rippling beat descended over her cheeks, across her lips, down her throat, then, easing her nightgown open, it flowed waterfall-like down to her breasts.

"This is wonderful," she breathed.

"It comes from playing the piano every day." There was a smile in his voice. She couldn't see it on his face; she was mesmerized by the rippling of his tapering brown fingers on the rise of her breast. "No one can make love like a piano man."

Indeed.

Her nightgown was off. His mouth followed the path of his fingertips, from cheekbone to cheek, from chin to throat, from collarbone to breast. His hands were now open on her body, his palms hot and molding, finding the curves of her hips, the length of her thighs.

She was gasping. This was wonderful. Quinn was paying the most intimate attention to her body's wants and appetites. He noticed every gasp, shiver, and tightening, and he responded with more of whatever had pleased. His lovemaking was careful, crafted, and gallant. But it wasn't quite lovemaking. It was too perfect, too deliberate.

But how else could a man please a woman he didn't

know? How else did you make love to a woman you
didn't love?

But they did know each other. They did love each
other. And this should be as unique for him as it was
for her.

Even though his kiss was sliding down her body,
even though she could feel his thick hair brushing
against her ribs, her abdomen, even though her body
was singing out for what was about to come, she
stopped him.

He looked up, puzzled.

She took his face in her hands. "Tell me what you
are feeling."

This was what she had said to him when he had
believed he couldn't sing the songs on *Self-Chosen
Snares*. In the light of the bedside lamp she saw his
eyes darkening. He remembered. "Tell me how you
feel," she repeated.

He didn't answer; he didn't speak.

"Tell me."

A silent heat rose in his body; she could feel it, a
surging wave of honest passion, an energy far stronger
than learned courtliness.

"That night in your dressing room . . ." She ran her
hands up his arms, down his back. "Do you remember
that?"

The lips on hers were suddenly rough and urgent.
His body was pressing hers back, his legs moving between hers, forcing them apart. A hot shaking hand
low between their bodies, the slightest resistance followed by a strong stroke, and he was in her, his thrusting body propelled by uncontrolled fever, his
movements driven, his needs too insistent for rhythm
or grace. This was Quinn as she had never seen him,
perhaps as he had never seen himself. She gloried in
his passion, in his loss of self-control.

Suddenly gasping, he stopped, still encased in her,
his chest momentarily heavy on hers. "We can't . . . I
haven't . . ."

She understood. "It's all right. Really it is."

"No." His voice was ragged, uneven. "I can't." He pulled out, a swift liquid withdrawal, leaving behind a weighted, damp emptiness.

He fumbled for the nightstand, then remembered where he was, his boyhood room. He had to get out of bed and go into the bathroom for what he apparently carried in his shaving kit.

A moment later he was back. The delay had restored some measure of self-control. An arm circling her shoulders raised her up. He lay on his back, and his hands closed firmly on her hips, lifting her and then slowly easing her down on him, watching with narrow, hooded eyes as the most vital part of himself vanished into her body.

Krissa had been watching his face. Now she looked down to see the lamplight shining on her golden breasts, on the inwardly sweeping curve beneath her ribs, down to the coppery tangle of hair brushing close to the golden-brown hair of his body. She pressed her hand against her flat stomach, loving the idea of what was inside her.

He was stroking her shoulders and her arms, cupping her breasts, his own chest rising and falling in quick passion. "I do remember," he said. "That night in my dressing room, I do remember. You hated it, I know that. But for me, it was the best. It was everything, bringing the songs back to where they belonged, back to you. I loved you so much. I can't believe how much I loved you."

His hands were on her hips again and he was moving her. Her head was back, she could feel her hair cascading down her back. Then she felt one of his hands cupping her breast again, lifting it, his thumb rolling over the nipple as his penetration sought deeper and deeper inside her. The thumb gave way to the wetness of his tongue, to the sucking of his lips, his hand still holding the soft weight, lifting it to his mouth. She was weightless, boneless, unable to support herself. Quinn caught her, his arms supporting her, pulling her legs back around him, so that facing each other, breast to breast, kissing, they made love.

For a moment they remained like that, her legs over his, her head on his shoulder. Then he lay back, pulling her close in the narrow bed. She murmured something. She was too warm, too deliciously cocooned to speak. She couldn't remember when she had last felt so at peace and so fulfilled.

Suddenly the spell was broken. Quinn sat up. He flipped the covers off her, then reached over to the nightstand and bent the stem of the gooseneck lamp down toward her abdomen.

She was awake now. What was he doing? Looking for stretch marks? She watched, fascinated, as he parted her navel with his thumbs.

"This is a new level of sickness," she told him. "What's so interesting about my belly button?"

He squinted, peering more closely. "I don't get it. You don't have a scar here."

"A scar in my navel? Why would I have a scar in my navel?"

"If you had had a tubal ligation."

"A tubal—" Then she understood. "Is that what you thought? That I had had my tubes tied? No, it's just a safe time of month. I'm the most regular person on earth. But Quinn, why did you want to see the scar?"

He pushed the lamp away and covered her back up. "Last time I made love to you, I was a poet. Now I'm a surgeon. The idea of someone else working on you . . . I wanted to take a look."

"You can relax. Surgically, I am a virgin."

"Except for your episiotomies."

Krissa sat up. "I beg your pardon?" An episiotomy was the incision made during vaginal childbirth. It was not the first thing other people noticed about you.

"I shouldn't have said that, should I? I can't help it. I'm a physician, I notice." Then he made a face at her. "But you can drop the outrage act. You don't mind."

She didn't. "How many stitches did I have?"

"I didn't get that good a look." He reached for the lamp.

Krissa batted his hand away. "Sex is free. Pelvics I pay for."

"Ah, pelvics. I haven't done one of them since I was a resident. I was good at it. My fingers are so long." He waved his tapering digits. "There was another student, she was this very tiny woman, and her hands were so small, her fingers so short, that she really had a lot of trouble doing pelvics."

"There are people out there who revere their doctors, Quinn. They do not want to hear this."

"I know that. And I applaud those people. I like them. But I don't happen to see any of them at this particular moment, do I, Mrs.-150-cc's-of-Amoxicillan-250?"

"No, I guess you don't." She laughed with him. "But I don't get it. If you thought I had had my tubes tied, why the rubber?"

He looked down at her from the corner of his eyes; he was half smiling. "You've been out of circulation too long. Condoms aren't just about birth control anymore."

Oh. Of course. Krissa felt like an idiot. "But with me?" If she had a sexually transmitted disease, someone was going to have to do a lot more research on how these things were transmitted. She had quit having sex even with her own husband.

"With anyone," Quinn answered firmly. "It protects you as much—or more—than me. But my patients are the real issue. Whatever risks I might take for myself, I simply do not have the right to take for them, however infinitesimal Congress and the A.M.A. says the risk might be. I may not like it, but that's the way it is."

His right hand was lying on his chest, the palm and fingers lightly arched over his sternum. She had always thought of him as having a musician's hands, but these were now the hands of a surgeon, a healer. That's who he was now, a doctor.

She spoke lightly. "That's why you don't have anyone to leave those diamonds to. If you're ever going to have offspring, you'll have to rethink this policy of safe sex."

"That is undoubtedly true," he agreed. "What about yourself? Why haven't you had a tubal? Did the question just never come up?"

"Goodness, no. My o.b. suggested I do it when Patrick was born and then bugged me about it every year afterward. I guess I could never look at Patrick and stand the thought that he was my last baby."

Quinn lifted his head off the pillow. "Is that emotional wistfulness or"—now his voice grew cautious—"can you imagine scenarios in which you would be willing to have another baby?"

A year or two ago Krissa might not have known the answer to that, but now she did. Another baby, perhaps a little girl, Quinn's daughter . . . oh, yes, dear Lord, yes, she could imagine that. "I won't leave Minnesota, Quinn. I told you that."

"You're worried about my practice? Don't. I'm proud of having built it. I needed to prove to myself that I could do something without Danny. But now I've done it, and I don't have to stay with it forever."

Krissa took a breath. He was speaking so quickly, saying so much. She wanted to be sure that she understood it. "Are you saying that you'd leave Washington?"

"Yes. It's hard to believe that I couldn't find a decent practice in the Cities to affiliate with. Even if I couldn't, I don't view my specialty as a life sentence. I'm a licensed physician, and I don't care how much money I make. The Indian Health Service, just to give one example, would find that an appealing combination."

"You'd move to Minnesota?" Krissa's heart was singing. This wasn't possible. He couldn't be saying this. It was so amazing, so unlooked for, so undreamt of. "Have you really thought about it? It's such a big step. You can't change your whole life because I'm good in bed."

"Why not? And what's there to think about? It's really very simple. We want to be together. You can't move. I can."

Krissa pressed her hands to her cheeks. Everything about her was skating, swooping. She was flooded with silvery joy. Maybe he was right. Maybe it was that simple. Maybe the bad part was really and finally over, and it was now their turn for the happily-ever-after. Why shouldn't it be perfect from now on? Surely there was nothing left to go wrong.

Chapter Twenty

BALTIMORE, MARYLAND, MARCH 1993

On Thursday, the day after his parents' funeral, Quinn, the probate lawyer, and an I.R.S. agent went to the bank to inventory the safe deposit box. Quinn had doubted the need of the I.R.S. representative. His parents had had no stocks or securities, and indeed the safe deposit box had such untaxable valuables as the negatives for their wedding photos and two withered corsages. But their will was there. The lawyer glanced through it and shook his head.

"They never updated it since their marriage," he told Quinn. "You are 'any subsequent offspring,' and there's no provision for guardianship."

"That's hardly a problem, is it?"

"Not now. But if they'd died when you were a minor, since there's no other family, you could have ended up a ward of the State of Maryland and grown up in foster care."

Oh, lovely. How could any two people be so irresponsible, so unaware of their obligations to others? They had had their own safe little cocoon, the two of them, and they didn't give a damn about anyone else. They—

Quinn stopped himself. Surely at his age there wasn't much point in getting upset over not having a guardian.

Krissa wasn't at the house when he got back. She had decided to keep the boys out of school for another day and take them into Washington to see the museums and the monuments. They'd have to leave in the morning; the twins needed to get home for the quarterfinal round of the state hockey tournament. Quinn longed to go back with them. Now that he had decided to move to Minnesota, he wanted to do it instantly. But he had professional partners and civic commitments. He would close up his life in Washington systematically. He was not his father.

He sat down to work at the Queen Anne writing table in his parents' living room. It was a charming table, with graceful, curving legs. He had a drink at his elbow, but he couldn't help thinking that if this were Krissa's home, there would also be a little tray of cheese and a basket of golden-green pears. The cushions would have been freshly plumped. A fire would be in the fireplace, its glowing blaze warming the heavy brass andirons. That would have been nice.

He worked away in the lovely, cheerless room. Well after seven he heard the front door open. He dropped his pen and hurried out to greet what was now the closest thing he had to a family.

They all started talking at once.

"It was so cool, Quinn. You should have been there. All the moon stuff—"

"No, no. It was the Lindbergh plane. It was so amazing. It was so small. Can you imagine? Crossing the Atlantic—"

"—this film of the Hindenberg. It just like exploded—"

Obviously the boys had spent the day at the Air and Space Museum. "Did you get to the East Wing?" he asked Krissa. That had been the plan, for her to drop the boys off at Air and Space and spent the day gloriously by herself in the art museum. "What did you think of the building?"

She sighed and pushed her hair back from her face. "I spend too much time with men. I never made it out of Air and Space. I hate myself. My one chance to see some art by myself, and I'm ga-ga over the planes."

She was laughing at herself. Quinn longed to put his arms around her. And make her life such that she did have time to go to art museums.

The boys were still talking. Krissa held up her hand, silencing them. "You guys have to go upstairs and do your homework. That was the deal, remember?"

They groaned, but in more or less good order, trooped upstairs. Quinn took Krissa's arm, drawing her into the living room. "I have something for you." He pulled open the center drawer of the writing table and took out a velvet jeweler's case. He handed it to her.

"What is this?" She looked startled, then eased the case open. She gasped. "Oh, Quinn, they're beautiful." She lifted the long, double strand of perfectly matched pearls from the white satin bedding. "But I told you—"

"They aren't Mother's." These were better than his mother's, much better. "And you told me that I could buy you a strand for your birthday."

"But it's not my birthday. I was just talking. I didn't expect—"

"Well, too bad. Next time you should think before you speak." He took the pearls from her and stepping around her, fastened them around her neck. He had considered buying her a ring, but he had decided to wait until his timetable for moving was clearer. So he had bought pearls instead. *Pearls are always right*, his mother had said.

She was still shaking her head. "It feels like you're paying me for last night."

But her hand had instantly gone to the pearls, her fingertips savoring their warm luster. She loved them. She couldn't help it.

"Oh, no. Even I couldn't afford sex if this were the price. I'm honoring last night, not buying it."

And I'm showing my dad. Look at these pearls. They're better than what he bought. And he was spending inherited money. This money I made.

Quinn stepped back abruptly, stung by the unpleasantness of his own thought. His parents had just *died*. He shouldn't think that way about them. He went over to the sideboard where a crystal decanter of sherry sat. He poured Krissa a glass. He tried to focus on her. She did look tired. "Sit down, drink your sherry, and fondle your new toys."

She curled up on the camelback sofa, her legs tucked under her, her cheek against the cushions. Quinn sat back down at the writing desk and picked up his pen.

"What are you doing?" she asked.

"Writing thank-you notes for the flowers at the funeral."

"You are? I thought thank-you notes were like the first seats on the lifeboats, the property of women and children. Men don't write thank-you notes."

"I do."

"Then don't let me stop you. I spend the first week of every year forcing the kids to write thank-you notes for Christmas. The idea of a man writing a thank-you note voluntarily has great appeal."

One of his mother's friends had clipped all the cards from the flower arrangements. Quinn picked up another one of the small florist envelopes, pulled out the card, wrote a note, looked up the address in his mother's little book, and then addressed the envelope. The next card had been put back in the envelope backward so he first saw Elizabeth Rhodes's description of the flowers, "carnations, yellow and bronze, with greens." Quinn turned the card over to see who had sent the flowers. There was a single word on the card.

Danny.

Danny? It wasn't possible. His parents must have known someone with that name. Dan Burgess. Yes, this was Dan Burgess.

No, it wasn't. Mr. Burgess never went by "Danny" and his wife would have signed the card for both of them.

But how? Danny sending flowers to his parents' funeral? It was inconceivable.

"Krissa, come here." Quinn held the card out to her. She looked at it and blinked. Yes, she was surprised too.

But she spoke mildly. "Chris Oberlin must have told him."

"Wait a minute. Is that all you find surprising? That he knew? How can we even be sure it's him? What on earth would prompt him to do a thing like this?"

"He has been bugging me all winter for news of you."

"He has?"

"If you're not sure it's him, call the florist." Krissa picked up the envelope the card had been in. It had the name and phone of a Baltimore florist.

"It's after six. They'll be closed."

"But someone might be working late."

Quinn dialed and the owner of the shop answered. Quinn described the carnations, saying that they knew several people of that name. Could the store provide any more information so that the family could write a proper acknowledgment? The owner said he would check. In a moment he came back on the line, saying that a wire service order had been placed by one Danny French with a Hispanic-named flower shop in New York. "He put it on his MasterCard."

Quinn covered the phone and spoke to Krissa. "He put it on his MasterCard."

"So?"

"He has a MasterCard?"

"Of course. I mean I didn't know it was a MasterCard, but he travels a lot, giving lectures to raise money. He has to have credit cards."

She was probably right. But for all Quinn had heard of Danny's life, it would be surprising if the man had a toothbrush.

Yet he had sent flowers. He had picked up the phone, had taken his MasterCard out of his wallet, had spoken Quinn's name. He must have been thinking, remembering ...

The florist was clearing his throat. "I remember this

order. It came in with a message that my girls didn't think was appropriate. I know they were talking about not including it. I guess they didn't."

There had been no message on the card, just Danny's name. "What was it?"

"We know the Hunters," the florist answered. "I don't think the family should be subjected to this."

"I'm not family," Quinn lied, unable to remember if he had given his name at the start of the call. "I'm just a friend, helping out. I will keep it from the family if it is that unpleasant." He tried to sound adequately prim.

"Well ... it wasn't really our place to delete it so I guess ..." The florist took a breath. " 'They were s,h,i,t,s,' " he spelled, " 'but what the hell.' "

At least Quinn had the presence of mind to hang up before he burst out laughing. What a thing to send to a funeral. What a *perfect* thing to send to his parents' funeral.

Krissa was staring at him. Unable to speak, he shook his head.

She waited a minute. "Okay, what is it?"

He took a breath and tried to tell her. Halfway through he put his head down on the desk, laughing again.

"It's not that funny," he said at last. "But the truth is they were shits. They were horrible people. They were selfish, they had no sense of any responsibility to anyone but one another ... including me. I wish I'd said this years ago. Danny's right. They were shits, and I'm so goddamn angry with them that I can't see straight."

For three days he had been fighting this, his fury at them. "How could they be so self-absorbed, so utterly out of touch with reality that they could get in a car after my father had had three Bloody Marys and not put on their seatbelts? Nothing got through to them. Nothing penetrated those lies they surrounded themselves with. Part of me wishes that I never had made any money, just to see if they would have finally gotten it if we had all gone bankrupt.

"You know what's always bugged me?" Now that he had started, he couldn't stop. "That I couldn't imagine them having sex. Here they were, they were supposed to be so in love and I could never see how sex fit into it."

"Quinn, no one can imagine their parents having sex," Krissa remarked. "First you think of sex as too disgusting. Then you think of your parents as too disgusting."

"You may be right, but there's more than that in this case. There really is." Quinn could see this now. "Sex is a life force. It's invigorating, and there was something so airless, so suffocating about their love."

His parents had nutured their love in a little hothouse. Didn't they believe that it could survive in the real world? True passion would survive a man not being home at five o'clock every night. Just yesterday Krissa had told him that she would love him to the end of her days, but she wouldn't disrupt her children's lives for him. Was her love for him any weaker because she also had obligations to others? No.

His parents must have been afraid. Quinn had never seen that before.

"I'm going to call that son of a bitch," he heard himself say. It was out of the blue, that thought, but it was the right thing to do. He was sure of it. "Do you have his number?"

Krissa obviously knew that there was only one person on earth he would call a "son of a bitch." She set down her drink and came across the room to dial the phone. She handed it to him.

A light female voice answered. "The Colony Shelter."

"May I please speak to Danny French?"

"May I tell him who's calling?"

What was this? A bank? "No, you may not." Quinn felt exuberant, giddy. Last night he had made love to Krissa again, and now he was about to speak to Danny again. "Since when does he care who he talks to?"

He heard the phone being set down on a hard surface and then the click of footsteps walking away. Apparently the shelter did not have a hold button on its phone. He had to wait some time, and then he heard another set of footsteps, the footsteps of a man.

"Yo, unidentified stranger, what can I do for you?"

It was Danny. Quinn would have known his voice anywhere. He could be on his deathbed, sightless, full of morphine and pain, and he would know Danny's voice.

He kicked aside the sharp surge of emotion. And he broke the vow he had made fifteen years ago in Madison Square Garden. "Yes, they were shits, but they were *my* shits."

There was a sharp intake of breath, the briefest of pauses. "Well, well, if it isn't Dr. Knee, the bereaved Dr. Knee."

"You scared the florist. He wouldn't print your message."

"But it seems to have reached you."

"We had to call the shop. You didn't sign your whole name. I had no idea who it was."

"My apologies," Danny drawled. But Quinn knew, he knew as surely as he knew anything, that Danny's dark eyes were dancing.

"I read your *Playboy* interview. You're getting generous in your old age."

"If I remember correctly, I called you an asshole doctor."

"That's no more than the truth ... except I'm not a proctologist."

"Now that's what I don't get. Why knees? Why do you want to spend your life working on knees? Who cares about knees?"

"People whose hurt, that's who. I could ask you 'why the homeless,' but I won't. I'm afraid you'd answer."

Danny's laugh was quick, sharp. "I would. How long are you going to go on being a jerk about the song rights?"

"Forever. I don't want them to be used to peddle running shoes, and I think the shelter movement is shortsighted. Build some affordable housing, that's what those women want for their kids, not another shelter."

"Okay." Danny must have heard all these arguments before. He knew that debate was pointless. "As long as we are criticizing other people's work, I didn't think much of that story set in Vermont."

Quinn sat up. "Oh?"

"You've got no business writing about places like that. New York, Philly, even that one set in Charleston, that worked better than I ever thought it would, but Vermont, you're no country boy."

New York and Philadelphia were where Quinn set most of his short stories, and he hadn't particularly liked the one set in Vermont either.

Danny went on. "And what brought on that one set in Virginia with the italics and elipses? You must have been reading Tom Wolfe."

Quinn was amazed. The Wolfe influence was subtle in that story. He had edited most of it out. To pick up on it, someone had to be reading carefully and thinking hard. Danny apparently had been. "It was fun to write, but it didn't quite work. I was surprised they printed it."

"They shouldn't have." Danny was his old blunt self. "Why haven't you collected them in a book?"

"I don't need the money."

"Then give the copyright to the Colony. We always need money."

Quinn had to laugh. "You never give up, do you? Get it through your brain—I am not interested in your shelter."

"Then what about a night basketball league, opening a rec center from ten to one a couple of nights a week so kids have some place to go besides the streets. Organized sports, that's right up your alley. Would you pay for that?"

"Oh, I suppose." He was being worked by a master, Quinn could tell that. "All right, sure, I'll fund that."

"And you aren't going to make us wait for the copyright thing, are you? We could get this thing started right away if you can cough up the cash."

"Call Chris. Tell him what you need. He'll cut a check."

"Hell, I don't know what we need. I just thought of it now. But we'll name the league after you if you want."

"Don't you dare."

"Or we could name it after Jim and Frank."

"Jim and Frank?" Quinn didn't know who Danny was talking about.

"Oh come on, you know. Jim and Frank. Mr. Laurence and Mr. Churchill, those guys."

Quinn blinked. The James Laurence and Frank Churchill Foundation gave away pianos. So far, no one, not one single person had ever traced it back to Quinn. "How did you know about that?"

"Because I still have most of my marbles. All the other shelters in town were getting used Chickering uprights, and we got three new Baldwins. It didn't take all the smarts in the world to guess who was the one person who would do that."

So all this time Danny had known the pianos were from him. "Do you keep them tuned?"

"Oh, come on," Danny scoffed. "Do you know what it costs to keep a piano in tune?"

Quinn knew. He also knew this man. He knew how he avoided answering questions. "Do you keep them in tune?"

"Yes."

Suddenly Quinn heard a commotion coming from Danny's end of the call. Danny muttered some excuse and Quinn could hear him talking to people in the room. "Can it wait ... I'm on the phone ... In a minute, I'll be there in a minute."

"It sounds like you're needed," Quinn said.

"Shit, I'm always needed. This is not the calmest place."

"I can imagine."

"Don't be so sure. We can be pretty weird, beyond normal human imagination. I'm coming, I'm coming." The last was to someone in the room with him. Then he spoke to Quinn again. "So you've taken up with my sister again. What's the story there?"

"There is no story. At least not one you are going to hear." Quinn had to raise his voice; more and more people were talking to Danny on his end.

"Oh, come on—" Danny stopped, needing to speak to people around him again. "Two minutes." His voice was sharp. "Can't I have two minutes to have a personal conversation?"

"Apparently not," Quinn said. "Go deal with it."

"Oh, all right . . ." Danny did not want to hang up.

"Go on, man, do what you have to," Quinn told him. "It's your job."

"Okay, okay. But your voice . . . you still sound like yourself."

Quinn's heart turned over. Their voices. This was what he wanted, what he had wanted for years and years, to sing with Danny again, to feel those powerful songs welling up from his body, to have every breath rich and manly, involving every sense so you were smelling and tasting the song. That's what he wanted, that's what he had always wanted, more than anything, he had wanted to sing with Danny again.

"You too," he said. "You still sound like yourself."

The noise in Danny's office had crescendoed, and he had to go. "Good-bye, Quinn."

It was the first time either had used the other's name. "Good-bye, Danny."

Chapter Twenty-one

MINNEAPOLIS, MINNESOTA, MARCH 1993

The score was tied one-one from the opening moments of the quarterfinal game. Edina, the suburban powerhouse favored to win the championship, was held off from more scoring by the scrappy city kids. The city team, the one the Aarnesson twins skated for, was such an underdog that simply taking the game into overtime would be a triumph.

That was clearly what was going to happen. The tension in the crowd eased in the game's closing seconds as everyone prepared for the drama of sudden death overtime. Coming around the net, the city right defense man picked up the puck. He saw his left man breaking along the boards. He tried a cross ice pass. Edina's center picked it off and took it in to score.

The Edina team exploded, skating madly for one another, their arms pumping in relief and joy. The other fans sat in numb silence. They had been so close. And then in an instant, when no one was really looking, it was all gone.

"Oh, guys," Krissa sighed. She put her arm around Patrick and rubbed her hand along Adam's leg. The twins were on the ice, their heads down. At least they were forwards. They couldn't blame themselves for the final play. "What a disappointment."

And now Quinn won't come.

As important as this game was, Quinn simply couldn't come. It was two days after his parents' funeral. He hadn't been in his office for a week. All the procedures he had canceled to be in Baltimore were now sitting on top of everything postponed the week before because of equipment failure.

But he had promised the twins that if they won this game, nothing would keep him away from the semis and the finals. Krissa had believed him.

The rest of the weekend was awful. Everyone was dispirited about the loss. All four boys had tons of homework to catch up on after a week out of school, and Krissa herself was way behind in her work. The tape on the answering machine had run out, completely filled with calls from frantic designers. Where was she? Mrs. Hume was expecting those chairs this weekend. Didn't she know that that rolled-arm sofa was for one of the Pillsburys?

It depressed her. But she had to work. Since Quinn had started coming, she simply hadn't been working as hard as usual. She had been happier, much happier, but the state of her checkbook said that she couldn't afford to be happy.

Sunday before supper the boys went into their usual pre-spring-break mope. They had seen their friends that afternoon. They had heard about the trips which other families had planned for spring break—Florida, Cancun, or Jackson Hole.

"How come we never go away?" Adam complained as they were sitting down to supper.

They had just been to Baltimore, the little ingrates. "You're going up to the Range," Krissa reminded him. "You and Brian will go the first week. Then Curt and Pat will go."

Or you could all go together and I could go to Flor-ida, Cancun, or Jackson Hole with Quinn.

But she couldn't do that. She'd never make the boys stay with her mother unless she would be there to deflect the criticism.

"You guys know we can't afford to do the kind of traveling other families can," Krissa said as she ladled a creamy leek soup into a tureen.

"Quinn could pay for it," Brian muttered.

Krissa spun. Dripping ladle still in hand, she glared at Brian. That was utterly unacceptable.

And he knew it. He ducked his head sheepishly.

But Patrick thought it was a great idea. "Oh, *yeah,* then we could—"

Brian cuffed him across the arm. "Will you shut up?"

Another wonderful moment in the life of the Aarnesson family.

Krissa wiped up the drips from the ladle, sprinkled some chopped parsley on the white soup and set the earthenware tureen on the table. There was a crisp green salad and a loaf of French bread. It was a light, pretty meal, wasted on her foul-tempered children.

She went to take the phone off the hook as she always did during Sunday night supper. Just as she reached it, it rang. She was going to unplug it anyway.

"Oh, Mom, *no.*" Curt's plea was agonized.

"All right. I'll take a message. But only a message." She picked up the receiver and said hello.

"So did you tell that jerk to call me?"

It was Danny. She signaled to the boys to start eating. Curt protested, outraged. If someone had been calling him . . .

Now Krissa glared at him as moments before she had glared at his twin. It didn't work this time. Curt glared right back.

She turned to answer Danny. "If you mean Quinn, I didn't. And you made the first step. You sent the flowers."

"But that didn't mean I wanted to talk to him."

She had tried to warn Quinn about this. Danny didn't have one-to-one relationships with individuals anymore. The other members of the Colony adored him, but he was their leader, and they his disciples. His compassion for the homeless was not a simple bond between equals. He loved them *en masse* for their human vulnerability, their neediness. Danny had given his heart and his spirit to his work. With individual people, he was short-tempered and inflexible. Quinn had to understand that.

"I'm a grown man," Quinn had said when she had raised the issue. "I can take care of myself."

And you, Krissa told herself, *are a grown woman. You aren't competing with Danny for Quinn's attention.* That's why she was being such a bitch this weekend. She could cope with the twins' team losing in the quarterfinals. What she was having trouble with was the way Quinn had looked when he hung up from talking to Danny. Was a five-minute phone conversation enough to put such stars in Quinn's eyes that he'd only be able to see Danny?

She shoved such thoughts aside. "There's nothing wrong in wanting to reach out to him," she said to Danny. "You might both be happier if you made peace with one another."

"I don't feel like my task on earth is to make myself 'happy.'" Danny's voice was sarcastic. "And we've done fine all this time. Why should he think that anything's changed?"

"You did almost die this fall, that has— "

"Die?" Danny interrupted impatiently. "Will you lighten up on that? How many times do I have to tell you I wasn't going to die? There wasn't a chance."

Not a chance? He had been in a coma, his fate had been entirely in the hands of other people. Krissa shook her head. When it came to admitting reality, he was as bad as Quinn's parents.

"Have you ever heard of a guy named Robert Marcel?" he suddenly asked.

"No."

"He's a big contributor, and I went to see—"

Krissa stopped listening. The ups and downs of the Colony's finances did not interest her. She looked over her shoulder to check on the boys. Brian and Curt had ganged up to pick on their younger brothers. It didn't happen often, but it was not a pretty sight. Patrick was almost in tears.

Vaguely she heard Danny's voice. ". . . and he said that with lessons, I could get back in shape."

"Lessons?" Danny wanted to get back in shape?

The only physical activity he had ever done was splitting wood. "What kind of lessons?"

"Voice lessons. Didn't I just tell you that he was a vocal coach?"

"Voice lessons? Danny, *why*?"

Oh God, this was all she needed. Back in January Quinn had made her propose to Danny the ridiculous idea of a reunion concert—*Dodd Hall: Back to the Garden,* some such nonsense like that. At least Danny had shown some remnant of sanity. He had complained that his voice was a mess, that he didn't have time to get coaching . . . and now, lo and behold, after that five-minute phone conversation, he too had stars in his eyes.

She wasn't sure what to say. Part of her wanted to let the pair of them rot in their own mess. "You aren't thinking of—"

"I'm not thinking of anything. I was seeing him about money for this stupid kitchen. He brought it up."

Sure. Krissa really believed that. Technically this Marcel person might have brought the subject up, but that was because Danny had gone there determined that he would. A determined Danny was not to be inflicted lightly on ordinary mortals.

He kept denying the importance of the lessons, even though Krissa wasn't arguing with him. She stayed quiet, listening with a sinking heart, knowing what he wanted her to do—to tell Quinn.

For two days she considered not telling Quinn. The reunion concert seemed like such a bad idea to her, so really and truly awful. Danny and Quinn couldn't possibly want the same thing. Danny had organized his whole life to avoid making any commitment to an individual, even in friendship, and of course, their intense friendship was what Quinn wanted to reclaim.

But in the end she knew she had to tell him. She didn't trust her own motives for keeping silent. Did she resent the concert idea simply because it felt like Danny was taking Quinn away from her?

So when Quinn called that night, she told him that Danny had started work with a vocal coach.

A long, long pause came over the phone line. "What does that mean?" he said at last.

"I don't know." She plucked irritably at a spot on her cuff. "It's hard enough to be Danny French's sister. I refuse to be his interpreter."

"Do you think . . . Is he considering the concert? Something to raise money for his shelter?"

"I couldn't possibly say."

But they both knew the truth. Of course, Danny was considering it.

And as she could have predicted, the next time Quinn called—less than a week after he and Danny had spoken for first time in fifteen years—he said that he too had started voice lessons.

Rumors fly . . . Danny French, New York's hunger striker *extraordinaire,* has been seen entering and exiting the studio of Robert Marcel, vocal coach of the stars. Rita's alert inquiry produced the information that Quinn Hunter, Washington's sexy surgeon, is also taking voice lessons. What does this mean, Rita Readers? Is there a Dodd Hall reunion in the works?

—Rita Ryan, "Return to Things Past?" Rita's People (column), *USA Today,* March 15, 1993, Sec. D, p. 2.

Quinn was swamped. Krissa could appreciate that. His parents' estate was a mess. He had hired lawyers and accountants, but there was still a lot he had to do himself. His resolve to get his voice back in shape was taking considerable time, and he was listening to all the old albums, thinking about each song, looking for ways a man of thirty-nine could sing lyrics written by a youth of twenty-two.

Nonetheless he seemed happier, giddier, than Krissa had ever seen him. She even accused him of enjoying the aggravation of his parents' estate. "You're wallowing in being pissed off. You're so glad to have a clear-cut reason to be mad at them that you're having a good time."

"Oh, probably," he admitted. "But tell me, how's Danny doing with his breath support? What about that break in his upper register?"

That's all he wanted to talk about—Danny, Danny, Danny. And Danny was calling her more than ever before because he wanted to talk about Quinn, Quinn, Quinn.

They were not speaking to each other. Danny was still refusing to admit that he was taking the reunion idea seriously, and Quinn, who was taking it seriously indeed, was at least semiconscious of the risk that they could both make complete fools of themselves. "Singing the songs badly," he said, "would be as much of a betrayal as selling them to Madison Avenue. We each have to decide independently if we can do it. We can't put pressure on each other."

Despite all that he promised the night of his parents' funeral, Quinn was too busy to come to Minnesota. Week after week he was full of apologies and explanations, but he did not come. Only one thing mattered to him—getting his voice back in shape so that he could sing with Danny, so that he could sing "My Grandfather's Chocolates," the song he had once sung to a tape machine.

> "Any speculation about the reunion of Dodd Hall is premature."
> —Statement issued by Joel Finenberg, former Dodd Hall manager, March 16, 1993

"I have a good idea, Mom. Maybe we can do it the next time Quinn comes."

"Maybe, Patrick, maybe."

> "Any discussion of the reunion of Dodd Hall is premature."
> —Statement issued by Jingle Smith, former Dodd Hall bassist, March 19, 1993.

"When is Quinn coming next, Mom?"

"I don't know for sure, Adam, but soon. Soon."

"Any contemplation of a Dodd Hall reunion is premature."
—Statement issued by Calhoun Bates, former Dodd Hall keyboard player, March 19, 1993

"Mom, you can tell us. We won't say anything to Adam and Patrick. Is Quinn coming back? Did something happen between the two of you? Mom? . . . Mom? . . . Oh, jees, Brian, she's going to cry. Don't cry, Mom. Please don't cry."

"If all this talk is so incredibly 'premature,' how come everyone is denying it in the exact same language? Don't tell me they aren't all working on it."
—Steve Project, morning drive-time dee jay, WATL, Atlanta, Georgia, March 22, 1993.

"It's your call. 1-900-856-7701 if you think Dodd Hall will get back together. 1-900-856-7702 if you think they won't."
—Poll sponsored by VH1 cable television network, March 29, 1993.

"Heard melodies are sweet, but those unheard
Are sweeter."
—John Keats, "Ode on a Grecian Urn," May 1819.

Krissa could not believe what a mess her family was. Little Patrick was desperate. He wanted to talk about Quinn all the time. Adam, the child most like herself, grew defiant, mocking Patrick for his neediness. And to give himself time to torment his younger brother, he quit doing his homework. Krissa was alternately sick and furious.

The twins were being determinedly cool, acting as if the only thing in the world that mattered was the NCAA basketball tournament. But Brian had broken up with Pam, and neither he nor Curt would say one

word about it to Krissa. Pam's mother, Barb Rose-
berry, said that Pam didn't understand. The girl was
crushed and bewildered.

But Krissa understood. It was all her fault. What
did the books say? Children of divorce don't trust relationships. Jerry had left. Quinn had disappeared.
King Arthur kept leaving the Round Table, and the
young knights didn't know if they were supposed to
go on looking for the Grail without him.

It was one thing to risk your own heart, and yes,
you have to do that if you are ever going to have a
life. But it was another matter when you laid your
children's on the table as part of the ante. That's what
Krissa had done, and she didn't know how she could
forgive herself.

At least all the wild rumors and publicity about a
Dodd Hall reunion made it easy for Krissa to explain
things to her friends and neighbors. *He's so busy with
his parents' estate and these voice lessons. As soon as
things quiet down, he'll start traveling again.* They believed her.

So why didn't she believe herself?

Because she knew what the important story was. It
wasn't about Quinn and herself. It was about Danny
and Quinn. That's what had prompted Quinn to break
fifteen years of silence—he needed her to talk to
Danny. That's what had made Quinn admit his anger
toward his parents—the card on Danny's flowers.
Nothing she did could ever matter as much to Quinn
as what Danny did.

Fifteen years ago such behavior would have felt like
a judgment on herself, a sign that she was inadequate,
that she did not measure up to her brother. She believed that no longer. This was Quinn's problem, a
result of his conflicts.

But that didn't make this easy.

Ben Zagursky next door was aware of her unhappiness.
She could see the look of concern in his eyes, the pity in
his voice. He had been avoiding her during these months

of Quinn's visits; now she was determined to avoid him.
One evening she finally had to face him.

Someone in the neighborhood had had an all-chocolate
party on a Sunday afternoon. For her contribution
Krissa had tried a new recipe, a chocolate-laced chili.
It was not up to her usual standards, but at least it
had protein in it. Everyone else had brought sweets—a
chocolate fudge pie with a chocolate crust and a chocolate meringue; a white-chocolate, dark-chocolate
marble mousse cake. The drinks included cafe mocha,
chocolate soda, and Frango Mint liqueur that someone
had brought up from a Marshall Fields store in Chicago. By five-thirty Krissa was feeling sick.

She got her coat and as she was saying good-bye to
her host and hostess, she felt a stirring at her elbow.
Then she heard Ben speak. "I'll walk you home. It's
getting dark."

She didn't need to be walked home. It was three
blocks through her own neighborhood. Nor was it that
dark outside. But protest would be pointless. Lynn
had not come to the party. She was out trying to sell
houses. This was Ben's chance to be alone with Krissa,
and he was determined.

Of course four months ago she wouldn't have thought
of protesting. She would have welcomed his concern. She
spent so much time taking care of others that she had hun-
gered for someone to take care of her.

But Quinn had been doing that.

She and Ben started down the sidewalk. Had the
way been icy, he would have taken her arm. But it
was spring and he had no excuse.

He spoke quietly. "Those are beautiful pearls. Everyone was talking about them. I suppose Hunter gave
them to you."

"Yes, yes, he did."

They were at the end of the first block. There was
no traffic.

"Krissa, I—"

"No, Ben. Don't. Don't say it."

This was as close as they had come to acknowledging that there was something to say.

"But I hate it that you're so unhappy." His voice was anguished.

"I'm not unhappy," she lied.

"Let me help you. Please let me help you."

Krissa tensed, irritation flashing through her. Couldn't he see that there was nothing he could do?

Why had she allowed someone else's husband to know her this intimately? She knew the answer to that. Because she had been lonely, far more lonely than she had had any idea.

Until January she would have told anyone that she loved her life. Now all she could think about was what was wrong with it.

She felt as if four copper grounding wires extended out of her. Each wire was attached to one of the boys, and all their sudden surges of electric energy, of moods, temper, and hormones, flashed along those wires. She conducted the electricity through her own body, directing the powerful lightning bolts safely to the ground. It was necessary work, a mother's work.

But she was not made of copper, the one metal that provides the least resistance. Electricity flows through copper, scarcely heating it. But human flesh burns and scars.

She too needed a grounding wire. She needed Quinn.

She now understood so much about herself. Through her domesticity, her love for warm, intimate environments, the sensual richness of her taste, she had been trying to meet needs that other women had met with men, not objects. She had created a caressing, enveloping environment because no one caressed her, no one enveloped her.

Even when she and Jerry had been washing dishes in the bathtub, she had lit scented candles, believing that she could not live without beauty. She had been wrong. With love, she could live anywhere.

No wonder her children were spaced as they were. Once they left toddler-hood, once they became sturdy little rascals who no longer wanted cuddling, she had had another baby, a sweet, delicious baby who wanted no more than to be held by his mother.

So much of what she had done over the past fifteen years, she had done simply because she did not believe that anyone except her children loved her. That was why she was so sure, so deeply sure, that if Quinn had to choose, he would every time choose her brother.

This was pain she could not run from.

As April began, things did not improve in the Aarnesson household, and in another few weeks, outdoor soccer would begin. Krissa loathed the soccer season. The boys' soccer schedule was much more geographically diverse than the hockey schedule. Last year Krissa felt like she had spent the whole spring driving an hour and a half to Rochester for an hour-long soccer game, then piling everyone in the car and driving an hour and a half home. With all the games this spread out, the twins weren't going to be able to drive their brothers and make their own games. Krissa would be back in the carpool regime.

Quinn still did not come, and with each passing day Krissa grew more and more certain that he would not.

Then, surprisingly, Danny said that he was coming for a visit. He had a talk to give. "Things are going to be grim around here if I don't get out and hustle myself. The lecture's Sunday afternoon, but I could come out on Friday morning if you wanted me to."

Friday was the Minnesota Twins' first home game of the baseball season. The boys were aching to go. Pam's grandfather had a box, but needless to say, Brian and Curt had not gotten invitations this year. "Friday's fine," Krissa answered. "I'm always glad to see you. But isn't this short notice?"

"Not really. It's been scheduled for a couple of months, but I wasn't sure I'd go through with it."

This surprised Krissa. Danny was smart and practical. He understood what reporters, foundation directors, and socially conscious socialites needed. He was never late for press conferences, he never embarrassed the socialites, he never canceled lectures. He did not torture people in little ways . . . only in big ones.

So for the first time in weeks and weeks Krissa was at the airport again on Friday. Only this time it was in the morning and she didn't go to the World Club. At less crowded moments such as these, the guards were not so rigorous about letting only ticketed passengers beyond the security check. Krissa was able to go down to the gate and wait for Danny's plane. Through the floor to ceiling plate glass, she watched the silver 757 roll majestically to the gate. The expanding jetway snaked out through the air to meet it.

The business-suited first-class passengers disembarked first; Quinn would have been among them. Then came the people from tourist class: more businessmen and some crisply dressed professional women, the young students in faded shirts and jeans, the not so young baby boomers, also in faded shirts and jeans, but carrying expensive leather satchels. Krissa expected Danny any moment. He did not come. Then the families got off, laden with their carseats, diaper bags, and restless kids. Still no Danny. Finally two flight attendants came off, each holding a child by the hand—the unaccompanied minors. No Danny. Krissa stepped forward, peering into the jetway. Another moment passed. Behind her, the flight attendants were checking the identification of the people meeting the children. The pilots and the rest of the flight crew would be next.

Krissa went over to the gate agent still behind the podium. "My brother was supposed to be on this flight. Can you see if he got on the flight?"

"Of course, what's the name?"

"French. Danny French."

The agent's fingers darted over keyboard. Then he looked puzzled. "He boarded in New York. Perhaps you missed him. Shall I have him paged for you?"

"Yes, please."

Before he could do it, the phone under the podium

counter rang. The agent answered it in a low voice. He listened for a moment and then he looked up at Krissa. "Are you Mrs. Aarnesson? Krissa Aarnesson?"

"Yes."

"Would you please come with me?"

Come with him? What on earth was wrong? Had something happened to Danny? She followed the agent through the now empty waiting area, past the glass door, down the jetway, and onto the plane itself.

The pilots were standing in the door of the cockpit. A flight attendant came forward. "Mrs. Aarnesson?"

"What's happening? What's wrong?"

"Mr. French says he can't seem to get off the plane."

"What?"

"It happens," the flight attendant said in a consoling voice. "People have panic attacks, flying is unfamiliar, they—"

Not Danny. He didn't have panic attacks; flying was as familiar as breathing.

"He's back in row 18," the flight attendant was saying. "Perhaps if you could talk to him."

"Yes, yes, of course." Krissa hurried through the first class compartment, past the forward rows of the coach cabin, and there in row 18, his head down, was Danny.

She knelt in the aisle. "Danny."

He looked up.

She was horrified. She had seen Danny over the years, and she was used to the way he looked, the ruined magnificence of his wild, youthful beauty. But even knowing what he looked like, she could hardly believe this. He was ashen, exhausted, his eyes were dead, his skin dull. He didn't know her, he didn't know anything.

"Oh, Danny . . ."

He had the heels of his hands pressed to his temples. The veins on back of his hands were bulging. "I thought it would be okay. I thought if I did it in the morning. I am better in the mornings."

Krissa could not breathe. There was no air in this

plane, it was tight and claustrophobic. She did not know what to do. Suddenly she was twenty-two again, sitting on a doctor's examining table, dressed only in a paper wrap, being told that she was having twins.

She heard a man speak behind her shoulder. "Shall we call the paramedics?"

"No." Danny was speaking slowly. "No, don't call anyone." His voice was slurred; every syllable was an effort.

Krissa was not twenty-two. She was a grown woman, the mother of four sons. And no woman with four sons can be lost for long. She spoke clearly and firmly. "Then you have to come with me. I know that you don't feel well, but you have no other choice." She stood up and put out her hand. "Danny, come with me. Let's go home."

He looked at her for a long, long time, and she looked back with a mother's certainty, that absolute rock-hard confidence in your own judgment that is ultimately a parent's only weapon against a surly adolescent. *I know you don't want to do this. I know that you're old enough to make many of your own decisions. I know you're bigger than me. But at this moment I am right.*

Danny stood up. Krissa sighed in relief. Now she had to get him through the airport and into the van. What she would do at home she didn't know. She couldn't worry about that yet.

She carried his duffle. It was heavy and he walked slowly. In the van she fastened his seat belt for him as if he were a child. Traffic was light. Danny had his head back as if he were sleeping, but his eyes were open.

She took him up to the guest room and helped him out of his coat. His shirt was a green plaid with a brown stripe. The breast pocket sagged heavily and something within it rattled as he moved. He sat down on the bed.

"Danny." Her voice was gentle. "Something's wrong. You need to see a doctor."

"I have. I went to one of the clinics. That's where

I got these." He dug in his shirt pocket and pulled out four amber pill bottles. "I've been taking them."

Krissa looked at the names of the prescriptions. She had never heard of these drugs. They weren't anything the pediatrician had ever given the boys. "You went to a clinic? What kind?"

"Some doctor comes to the shelter. His English is lousy but I suppose he knows enough."

"You went to a clinic for the homeless?"

He looked at her heavily. "Why should I have better medical care than any of them?"

Krissa didn't know the answer to that. But she was not going to allow her brother to have substandard medical care. She simply wasn't.

She gathered up the pills, assuming that they would mean something to someone. "Danny, I'm calling my doctor. You have got to see someone."

"No." Danny's face was set, rigid. "I am not talking to any more strange doctors. I have had it with people thinking they know what is wrong with me. Reporters, government people, doctors, they all think they know me, but they don't." He was growing agitated, nervous. He stood up, then sat back down, running his hands up and down his arms as if he were cold. "I'm not talking to some doctor I've never met."

Some doctor I've never met . . .

Quinn was a doctor. Danny knew him.

Was this what Danny was asking? Was he asking her to call Quinn?

Whether or not he was, that was what she was doing. She stood up, taking the pills. "You wait here. I'll be right back."

There were dozens of reasons why she wouldn't be able to reach Quinn. He could be in surgery, he could be with a patient, but it was as if the fates knew that she needed him. He was in his office, and within moments of her giving her name to his receptionist, he was on the line.

"Krissa!" He was concerned; she had never called

him at his office before. "What's wrong? Has something happened to one of the boys?"

"No, no. It's Danny." Krissa could feel her self-control start to crumple. "He's here, and Quinn, he's such a mess. I don't know what to do." She had to blink and swallow or she would have been crying. "Oh, Quinn, it's so awful. Something's so wrong with him, and I'm scared. I'm really scared. I feel so alone."

For all the years she had been raising the boys virtually alone, she hadn't admitted to being lonely and scared. She couldn't. There would have been no solution. Now there was one. At the other end of the phone was the man she loved.

"Slow down, love. And tell me. When did he get there?"

That she could answer, and under his steady questions she was able to tell him what had happened. He asked her what the pills were. She read the labels.

She heard him take a sharp breath. "What is it, Quinn? What is it?"

"I don't know much about it, but those are powerful drugs. No wonder he felt like he couldn't move."

"What are they? Are they—"

"One's an antipsychotic, the others are antidepressants."

Antipsychotic. Antidepressants. Psychosis and depression. So it had happened, what Danny had always dreaded. Their father's mental illness had snapped its sharp iron teeth into him.

Quinn was still talking. "I need to look them up, but— He's at your house? Go sit with him. Stay with him. I'll be there as soon as I can. Don't leave him alone for more than a minute or two. Don't let him lock the bathroom door. Stay with him."

And Krissa understood. She knew what had happened to Mitch Snyder, the Washington D.C. homeless activist Danny had admired so, the man whose work Danny had pledged to continue.

Mitch Snyder had committed suicide.

Chapter Twenty-two

The new album was almost done; ten tracks were mixed and ready to go. If Danny would agree to record "My Grandfather's Chocolates," Dodd Hall would be out of the studio in a few days. But Danny wouldn't agree.

They were stuck. They had other songs that they hadn't recorded, but none of them fit this album. It was about loss—losses you'd faced, losses you knew were coming, losses you'd survived, losses you hadn't. "My Grandfather's Chocolates" pulled all those themes together—the grandfather you didn't remember, the father you couldn't catch hold of, and the forgotten bar of chocolate melting in the sun on a white porch railing.

It was a great song. And Quinn was going to be damned if he'd write another one to replace it, not when the only problem was that Danny was being a shit. That's what was going on. This was a power struggle. The capitalism in the song wasn't the issue; who made Dodd Hall's decisions was. Danny was trying to knock everything out of balance. He was trying to be the one in charge.

So Quinn went sailing.

For six years he and Danny had not looked up. The day after a tour was over, the two of them were at work on the next album. But out on the aquamarine sea with the salt-scented wind filling the white sails, Quinn felt like he could breathe again. Men in prison must get used to chemically purified, recycled air; you must forget what it was like to fill your lungs with Nature's clean, clear gift. Quinn certainly had. Dodd Hall had smothered him.

He didn't write a word on the trip. He didn't think about rhymes, meter, middle eighths, or metaphors. But as he boarded the plane back to New York, his mind began to tumble with words and images, enough for three or four songs. They'd be strong songs, songs about accepting that loss is necessary to change. They'd be about people who had said farewell and then had gone on.

First thing tomorrow morning he'd sit down with Danny. They would both have to compromise more, they'd have to be more workmanlike. It wouldn't be like the old days anymore when everything was raw guts and inspiration, but that was okay. If the album got finished, it would be worth it. Dodd Hall would get back on track. Perhaps it would be a different track than before, going somewhere else, but it would still have those two parallel rails, Danny and Quinn.

He got into New York late. So it wasn't until the next morning when he went out for coffee and a newspaper that he saw the posters.

They were fastened to the plywood boarding up the window of an empty store—six day-glo orange posters stapled edge to edge, forming a long flourescent stripe, impossible to miss.

Quinn ripped one off the plywood. The coated paper tore free of the corner staples, leaving four little orange triangles surrounding a blank space on the weathered plywood.

The poster was announcing a benefit at Madison Square Garden for an environmentally conscious group that was run by a couple of the crazy radicals Danny was starting to hang out with. Quinn had heard about the concert before he had left town. The bill was a few second-rate art rock bands. Apparently ticket sales had been flat. Quinn had—for the first time in his life—been glad that Dodd Hall didn't perform benefits. Otherwise Danny's friends would have asked them to rescue this one.

Except, according to this poster, Dodd Hall did perform benefits. It was right there in bold type: WITH A SPECIAL GUEST APPEARANCE BY DODD HALL.

Quinn stepped off the curb and stuck out his arm. A cab stopped. He got in and gave the driver the address for the office of Joel Finenberg, Dodd Hall's manager.

The receptionist was surprised to see him. Oh, yes, she said, Joel was in. Of course he would see Quinn. He was on the phone at the moment. Quinn could—

Quinn could do whatever Quinn wanted. He jerked open the door to Joel's office and dropped the poster on the wide glass-topped desk. "What can you tell me about this?"

Joel muttered something into the phone and hung up the receiver. "I saw it on the street last week. It was the first I had heard of it."

"I assume you told them that they were about to be sued off the face of the earth."

"I did call them," Joel replied, "and they were delighted to hear from me. They were expecting me to call. Danny said I would be messengering the contracts to them."

Danny.

In his heart Quinn had known this. He had known that Danny was behind this. For six years they had refused every benefit because Danny didn't like the idea. They had refused to help a hospital that Quinn's family had supported for four generations. They had refused a request from George Harrison. This was absurd. They had said no to an ex-Beatle, and now they were going to appear with a couple of weak Moody Blues imitators. Did that make sense?

If Danny had asked him, if he had asked for a mutual decision about changing their policy, the discussion would have lasted only as long as it would have taken Quinn to say the word "yes."

But to wait for the first moment Quinn's back was turned . . .

"And what did our friend Mr. French have to say?"

Joel leaned back in his chair, pressing his fingertips together. He knew how inadequate his answer would be. "That you always wanted to play benefits, that you couldn't be reached on board the boat. Apparently they had only sold about a third of the seats, and—"

"I trust the concert is now sold out."

"Yes."

Of course. Dodd Hall hadn't performed anywhere in six months; there hadn't been a concert near New York since last June. Of course the Garden was now sold out. It only had 20,000 seats. Dodd Hall could have sold it out for six nights running. If they were finally going to start doing benefits, at least they ought to be doing something that would generate some major money.

Quinn looked down at the poster. *This is such chicken shit, Danny. Why are you risking so much over something so small?*

"It's not a bad cause," Joel spoke in his best let's-smooth-this-over voice. "I looked into it, and—"

Quinn held up a hand, stopping him. He didn't want this smoothed over. The cause had nothing to do with it. This wasn't about charity. It was about control, Danny's need to control him.

Why? There are no issues here. Only "My Grandfather's Chocolates" and you've already won that. Do you just need to see how far you can push?

Dodd Hall was Feninberg Management's biggest client. Evidence of their success covered the grass-cloth walls of Joel's office—gold records, framed copies of their *Rolling Stone* covers, the *Billboard* chart from that astonishing week when Dodd Hall had had four albums on it.

Dodd Hall was a lot more than two jeans-clad troubadours humping around used equipment in a battered van. It was a complex business organization employing secretaries, accountants, and lawyers. But none of that would matter if there weren't still those two troubadours at the heart of things, making music together.

Trusting each other enough to make music together.

"You didn't sign the contract, did you?" he asked Joel.

"No, of course not. But Quinn, they put posters up all over the city. People bought the tickets expecting you."

"That doesn't feel like my responsibility."

"Do you want to put out a statement?"

"No. Let Danny show up there all by himself. Let him rot. I'm not going to be there." Quinn started to leave, then turned back. He held up a finger, warning Joel. "If anyone dares say that I'm sick, that I've checked into the hospital for a kidney transplant, I will spend that whole evening in Studio 54."

Quinn never went to that disco for the publicity-mad, but he would if that's what it took to show Danny that he couldn't get away with this crap.

He stormed out of Joel's office. There was no point in going to the Dodd Hall loft now. He didn't want to see Danny, much less sing with him. Danny had some serious apologizing to do, but Quinn wasn't about to accept an apology until after the benefit, until after Dodd had gotten up on stage and tried to harmonize without Hall.

But the concert was a week away. What should he do with himself until then? For the second time in the last two weeks Quinn found himself with time to kill.

Down in the islands he had met someone who was the tennis pro at a country club out on Long Island. When Quinn had moaned about how rusty his game was, the man had invited him to come to the club for some work. Quinn had thanked him, but had been honest. "It's the sort of thing I'll always think about doing, but will never get around to."

Things had changed since then. He picked up the phone.

His game was so off that he could hardly stand to

play, but the instructor put him through drill after
drill, and gradually things started to come together.
He was exhausted at night, aching in the morning. It
suited his mood exactly.

Joel knew where he was, but had the sense to leave
him alone. Halfway through the week Jingle, Dodd
Hall's bass player, called.

"So"—Jingle's voice had a wise, lazy rhythm to it—
"what are you up to all the way out there?"

"Tennis. I'm working on my game."

"Tennis, sailing, my, my," Jingle drawled. "You really know how to pick them, man."

"What's wrong with tennis and sailing?"

"I wouldn't know. Never done either."

Quinn drummed his fingers impatiently. Surely they
weren't back in Class Struggle 101, were they? "Is that
why you're calling? To criticize my leisure activities?"

"You're full of sweetness and light. No, I wanted
to put in my two cents about this benefit. Isn't it a
pretty rinky-dink issue?"

"I didn't chose the battlefield. He did."

"The man has demons. I don't get what they are,
but they make him do weird stuff."

Quinn wasn't going to accept that as an excuse.
Maybe Danny did have demons, but he didn't have
to force them on everyone else. "Dodd Hall is a duo.
He'll have to choose. He can sing with me or he can
sing with his demons."

"You sound like you've made up your mind."

"The minute I saw that poster. I'm not going."

Quinn believed that, but on the morning of the benefit he found himself heading back to the city.

He told the driver to turn on the car radio. All the
stations were full of talk about the concert. A contest
for tickets the day before had overloaded the telephone circuits, causing angry complaints from Wall
Street.

It was nearly one by the time they got back to Chelsea. Quinn dropped his bag off and walked over to
the little cafe where Krissa had once worked. A couple

of people came over to his table. They were all looking forward to the concert, they said. The hostess who
had seated him came back to ask about a ticket for
her boyfriend.

"I'm sorry. I don't have anything to do with that
this time."

*Tell her her boyfriend should stay home and watch
the Mets on TV. Tell her there won't be any concert.
Tell her one half of Dodd Hall wouldn't be going.*

But there would be a concert. He would be going.
He knew that. Dodd Hall didn't let their fans down.

He spent the afternoon walking around the city. He
stopped in shops and bought stuff. It was almost like
he was equipping himself for a new life, not the one
he had been living, but the one he had been raised for.
He bought Topsiders and khakis, polo shirts, tennis
sweaters, ties, and cuff links. People were surprised to
see him on the streets. What was so miraculous about
that? How did they think he got from one place to
the next?

He wasn't going to the Garden for Danny. He felt
close to hating Danny. He was doing it for the people
he was seeing around him, the people who had bought
tickets because they expected him to be there.

And Danny had known this. Danny had found a
way to manipulate him. All he would ever have to do
from now on was set up a situation like this, where
Quinn's ingrained, out moded sense of honor was on
the line.

*You didn't trust me, did you, Danny boy? You didn't
believe that I'd stay unless you tied me up.*

Dodd Hall was never going to be the same again.

Quinn waited until the last possible moment, then
had trouble getting a cab. He almost didn't care. If
New York's taxi fleet wanted to take this decision out
of his hands, that was fine with him. Another cab came
down the avenue. He stepped out to hail it, then saw
that there were people in the back. He dropped his
arm and moved back out of traffic.

But halfway down the block, the cab slowed and

moved over to the curb. The rear window was open, an arm was stretched out, gesturing to him. As soon as the cab had stopped, the passenger door opened and a clean-cut guy in a blazer and jeans came running down the block. "You need a lift?" he called out.

Clearly he was a fan. Quinn nodded. "I'm going to the Garden."

"So are we."

Quinn got in the cab. A fair-haired young woman was there. For an instant Quinn thought it was Brooke Shippen, Krissa's former roommate, but it wasn't.

"I thought *we* were late." Her voice was breathy. She could hardly believe they were sharing a cab with *Quinn Hunter* on the way to a *Dodd Hall* concert.

"You are," Quinn told her. "But I'm even later."

"At least they can't start without you," her boy-friend said.

The cab dropped the two fans off at the main entrance on Seventh Avenue. The man tried to settle up with the driver. He didn't want Quinn to be stuck with the fare.

It was a nice gesture. "Don't be silly," Quinn said. "I'm grateful you stopped. Let's not argue about this. You've already missed enough of the fine opening acts."

"How did you come to be playing with these bands?" the man asked.

"That," Quinn answered, "is one very long story."

Performers entered the Garden through the truck dock entrance on Thirty-third Street. A long ramp allowed their cars to drive up to the main arena on the fifth floor. Off to the left of the crescent-shaped marshalling area was the long dressing room corridor. To the right was the Rotunda where the preshow party would have been. Quinn avoided both. He stayed in the cluttered backstage, waiting quietly by a stack of plywood sheets that he guessed was the basketball floor. A couple of stagehands were there, drinking coffee. They didn't recognize him.

Deb, one of the Dodd Hall secretaries, was the first

who did. She gasped in relief and hurried off. Two minutes more and Joel was at his side.

"I honestly thought you weren't coming."

Then why was all the Dodd Hall equipment here? "Did I at least scare him?"

"I don't know," Joel answered. "I don't know."

Quinn did. He hadn't scared Danny in the least. Danny knew that he had Quinn pinned to the wall, a helpless squirming little butterfly bruising its pretty wings in agonized death.

He went over to look at the Zamboni machine used to make ice for the hockey games. He stared at piles of colorful circus props. There were lots of people milling around, girls in leather minis, guys in earrings, all trying to look cool. Quinn refused to meet anyone's eye. He went back closer to the stage and tried to listen to the last of the opening bands. They weren't anything to write home about, but he shook their hands as they came offstage, said a few words to them.

Then he felt someone come up behind his shoulder. It was Danny. He couldn't see him, hear him, or smell him, but he knew it was Danny.

Don't you dare say a word, don't speak, don't gloat.

The band gathered. They must be relieved that this had worked out. No one said a thing. The roadies had finished shifting the equipment. Jingle shot Quinn a questioning glance. Quinn nodded. Jingle signaled to the others and they ran out onstage. Stan swung onto the stool behind his drum kit. Jingle strapped on his guitar. Calhoun took his place behind the keyboard.

Quinn followed the spotlight on stage, lifting his hand to acknowledge the applause, the swelling waves crashing at the foot of the stage. Again he felt Danny at his back.

The twin mikes, those thin steel phallic symbols, stood side by side, close. Quinn ran his hand down his. The metal was cool, the crowd was still roaring.

He had no idea what they were going to play. After four opening acts, a "special guest appearance" would usually last twenty to thirty minutes. Dodd Hall usually played for two and a half hours.

Twenty minutes, Danny. You'd risk this much for twenty minutes?

Quinn had already lost Krissa to his career. He was not going to lose his self-respect too. If being Danny's puppet was the price of keeping Dodd Hall together, Quinn wouldn't pay.

The band knew a playlist hadn't been set. From the corner of his eye Quinn saw Jingle move. He said something to the others, and a little pretty tinkling rose from the organ. The audience quieted instantly. This was the opening to "Cinnamon Starlight," Dodd Hall's first hit. It seemed like an odd, nostalgic choice. The guitars joined the organ.

This band was the best. They'd carry Dodd Hall through this show. With these three guys behind them, Dodd Hall would make it through tonight. Tomorrow could bring the apologies and the explanations. Quinn stepped close to the mike and looked at Danny.

And Danny smiled.

It was a cocky smile, an arrogant smile, the "I've got you" smile of a gloating winner, of a corrupt puppet master.

Quinn jerked one hand back over his shoulder, holding it out flat, stopping the band. The bass, the keyboards, then the drum stopped. The audience was startled. The Garden was heavy with a bewildered, restless silence. Quinn covered the mike with his other hand and hissed the last words he ever intended to say to Danny French.

"Enjoy this because it's the last. I will never sing with you again. I will never get up on a stage with you again. I will never speak to you again."

He waited, looking at Danny, waited as the crowd stirred. A few people called out things, someone started to chant something—Quinn didn't know what. He was going to stand here until Danny believed him.

He would stand here all night if he had to, one hand over the mike, his body still turned, his other arm outstretched, stopping the band. The crowd could riot, the stagehands could leave. He didn't care. He wasn't singing a note until Danny understood that this was it, that Dodd Hall was over.

And finally Danny did. Quinn could tell the instant that he understood. His eyes darkened; there was a change in the set of his shoulders. He understood that the game was over. He knew that he had broken the toy.

Only then did Quinn lift his hand, signaling to the others to start. Only then was he ready to sing.

MEMO

DATE: May 3, 1978

TO: Kevin Farragut, Presto Records

FROM: Joel Finenberg

We have something that will work. Danny has agreed to record the chocolate song. Quinn will be involved only if he does not have to speak to or see Danny. So each will come into the studio separately and tape his part.

The album will be delivered on time, but it will be the last one. This, my friend, is the end of Dodd Hall.

ST. PAUL, MINNESOTA, APRIL 1993

It was a long day. Krissa knew that she couldn't expect Quinn until nearly evening. Flights between Minneapolis and Washington were scheduled for the convenience of the business traveler. They were clustered in the early morning and the late afternoon.

Krissa's guest room was heavy with Danny's restless misery. He said almost nothing, but he was like a person struggling through a cobwebby fog. Every moment had a frantic quality, but the frenzy played in slow motion. Every anxious gesture was weighted and ponderous.

Krissa stayed with him, leaving him only for a moment or two when she had to answer the phone or get an apple for herself. She was not going to let her brother commit suicide. At two o'clock the phone rang. It was a nurse calling on behalf of Dr. Thomas Fricke. She had the information Dr. Nguyen had requested for Dr. Hunter. Krissa obediently copied down the number and address of the Davis-Lansky Institute. She had never heard of it before.

Just before three the doorbell rang.

She winced. She murmured a word to Danny and hurried downstairs, taking a breath before she opened the door. The last thing she felt like dealing with at the moment was a self-important designer with an armful of fabric.

It was Quinn, his tie loosened, his eyes drawn and anxious. Krissa had never been so glad to see anyone. "How on earth ... I didn't expect you for hours."

"I know people who have their own planes," he said briefly. "How's Danny? Is he any worse? Did Tom Fricke call?"

Krissa handed him the piece of paper. Quinn looked at it quickly, nodding. "He's in the guest room?"

Krissa nodded.

Quinn took the steps two at a time. Krissa sensed the urgency pulsing through him. This wasn't just medical concern. His heart must be beating with one refrain—he was going to see Danny again, he was going to see Danny again.

The door to the guest room was half open. Quinn knocked lightly and went in. Danny was sitting on the bed's patchwork quilt, hunched forward, his hands clasped between his knees. At the sound of the door, he turned his head, looking up.

Quinn stopped dead. Krissa had caught up with him, and his eyes shot to hers, shocked.

She was at least used to the ruin of Danny's beauty; she had seen the lines on his face deepen and the hollows under his eyes go gray over the years, but even she had been horrified by how bad he looked today. Quinn had not seen him since they had both been twenty-five. Danny's eyes were glazed and lifeless. He was weary, his fire extinguished. Quinn must be shattered.

But before she could speak, Quinn was moving, crossing the room, pulling the chair out from the table. He swung it around to face the bed. He sat down in front of Danny and leaned forward, touching his arm. "Krissa called me because she's worried about you." His voice was strong and calm. The shock was gone. "Can you tell me about it?"

Danny didn't answer.

"When did you start feeling this way?"

They looked so different, the two of them. Quinn was fit and healthy, his thick, glowing hair was cut with just the slightest fall over his forehead, his gray suit skimmed over his shoulders with quiet elegance. Danny was ashen and unkempt, his wild black hair dulled, his baggy khakis crumpled.

"Has it been long?" Quinn spoke again. He was keeping his voice warm and concerned, but there was no personal distress. "More than a month?"

Danny shrugged. "I don't know ... since the hunger strike, I guess. I felt so great this summer, like I could do anything, and now ... I don't know, everyone expects so much."

"When did you see the doctor at the clinic?"

"I don't know ... ten days, two weeks, something like that."

"Can you tell me about the pills you were taking?" Quinn glanced at the nightstand looking for the bottles, but Krissa had locked them in her dresser drawer.

"I take the big ones twice a day, or maybe it was three times, and the yellow ones ..." Danny stopped. "I don't remember."

"Did the doctor have you increase the dosages gradually?"

Danny shook his head.

Krissa was standing behind Quinn, but there was something in the set of his shoulders that told her this was the wrong answer, that the drugs had been prescribed improperly.

"Did the doctor say anything about a drug called Lithium?"

"Yeah, I guess he did ... but he was giving me samples, and he didn't have any more of that one."

This had to be one of the fantasy moments in rock history, Danny French and Quinn Hunter, Dodd and Hall, meeting again for the first time since the concert at the Garden. Reporters would stake their careers to be here. Oprah would have paid the earth to have it happen on her show.

But what was happening in this room had nothing to do with the past. In fact, it had nothing to do with the Quinn who had once been in Dodd Hall. This man sitting in the chair was Dr. Hunter. This was how he would have spoken to any patient. He would have been this sincere, this understanding with any patient. Whatever anguish Quinn might feel at the wreck of his partner, Dr. Hunter had set aside in order to do his job.

Dodd Hall was truly over. The two vagabond singers had become doctor and patient.

Quinn spoke again. "How bad is it? Have you thought about killing yourself?"

Krissa drew back. That seemed like a horrible question. Yes, that's what they had been worried about, but to speak about it ... she hoped Quinn knew what he was doing.

Of course he did. For an instant it seemed as if this moment made sense of everything he had done since leaving Dodd Hall. This was why he had become a doctor, so that he could save Danny.

Danny answered. "Everyone does, don't they?"

"Have you thought of how you'd do it?" Quinn asked.

"No." Danny stirred restlessly. "I just know that if I were run over by a truck, I wouldn't care."

"This sounds serious. I know you're suffering but we can get you help. There's a place nearby. It's small and quiet—"

"No." Danny interrupted. "I can't go anywhere." He was starting to sound agitated. "Don't you see? My work ... my credibility ... if people knew ... they'd dismiss everything. 'Oh, he's just crazy.' 'What do you expect of a lunatic?' They already say that."

Quinn put his hand on Danny's knee, trying to calm him. "This is an illness, Danny. Some people have cancer, some have—"

"I can't go somewhere. Give me some different pills if you want. You give me something else, and I'll take it, but I'm not going anywhere."

"I can't prescribe for you. I'm not a psychiatrist. You have a lot of drugs in your system now. Those have to be cleaned out, and new one—"

"Then there's no point because I can't go somewhere."

"We'll be able to keep it out of the press. We can handle it quietly."

"No. I can't. I would if I could. It would be different if I were someone else. Maybe it would be better if I were someone else, but I'm not and so there's nothing to be done." Danny was shifting on the bed nervously. He seemed about to get up, but then slumped even lower. What was the point of getting up? Where would he go? "I can't."

Krissa had not spoken a word throughout this. Quinn looked up over his shoulder at her. Did she have any ideas? How were they going to get Danny to agree?

She stepped forward. "Okay, Danny, it's time."

Both men looked at her questioningly, Quinn's eyes faintly puzzled, Danny's in turmoil.

She sat down on the bed and took Danny's hand. It was heavy and limp. "You remember, the day after Dad's funeral, we made a pact. If one of us thought the other needed help, then that one would get treatment, no questions asked. You remember." The memory bit at her. Her wild, gifted, exuberant brother, so full of life and ambition, how could this have happened to him? It wasn't fair. It simply wasn't fair.

"But that was so long ago," he protested. "We were kids."

"No, we weren't. And it wouldn't matter if we were. Quinn can protect you from the publicity, and even if he couldn't, that doesn't change the fact. This was a vow we made, and I expect you to honor it."

She braced herself for argument. She was prepared to hold firm. "Danny, it's time."

And he must have wanted to hear this, he must have wanted someone else to make the decision for him. He put his hands on his knees, and after a moment stood up.

"Okay," he said slowly. "Okay, let's go."

Chapter Twenty-three

Quinn had never been in combat, but he had talked to people who had. They all said the same thing. In the first instant of hostile fire, you might go giddy with panic, but then the training kicks in and you do your job. Medicine was the same.

Krissa's anxiety had not prepared him for how bad Danny was. It should have, but in some blind spot of his heart he had always imagined Danny as preserved forever at age twenty-five. That had been essential to his fantasy, to the dream that had been steadily growing within him for the past fifteen years, the dream of being Dodd Hall again. How could he and Danny go back to being Dodd Hall unless at least one of them remained twenty-five?

But when he finally saw Danny again, his dearest friend had been sitting on the bed in Krissa's guest room, his head slumped down, his eyes vacant and weary. Quinn couldn't believe it. How could this be Danny? He and Krissa were playing some kind of joke. In a moment Danny would leap up, laughing—*Gotcha.*

But Danny did not move. His eyes remained vacant. This was happening. This was what Danny was like now. The wave of horror and grief crashed down around Quinn. It jerked him off his feet, twisting him around, grinding his face into the sand.

But a second later he was pulling out a chair, in complete command of himself, a doctor able to do what had to be done.

And he had remained that way through the rest of the afternoon. Krissa had stayed home to meet Patrick's bus, so he and Danny had driven to the small private hospital in the limo that had brought Quinn from the airport.

As they were being driven over, Danny had admitted to having similar, although far less severe, episodes before. That did not surprise Quinn now. Reconstructing Danny's behavior during the last year and a half of Dodd Hall, Quinn could see the beginnings of the bipolar pattern of manic-depression—periods of wild exuberance followed by self-destructive depressions. Danny was a manic-depressive, and he had been so for a long time.

Whether or not the hunger strike had interferred with Danny's body chemistry enough to intensify the two poles of mania and depression, Quinn did not know. This was not his field. But he certainly did know one thing. A person struggling with undiagnosed mental illness would not have done well with the pressures of singing, recording, and filming a concert in front of 20,000 people. The voice lessons and the hopes of a reunion concert might well have helped trigger this breakdown.

A Dodd Hall reunion, even for a single night, was out of the question. That was hard for Quinn to accept, bitterly hard.

For years after Dodd Hall broke up, Quinn had dreams from which he would awaken shaking and nauseous. In the dream he would be onstage, and all the people would be there, a black mass of faces and waving arms. The music would be there, perfect in its swelling energy. The band would be there, everything would be right, a performance at its very best, and he would turn to look at Danny, to share this with him. Only he wouldn't be there. Quinn would be standing next to a tape machine.

The last weeks had been glorious. Starting to sing again, knowing that he was doing it because he was going to sing with Danny again, he had been delirious, obsessed. That intimacy of standing so close that your bodies are one, that sense that your voice isn't simply yours, but yours and his soaring together, he was going to have that again. He was going to have it again. With Danny.

But he wasn't. Danny wasn't capable of it.

He now understood that for years and years he had silently been filling up a package with things that he wanted from Danny—connection and familiarity, knowledge and trust—things from the Dodd Hall days that had mattered as much as the music. But Danny couldn't meet his own needs now, much less anyone else's. Quinn and Krissa would, Quinn knew, spend the three weeks of Danny's hospitalization worrying about Danny, driving to see Danny, picking things up for Danny. Quinn would pay for his treatment; Krissa would visit him twice a day. Danny would do nothing for them. He couldn't.

The limo turned down Krissa's street, now almost as familiar to Quinn as his own. He saw Ben Zagursky in the driveway next door playing catch with his older son. The boy had on a Minnesota Twins sweatshirt and cap.

What folly it had been to think he could turn back time. And what did he think it would have accomplished? Why had he, for years and years, focused on the hope of someday singing "My Grandfather's Chocolates" with Danny? What would truly bring him contentment? The six minutes and seven seconds of that song or a driveway and a kid of his own to play catch with?

Ben and his son had paused in their game, looking at the limousine curiously. As soon as Ben recognized Quinn, he came over, his hand out, offering condolences.

Quinn knew he was looking at Ben blankly. What was Ben talking about?

"Your parents." Ben was a little puzzled. "Krissa said your parents died."

Oh, of course. Quinn felt like a moron. "Thank you. That's kind of you."

Dodd Hall wasn't the only thing he had neglected to mourn. It was probably as crazy to pretend that you could be twenty-five again as it was to pretend that your parents could die without your minding. Yes, you had to admit your anger toward them, but sooner or later you had to face your grief too.

"I didn't realize you were coming this weekend," Ben said. "I thought Krissa's brother was . . . or are all the rumors true? Are you two getting back together?"

"No." Quinn shook his head. "There's no chance of that."

Ben's eyebrows were arched questioningly. He was waiting for Quinn to say more. Quinn didn't.

"So are you taking the boys to the game?" Ben asked. "I know they were all dying to go."

Game? Oh, yes, tonight was the opening of the baseball season. The limo driver had been talking about it. "I thought the older ones went with Pam's family."

Ben had been examining the stitching on his worn leather baseball glove. He looked up, a little surprised. "Didn't Krissa tell you? Pam and Brian broke up."

"I didn't know that." What a shame. He wondered why Krissa hadn't told him. "When did it happen?" It must have been within the last day or so.

"I don't know for sure. Three weeks, something like that."

Three weeks? That wasn't possible. He had spoken to Krissa nearly every day since his parents' funeral, and she hadn't mentioned a thing.

"She didn't—" Quinn stopped. Suddenly he didn't want to admit to Ben that Krissa hadn't told him. He sensed a flash of hostility in Ben. An answering tension surged up in himself. This was suddenly a competition—who cared about Krissa the most, who helped her the most.

His eyes shot to Ben's. *You've got no rights over her. You're married.*

And Ben returned the look, equally flat, equally accusatory.

What are you accusing me of? What have I done?

Ben went on. His voice was deceptively mild, but

the competition was still on; he wasn't backing down. "I think she's pretty worried. About all the boys, not just Brian."

"Oh?" Quinn kept his voice careful.

"Kids don't do so well with an on-and-off thing. I know it's tough when you get busy, but- "

On and off? Where was Ben getting that from?

From Quinn's own behavior.

The night of his parents' funeral he had promised Krissa he would leave Washington, but he had done nothing to make that happen. He had said no more about it. The past had beckoned and he had turned away.

"Come on, Dad." Ben's son pulled on his arm. "You said if we left now, we might catch the end of batting practice."

Ben put his hand on the boy's head. "They'll be glad to see you next door," he said a little awkwardly. He had won the battle. Now he wished that it hadn't been fought, that he could have handled his words of caution differently. "I know they will."

Frantically, Quinn glanced at his watch. It was only two hours before the game. All the decent seats in the Dome would have been sold out for weeks. Getting tickets wouldn't be easy.

But it would be possible. Quinn didn't care what he had to pay as long as he could make this up to the boys. He might not be able to get five seats together, but a two and a three would—

He stopped. Krissa would murder him. If he had planned ahead and bought tickets through normal channels, she would have been delighted to have him take the boys to the game. But this guilt-ridden excessive expense—that was against every standard of child-rearing she had. He wasn't going to be able to buy his way out of this one.

Slowly he walked up the front steps of the house and rang the bell. In a moment he heard Krissa's footsteps.

Why hadn't she told him that she was worried about the boys? Didn't she think he'd care?

She opened the door, a rush of everything clean, fragrant, and loving. "How's Danny?" Her voice was urgent. "What did they say? Is he going to be okay?"

But for the first time since a dormitory suite in Princeton's Aughty One, since that moment when he had first heard Danny's voice, Danny didn't matter. All that mattered was Krissa, and how much he had hurt her. *I love you. How can you forgive me?*

Edna St. Vincent Millay was wrong about candles that burnt at both ends. The loveliest light came from the candle that did last the night. And this was it, this love between Krissa and himself; this was what would last. It was the string upon which all the other beads of their life would be strung. He and Danny and Krissa were no longer a triangle, each leg drawing energy away from the others. Danny was another bead. Sometimes he would glow with a jewel's brilliance; sometimes he would be weighted with lead. But the intricately wrought gold chain that connected Quinn and Krissa was strong enough to carry him, beautiful enough not to need him.

He followed Krissa back into the kitchen, answering her questions about Danny, saying how encouraging the doctors had been. There would be no easy miracles, but there was much hope.

She had been rolling out dough. A large floury rectangle lay on the counter. She had already cut circles out of half of it, and lined up on a platter sprinkled with cornmeal were pale half-moons crimped at the edge.

"Pierogis," she explained. "Polish dumplings. We had them as kids. I always make them when Danny comes."

"He'll probably be in the hospital for three weeks."

"I know. But the dough was made, and it's soothing work."

Why were they talking about this? Why wasn't he opening his heart to her, telling her how much he loved her, how desperately he regretted what he had done?

Because he was afraid that she would not accept his apology. He was afraid the damage he had done was too great.

She went back to work, cutting out circle after circle, her slender wrist turning and lifting. He had to speak.

"I always believed that I would see Danny again some day, and now that I have, I see that I've been keeping a space in my heart for him for too long. Just like people who can't form new relationships after a divorce because they've never said good-bye to their ex, that was me. I'm not repudiating him now, not when he needs our support, but I am repudiating the myth that we can go back to being Dodd Hall again. We are never going to sing 'My Grandfather's Chocolates' together."

Krissa had stopped working. Her eyes were soft, she was ready to grieve with him.

"No, no." He wanted her to know that he was all right. "We have to see this as good news—not what happened to Danny, but what's happening to me. Even if he weren't so troubled right now, I wouldn't want to be Dodd Hall again. I know that now. You remember what Jingle used to say about us, that if you put a quarter in me, you get the dial tone out of him? That kind of intertwining of identity was strange enough then. I would hate it now. I want to be my own dial tone." He took the cookie cutter out of her hand. "I know I've been a real prince for the last month, ignoring you while I chased this unwanted dream. Tell me, how close have I come to—once again—losing you?"

Krissa took a breath and slowly, reluctantly, pulled her hand free. "It's not me, Quinn. I meant everything I said about loving you. I don't expect to come first all the time. I don't need it, I don't want it. I'm not like your mother."

"But the boys have felt abandoned."

She looked surprised. He shook his head. "No, don't give me too much credit. I didn't figure this out on my own. Your neighbor speaks with a mild voice, but in his heart he is angry with me ... although no angrier than I am with myself. I can't believe that I didn't see it."

"I probably need to accept some of the blame," Krissa said. "I was the one who saw what was happening. If I called and said, 'The boys need you. Please come,' you would have, wouldn't you?"

He nodded. "I would have resented it at first," he said honestly. "I hated anything that took me away from singing, but I would have come, and once I got here, I wouldn't have resented it at all. In fact, seeing them probably would have broken my obsession with the past."

"I should have said something. I was being nineteen again. My pride was hurt."

He put his arms around her. "Krissa, I'm going to make mistakes with them. That's simply the way it is. You're going to have to help me." He pulled her out of her chair and put his arms around her. "I don't know if I asked you to marry me when we were kids. I can't remember if I did last month when I said I was going to move out here. Both times it seemed so inevitable. And this may be the wrong time now. Does it seem premature? Do you want more time?"

"No ... I mean, yes." Krissa was laughing. It was like holding an armful of starlight. "No, I don't need more time. Yes, it's ... I don't know if it's yes or no. I've forgotten how you worded the question."

THE FIRESIDE ROOM AND THE RAMSEY ROOM WILL BE CLOSED SATURDAY, JUNE 19, FOR A PRIVATE RECEPTION.

—Sign in the lobby of the University Club, St. Paul, Minnesota

ST. PAUL, MINNESOTA, JUNE 1993

Curt was missing. Krissa couldn't swear when she had seen him last. She thought he was in one of the cars caravaning over to the church, but she wasn't sure. Of all her children to act weird on her wedding day, she would have thought Curt, the more orderly, more reliable of the twins, the least likely. But there was no question. Here she was in a small room off the church foyer, dressed in a sensationally fitting tea dress of the palest cinnamon chiffon, with only Brian.

Sixteen years and she had kept track of both of these boys. She had never let one run into the street, she had never lost one at the grocery store. Sixteen years, and now one was gone.

"Calm down, Mom," Brian said. "He'll be here."

Calm down? Calm down? Krissa had woken up this morning, every nerve ajangle. It was quite simply that she had nothing to do. The reception was at the University Club. She had not stayed up all night making canapes. She and Quinn were going to France for two weeks, but not until school was out, so she didn't have to pack. And her mother was in town for the wedding. Whenever Krissa tried to do anything, she was, as her mother so patiently told her, doing it all wrong.

Actually, the last two months had been lovely.

Like any man, Quinn had proposed as if he were willing to move the moon and stars for her. The next day, again like any man, he turned out to have a bunch of conditions. Fortunately he was open about this. He had three.

"First is my parents' furniture. If it were just theirs, I wouldn't care, I'd torch it all. But it belonged to my grandparents, my great-grandparents, some of it is even older than that, and if I'm going to have a home, especially in a house built by another man, I want at least some of the things from my family."

As he was speaking, Krissa had glanced through her kitchen door to the rest of her house. Her dining room table was always covered with a cloth because it was made of particle board. Her living room, however comfortable and warm her upholstery made it, was still other people's cast-off wicker and mismatched tables. "All right," she said magnanimously. "In fact, if you change your mind about getting married, just send the furniture. It will make me as happy as you will. What's next?"

"Jewel. She's always said, even when my parents were alive, that if ever I had a child, she would want to work for me. I know you love cooking and all, but is there anything she could do?"

Krissa did indeed love cooking, but the "and all" she was not always so fond of. A wonderful vision filled her mind, all the laundry, the cleaning, the unending picking up drifting out of her life, carried away as steadily as the ebbing tide carries out a used Popsicle stick. A full-time housekeeper. Not a nanny, just a housekeeper. "This is a hardship I can cope with."

"She may not come. I don't imagine she thought she'd have to move to Minnesota, but I owe it to her to ask."

"Don't ask. Beg."

"Then there's my piano. I don't come without my piano, and she's big."

"I don't have any problem with that." Quinn had often been pretty rude about the quality of the old upright in her library. "I've always thought a grand piano would look great in the corner of the dining room where we had to brick up windows for the garage."

Quinn smiled. "No, love, you're thinking of a baby grand. Mine is a nine-foot concert grand, and while she is beautiful, how she looks—you Philistine—is irrelevant. What counts is how she sounds. I play at weird times and I don't know how I am going to feel about sticky-fingered people practicing 'Flight of the Bumblebee' on her. I may be okay about it, but I may not be."

Quinn would have rights when he joined this family.

He wouldn't be a visitor, a guest. The Census Bureau—to say nothing of the bank—would consider him the head of the household. As large as it was, the piano was a good thing, Krissa thought. It clearly stated that he didn't have to make all the changes. They would also have to accommodate him.

"There may still be room in the dining room," she said. "But that's not always the most peaceful of places. Why don't you take over my workroom? I know it's in the basement, but it's huge and the light is great. You could play at two A.M. You could write there. You could forbid everyone from ever setting foot in it. It would be there when you need to hide out."

"But what about your business? Where would you work?"

"I wouldn't. I'm like you. It's important to me that I built up a business. I like knowing that I can take care of myself. But I don't have to go on doing it. I could keep working or I could have another baby. I'm not doing both. You choose."

He didn't look as if he were going to find that a difficult choice.

So as conditions went, these were not bad ones. She and the boys had already adapted, and they could continue . . . at least if she still had all four of them.

"Brian," she pleaded with her one remaining twin, "do you know where Curt is?"

"At this very moment? The exact spot?" His eyes were dancing.

"You're up to something, aren't you?" The pair of them had made a plan. "Does Quinn know?"

"No, he'll be as surprised as you."

That didn't make Krissa feel any better. She looked at her son. He looked splendid, broad-shouldered and clear-eyed, his blond hair set off by the dark elegance of his tuxedo. The only thing standing between him and death was the fact that his mother couldn't think of a way to murder him without wrinkling her dress.

So instead she hugged him.

He patted her shoulder. "That's okay, Mom. Pam's mother"—Pam and Brian were now a couple again—"says all brides are nervous."

"I'm hardly a bride," Krissa said stiffly.

The door opened. It was Curt, as broad-shouldered, clear-eyed, and as formally dressed as his twin. Curt stepped back, and through the door came a man, a man in jeans and a plaid shirt.

"Danny!" Krissa gasped. "What are you doing here?"

"You invited me."

"Yes, but—"

He looked great. Well, maybe not great, but far, far better than he had that terrible day in April, better even than when he had left the hospital. He had gained weight, his color was better, his glance was more certain and direct.

Krissa had since learned a great deal about the drug Lithium and was now aware of how controversial it was. She did hope Danny continued to respond well to it without significant side effects ... and she profoundly pitied the medical establishment if he did not. He was capable of making his opinions extraordinarily well-known.

How delighted she was to see him. "This is wonderful," she breathed. "Why didn't you tell us you were coming?"

"Because I couldn't be sure I would make it. Do you mind that I'm not dressed up? They hid me out since lunch at Brian's girlfriend's house, and her dad wanted to lend me his rig, but I didn't want to tax the system."

"I don't care," Krissa said, hugging him. "I'm just so glad you're here. The day wouldn't have been complete without you." Then she noticed that the twins had disappeared. "Are you going to give me away?"

"No, you aren't my property. But I will walk in with you."

She had to laugh. Nothing would ever interfere with

the purity of Danny's politics. "If I were your property, you would sell me to raise money."

"Undoubtedly." For a moment his dark eyes sparkled like the Danny of old. Then he was serious. "Are you happy, Krissa?"

"Yes. Two minutes ago I was a wreck, but now I'm fine, and I am gloriously happy."

"Then let's get this thing over with."

Krissa hardly remembered the actual ceremony, just that she was halfway down the aisle before Quinn even noticed whom she was walking with. At the altar Danny put out his hand, Quinn gripped it warmly, but then Danny moved back to the pews to sit with his mother who was, no doubt, writhing because he was not dressed as nicely as Quinn. So at the altar, as Quinn and Krissa exchanged vows, were only the two of them and the four boys.

Surprisingly--although the minister seemed to expect it—after the ceremony Brian touched Krissa's arm, moving her to sit in the front pew with Adam and Patrick. Curt came out of the vestry carrying two guitars. He handed one each to Danny and Quinn.

Quinn looked puzzled; the pleated front of his white dress shirt shone above the guitar's warm wood. But Danny stepped forward confidently. He and Quinn looked at each other, and Danny murmured three words.

Quinn shook his head. He did not need to sing "My Grandfather's Chocolates." It was too bitter a song, a record of feelings he no longer had. Without speaking he began to play a light, starry melody. Danny nodded, agreeing.

So, in a performance unrecorded and never again to be repeated, in front of a churchful of hockey parents, members of the Quality Trash Book Club, a few East Coast doctors, a couple of aging rock musicians, and a Cub Scout troop, Dodd Hall sang the beautiful, innocent "Cinnamon Starlight," the first song Quinn had written for Krissa. These feelings he still had.

It was not a perfect performance. Quinn's voice,

brilliant and warm, carried Danny's, although what Danny had lost in technical purity he compensated for with grit, with a seasoned knowledge of suffering. And as they came to the last chorus, to the closing chords of the absolutely final performance of Dodd Hall, it was not—in this moment of sweet elegy—Danny whom Quinn was looking at. It was Krissa. He now knew where starlight came from.

"Do you believe it? God *damn* it all. They sang, and we missed it. I can't believe it. We missed it."

—Steve Project, morning drive-time dee jay, WALG Radio FM, Atlanta, Georgia, June 21, 1993.

Turn the page for
a preview of
Kathleen Gilles Seidel's
glorious new novel . . .

Again

coming from Onyx
September 1994

Chapter One

"You know what they say about him, don't you?" This was from George, the executive producer. He was more or less Jenny's boss.

"I know, but he's terrific."

"He's supposed to be impossible, very demanding." This was from Thomas, the show's casting director. He and Jenny had been friends since their days as lowly production assistants.

"Maybe the people calling him impossible are impossible themselves."

"But you've never met him. We could be letting ourselves in for all kinds of trouble. It can't be worth it." This was from Brian. He was Jenny's boyfriend.

These were reliable people, George, Thomas, and Brian. Jenny trusted their judgment and their taste. But she had instincts. *This is it*—the knowledge would flash along her arms. She would feel bubbly and confident

"I don't get it," Brian went on. "Why are you so sure?"

"I like his eyes."

Two years ago two daytime soap operas debuted on network television at the same time— the big, splashy, generously budgeted *Aspen Starring Alec Cameron*; and the quiet, quirky *My Lady's Chamber*. No one except the people on *My Lady's Chamber* thought of it as a competition. *My Lady's Chamber* had too much against it. It was a half-hour, it was scheduled against daytime's number-one show, it had an historical setting. "Quixotic" was the word most often used to describe it, followed right after by "doomed."

But in spite of the predictions, the scrappy underdog held on. Slowly it built an audience. Its attention to historical detail and the elegant BBC–*Masterpiece Theatre* tone of its production brought in new viewers, people who had never watched soaps before. Lawyers with expense accounts, college professors, graphic artists, and symphony volunteers programmed their V.C.R.s and watched *My Lady's Chamber*.

And the megabudget *Aspen Starring Alec Cameron*? It was a bomb. No one watched it.

Alex Cameron hadn't asked anyone to produce a show starring him. The network had approached him with the idea and he hadn't thought it a very good one. He had said so frankly and clearly. Soaps shouldn't have one particular star; the cast should be an ensemble. Daytime should never feature one actor so prominently.

Of course if daytime was going to feature one actor so prominently, Alec would just as soon that it be him rather than someone else. The network executives kept talking about his proven audience appeal, his unquestioned talent. The idea started sounding better and better. Pretty soon it seemed downright excellent.

It wasn't.

The network had hired a new writer, a playwright who had never written for television, much less for daytime. The man watched three weeks' worth of soaps and then, based upon that vast experience, announced that he was going to revolutionize the structure of the soap opera. There would be no core families, no super couples, no amnesia.

"What do you mean, my character has no family?" Alec asked during his first meeting with the man.

"Oh, we're not going to be doing families. We're not interested in families."

A soap that wasn't interested in families? That's what soaps were about—families, connections, blood. The family stories held everything else together.

Jenny Cotton knew that. She was the creator and headwriter of *My Lady's Chamber,* and she was very interested in families. Her show was set in the past, her characters wore intricately tied cravats, and flowing, high-waisted gowns, but they were still part of families. Jenny wasn't interested in revolutionizing the structure of anything. The structure of the soap opera was fine. She worked on what needed to be worked on. *My Lady's Chamber* had better writing and more consistent, believable characters than anything on daytime.

Day after day Alec would get his scripts for *Aspen,* and he would stare at them, disbelieving. Everything was wrong. There wasn't enough recapping of prior episodes. Viewers who had missed a few shows got lost. Two, sometimes even three, stories were peaking at the same time, diluting the intensity of all of them. The characters were glamorous, but not engaging. Whoever was writing these scripts didn't know anything about soaps.

If he had been just another actor in the cast, Alec might have kept his mouth shut, but his name was the one featured in the credits. His reputation was on the line. With the morale of the cast dropping like a stone, he had to do something.

He tried to play fair with Paul Tomlin, the writer. He kept his criticisms away from the greenroom and the dressing room corridors where the actors hung out. His business was with the writing staff and the production staff. He met with them, reasoned with them, pleaded with them. This was his fourth soap role, he had won back-to-back Emmys. He knew a lot about what made soaps work. *Get back to basics,* he begged. *Characters that the viewers care about, stories that touch the heart. And families, please give us some families. Mothers, grandfathers, unknown half sisters, adopted third cousins, anything.*

"Families are passé," Paul said with a sniff. "No one cares about families anymore."

No one cares about families? Alec could only stare

at him. Where was this guy from? Didn't he know anything about the daytime viewer?

Alec kept on. He wasn't doing this only for himself. *Aspen Starring Alec Cameron* employed a lot of people. Actors, craftsmen, tradespeople, gofers, and hairdressers would be out of work if the show got canceled. Just as surely as if he had to meet the payroll himself, Alec felt responsible for these people's livelihoods.

At the end of the first year, the network became desperate too. Alec found himself working five days a week, with forty pages of dialogue to learn a night. The show started going on location, expensive jaunts to Peru and Finland. It didn't help. A story that was boring at home was going to be boring in Italy.

My Lady's Chamber, on the other hand, actually had a foreign setting: Regency England. But it never went on location. It couldn't afford to. It didn't need to.

At last after a wearying, mind-numbing eighteen months Alec's ordeal came to an end. *Aspen Starring Alec Cameron* changed its title to *Aspen!!* and Alec's character skied into an avalanche.

Never had being fired been such a relief. Someone else had taken the sword out of his bloodied hand. "You have fought long enough, my friend." The doctor had closed the chart. "You may die in peace."

Alec slept for a month and then went home to Canada to visit his own family. He returned to New York, renewed, refreshed, ready to work again, and discovered that he might just as well have stayed home. His name was as muddy as his father's potato fields. No one would hire him. He was finished at the age of thirty-two.

He was being blamed for *Aspen*'s terrible ratings. He was difficult—the reports went—temperamental, obstinate, a perfectionist.

He couldn't believe it. He had always been one of the good guys—punctual, professional, dedicated. How could anyone call him difficult? He was Canadian. The world's longest unprotected border and all that. Canadians didn't know how to be difficult.

"But these people know me," he protested to his agent. "They know I'm not like that."

"They also know that you were part of a bomb."

There was no quarreling with that. Except perhaps with the "part of" bit. He hadn't been "part of" a bomb. He had starred in it. *A Bomb Starring Alec Cameron.* Not a perfect career move.

Putting bread on the table was not a problem. He did voiceovers for commercials, not very satisfying work but lucrative. He got a decent-sized part in a good movie, but he had never liked film work—standing around and waiting while people fussed to get the lights exactly so. Nor did he like the spaceship/desert island atmosphere of a movie production. He belonged on a soap. It suited his acting style; it fit in with his desire to be a regular guy. Someone with a job. A person who went to work every morning. Acting in the soaps was clearly what he was meant to do with his professional life, and all of a sudden no one was letting him do it.

Then that strange little historical show, *My Lady's Chamber,* needed to recast the part of His Grace Frederick Charles Edmund Stairs, the fifth Duke of Lydgate, and an instinct flashed along Jenny Cotton's arms.

My Lady's Chamber was housed in an old, three-story brick warehouse in Brooklyn. The network's other daytime shows were taped in a modern, midtown Manhattan facility, but *My Lady's Chamber* had expensive costumes, expensive sets, and a very limited budget. Everything from lumber to midmorning Danish was cheaper in Brooklyn than in Manhattan.

The network did provide limousines to bring the actors out to this wilderness of a location, but Alec decided that he would get to Brooklyn on his own. He didn't want to begin his stint here sharing a car with other cast members. He didn't want to get too chummy.

Things were going to be different this time. He was going to come in, do his job, and go home. He wasn't going to carry the weight of the world on his shoulders. If two of the actresses loathed each other, well, that was a shame, but he was going to keep out of their way. If one of the directors was too hard on the gay men—or on the straight men—again Alec would be sorry, but he wasn't going to fix it. It was someone else's turn to play savior. It was someone else's turn to be crucified.

The security guard sitting inside the warehouse's street door recognized him. "Mr. O'Neill wanted to know when you got in." The guard picked up the phone that sat on his desk. "He'd like to show you around."

"That's not necessary." Alec did not want to be led around like some kind of returning prince who had failed to distinguish himself on the Crusades. This was his fifth soap. He could probably tell the makeup room from the wardrobe department. "Just point me toward the dressing rooms."

"But Mr. O'Neill, he said that you were to wait." The guard was looking worried. He had his instructions.

And Alec was being difficult. His agent had warned him to be careful. "Everyone will be watching you," she had said. "Stop at the water fountain, and someone will say that you're being difficult."

This really stank, that he should have to be so careful at this point in his career. But that was the way things were. No use in pretending that they were otherwise.

He beamed at the security guard and spoke in good hearty tones. "If Mr. O'Neill said I should wait, then wait I shall do." He moved to the wall to wait.

He assumed that "Mr. O'Neill" was Brian O'Neill, an actor he had met several times over the years. Alec didn't really know the man, but he had a good reputation in the daytime world. He was known to be pleasant and hardworking, particularly able to do something with a character who wasn't getting much of a story.

Indeed it was Brian O'Neill who approached the security desk a few minutes later. He was a slender man with a willowy torso and the sort of slim, long fingers seen in Renaissance paintings. He had the fair skin and very dark hair of the black Irish.

Alec's own ancestry was Scotch, and he had a firm, broad-shouldered build, warm skin tones, and auburn hair. His eyes were wideset, and while in life they didn't seem remarkable, on camera there was some sort of magic to them. Whether it was the spacing, the color, or the way they reflected light, they made him seem instantly interesting. From the moment his character was introduced, people were drawn to him. They wanted to see more of him, know more about him.

He shook hands with Brian and let the other actor show him around. There were no surprises. Wardrobe, the greenroom, and the studio floor were on one. Makeup and the dressing rooms were on two. The rehearsal hall and the production offices were on three.

"You're sharing with Ray Bianchetti," Brian said as he opened the door of Dressing Room Six. "He's a nice guy."

"I'm sure he is," Alec replied.

"In fact we all get along pretty well."

"I'm sure you do."

Brian paused. He must have heard the caution in Alec's voice. "This isn't *Aspen*," he said quietly. "Jenny is nothing like Paul Tomlin."

"How could she be?" Alec's answer was brisk. He didn't want to talk about *Aspen*. "She writes a show that people want to watch."

"It's also one people want to work on."

Was Brian warning him? Alec wasn't sure. *We don't want your kind in this town.* Was Brian reminding Alec that this was not the place to be difficult? Or was Alec overreacting?

He would like to know. Brian was not just one more actor in the cast, one more name on the credits. He was Jenny Cotton's boyfriend, her long-time "significant other," her live-in companion.

The head writer's boyfriend. That must be a little like having your name a part of the show's title. Brian must be in the middle all the time, having to defend the writer to the actors, the actors to the writer. He must be the one who negotiated, advised, and warned.

It was a thankless job. Alec was glad that someone else was doing it.

"We all hope you like it here," Brian said. He was indeed sounding like the official cast ambassador. "Jenny certainly did go out on a limb for you."

"Oh?" Someone went out on a limb for him? He did not like the sound of that.

"She was the one who pushed. She's really looking forward to meeting you. People assumed that she already knew you because she was so willing to discount . . . well, you know. . . ."

Yes, Alec knew. She had been willing to discount everything Paul Tomlin was saying about him.

Alec was from a family of six children. The first three children had been born one right after the other. Then there had been a gap of six years, after which had come three more, closely spaced children. Alec had been the first of the second wave; he was the oldest of the "Littles."

He had always felt responsible for his younger brother and sister; he was the one who spoke on behalf of all three of the "Littles." He supposed that was why he had felt responsible for what happened to the people on *Aspen*. He had always felt responsible for Ross and Meg.

While he had an oldest child's sense of responsibility, he didn't have the self-assurance. Watching out for Ross and Meg didn't keep him from comparing himself to Bruce, Gordon, and Jean. Of course he couldn't measure up to them; they were years older than he was. But he hadn't liked it. He didn't want people patronizing him, making allowances for him.

Those had been childhood feelings which he had thought himself long over. But now, thanks to *Aspen,* he was back to having people make allowances for him.

"I'm looking forward to meeting her too," he answered smoothly, untruthfully. "What day does she come in?" Writers worked at home and usually came into the studio only one day a week.

"She's here all the time. She likes being in the thick of things." Brian had his hand on the dressing room door, motioning for Alec to pass through. "She should be here now."

Alec followed Brian up to the third floor, down a short hall, and into an office.

He had a quick impression of clutter: bookcases wedged tight with books, maps and drawings taped to the walls, piles of dog-eared legal pads, and stacks of colored index cards. Then his eye went to the person behind the desk.

She hadn't noticed them come in. She was staring at the computer screen—intent, concentrating. It was probably very grown-up work she was doing, but she was sitting like a kid, one leg drawn up, her arm wrapped around her knee, her chin resting on the back of her hand.

"Jenny, here's our new duke."

She looked up. The leg dropped, the chin lifted, and a smile flashed across her face. Alec had to admit that it was a cute smile, bright and gamine-like. "Hello, hello." An instant later she was out of the chair, in front of the desk, putting her hand out.

She was small. Her light brown hair was full and short, rumpling around her ears. She had freckles across the bridge of her nose, and everything about her sparkled with energy. Alec had heard she was about twenty-eight; she looked at least ten years younger.

She was dressed casually. Her trousers were wheat-colored, light and loose. The collar of her white shirt was open, and her cuffs turned back. They were good garments, well-cut, nicely fitting, but she was wearing no accessories—no earrings or bracelets, not even a belt, although her pants had belt loops on them. Clearly she was not one of life's better dressers.

She banged her elbow against Brian's ribcage. It was a nice gesture—lighthearted, affectionate. *I like you*, it said. *I'm glad you're here*. Then she put her hand out to Alec. "Welcome to the nineteenth century." She was lightly tanned and her voice was a little husky as if she had been outside all afternoon playing ball in the wind and the sun. "I'm so glad to finally meet you. I think you'll love it here. I mean I *hope* you will. You should. Everyone's so great, we're—"

"Jenny," Brian interrupted. "You're bragging."

"No, I'm not," she protested. Then she made a face, wrinkling her nose, laughing at herself. "So what if I am? A half-hour show is really great. You've only been on the hours, haven't you?"

Alec realized that she was speaking to him. "That's right."

Those were the first words he had spoken.

"I think you'll be surprised at how much more fluid and flexible we can be here, how much more—"

Brian interrupted again. "It's just that *she* loves the show," he explained to Alec.

"I gathered that." He had to smile. No one on *Aspen* had had fun. Jenny Cotton was still having fun.

Why didn't a person meet more women like this? She was enchanting, so fresh and uncomplicated. Alec could imagine her on that limb she had supposedly crawled out on for him, a compact little nugget of a person sitting up in a tree, her feet swinging, with her freckled nose, and bright eyes peering down through the leaves.

He had worked with many gifted, successful actresses; he had been married to one of daytime's most gifted, most successful. As astonishingly lovely as some of these women were—his ex-wife was almost supernaturally exquisite—he couldn't recall any of them making such a marvelous first impression.

Well, as long as his career was perched out on a limb, he might as well be in the tree with someone who is having fun.

The daily routine on a soap had been developed in the days when shows were aired live. What was taped in a single day aired in a single day. If a Friday show ended with a character rushing into a room shrieking that the building was on fire, and Monday picked up two seconds later with everyone scrambling to get out, those two scenes, even though all the actors were in the same costumes, standing in the same places on the same set, were taped on two different days.

The day began in the rehearsal hall with the cast sitting at a long table reading through the script. The rehearsal hall was a bare, vinyl-floored room furnished with folding chairs, a couple of long tables, and a trolley for coffee. The one here was no different from rehearsal halls anywhere.

The show had two core families, the Varleys and the Courtlands. The Varleys had raised two nieces, a wealthy one and a poor one. The rich one had married the Duke of Lydgate, Alec's character. The duchess was a sympathetic character, played by Karen Madrigal, a lovely swan-necked actress with clouds of dark hair. The viewers were crazy about her. Ray, Alec's dressing-room mate, played another popular character, the duke's younger brother, Lord Robin Stairs, a dashing and gallant calvary officer. An actress named Trina Nelson was the duchess's maid, Molly, and Brian played the family's butler. There were about ten actors getting themselves coffee and finding places at the table in the rehearsal hall.

Alec didn't know any of the others. Except for Brian—and now Alec himself—everyone in the cast was new to daytime. But they were all welcoming. "Oh, you *are* going to love it here." "It's because we're only half an hour." "We're so different from

the hour shows." "You'll love it; we're a family here."
"Yes, yes, that's right. We're one big happy family."

One big happy family. Alec listened to the cast talk.
As sad as it was, most actors had little experience with
happy families. They were likely to be confusing such
superficial pleasantries as the absence of spurting
blood with family happiness. Since four of the six children in Alec's family had been boys, there had been
a great deal of spurting blood as well as prolonged
dearths of superficial pleasantries, but as a family they
had been happy, a condition far too complicated to
compare to anything else, especially a professional
situation.

Moreover, how did any of this cast know that a half-
hour show as so much better? None of them had ever
been on an hour show.

But Alec let these suspicions drift away. It was so
good to be back at work, to be getting a cup of coffee
with a script tucked under his arm, hearing people ask
one another about their weekends. He didn't want to
be suspicious and cynical. He don't want to feel like
the weather-beaten old gunfighter in a town full of
well-meaning settlers. He wanted to work.

He found a seat at the table. A minute later the
director of the day's episode, Gil Norway, took his
place on the tall stool at the head of the table. He
welcomed Alec, paying a brief tribute to his experience and his back-to-back Emmys. Then the day
started.

The show was just coming off the climax of an extremely passionate love story. The dramatically beautiful, but married Lady Georgeanna Courtland had
been desperately involved with Sir Peregrine Hen-
slowe, a dashing, young, bankrupt gambler. Lady
Georgeanna was now pregnant with her first child,
whose father all polite society knew to be Sir
Peregrine.

The story had shifted to a side-burner—Peregrine
was off on the Continent trying to rebuild his purse
at the casino tables and Georgeanna was in the coun-

try, being pregnant in seclusion. In truth, the actor playing Peregrine was on a write-out to do an off-Broadway play and the actress was on her own maternity leave. Much of today's script was devoted to clearing up the loose ends from that story.

The first scene in the episode— "Prologue A" it was called—featured the Duchess of Ludgate and her maid. Alec leaned forward, listening, interested in Karen Madrigal. He would be having many scenes with her.

He knew from the shows he had seen that she was very good. But he still had everything to learn about her process. Did she like to rehearse endlessly? Or did she sleepwalk through the day and burst into life when the taping started? Did she. . . ?

It was wonderful to be back. The voiceover work he had been doing was all technique, no emotion. Until this moment he had not let himself admit how much he had missed being a part of a daytime cast. He noticed his foot jiggling. A light, jubilant, almost a fizzing sensation, was spreading through his body. He could hardly wait for his turn.

The door to the rehearsal hall opened. He glanced back to see who it was.

It was Jenny.

She pulled a chair away from the wall. Alec watched her. She perched on the chair's back, her feet on the seat. She leaned forward, her elbows on her knees, her hands clasped between her legs. Her white shirt fell open slightly.

Karen and Trina finished their scene. The production assistant's stopwatch clicked off. While Gil was noting the scene's time, Trina turned her script over and wrote some big letters on the back. She held it up like a sign for Jenny to read. Alec leaned forward so he could read it too. "BELT!!" it said.

Startled, Jenny peered down at her waist and noticed the empty belt loops there. She stuck her thumbs through them and grinned at Trina, not in the least embarrassed.

"I have a problem with 2C—"

Alec dragged his eyes away from Jenny. It was Brian who was speaking, directing his words to Gil. Why was he talking about scene 2C? They had just finished with Prologue A.

"I don't get this business with the butler taking a tip from Jaspar."

"What do you mean 'taking'?" demanded the young actor who played Jaspar. Alec wasn't quite sure how that character fit into things. "The way I read it, it's a shakedown. That's not nice." The actor was exaggerating, pretending to feel this outrage. "I'm dead broke."

"That's just it," agreed Brian. He wasn't exaggerating. "Do you really think a duke's butler would do something like that? Isn't there a question of dignity here?"

Whoa. Alec sat back. What was going on? Brian was querying a little piece of business, nitpicking, holding everything up. What had happened to the big, happy family?

This was the sort of thing that could turn daily life on a soap into a nightmare—an actor quibbling about every single detail. As bad as things had gotten during *Aspen,* Alec had never held up rehearsal. He had met privately with Paul, with the producers, even with the network. But once it became clear that he had lost, he had shut up and done his job.

He glanced around the table. How were the rest of the cast reacting? If this was an everyday occurrence, they would all automatically switchoff. *Wake me up when this is over.* Some would get more coffee; others would draw close to their neighbors and start talking about the Mets.

But clearly Brian's objections were not a part of the routine. People were alert, looking at each other, puzzled and questioning.

How important a scene was this? Alec supposed that having been in the cast for all of twenty-five minutes, he shouldn't judge, but it certainly didn't seem like it was worth wasting time on. Gil, the director, needed to take control here; he needed to cut off this discussion and get things moving.

Of course there was an interesting wrinkle. The actor complaining was the head writer's boyfriend, and the head writer was in the room.

Gil had been listening to the actors, looking at them over the tops of his half-glasses. Then he deferred to Jenny. "What do you think?" he asked. "Is it going anywhere?"

"Actually it is. People did tip servants after house parties and such—it was called 'vails.' "

"But this has just been a dinner," Brian protested. He had pushed his chair back so he could look at Jenny directly.

This didn't make sense. Alex felt his weather-beaten, old gunfighter suspicions re-emerging. Brian had had this script for a week, and he lived with Jenny. Surely he could have discussed it with her privately. He must want to challenge her in public.

"I know." Jenny didn't seem the least upset. If Brian was challenging her, she wasn't taking up the gauntlet. "That's why Jasper's surprised. He wasn't expecting it."

Maybe she was stupid. This was a complicated moment, an actor using his personal relationship with the writer to embarrass her and undermine the director's authority. She didn't seem to have a clue. She was breezy, unconcerned, unaware. The simplest explanation was that she was stupid.

No, she wasn't stupid; she wasn't unaware. A person didn't get to be head writer of a network show by being stupid. Little moments charged with greater significance were the heart's blood of a soap. Jenny had to understand absolutely everything that was happening. She probably was seeing a whole lot more than Alec was. She wouldn't be able to write a soap if she didn't live and breathe in a world of nuances.

"Fine. I understand Jaspar's reaction," Brian said.

"The problem is with the butler. I can't see him doing this."

"It is a little out of character," Jenny admitted.

Oh, no. A little out of character. On daytime television. How could that be?

This was a soap opera. The story had to get told, and a rare week went by when someone didn't have to do something out of character. If you couldn't live with that, you shouldn't be working in daytime.

"If you're uncomfortable with it, it's not a problem," Jenny's voice was still as cheery and as unconcerned. "Jasper goes to Lady Varley's next week, and her footman's in the scene. I'm sure he won't mind another page or so." She hopped off her perch on the chair. "But I'd better go make a note of it. Otherwise I'll forget."

Alec kept his expression even, but silently he cheered. Jenny Cotton might be playing the blithe tomboy, but she had just made one clever move, the kind that does not happen by accident. *You don't have to say these lines. You don't have to do this business. We'll just give it to someone else.* No actor wanted to lose screen time. She had cut her boyfriend off at the knees.

Brian reddened. "That's way too much trouble for you. I'll do it." He spoke as if he were being magnanimous and accommodating, as if he were doing her a tremendous favor ... which of course he was not.

Well, well. Alec picked up his Styrofoam coffee cup. His interest was now thoroughly engaged. Here was a cast that needed to believe that they were happy, a head writer who was pretending that she was Huck Finn, a boyfriend who had something to prove to someone. This was going to be one interesting place to work.

Look for AGAIN
coming from Onyx
September 1994